A PERFECT BLINDNESS

W. Lance Hunt

ⓘUniverse®

A PERFECT BLINDNESS

iUniverse books may be ordered through booksellers or by contacting:

iUniverse
1663 Liberty Drive
Bloomington, IN 47403
www.iuniverse.com
1-800-Authors (1-800-288-4677)

ISBN: 978-1-5320-1012-5 (sc)
ISBN: 978-1-5320-1013-2 (e)

Library of Congress Control Number: 2017900664

Print information available on the last page.

iUniverse rev. date: 04/24/2017

There are two ways to be fooled. One is to believe what isn't true; the other is to refuse to believe what is true.

—Søren Kierkegaard

Acknowledgments

I thank the following people for reading and commenting on the various drafts of this book in its various incarnations over the past fifteen-odd years: Greg Beaubien, Sofi Stambolieva, Linsey Abrams, the workshop (especially Edith, Rod, Laura, and Rosary), and my wife, Karina, not only for her comments but also for putting up with my hours alone, staring at a computer screen.

Chapter 1
Only a Party
—Jonathan—

If only I had seen it sooner. Kenny might be here. Scott and I might still be friends, and Jennifer ... well, she wouldn't have felt pushed to escape. As for us, Amy, there'd never been any real chance.

Yet I've come to understand that none of us is entirely to be blamed for what happened. How could we possibly have understood what each other needed when we couldn't even see what we needed for ourselves? We'd had no guide to lead us through this thicket of ignorance. No one ever does.

Looking back, it all seems so obvious. That makes me angry. But it makes me sad more than anything. There was so much pointless pain. We were making the same mistakes over and over, never grasping that the stories we kept telling ourselves were only what we wanted to be true—not what was true. For this I'm sorry—for all of us.

While each of our stories ends differently, they all begin on that first trip to Chicago, three years ago, the first Saturday of May 1988.

Scott and I came only to visit a couple of friends, Tanya and Randal. We were to go to a party at their place, crash on their couch, and then head back to Columbus the next day. It was to be one night—nothing life changing. Certainly nothing for anyone to die over.

Driving Scott's Sentra on our first trip to Chicago, I listen to the hum and rattle of the road, the steady vibration numbing my butt. I've spent six hours on flat, straight freeways, driving through corn and soybean fields, and past cattle and horse farms, first west on I-70 and then north on I-65, with the trees, hills, and fields all violently green in a Midwest spring.

Scott's sleeping because he worked late and got only two hours of sleep before we left. He must be completely cashed out to get any sleep the way he's awkwardly crammed into the passenger seat. He's too big for it: a bit over six feet tall, and thick from years of having worked out. His shirt buttons strain across his chest, and jeans wrap like skin around his legs. I'm sort of his opposite: five ten, skinny, with long light brown hair—dirty blond I've been calling it lately. When I first met him, I imagined a real stud with the ladies. But he usually spurns their attention—claims they're needy and take up too much time. Even so, I've seen the way he looks at them. I doubt he's as in control of his lust as he'd like to imagine. I suspect that's why he wears his dark brown hair parted above his left eye, as if he were still in high school; it's his veil of dweeb.

Right now I'm awake, but I need some tunes to stay that way, so I turn the volume down and the radio on. Out comes Depeche Mode, and I bop my head to the beat of "Just Can't Get Enough," which has about the perfect energy for driving.

It's not until we get near Gary, Indiana—where I see the first exit sign pointing to the Skyway and Chicago—that it really hits me: we're actually going to Chicago. Yesterday Tanya called and invited Scott and me to visit them in their new place in Wicker Park. Our band White Heat didn't have any gigs this weekend, so last night we gave away the rest of our shifts at the restaurant, and this morning we packed our bags, gassed up, and hit the road.

Sitting here now, steering wheel in hand, I feel bad about the way I left things with Amy.

She was pissed when I called this morning to let her know that Scott and I were going to Chicago. I told her the truth: "We're going to visit Tanya. We're staying at her place. You guys can't stand each other. Plus, six hours with you and Scott in the same car?"

"You going up there to join her entourage again?" she asked. "She hooking you up with a place? A job?"

"It's a party."

"Six-hour drive for a party?"

2

"Yep. Be back tomorrow, late."

"Better not be lying."

"Only a party. Back tomorrow. Nothing else," I said. "Promise." I meant it too.

As we pass Gary, the farmland turns into factories. To the right, the US Steel mill never seems to end: one smokestack follows another, some spewing smoke, others flame, others nothing, scattered across a field of jagged roofs like sharks' teeth. Beyond that lies the endless water of Lake Michigan. On the other side of the Indiana Tollway are small brick and aluminum-sided houses, each in one of a few styles, repeated endlessly, lined up on straight streets, spreading outward in an orderly grid.

We approach the Chicago Skyway Bridge, the last thing between us and Chicago. I nudge Scott awake as we drive across the almost eight-mile-long bridge over the Little Calumet River. Glimpses of the city flash between the girders.

Then, right as we pass the crest of the bridge, Chicago appears like a revelation: buildings erupting out of the plains, stretching up until they penetrate the clouds. At their feet is water as far as I can see on one side; on the other are the plains, covered in ordered rows of houses, spreading out until everything disappears at the horizon. Scott looks awed. I imagine showing this to Amy: *See why we came?*

Then the road sinks, plunging below street level until we're in a canal where streams of cars and trucks gush through the city.

"Crappy view," Scott says. "I can only see rooftops. And light poles."

I want to look up; instead I have to concentrate on the traffic, as cars are constantly switching lanes, pushing themselves into tiny gaps, cutting off trucks, busses, and us. I have to jam the brakes or accelerator every few moments.

"It's six twenty-five in Chicagoland," the radio announcer says. "A beautiful sixty-eight degrees on this Saturday, the seventh day of May. And the rest of the weekend looks perfect for grilling out."

When an ad starts, Scott pushes in a Joy Division CD—*Closer*—and "Atrocity Exhibition" starts its bleak, stripped-down soundscape.

"Yeah," I say. "That'll work." Better than the usual George Michael, Rick Astley, or Whitney Houston that have taken over the airways lately.

A lot of people have said that I sound like Ian Curtis. I don't hear it. People probably see me behind the mic, conjuring moody soundscapes on my keyboards, and think I'm trying to be some modern version of him. I'm not.

Scott rifles through the glove compartment and then flips through my song notebook. "Where'd you put the directions?"

"Should be right there," I say, pointing my elbow at my notebook.

"Well, they're not." Sighing, he pulls out an old gas station map and unfolds it to a section with a heading reading, "Chicago: Downtown Detail."

After a half hour, the signs tell us that the Dan Ryan has become the Kennedy Expressway.

"Why the hell don't the signs use numbers for highways? You know, three fifteen, seventy-one, two seventy," he says. "How are you supposed to find anything on a map?"

"She told me we're supposed to stay on the Kennedy until we get to North Avenue," I say. "Wherever the hell that is."

"We've still got their phone number, right?" he asks.

"On the directions."

"That I can't find. Wonderful."

Quickly, we pass the Ontario Street exit. Then comes Chicago Avenue, Augusta, Division. And then the sign we need—North Avenue—appears.

Exiting, we rise from the Kennedy Expressway and come to a traffic light. The traffic light isn't like the ones I'm used to, hanging overhead, but is propped up on a lamp pole off to the side of the intersection.

Turning onto North Avenue toward the sinking sun, we really enter the city. I can see whole people for the first time; they are walking, entering buildings, waiting for these weird traffic lights to change, and talking on pay phones. As we drive west, the people vanish from the sidewalks. The buildings get sparser and are short, industrial, and shabby. Some have fenced-off parking lots sprinkled with a few cars and a delivery van or two. Several have boarded-up windows, and a few look derelict. Convenience stores and the occasional auto-repair/tire-fix shop or check-cashing place pop up at corners here and there. It's not pretty; it's functional. As the signs say, "Chicago: The City That Works."

"Where is it we're turning, again?" he asks.

"Win-something. But I remember that we turn right."

"Wow, that's almost helpful."

"Win-*chester*," I say. "Like the gun. That's the name."

One slender building rises taller than all the rest around: the Coyote Building, its tall spire a minaret calling the faithful to play. It brings the streets back to life. Around it the industrial buildings end and three-story brick and stone buildings spring up like uneven teeth: crowded blocks of apartments sitting atop small shops, most of which are painted in bright colors, with homemade-looking signs featuring stick figures. Bicycles are chained up along the sidewalks. Handbills plaster empty walls, the words spelled with cutout letters like in movie ransom notes. It's shabby but alive.

Closer to the Coyote Building, I see a train passing above North Avenue on elevated tracks as it slides between buildings. I feel as if Amy is seeing this with me. *You gotta admit it's cool, girl.*

Then I see Winchester.

Turning right, we slip onto a residential street; on either side are apartment buildings, pocked with an occasional vacant lot scattered with mattresses lying on piles of junk. Most apartments have stairs going both down a half flight to a garden apartment and up a half flight to one or two doors. A few stand-alone homes squeeze in between. All look mangy, and some, decrepit: fading paint, broken gutters and handrails, listing screen doors, shattered flowerpots, and cardboard stuffed behind broken windowpanes. Potholes clutter the street. Many street lamps are gone but for their stubby bases, left there like steel stumps. Here and there, windows are boarded up, and several times we pass completely boarded-up buildings with junk sprouting from their skinny yards: abandoned box springs, dinette sets, refrigerators, toys, mysteriously shaped scraps of metal, and bags bursting with clothes. The street reeks of neglect. Yet it's studded with buildings that have been reborn—new windows, fresh paint, and rich-looking curtains, behind which are bookcases and chandeliers.

"Sixteen seventy-five Winchester," Scott says, holding up the page of my songbook I'd scribbled Tanya's address on.

We're close. On the next block, I slide the car to the curb almost in front of the house.

"Rock-star parking," we both say.

We bail and grab our bags. The radio, CDs, and the rattle of the road have filled the past six hours, and now that we're walking down a sidewalk, the only sounds are our footsteps and the soft drone of cars in the distance. It feels strange—especially since Tanya told us this was still mostly a Spanish-speaking neighborhood, with the Latin Kings and Party People fighting for turf to sell crack around the edges. She's even heard gunfire at night a few times—drive-by shootings that she saw later on the ten o'clock news. Lately, though, a lot of artists have moved here, opening up shops, galleries, and restaurants and refurbishing run-down buildings and houses.

"Let's go," he says, pointing at the doorway.

I press the doorbell button. The muffled electronic *ding-dong* of the doorbell is followed quickly by the shuffle of shoes and jangle of the doorknob turning. The door swings open.

Dramatically lit in the foyer, a lone man stands. His wavy black hair is pulled into a tail, hanging past his shoulders. He's wearing snug, well-worn blue jeans, shiny black boots, and a white V-neck T-shirt. Curly black hair pokes out from the collar. A camera hangs from his neck. He examines us, his eyes moving quickly down and then back up each of our bodies.

"Tanya's downstairs," he says, drawing the camera to his eye; two flashes fire off in a row.

With spots in the middle of my vision, I step inside and find I'm standing on a bridge spanning the space from the foyer to a hallway in the back of the second floor. Midway across, there is a spiral stairway leading down. Looking over the right side of the railing, into the lower level of the house, I see the expected crowd. They're like they were at her parties in Columbus, but more so: more hip, more artsy, more punk, more stylish.

I know you hate these parties, Amy, but that's your fault. She's the star— not you. You should've known better.

The photographer looks around and then down into the living room. His eyes seek; they're always hunting, locking onto things for a moment—usually a face, or a body posed just so. He's like a hawk scanning the ground for something small and hard to see to swoop down upon and catch. His fingers even resemble talons the way he holds them slightly curled. So often he seems about to grab the camera but rarely does.

Scott pushes past me to the stairway. He bounds down the stairs, which look frail for his size. I'm soaking everything in first. Leaning on the handrail, I breathe in the smoky air: layers of cigarette, charred meat, and charcoal, with a hint of dope.

"Serious party." I turn to the photographer. "Drinks?"

Gazing through the viewfinder of his camera at the crowd below, he says, "Kitchen. Downstairs." The camera clicks and flashes three times in rapid succession. "All the way back. Grill's outside."

I climb slowly down the stairs, checking everyone out; I scan the faces for our hostess and host, Tanya and Randal, but I see neither, so I walk down the hallway. A redhead—maybe old enough to drink—walks by in a tie-dyed tube top dress laced with multicolored waves and gives me a playful cruise. *Oh, I like this city. A lot.*

The kitchen is crowded, but Scott's easy to find, and next to him— the hostess. She's looking good as always. Not that it's hard for her—she modeled about a decade ago, in her late teens, and still has the looks: not quite six feet tall, with long, wavy light brown hair pulled back into a ponytail, her full figure poured into a tight-fitting flapper's dress with fishnet stockings and high-top grandma shoes. She's laughing.

Stopping almost in front of her, I stare, waiting for her to look up and notice I'm here. I like getting the surprised look that breaks into a smile, and then her dramatic hello.

I feel a hand tug on my shoulder. Expecting someone from Ohio, I turn to find a woman who's moving me out of the way. She has distinctly Eastern European cheeks and nose, and spent time putting herself together: deep red lipstick; chestnut-brown hair, perfectly parted and falling across one eye; an apricot-colored scarf knotted off to the left; a dark brown velvet jacket; and a low-cut black top that exposes the perfect amount of her small chest. She raises an eyebrow at me and then sinks back into the party.

7

"Jonathan!" Tanya calls. "Oh my god! You *did* make it." There's the smile I love getting. It's pure show—a special introduction for me. Everyone turns to look.

"Of course," I say, playing along. "How could I miss all this? Six-hour drive be damned."

"Come here, come here," she says.

I slide through a few people and reach out for her. She grabs me, and we kiss each other's cheeks. Tanya's the sun around which everyone's social life spins, so the chatter has gone quiet in anticipation of my introduction.

"Everyone," she says, "Jonathan. From far, far away. Came just for this little party of mine."

I give a quick wave.

"Now, who have you met?" she asks.

"Well ..."

Scott mimics taking a photo.

"Ron the photographer, of course," she says. "Now, weren't you looking at someone?"

Near Tanya, I see the Eastern European–looking woman, and I nod at her. "We weren't formally introduced." She strikes me as, somehow, out of place.

"Oh, my," Tanya says, arching her eyebrow. "Michele, Jonathan. Jonathan, Michele." Then she shakes her head in theatrical disappointment. "We really have to do better than two people."

Letting slip a smirk, Michele turns to the sink, which bristles with wine bottles plunged into ice.

"Well, to start," our hostess says, pulling the shoulder of a woman to get her to face me more completely, "AnnMarie, Jonathan."

AnnMarie has a dark brown bob, cat-eye glasses, and is good looking in a funky-hip way, yet she isn't sexy, in spite of the skimpy, tight-waisted Jane Jetson dress she's wearing. "You two have a lot to talk about. But"—Tanya raises her finger—"it's business. So not until later."

She turns to a pretty, androgynous blond. "This is Kenny. Kenny Magnum. One of Wendy's boys. She's around here someplace."

"Wendy's boys?"

"Oh yes. You're a foreigner," Tanya says. "She's a founder of Les Femmes. The modeling agency. She's trying to rent him out to go look pretty in front of cameras. But enough for now. You have a cocktail to get." She points to the sink. "There is a selection of white wine, white wine, or white wine. So, hurry up. Randal wants to see you too. He's out back tending the fire."

My time in her spotlight done, the talking resumes, and I head to the sink. Scott pushes himself next to me.

"Like back home," he says. "Including *your* red carpet intro."

"I've known her longer."

He rumples his nose. He's always had a problem with appearing second. In all our bands, I've been the lead singer and the keyboardist, and always the person people recognize first, so whenever he can, he makes a point to say he plays lead guitar and the band is both of ours.

I get it. But it's not like I'm trying to steal the thunder.

Lifting a bottle out of the sink, I feel that same thrum inside I always do at her parties. Here even more so, as everyone is totally new. Any of them could be a lover, friend, fan, band member, or A&R person—the artists and repertoire executive we need to get our recording contract. It's all newness and possibility, and so far from Columbus, everything I am there vanishes. I have no weight to carry; I can choose to be anyone I wish. It's as if all my mistakes have been washed away or been forgotten and traded for all this possibility.

That Eastern European–looking woman, Michele, is talking to Tanya, giving me the chance to really look at her. Then it clicks; what's so strange about her is that she's here at all. Tanya is the star of the gang. No one outshines her, and everyone depends on her somehow—even the host, her longtime beau. A girl can be beautiful as long as she is young and inexperienced. Everyone here depends on her to get into the right places or to be introduced to the right person. That's how Michele doesn't fit. She's no young girl. Looks to be in her late twenties like me. She's like Tanya's inverse. Tanya was a catalogue model for J. C. Penney and Sears a few years back; she is good looking in a curvy and suggestive, yet safe, suburban American way. Michele doesn't have the curves; her body is long, slender, and almost smooth. There's nothing remarkable about her face. But with the way she has put herself together, she looks as if she fell, moments ago, out of a glossy ad for some expensive, impossible-to-pull-off, edgy couture. She looks like a woman who really doesn't exist, except in magazines. Amy's like that, except Amy walked straight off a page of some highbrow erotic novel.

I can't imagine why Michele was invited to the party. *What do you have that Tanya could want?*

"You always talk to yourself?" AnnMarie asks, stepping into my gaze.

"Talk to myself? Oh, that. Yeah, all the time," I say. "Always say it's the reason I've never been mugged. Thugs think I'm crazy."

"Insanity defense. Like that," she says. "I should use it myself."

"Be my guest. Just don't start talking back."

"Right," she says. "By the way, Tanya gave me your demo tape. Very post-punk: Joy Division."

"Get that a lot. Or Bauhaus."

"Sounds like the last few bands I gigged with. When are you going to play Chicago?"

"No idea. Takes connections in a big market like Chicago."

"Not really," she says. "Only seems like it. I've been playing around in this town for years. I know about every place you can play. Here, Milwaukee, West Bend, downstate. All you actually need is good demo tape. Like yours."

"Aaaah, I see what our hostess meant about business to talk about later. What's your axe?"

"Drum machines. Delays. Sing backup."

"So you know your way around sequencers, patches?"

"Not bad. But I'm no geek."

"I wish I knew more. I'd love to move on. Change our sound."

"To?"

"Not sure. New Order, RevCo, the Cure. You know: 'Blue Monday,' 'Attack Ships on Fire,' 'In Between Days.' Or not. Just ideas floating around in my head."

"Well, I'm available if you need help here," she says. Then she drinks, pushing her cup up and up, and then down, and she scowls into the emptiness.

"Ooh, seems we've a problem," I say. "Not to worry."

Scott is standing by the sink, and I wave, holding up my cup. "Hey, Scott!" Getting his attention, I point at her and then my cup. I hold up two fingers.

"You're the lead singer," AnnMarie says. "That's obvious. And keyboards, right?"

"Yeah."

"Lead guitar would be?" she asks, nodding her head at Scott.

"Yup."

With the three newly full cups in his one hand, he's gliding through the crowd, spilling nothing. This ease of movement seems impossible for his size; he's big, even intimidating, yet supple—a moving contradiction.

He pulls up to us, snapping his scuffed, thick-soled black shoes together.

"Now, about that business our hostess mentioned," I say. "AnnMarie here knows everyone we need to know to play Chicago. Every place around too. And ... she plays. Drum machines."

"Choice. What's the scene like here?" he asks. "I mean really."

"Pick up a *Reader*. Pick any night of the week. Three, four, five shows. Shows that you *want* to check out."

The photographer has strolled over, and they start talking about places he's shot bands and that she's played around here: Lounge Ax, the Beat Kitchen, the Double Door. But when Cabaret Metro is brought up, the tone gets reverential. Every band that matters has played there, both national acts and hot local bands. To play Metro *is* to matter.

As they talk, I imagine playing Cabaret Metro. The stage unfolds before me: the wood of the stage floor, cables snaking across it, duct tape, monitors. I'm about to sing. Standing behind my keyboard, the lights washing away the audience, I can hear them chanting the name of the song I'm about to sing: "Amy's Face." My heart starts to pound. *This is why we came, Amy. Get it now?*

"Cabaret Metro," I say, raising my hands up as if I'm about to play my keyboard. From the corner of my eye, I catch Michele watching. I strike the keys in a furious opening chord for her, but she's already turned away as if she'd never glanced this way. *That's such an Amy move.*

11

"Mister photographer!" Tanya calls out, having made her way next to Scott, "Wendy says she's got some new boy to shoot."

Ron makes a slightly sour face. "That's fine. But I'm still working out Charlene's comps."

Right then, a woman starts toward us. She's not tall—about five feet five—and wears her hair slicked back like Rudolph Valentino's.

"Hello, Wendy," Ron says to her.

"I know you're all hot to shoot Charlene," Wendy says, standing in front of Ron insistently. As short as she is, there's no question as to who's in charge. "Don't worry. That's a done deal. We're working out the time. But meanwhile, here's someone else to shoot. Come here, Kenny," she says, waving over that pretty blond boy with hazel eyes and a slight build. With makeup and a skirt, he'd make a good-looking girl. He reminds me of David Bowie from the seventies—boy or girl, depending on what he wanted someone to see.

"This is Kenny Magnum," Wendy says. "He's got talent but needs a portfolio. From a pro like you, not the usual amateurs. He's more flexible than Charlene right now; she's working a couple of jobs on spec, so she's busy."

The photographer looks the girlish boy over. "I can see it. Sure, Wendy. What I really need is a reliable studio. Someplace I can stash my lighting equipment. *Without* having to worry about it getting ripped off."

"We'll get that worked out on Monday. And, if I can finally convince her"—Wendy pulls a woman out from behind her, where she's been hiding—"Jennifer here. She needs comps as well."

Jennifer is slender and slightly built, a sylph in cutoff shorts and black nylons, though no one would mistake her for a boy. She's Eurasian, with slightly rounded almond-shaped eyes and a button nose with a small piercing I can't quite make out. She looks young—a college kid.

"I've seen you around, right?" Ron asks.

She nods.

"Yes," he says. "You work at Les Femmes. In Wendy's office."

With a deadpan expression, she nods again.

"Real Chatty Kathy out of the office." He turns back to Wendy. "Okay,

Monday. Let's set up Kenny and Charlene. Let me know if the mute here wants to shoot. Great look. Could get her places."

"Hey, Ron," Scott says. "Tell me more about Metro."

"Why don't you two just move here?" Ron asks. "Find out all you want about Metro, firsthand."

It's a simple question that I've no answer to.

Scott goes quiet.

Why don't we? Columbus is going nowhere. Chicago's huge. It's got what we really need. We have Tanya and AnnMarie.

Scott gives a never-thought-about-it shrug.

"You should," Ron says.

"You know Tanya can hook you up with an apartment," AnnMarie says. "A job. Anything. I know the scene. Plus, I need a new band to play in, and you'll need a drummer, right?"

I look to Scott and start nodding, and then Scott nods, and our nods go faster and faster until I know we've decided. *We're moving to Chicago.*

"All right." Ron grabs his camera and fires off several flashes at us with our arms around AnnMarie. "There, I've you documented from the start."

I've no idea what I'll tell Amy.

Chapter 2

Heading Back
—Jonathan—

The next morning, a couple too many cocktails last night have left me feeling rough. Scott's driving us back to Columbus, which helps, but the sun's still out to torture me.

"You know," Scott says, "we can't tell anyone about this. Not yet. Not anyone in the band. No family. Sure as hell not Amy."

I let out a groan. *Oh must you? Now?*

"We've a lot of plans to make. Can't afford any problems. Any drama."

"Drama?" I ask, regretting it immediately. I need to play too sick to talk so I can think things through.

"Yeah, like being stood up for a gig by Sean and Marsha. Who are not coming with us. Like the melodramatic tantrums Amy'll throw. Like parents getting all in our stuff. Every one of them trying to convince us to not go. To trip us up. Keep us down there. With them."

"Why ..." *Would you do that, Amy? Hold me back?*

"No one wants to be left behind."

I really need to think here, man.

"Columbus is a cow town," Scott continues. "Chicago's the next step we need to take. *Must* take. Or else we'll end up getting old and dying here, playing in cover bands for a few bucks and free drinks. No. That's for people who can't. We're people who can."

"Sure. Right," I say. "Yes. You're right. You are." I curl up as much as

I can, trying to get him to shut up for now. "I'm not feeling well. Let me settle my stomach."

"Gonna boot?" He points into my footwell. "There's an empty bag there if you have to."

"Right. Thanks."

I twist my head away from the sunlight and close my eyes. I know Scott and I *have* to move. We've gotta get out of that place to get our shot—to grab everything we've been busting our asses for. For years.

But without Amy?

In the quiet, Scott flips on the radio and "The Theme from S Express" comes on.

"Could you," I say, undulating my hand downward. "Just a little."

He turns it down: a little.

This should be so simple: Move. Grab the ring. Be what you talk about being. In Chicago—a real town. A serious market.

My eyes pop open.

Hold on. That could be a promotion for her. A more prestigious market. So she can move. Sure she will; it's a promotion. She can even live with us at first, till she finds her own place.

"So," I say. "If she moves in with—"

"*No!*" Scott bellows, the sound of his voice ringing around the inside of my headache, making it more intense.

I grab the sides of my head.

"Amy? Not living with us. No chance in hell."

"Yeah, okay, okay. Just thinking out loud. Forget about it."

"This is for us."

"Right. Got it," I say. "Where's a puke bag?"

"Down there."

Reaching down, I start pushing the trash around the footwell. I knock over a crumpled burger bag and then see the *Chicago Magazine* we snagged for home. It's lying open to a photo that peers through a kitchen doorway at a party full of people drinking; the scene looks very much like the party where I met Amy four and a half years ago. It was a Friday, in early May like today, after work, during the only time in my life I almost had a real job, back when Scott and I were so broke it hurt. Nothing had gone like we'd planned. We'd gotten our degrees like the Ps wanted and then devoted all our time to playing. We'd figured that was what had been holding us back: full commitment. We had part-time waiting jobs to cover rent and electric. But after we gave it everything we could, all our band Arcade Land did was leave us more broke than we'd been in college. Scott had to give up his gym. We were down to eating ramen noodles, and whatever was in the discounted dented-can and bent-box bins next to the cash registers. The money got so meagre. The next step was to move back home.

Since I could type fairly well and use a ten-key calculator, we decided I'd get a regular daytime job to keep nights free, and he'd keep working on the band for us.

I took the only job offered: a temp.

It was as if I had died.

Alarm clock at seven. Car at eight ten. Cubicle at nine. Every place was the same: "Do something with this piece of paper and then something with that one." Lunch at noon. Back to the cubicle at one. Glance at the clock until it's four, and then stare at it in order to drag the small hand down with the sheer weight of my eyes, until it nearly touches the five, then push the big hand up from the six at four thirty, past the seven, the eight, the nine, the ten, and the eleven, until at last it touches the twelve, freeing us all. *Five o'clock!* Chairs go back, jackets get snatched, lights go out, and the parking lot drains of cars. On Fridays, five o'clock turns magical, filling the room with excitement. No one is nearly nodding off, everyone's feet are tapping, fingers gently rapping desks until the hour has struck, granting freedom for days.

"Freedom to do what?" I'd asked so many people, yet everyone's plans sounded nearly the same, all equally bleak: Dinner, then a date with the tube for *Moonlighting*, *MacGyver*, or *Mr. Belvedere*, and then bed. Or perhaps a movie like *Twins*, *Crocodile Dundee II*, or *Die Hard*. Maybe a video. Occasionally a singles bar, hoping for a chance in the money machine to grab as much cash spinning in the air of that clear box as possible in thirty seconds. Week after week I heard this. It was desolate, passionless, and devoid of dreams. I stopped asking and kept to myself.

The months went by. Our band Arcade Land stumbled badly; people kept quitting, and we had fewer and fewer gigs until there were none, but by then I'd stopped caring that much. The rut of nine to five had metastasized, spreading to every part of my life; I thought more and more about five o'clock and my escape from those cubicles.

Sometimes I could hear songs struggling to form in my mind—desolate melodies and quiet, desperate lyrics imploring an indifferent universe to reveal to them that there was something else: something more than merely surviving yet another day. Something that felt like being truly alive. That there *had* to be. One hideous afternoon, I realized that these were also the sounds of *my* own life—sounds so different from those I'd always heard before, that I'd caught on paper and then loosed on stage: the sounds of growing up, of always being hungry, of always wanting to be older, to be bigger, to be more real, of needing to matter to anyone—at all—and, most urgently, to know who or what I am. These new sounds repulsed me. They scared me even more, for they howled that there was no answer, no end to this yearning. Not ever.

By then Scott had changed too, acting more like a happy homemaker than a driven band manager or striving lead guitarist, as if this, our living together, and talking about putting Arcade Land back together again, someday, was good enough.

The Friday I met Amy, I'd arrived home from my cubicle, unsure if I'd tell Scott about this party I'd heard about. I hadn't decided if I'd go yet and could bail easier if I didn't say anything. I found Scott in the kitchen, chopping vegetables on the counter next to a large salad bowl. Bags of groceries were on the table. He looked up at me and smiled.

"So," he said, "How was your day?"

Right then, an icy slush filled my gut. This was it; I'd failed. Making it as a musician was a chimera, and 5:00 p.m. would be all that I would look forward to, free to come home, have dinner, and watch TV. The idea of being onstage—something that had buoyed me through all trials, every setback we'd then overcome, and had filled my days with purpose and told me who I was—finally collapsed and shriveled up. *It's all been a waste of time.* The three clean white walls of my cubicle marked out the silhouette of who I'd become.

Had it remained like this, I would have gone out at the end of a leather belt I tied around a chandelier, kicking at the smoke-filled air.

Though I didn't know it, at that very moment, my deliverance was dressing herself for a party I'd decided I couldn't bear to attend.

I shudder to think of that now; I'd almost stayed home and watched something on TV with Scott. I'd had every reason not to go. I would avoid having to face people who knew I didn't have a band anymore, and avoid admitting that I was now a cubicle automaton, that I wasn't who they thought they knew—that I wasn't the person *I* thought I knew.

After dinner, I went out for cigarettes, but on the way back home, for reasons I still wonder at, I turned left on Neil Avenue and walked the three blocks to that party and straight into a different life.

The party was in a third-floor apartment, and once inside, the smells of cigarettes, kef, and incense; the sounds of the Eurythmics' "Love is a Stranger"; and the sights of people like I used to hang with jarred me, as if I'd walked head on into a glass wall. It took me a few moments to get my bearings and find out that the drinks were in the kitchen. "Over there, down that hall," somebody told me.

There, through the doorway, in the cramped, smoky kitchen, she stood next to a table, indifferently sipping from a half-filled plastic cup. She was nearly as tall as me—a couple of inches shy of six feet—and had very dark brown, almost black, wavy hair to her shoulders, with bright blue eyes; they looked like a cat's eyes in the dark. Meticulous makeup highlighted those eyes, raised her eyebrows, accentuated her high cheeks, and plumped her lips. The whole effect betrayed that she was older than the touch of baby fat under her chin suggested, with a body that didn't seem quite real. She looked like a cartoon bombshell—a taller, sleeker Betty Boop: full breasts, a wasplike waist that flowed into round hips, and long, lively legs. She was dressed to show herself off: the thick seams on the backs of her black stockings drew my eyes along her calves and then her thighs until the edge of a micromini abruptly ended the trip up her legs. A snug-fitting gossamer top revealed a tattoo on her left breast—of what I couldn't make out through the hunter-green fabric. All of her clothes were ten or twenty years out of date, worn rough in places and threadbare in spots. She, though, pulled off this type of secondhand-store shabbiness in a way few could: fiercely.

You have to be sleeping with someone here.

Then I remembered I was a cubicle drone now, and that I was here only because it was after five on Friday—not a school night. *What the hell does it matter if you're free? What am I going to say? "Oh, today was a bitch. My batches wouldn't add up. Three times in a row?" I'm ashamed of who I've become. I'm sleepwalking through the empty hours that make up another day.*

Still, I kept putting off leaving for another few minutes, time and again, lurking as I watched people laugh, talk, and simply enjoy being here. I wanted that too, but I felt embarrassed for myself and so out of place. It hurt being here like this. I decided to leave after one last cigarette.

She was standing almost next to me when she bummed a cigarette from someone, and I had my Zippo in hand so lit it for her—a meaningless gesture that led to a smile, a first few words, and then more, and then to casual touches, purposeful caresses, and finally to a kiss. An hour later, we were in my apartment, sitting on the edge of my unmade bed, her arms draped around me. I slipped my hand between us and fondled the bottom button of her blouse. As our kisses grew deeper, I pushed the domed button through the slit that held it, and then I released the next and the next of those tiny black buttons until I came to the last.

As that last button of her blouse slipped from my finger, she pulled back and said, "You know you're raping me."

My fingers froze.

"I'm only seventeen. I'm not legal for six weeks." She watched me. "Rapist."

I stared at her, not understanding why she was saying this. *Do I stop? Do I—*

"You're not going to *torture me*, are you?" she said, running a hand along the inside of my thigh. "Leave me guessing when you're going to do it—going to have me?"

I shook my head. I don't know if I believed she was seventeen or not. I want to think that I didn't, but it wasn't until six weeks later, on her nineteenth birthday, that I actually found out she'd been eighteen, and then it became clear that her jailbait claim was a lie to push further, to see if I could keep up with her, to make touching each other mean something more than merely having sex.

That first night, she smiled and leaned back on my bed, her shirt falling open, revealing her tattoo: a butterfly, its wings teardrops of reds and blues within thick black lines, one wing grazing a nipple. I touched the edge of a wing and ran my fingers around it; then I ran my fingers around the other wing until I came to her lavishly pink nipple. I kissed it.

"Rapist," she said, unbuttoning my jeans.

My bedroom swallowed us whole that weekend, and every night for the next week, and then the weeks after. The clean white sides of my cubicles no longer fixed who I was; they morphed to mere walls, keeping me from my lover, and five o'clock transformed into the key that let me free of them and back into my newly vibrant life. On Friday, five o'clock meant whole days with her and late-morning hours spent in bed as we consumed every particle of each other's bodies and imbibed the merest details of each other's lives, the sheets knotted and twisted around us. I felt as if we had stepped off an infinitely high precipice and, as we fell together, that we were actually flying. Gravity ceased to be. I'd never lived this vividly.

While Amy and I spent every moment we could unearthing the pleasures of being with each other, Scott grew testy, sullen, and snippy, snapping that she left too little milk and grumbling that he found her things around *our* house. After three weeks, hints about my true commitment to reforming Arcade Land sprung up whenever we talked.

While Scott the grump grumbled, Amy expanded me. Opened me up to things I'd never known, such as Lawrence Durrell's *The Alexandria Quartet*. "Passionate existentialism" is how she described it.

I scoffed.

"Shows we truly exist only through our passions." She rolled up against me in bed. "One of my favorite quotes is 'There are only three things to be done with a woman,' said Clea once. 'You can love her, suffer for her, or turn her into literature.'"

"Love, lose, or preserve?"

"You're a writer."

"A songwriter. Yes."

"Then turn me into a song. Or three. Preserve me. Preserve us."

These words would soon change everything. For all of us.

The next Tuesday afternoon, I'd gotten home early enough to catch him in the hallway as he was leaving to work one of his two weekly shifts at Denny's he had to pull now.

"Jonathan," he said, blocking me from walking in any farther. "There's something wrong here. You're not acting right."

"What?"

"Yeah," he said. "Not acting like you give a damn about playing any more. You only care about sleeping with your girl—"

"Hold up here, now."

"You told me once nothing mattered to you more than playing. That it's your reason for being, or some shit like that. Now? I don't know. Do you even *want* to play in Arcade Land? Or is she your instrument now?"

"My instr ..." I said. "No. No. This ... No."

"When was the last time you even looked at your keyboard?"

"When I had a reason to," I said. "When we had gigs to play. When we had a band. Right now, Arcade Land is only the two of us. That's not a band."

He glowered.

"I took a miserable day job so you could 'work on the band,' and what?"

"Look. You need to make up your mind. Do you want to play in a band with me? Or are you more interested in balling her?" He slid past me to the front door. "Just let me know."

He slammed it behind him before I could say anything.

After that, Amy and I hardly saw Scott any more. Instead we got notes instructing what food not to touch, or asking why something got left out, or complaining that our dishes weren't done or that his towel was left wet.

This silent quarrel of notes lasted about a month until it got very loud one Sunday afternoon. Amy was looking over my shoulder as I poked around the refrigerator to find something to eat when Scott walked into the kitchen.

"Doesn't she have a home?" he asked.

I let go of the container of leftover Chinese I'd been looking at and pivoted on my heel.

Amy straightened up from a crouch. Her expression was severe—jaw jutting out, eyes thinned to slits—I'd never seen her angry before. Not like this. She turned, slowly, to face him.

"What's your problem?" she asked. "Jealous I've got all your boy's attention?"

His lips curled, and he pushed his head toward her. He squared off his thick shoulders like a bull about to charge. This I'd seen before, many times: Scott *supremely* pissed off. He's frightening like this.

I caught my breath.

"My *boy*?" he asked scornfully. "My *band's* lead singer. Songwriter. Keyboardist."

"Oh, is that all?"

"What the fuck's that supposed to mean?"

"Whatever you think it does."

"Look, woman," Scott said, jabbing a meaty finger at her. "This is *my* house, and—"

"Guys! Guys!" I shouted, jumping between them, my palms held up to both. "Just. Stop it."

"No. Not in *my* house—"

"*Our* house," I said, cutting him off, holding a finger up at him. "In *our* house. And"—I threw my thumb at her—"she's in *my* life."

He balled his fists and glared. I waited, my breath ragged, heart hammering. Amy watched.

"That mean you're quitting Arcade Land?" he asked. "Punking out on me? Giving up on us?"

"No," I said. "It doesn't. At all. But damnit. I need ..." I threw my arms down. "Not *this*."

"You wanna be in Arcade Land," Scott said, jabbing his finger at me. "Act like it." He turned and walked away.

Shaking, I stared at the empty doorway he'd walked through.

"Hey," Amy said softly.

The caress of her voice allowed me to let go of the tension. My body finally went slack, my breath slowing.

"Hey yourself," I said, still watching that doorway.

"I didn't expect that," she said.

"Him not liking you here?"

"Hardly. You standing up to him."

I made a puzzled face.

"He's not used to that. Big guys like him—bullies—they're always the boss. And he liked things as they were, being the boss. Domestic bliss. The happy married couple."

"What are—"

She put her fingers over my lips. "Shh." She shook her head. "Don't worry about it. He doesn't see it that way. Best not tell him."

She smothered my bewilderment with a long open-mouth kiss. I don't think I cared what she meant; I felt so intensely alive with her.

The next day, Monday, she went to work as usual, but I didn't have an assignment, and Scott was off doing something he hadn't bothered telling me about. For the first time in months, I broke out my keyboard and hooked it into the amp. I started dabbling with melodies, trying out whatever came to mind, the sounds I created groping after all the raw feelings racing around inside me, both those born of the fierce joys of stepping off the edge with Amy and those of the somnambulistic desperation of the five o'clock world. When Scott got home, he listened for a couple of minutes and then pulled out his guitar, and we started shaping these fragments into full songs, extending melodies, filling out choruses, and building rhythms. In the next days, I froze moments of passion as well as moments of desperation into lyrics and quickly found the sounds of passion far easier to work with, just as falling is easier than climbing. I strung only those ardent moments together like crystals on strings, song after song.

When we played these new, fiercely passionate songs in auditions, bassists and drummers strove to be the ones to play them with us. We dumped the name Arcade Land and the stain of failure it carried and renamed ourselves White Heat. We chose Sean for our bassist and Marsha for our drummer.

When we played out, we drew crowds. The Main High booked us again and again, and we practically became Crazy Mama's house band. In half a year, we were playing all original works, including our first seriously popular one—"Amy's Face."

I quit temping and went back to waiting part-time. Five o'clock melted back into being nothing more than one of the other twenty-four hours. The sanitary white walls of the cubicles receded into memory; their hold on who I was crumbled completely, though broken bits of them appeared in nightmares, which sometimes woke me late in the night. At these moments, all I needed to do was reach out for Amy, and her warm flesh would dispel them completely.

Being broke no longer mattered to me. Ramen noodles tasted fine even ten times a week. The mirages that chained us vanished. We needed more than commitment, more than good music, more than a solid band. We needed opportunity. As the weeks and gigs passed, and the cheering crowds led to nowhere new, it became ever more clear that the opportunity we needed wasn't in Columbus. Scott wondered about it out loud, but I turned my thoughts away whenever it led to leaving here, because that meant leaving Amy; Amy and I had never spoken of endings, making believe nothing would ever change, and fought off the bite of routine by acting out fantasies, whims, and melodramatic jealousies until it became hard to know what was real and what was play—until one Sunday afternoon, a line was stepped over.

Scott had gone out to run errands, and Amy and I were being bums, lying in bed, doing a lot of nothing, and really enjoying it. I didn't feel like getting out of bed and rushing to the phone when it rang, but the noise did make us get up and get dressed, and toy with the idea of going for a walk or something to get us out of the house. A half hour later, we'd only walked downstairs and decided to have coffee. It was two in the afternoon; we were in no rush to leave. From the kitchen, we heard Scott get home, and then came the sound of the answering machine: "I'm trying to reach Scott Marshall or Jonathan Starks. This is Maury Jenko at the Agora, and we're interested in talking to you about opening for Warren Zevon. We need to know in the next half hour. Give me a call at—"

"Jonathan!" Scott yelled from down the hall. "You got that, right? You called? Tell me you called."

"No," I said. "I didn't see we got a message."

"Christ!"

I heard Scott play the message again.

"Why didn't I ...? We ...?" I asked Amy, who shook her head, wearing a look of consolation.

"Hello, is Maury there?" I heard Scott ask. "This is Scott Marshall. From White Heat."

He said nothing for a few moments. I started for the hall, where Scott held the phone to his head.

"Oh, I see. Yes. Thank you."

"What?" I asked. "What?"

"You didn't hear the phone ring?"

"I ... I didn't get to it. So ..."

"You let the machine answer. But *didn't* bother to listen to it?"

"What did they say?"

"Already booked someone. Opportunity: lost."

I slammed the heel of my hand on the wall.

Scott pushed past me into the kitchen.

"Oh, exactly," he said. "She's here. No wonder. Why would I think otherwise."

Putting her cup down, Amy watched him approach, her expression turning from concerned to coldness.

"Can't we talk to them anyway?" I asked. "In case this other band drops out."

"What was it this time?" he asked, leaning over the table toward her. "Locked his head between your thighs? Getting off that important to you?"

"Back off, mister," Amy said calmly.

"Can we try?" I pleaded. "It's Warren Zevon."

"You're a menace," Scott said to Amy, pointing at her face. "To us. To everything."

"Look, you closet fag," she snarled back, her hand up to fend off his finger.

"Useless snatch."

"Goddamn! Stop it!" I shouted. "Now!"

They looked at me, ugly expressions hanging heavily on both of their faces.

"Now," I said, "is there any chance we can call them back?"

"You asshole," Amy said to me. "Go. You call 'em. And then go fuck yourself. Every night. Forever." She walked to the door and then turned back one last time. "Your wannabe boyfriend here should be happy as hell now."

The door slammed loudly after her.

Inside, I burned for days. No matter how many times I called, she never picked up; no matter how many messages I left, she never returned one. I filled the tape up with pleading until even the machine refused my calls. I couldn't pay attention at work—got me cut early twice that week. I couldn't concentrate when I was playing. Every time I thought I saw her, or the phone rang, I felt a surge of blinding hope that squeezed my breath out; but it was never her, and my hope broke into sharp pieces until every part of living cut into me.

After another difficult rehearsal that next Saturday, I let the band take me out for drinks at a hole-in-the-wall just south of The Ohio State University.

We ordered drinks, but I turned away from everyone else; I didn't want to talk.

Then I saw Amy—only two tables away.

She was talking to a boy, leaning closely to him as if she might kiss him.

I could only stare, screaming inside: *How could you when it hurts this badly?*

Then Scott noticed who I was looking at.

"We gotta leave," he said.

He tried to grab me, but I slipped through of his grasp and slammed into a table, knocking drinks over. People started shouting at me, and whole bar looked to see what was happening—including her.

She got up, knocking her chair over, and stomped directly at me, nostrils flaring. She got close enough I could touch her, and then her hand flew out and grabbed my throat.

"You," she said. "Fucking. Asshole."

"Psycho," Scott said, holding back Sean and Marsha. "Let them. He's gotta get that she's nuts."

Then she kissed me ferociously, digging her hands deep into my hair. I grabbed her waist, swung her around, and laid her over a bar stool.

"Don't you," I said as she wrapped her legs around my waist, "*ever* walk out like that again."

"Don't let me, asshole," she said. "I love you more than I can even think."

"I won't," I said. "Not ever. I swear."

That night had felt as life altering as the night we met, and pretending to break up so we could get back together has become another game we play to stay so fiercely in love. What's real and what's play has smeared together for us; yet which is which has never mattered. Until this ride home, when the real asserts itself so starkly.

The opportunity I need is Chicago. This opportunity does not include Amy. Our last breakup won't be play.

If I can cut her from my life.

I get sick into the bag.

Chapter 3

Eyes in the Mirror

—Jonathan—

Scott starts drilling my head about plans for the move right after we get past Indianapolis. I've been yeah-ing along, half 'cause there's not much we can do and half to keep from telling him I'm not so sure anymore. The only plan we actually nail down is to call Tanya to go back for another visit. He stops talking for a few miles, giving me time to think, but I can't shake the feeling of confused dread, so I stare at the freeway in front of us, watching the miles and minutes vanishing before we're home and I have to face her.

Then I notice Rick Astley's "Never Gonna Give You Up" playing on the radio.

Scott's mouthing the lyrics "Inside we both know what's been going on," and he puts his hand on my arm as if to comfort me.

"Excuse me," I say, looking at his meaty hand.

He glances at me, and then down, and yanks his hand away, quickly grabbing the steering wheel.

"Sorry," he says, shaking his head and frowning. "I only meant to apologize for busting out earlier. 'Bout Amy."

"Sure," I say. "Thanks."

He must be dying to say it'll be better this way, with her gone. He's never gotten Amy. Thinks she's only a distraction, and worse, a problem for White Heat, completely missing how I feel with her: fiercely alive. But that relationship's ending now, which is disorienting. My thoughts stumble around, and then I notice him searching the rearview mirror. Finding me looking into it, he holds my eyes, lip-synching, "Never gonna let you down," as if he meant the words for me.

This jolts me. I look down. Quickly finding the seek button on the radio, I push it to stop whatever's happening.

"Faith" by George Michael comes on.

"Hey," he says. "I liked that other song."

"Overplayed. Just like this one," I say, reaching down to change the station again.

He fends my hand away. "I'm the one driving."

"Driver's choice. Fine," I say. The hangover is still clawing around inside me, tangling itself up with Chicago and Amy, his arm-holding apology, and that weird lip-synching, and then a sign flicks past, telling me we're passing Ft. Wayne, Indiana, and it's only 137 miles to Columbus, pushing me nearer to facing Amy and forcing me to figure out how to tell her I'm leaving.

This should be great. We're taking a chance, getting our opportunity. Getting out of that cow town. But I hate the way I'm feeling now. I hate everything about this trip home.

Chapter 4

Lies and Other Fictions
—Jonathan—

I need someone to talk to. So much is going on inside my head.

Ever since getting back a week ago, Chicago's been the last thing I think of before sleeping, and the first after waking. The move is almost the only thing I think of at all. I'm always on the verge of blurting it out to Amy; she's my lover, the one who pulled me back into life, yet moving is essential for me. I want to tell her. I owe it to her. But I can't; she'd try to stop me, and I'm not sure I could resist. Sometimes I want her to find out and convince me to stay, ending all these lies.

That urge I can never reveal to Scott, so I have to tell one lie to Amy and another to Scott, and what seems like another to myself to keep from losing it: that everything will work out okay in the end.

Understanding that our past has no place in our future is easy. Here we failed. In Chicago, our future, we will be new—unstained. The past must remain the past—the back there, the forgotten, the cut away—so behind everyone's back, Scott and I have been making calls to Tanya and AnnMarie, plotting our next visit Chicago to find a place to live and pick a date for the move.

I'm also okay with not telling the two other members of White Heat, our final Columbus band. As Scott said, "They refused to give up a couple of shifts and come with us to even *visit* Chicago. And 'Persistence and determination alone are omnipotent.' They persist in waiting tables. They are determined to be waitrons. We persist in playing. We are determined to be musicians. Let them succeed in making fifty bucks a shift. They're not committed to the band. Not like you and me."

The move is clearly for Scott and me—for *our* new band.

Yet plotting behind Amy's back has never felt right, and I can tell she's catching on that something's up.

The last time I brought it up, Scott told me, "You cannot tell her. Even if she guesses. Can't."

"Maybe she'd want—"

"Do you really think that she'll quit that sweet design job of hers, pack up, and run off to Chicago with you? Go back to bartending?"

"Could be a promotion. Bigger market, right?"

"Moving to be with her boyfriend, a promotion? For a Madison Avenue firm? Only in fairy tales."

I shake my head. She's not even twenty-three and already the head of a design group for Kolby, Green, and Michelson, the New York advertising agency. She's got what I'm still striving for, and I'm not more important than her career; that I know.

To tell everyone fewer lies, I've started isolating myself, avoiding calls, sleeping in, and not going out; but as much as I can avoid other people, I cannot elude myself.

In some ways, it's been harder since Amy unwittingly let me off the hook a few nights ago. Since we'd gotten back two days before, she'd been treating me as if I were someone she was sizing up for the first time.

That night, after Scott left for work, leaving us alone together, she began scrutinizing me: my expression, the things I say, the way I answer her or don't, how much I look at her, and whether I can meet her gaze.

After an hour of this examination, I can bear no more and slip away to the bathroom. *Relax, man. Calm down. You're not going to say anything.*

"Like I said," I tell myself in the mirror, trying out my best nothing's-going-on expression. "It was only a party. That's it."

After giving myself a thumbs-up, I open the door, and Amy is standing right there, her expression hard, like an interrogator's.

"Um ..." I say. "Yes?"

"Chicago," she says.

"Chicago. What ... about it?"

"Did you have fun there?"

"Yeah."

"What'dya do?"

"Went to a party. Like I said."

"Did you meet anyone interesting?"

"Anyone interesting. Well …"

She's gazing directly into my eyes.

Waiting for me to tell her what really happened in Chicago. To admit to deceiving her.

She taps her foot impatiently.

"Hmm," I say. "I … No. I don't think so. Not really. Boring party."

The weight of suspicion tilts her head to the side.

You've figured out we're moving. My heart takes off running.

"Boring party?" she asks.

"Nothing's going on. Really. It was just a party."

"You're going to spoil it with these lousy lies," she says.

"Spoil it?"

"Come on. You've strung it out two whole days. Making me wonder what happened up there. With no one to watch you. It's been exciting. Hot." She puts on a severe expression. "So. What was her name?"

"Her name?" I ask.

"Who'd you get into bed?"

"No. I …"

"Don't lie about it. It's so obvious. The way you've been acting since you got back."

"I'm not. I didn't talk to anybody. About plans. We're not—"

"We?" She nods, smirking. "So you did get someone in bed."

In a flash, I realize she thinks that I'm been playing some elaborate erotic game, pretending to be covering up a tryst in Chicago.

Okay, Jonathan. Tell her a dirty story. About anyone. Easy as pie.

I draw a blank.

She lets out a disgusted grunt. "I hate lousy liars."

"Why would I lie?" I ask as coolly as I can. "See, I've nothing to lie about. No young girls. No one like you." *Think, Jonathan. Doesn't matter who. Any face.*

"Who was she?"

I squint in theatrical anger. "Oh, so you *really* want to know what happened a week ago? What I've been hiding from you? What's been making you so hot?"

"Yes. Oh god, yes. Tell me *everything.*"

"*Everything* that happened between me and the hot little tramp who kept letting me know how available she was? How eager?"

Amy's eyes grow wide in anticipation.

"Do you think I pushed her away after she led me to Tanya's bedroom? Huh? What do you think I did when she lay down right on Tanya's bed?"

Amy scowls melodramatically, balling her fists around her face. "What was her name?"

"I lifted up her skirt is what I did. No panties. Shaved. Just like you."

"Oh, that bitch," she says.

"Such firm, smooth thighs. Pale, like yours."

"What's her name?" Amy shouts.

"You want to know the name of the girl who begged me to fill her with my seed?"

"What the fuck's her name!" she shrieks.

"Jennifer." It's the only name that comes to mind. I bite my lip. "Such a hot little girl."

"Little girl?"

"Dark brown hair and young. Barely eighteen. Remind you of someone?"

"Eighteen—you pervert!" she yells, trying to slap me.

I jerk my head back, making her miss.

"You should know," I say, smirking.

She coils and launches herself—hands out to throttle me. I lean forward to catch the brunt of her weight, easily grabbing her wrists and shifting her to the side, right past me. I push her against the wall and pin her there with my hips, my hands pressing her wrists to the wall. Her body is taught. Our noses nearly touch. I slide a knee between her legs, and she starts grinding the seam of her jeans into my thigh. I release her wrists. She lets go of all her tension. Her mouth opens.

We kiss.

Pulling her around, I sweep the telephone, message pad, and pens off the hall table and lay her across it. I pull down the zipper of her jeans. She shakes her shoes off. I unbutton her jeans, and she lifts her hips, letting me pull them off. Her legs fall open.

"Jennifer isn't as good as me," she says defiantly. "No one is."

"Not even close."

I live for these moments. They allow me to make sense of the world and give me the will to get out of bed, climb onstage, and perform, trying to explain to myself why any of this is.

Holding her tightly against me, I whisper into her hair, "I'll never let you go."

Chapter 5

I'm Pregnant
—Jonathan—

Scott and I've arranged for this Friday to Sunday off work and have planned to leave late Friday morning. On Thursday we tell the other members of White Heat that we'll be gone for a couple of days and there won't be any rehearsal until Monday. They seem relieved, like schoolkids hearing it's a snow day. Friday, after I toss the last travel bag into the car, I call Amy and tell her we're going to be gone a couple of days scouting bars White Heat can perform in around Dayton and Toledo, and in Indiana and Illinois.

"And you didn't bother letting me know you were planning this?" she asks.

"It was kinda last minute. Wasn't sure if—"

"Wasn't sure if what? I'd care?"

"Scott thought—"

"Scott shouldn't think."

"Look, I just ..." I say. "I'll be back late Sunday. I'll see you—"

She hangs up.

I feel odd standing there with a dead telephone in my hand. *Yes, I'll be back Sunday. But one of these times—*

Averting my mind from that day, I put the phone back in its cradle.

A few minutes later, I climb into the Nissan next to Scott, and we drive the same route as before. The sight of Chicago—bursting like Valhalla from the gray industrial landscape of Gary, with the skyward reach of its towers, the immensity of the lake, and the plains covered with houses as we cross the bridge over the Little Calumet River—thrills even more this time. The coursing cars in the valley of the Dan Ryan aren't so intimidating, and the exit to North Ave and the way to Tanya and Randal's house are familiar.

Randal waves at us as we park the car. He's good looking in the same way Tanya is—tall, Aryan blond, and lithe. He dresses to show that off—today in a fitted, boldly striped shirt and skinny, straight-legged jeans. They've never married and probably never will. But they act as if they are. For him, I'm sure, sleeping with the boss's daughter is more intriguing than being married to her. Instead of merely being a part of the family, he's still sleeping his way to the top. More of a continual thrill. Like them living in Wicker Park. They should be in a romance-novel mansion, not kicking around the edges of Spanish gang territory. It's like a twisted fairy tale: "Looks, money, popularity—we didn't want them. But since they're here ... why not have fun with them?"

We climb the short staircase.

"Good to see you again," Randal says, shaking Scott's hand. "Soon we won't have to wait so long."

We stroll across the entrance bridge, down the spiral stairs, through the kitchen, and out the back door. It's a perfect sixty-eight degrees, with a light breeze. Smoke wafts off the grill in ragged white streaks. An eight-foot blond-wood fence blocks out the neighbors and the alley from the lush emerald lawn spreading across the yard. At the sound of our entrance, Tanya, Michele, and AnnMarie look up from under a huge, lime-colored parasol sprouting from the center of a bright, daisy-yellow flower-shaped table.

As our host leads us down the five steps, my shoes sink into the grass and the sweet, herbaceous scent of freshly cut grass blends into the rich, faintly petrol-laced odor of burning charcoal.

A wine bottle is hoisted from an ice bucket, and two glasses are flipped upright and filled. Michele brings over our glasses.

Why are you even here?

She thoughtfully purses her lips as if to answer the unspoken question, but instead, turns and walks to our host, who's fanning the coals in the grill. Flames jump and crackle. Smoke bellows out in a thick cloud. Next to him, steaks are laid out in a glass dish, covered with red wine, red onions, and herbs. Ears of corn are piled in a pyramid, their husks pulled back into handles. Around the parasol's pole, a tossed salad and potato salad wait in deep bowls next to neatly stacked plates. It looks like a magazine ad Amy would've put together.

"Where's that photographer, Ron?" Scott asks AnnMarie.

"Some job he didn't want to do," she says. "A wedding out in the 'burbs."

Our hostess raises her glass. "To distant friends," she says. "Hey, you two. Randal? Michele?"

Soda water, not wine, fills her glass, and I wonder what she has up her sleeve this time.

"After we're fed," she says. "Road trip. I don't think we have to go very far. This is the neighborhood to be in. But you need to see where *isn't* that good to know why this *is* so good. So then: Lincoln Park, Boystown, Uptown, Andersonville, Rogers Park, and then Bucktown, and home to Wicker Park."

"We'll take your word for it," I say.

"Oh, no you won't. I'll not have you blaming me. For anything. You'll see for yourself."

The sudden sizzle of the steak Randal tosses on the grill stops the talking. As the marinade dribbles off the meat, the coals hiss angrily, shooting dark smoke up in trails. The scent of searing onions and flesh floats over us. Next to Randal, Michele takes the corn, ear by ear, and lays each across the rear coals; burning husk joins the medley of scents.

Amy would hate this—two rich kids slumming: sham hip. She'd go off on them—bitch about 'em. Tanya especially. *Don't worry; you soon won't have to hear about them. Ever.*

After the meal, four of us—our future drummer, our hostess, Scott, and I—leave the host and Michele behind and pile into Tanya's Jeep Cherokee and start the tour of the neighborhoods. We leave Wicker Park, with the Chicagoans as tour guides. We head east toward the lake and through yuppie-infested Lincoln Park, and then we turn north up Halsted Street.

As I'm looking at all these new streets, thoughts of Amy keep intruding—especially of her lying on the hallway table, half naked, saying, "Jennifer isn't as good as me," and of my whispering into her hair, "I'll never let you go." I squirm to escape these sights and then get looks like "What's wrong with you?" from Scott, and I wave him off, saying, "It's exciting. That's all." To hide from Amy's intrusions into my mind, I concentrate on reading every store and restaurant sign, trying to figure out what each is like inside, or why the traffic lights are all on the sides of the streets.

After a few minutes on Halsted, the street becomes lined with bars with names like "Manhole" and "Rawhide," and the sidewalks bustle with mostly men, some holding hands.

"Gentlemen, welcome to Boystown, 60657. Nice place if you are of a particular bent."

Scott frowns and shakes his head. "Not exactly my cup of tea," he says.

A couple of turns bring us to Clark Street, and after a few minutes, we pass Wrigley Field and then, down the street, Cabaret Metro. *Where all the bands that matter play. Where I'll play.*

I don't remember the particulars of the rest of our tour: only lots of streets, three- and four-story buildings, and apartments over storefronts, going on and on in every direction I look. It all blurs into one vast *city.*

"This is one big town," Scott says. "We've been driving forever. What—three, three and a half hours?"

"This is only part of the North Side," AnnMarie says. "A little of the West. Most of the city, you haven't even seen."

"Those are the parts you really don't want to live in," Tanya says. "Visit, maybe."

"It's like I can take a vacation to a different city by hopping a ride on the subway," I say.

"The 'L,'" she says. "This isn't New York. No subway. We have the 'L.'"

"By hopping a ride on the 'L,'" I say.

"Much better. Now you're starting to sound like a Chicagoan."

Nearing her place again, the houses get shabby, but the restaurants and bars speak to me: an Italian place with live music, and a bar with a sandwich board covered with Gothic letters, listing specials, cocked open in front of windows with deep red drapes and candelabras stuffed with thick white candles atop frozen falls of wax, waiting for night and resurrection.

"Yeah," I say. "I get why this is the hood to live in."

"I knew you'd understand," she says, turning the Jeep onto Winchester.

"Definitely," Scott says.

All at once, the move feels real, as if I can touch it. I want to get things rolling, see apartments, pack, and start living my new life. We must grab our opportunity before something happens.

Before you can change my mind, Amy.

It's clear there's no way I can let her know. Not until we're already here. When it's too late. Then I'll have to ask myself all the questions Amy would have asked me, make the comments she would have made, explain to myself what I'm doing and why I'm doing it—have conversations for lovers, but with myself, alone. *I wonder if it'll make any sense.*

Once we're back, we walk through Tanya's place to the table out back, where Michele and Randal have cocktails and a spread of food for us. The evening feels calm. The traffic from North, Damen, and Milwaukee Avenues provides a soft white noise, accented by the rare car driving slowly by in the alley behind the blond-wood wall. Occasionally an 'L' train moves along its raised tracks far enough away that its rumble is a hum, and its screeches are like a distant bird's calls. The dusk's reds and yellows settle across the clouds. Everything is golden warm.

"By the way," Tanya says, picking up her glass and sipping from it. "I'm pregnant."

"Huh?" Michele blurts, looking to Randal, who raises his eyebrows and nods. Her expression clashes with the news: sour, as if she were watching a bad play.

Still cannot get my head around you, Michele.

"That explains the soda, you lush," Scott says. "Designated driver my ass."

"When did you find this out?" AnnMarie asks, pinching her lips, looking disturbed, as if she were the one pregnant.

"Confirmed it yesterday."

"And why didn't you—"

"More dramatic," she says.

"To say the least," Michele says.

"So," Scott says. "This mean you're going to get hitched? At long last."

"Not sure," Randal says. "We—"

"We don't know," Tanya says. "A shotgun wedding is so ... 1950s white trash."

"Tanya," I say, "that's about the weirdest thing I've ever heard you say." The to-be parents look pleased, so I say, "Congratulations. That's great. For both of you. Really."

I guess. *What does this mean—you can't help us now?*

Chapter 6

Artful Dodger
—Jonathan—

The next morning, Scott, I, and the parents to be head to the Northside for brunch. It's only a few blocks' walk. I like the Sunday morning feel of our new 'hood: it's quiet, but there's still life. I can hear cars, and see people walking on other blocks. The city is waking up from a party—a little hungover but alive.

At the Northside, we meet Michele and AnnMarie, and by the time we've killed our first round of drinks, Ron arrives at the table, camera hanging from his shoulder.

"Well?" AnnMarie asks him as he sits down.

"Well what?"

"Congratulate the new mother-to-be."

"You're pregnant?" he asks. "When did you start dating?"

She laughs. "Not dating. And *not* me."

He looks at Michele.

She shakes her head, "Hell no" all over her face.

He looks at Tanya. "Bullshit," he says. "Not possible."

She breaks into a smile.

As quick as a falcon, he has his camera at his eye, and the shutter clicks at her, and then at daddy, and then at the parents together.

"Good," Tanya says. "Now that we're all here, we can get down to business."

"Looking for a place to live," Scott says.

"Kinda depends," she says.

So then, this isn't happening, right?

"On?" Scott asks.

"How much work you're willing to do."

"How much work, meaning ...?"

"What I said," she says, sipping her "just OJ in a champagne flute." "You see, we, Harman Co., recently bought a building right around the corner. Big one. Former pencil factory. And we can make more money renting it as a work/live space."

"Residential makes more per square foot than commercial," the new daddy says.

"The only catch is that it needs work."

"Work," Scott says. "As in—"

"No," she says. "Not that much. Mostly cleaning up. Some light construction."

"For you," Randal says. "Three thousand five hundred square feet of open space. Empty. Twenty-foot ceilings. No kitchen, no bedrooms. Yet."

"Here's the deal," Tanya says. "The second, third, and fourth floors and the basement aren't occupied. The first floor is already promised to a guy who's opening a coffee shop. The second and third floors are in really bad shape, so we'll have to pay people to reclaim them. But the fourth floor and the basement—whichever you want—you clear them. We do the plumbing, cabinetry. You take care of the rest. Bedrooms. Supply the kitchen appliances. This for free rent."

"Free?" Scott asks.

"For at least a year. Then as long as I can keep it zero. Even then you'll get it at a steep discount. Thirty-five hundred square feet of empty space. A place to rehearse, to live. With a last condition: it's also a place for Ron, here, to shoot and store his gear."

"So," Scott says, "this is really for the three of us."

"No. It's for you two," she says. "He gets to borrow it though. *If* he helps you two."

"Free," I say. "As cheap as it gets."

"I'll shoot around your schedule," Ron says. "No problem. My equipment doesn't take up much room. This—it'll be sweet."

"As long as we can sleep and rehearse," Scott says. "I'm all over this."

Sorry, Amy.

"I thought you'd like that," Tanya says. "Like I said, Ron, you've gotta pitch in. It's not a small job."

"When can we see it?" I ask. "But thank you. Very much." *Can't forget that. Tanya never would.*

"It's only a couple of minutes' walk from here," she says. "But there's no electricity. No running water. No heat. Nada. It's a big, dirty, dark cave with crap in it right now. We've a couple of legal loose ends to wrap up before you can start doing anything. So, in six weeks, we'll get you the keys."

The clock starts: Chicago has a date, and the end of my old life appears. It's all getting very real, very fast.

"A toast," she says. "To Chi-town. Welcome."

Glasses clink. *Amy, it's a free loft. In Chicago. How can I say no?*

An icy cold sensation flows down inside me.

No, girl. I shake my head. *It's you. You* won't *move.*

I put down my glass and grimace at the empty seat right across from me as if Amy were sitting there all this time but was suddenly removed when I looked away.

But what? And I quote: "We're lovers, not each other's purpose." Those are your own words, dear.

I shake my head.

Metro matters. Playing there is a purpose. For me. I point my thumb at my chest. *Look, we've still got six weeks, Amy. There's still time for you to figure something out, right? You're the one who's good at this.*

Scott looks askance at me.

Closing my eyes, I take a deep breath and shake my head to knock this quarrel from my mind. To keep it away, I drink, smile, laugh, and talk, and the brunch melts into the afternoon, and the party moves back to their place. Then the afternoon turns into evening, and then into night. Then, around eleven, talk starts of going out again. A happy buzz floats through everyone's mood. The host and hostess head to their room to get ready.

"What's this place we're heading to?" I ask AnnMarie.

"Artful Dodger," she says. "A few blocks away. Think neighborhood bar plus dance floor. Locals only; no yuppies. Yet."

So Scott and I climb the spiral staircase to the spare bedroom to change for the night out.

Getting ready to head out at night is like casting a spell for a good time. That with the right mixture of clothes, alcohol, and music, there will be dancing and, perhaps, a chance to step into someone else's life, as I did one night with Amy. This is the purpose of tonight's ritual: the cocktail I have to be drinking, the selecting of what to wear. *These shoes or those? These pants? With this shirt? Or the other? This jacket? That? None?*

Though I've nothing to change into other than a second pair of black jeans and the single extra shirt I packed, I follow my ritual by lining up my wallet, pack of Camels, and Zippo as if I were at home with a closet of clothes to choose from. But this will work only with the right music.

I turn on the radio to WNUR from Northwestern. I'd love to hear "Temple of Love" by the Sisters of Mercy. That's a sign of a successful night, as it invokes the charm: "Life is short and/love is always over in the morning." Instead I hear Joy Division's "Isolation," a bleak landscape of shame, devotion, and loneliness—of blindness, touching perfection, but hurting—like anything else. Yet I remain an optimist; after all, everyone going out has spent time getting ready, so wants something, though they may all pretend they don't, and that something might be me.

I toast myself in the mirror and set my martini so I can see exactly half of it reflected. The twist floats, slowly, to a stop, one yellow-and-white end poking through the surface: I take that as a good sign.

Behind my reflection, I can see Scott taking off his shirt. He's very big. Not ripped; rather, he's thick. Like a college running back. Someone to avoid messing with.

Once I take off my shoes and pants, it's time to take another sip, but not more. The wine from dinner and gin from this martini warm me and give everything a pleasant glow; any more would tip the scales into drunkenness.

He's already finished and is in the bathroom, running water to splash his face.

I take the next ritual sip, and then I pull on my pants. They're snug, even on my skinny ass.

I see him watching me in the mirror.

"You're fine," he says. "No one can see your chicken legs."

In summer, when I have to wear shorts, the Mexicans in my restaurant call me *pollo loco*—crazy chicken.

After putting on my hefty black bus driver shoes, I brush out my hair using a steel-tine hedgehog brush. I make sure the part down the center of my skull is straight. My hair curls slightly at my shoulders.

Then, stretching out my neck, I give myself three quick sprays of Versus cologne. It smells exactly like tonight's going to be great.

The radio's providing the right songs for my soundtrack: New Order's "Blue Monday" comes up.

I'm ready to complete the charm by finishing the last sip of my cocktail. *Practice, for when I'll be alone again.*

Scott jerks this thumb toward the open door. "Let's roll."

At the bottom of the stairs, we hook up with the others, and take off into the night, walking a couple of blocks to Wabansia and then left into Bucktown, where it's deep residential: house after house, some detached, some three-story multifamily buildings—nothing to show any life except the flicker of TVs through windows.

Then a dark green hexagonal tower bulges from the corner of a three-story brick house, the tower rising up to the fourth story, taller than all the houses around. A sign juts out above the street corner, carrying a mock coat of arms reading "Artful Dodger." An oasis of fun in this desert of quiet.

"Yep," I say. "Looks like it's going to be a great night."

We follow Tanya through the door.

The Dodger envelops us. Smoke wafts in clouds over the bar, tables, and booths. Everything is wood: the benches, chairs, and even the walls. The Ramones' "Sheena is a Punk Rocker" plays from the back. In the semidarkness, drinks glow in people's hands like fireflies on a hot summer eve. I breathe in the smells of stale beer and cigarettes.

"Smells like ex-girlfriends," I say to no one in particular. Not that I'd know. Just sounds good.

Scott leans into Michele, close enough for her to pull back slightly. "What's with those?" he asks.

"Aqua Velvas," she says.

"They glow," he says.

"Glow sticks," she says as if she were talking to someone who's a bit slow, nodding toward someone lifting a glowing plastic tube from his cocktail.

"Thanks," he says curtly and leaves for the bar.

You're tough, girl.

She catches me watching. Her eyes linger a moment. Then, without any specific expression, she turns and joins the others at the end of the bar.

I click my tongue. *What is your deal, girl?*

Scott shoves a glowing glass of liquid and ice in front of my face. "Aqua Velva."

"What's that?"

"Cocktail." He drinks. "Strong one. Lots of tequila. And a glow stick." He swishes the ice around in his glass with the glowing plastic rod.

Then, from the back of the bar, the tattoo of a drum emerges. It curls around me and turns my head as a thick, throbbing rhythm bellows across the room.

I take off toward the doorway, whence the Revolting Cocks' "Attack Ships on Fire" calls. A voice cries out above the pummeling beat. Barely human—like that of a man trapped inside a machine—it cries out, "Time and time and time again," that it's freezing and hurting, having another bad dream. I feel the beat, lashing like a whip—a drum machine hammering out 150 beats a minute—while other, nameless machines, pummeling unknown parts, stamp out a steady, implacable time, like infinite marching. The inhuman voice pleads, "Someone, somewhere wake me up."

This voice and these machine sounds crawl through the relentless beat of the drum, the simple, brutal hammering filling the room. My body follows this battering signature across the dance floor. I lose myself to it. My head rolls the way the machines roll; my legs and arms thrash the way the machines keep the beat. The sound compresses me, winding me like a gigantic spring being tightened in some obscure factory, tighter and tighter and tighter, and the only way I can keep from flying into pieces is to expel this energy through my lashing head, my flaying hair, the jerking of my arms, and the spin of my body this way, then that way, until my eyes sting from the sweat, which tastes salty, like sex—like ecstasy.

Nothing exists but my body and the unremitting, remorseless sounds of machines. I'm untouchable.

This is what I play for: to get everyone to feel like I do right now. Infinite. Muscular. Only the body, the beat, the hammering rhythm, the machines, the voice exist; I am untouchable and beyond any care. It's like those first hours with Amy when we make up, thrashing in bed, devouring every particle of each other again.

Then, as always, the song ends, and the next one shifts too much, shattering the spell.

Strands of hair stick to my face. I feel the sweat dribbling down my nose and my cheeks, and off my chin. Patches of my shirt cling to my skin.

Turning back to the doorway, I notice a few people checking me out. I walk through their stares like cobwebs. *Damn right, folks. That's what I can do for you if you listen—if you hear what I create. You will. Soon. A few more weeks, and then you'll hear. Believe me.*

Stepping up to our table, I pull off the hair sticking to my face.

"There," Tanya says, pointing to my Aqua Velva, the ice mostly melted, the glow stick faded to a faint green smudge. "Saved it for you."

I take a long suck from it, and it feels good. *The cocktail, this place, my life. All good right now. I've songs to write, to play and sing. This is why I'm here, goddamn it. That's why, Amy. No matter how hard saying good-bye to you is going to be.*

Chapter 7

Electronic Body Music
—Scott—

Getting out of Chicago the next morning is easy. It's Sunday, and traffic's light. It's overcast, so not bright—fortunately for Jonathan. He took aspirin and pushed back a couple of glasses of water before we left Tanya's. He still looks rough.

Once we cross the Skyway and are on the expressway in Indiana, Jonathan leans the seat back as far as it goes. He turns away from the windows.

"Here," I say, handing him a T-shirt from the backseat. "Put this over your eyes."

Jonathan lays it across half of his face. After about ten minutes, his mouth starts moving as if he's talking something out to himself. He puckers his lips and bunches them off to the side. Then he starts pointing to things he's showing himself in his head. Next he'll make a suggestion. I never know what to expect.

"You know," Jonathan says, "we should change our name."

"Okay ..."

"And our sound," he says, adjusting the T-shirt. "We have to."

"Uh-huh."

"This isn't Ohio. Chicago isn't. We don't have to be us. I mean, who we were. We shouldn't be them. They've never made it there, so they can't make it here."

"All right." *I'm the one who told him all this.*

"We can't be who we were. Unless we want to fail."

"Okay." Saying anything more would mess with whatever's going on in his head.

"White Heat. We were trying too hard to be someone else. One of those post-punk bands—Joy Division. But"—Jonathan stares down into the footwell and pushes around a balled-up sandwich wrapper as if about to make a dark confession—"I keep listening to all this new stuff. Music made to move to. Less guitar, more machine driven. Keyboards. Loops. Using found sounds, like drills or stamping machines. A razor blade tapping out a beat on a mirror. It's music for your body to move to. Electronic body music. It sounds a lot less like a couple of punks trying to live out a rock 'n' roll fantasy and more like ... music for the rhythm zone. Clubs. Music to get sweaty to. Get erotic with."

I've no idea where he's going with this. I peg my eyes to the road and listen. Jonathan can lose his way rather badly in life, but his instincts about music are usually spot on.

"I know I'm talking dance music. It's not AOR material. We'll never get airplay on QFM96, 'Ohio's Best Rock.'" He says the tagline for WLVQ with the same dramatic voice as the announcer's. "College radio—could be. Clubs—definitely. And, I'm not talking East Dallas or some other danceteria crap. I'm talking the New York underground scene. London. Chicago. Belgium. Bands like Cabaret Voltaire. Front 242. A Split Second. Revolting Cocks."

"RevCo?" I ask.

"Their songs are cries from the pit of the machine. Someone screaming to wake us up, make us see we live in a world with a madman in the Oval Office—Ronnie Ray-Gun. 'In the East, where the bear is dancing/in the West where the Eagle flies.' Asking us how're we going to survive. About DuPont killing people in Bhopal and West Virginia: 'dead bodies everywhere' and 'the official number of the dead is now put at 38.'"

"Front 242 I can see. A Split Second—sure. But RevCo? Next you'll being saying we should do hardcore like the Dead Kennedys."

"Okay, not RevCo. You get the idea though, right?"

"I think so. But ..."

"But what?" Jonathan asks.

"I don't know," I say.

"What do you mean you don't know?"

"That I don't know."

"This isn't a stupid idea," Jonathan says.

"No. It's probably very smart," I say.

"Or psychotic."

"Didn't say it was."

"But what?"

"But you don't really write like that." Now that I hear it, I don't believe it.

"Not yet."

"What would happen to those—what do you call them—not-ended stories?" I ask.

"Unfinished stories."

"Unfinished stories. You keep talking about all those songs you can't finish because you don't know how the stories will end. Yet when you do finish them, that's what people like the most."

Jonathan frowns. "That's the whole point. It's gotten us all the way to—nowhere."

"We're moving to Chicago."

"Exactly," Jonathan says. "And what did you say about that? 'What *was* must be left.' Leave the members of the old band—Sean and Marsha. Leave the name too. The sound. Everything. What *will be* must *be* new—as new as possible. You can't walk away from yourself without realizing first who you actually are."

"True."

"Or what you change is only lipstick and haircuts. You'll end up the same as ever."

I wonder if that means giving up Amy as well. She has gotten into Jonathan's head like a disease.

"All we've done in Columbus is run on the fumes of what was left after punk. They've taken us nowhere."

Jonathan slaps his hand on the dashboard.

"But we want to be there." He points beyond the fields of corn to the horizon far in the distance. "This isn't 1980. I'm not Ian Curtis. Yeah, I sound like him. But I never wanted to be him. He hanged himself, for fuck's sake. Who wants that?" He points at the horizon again. "You know I'm right."

"Uh-huh."

"Been hearing about this guy Trent Reznor. Think he's calling his band Nine Inch Nails. Doesn't matter. Nobody gets the sound he wants to create, right. So he goes off like Prince. Plays all his own instruments. He's making a single with a goddamned Apple Plus—'Down in It.' Supposed to come out in September. I've heard it's wicked. This is in Cleveland. Not New York. We'll be in Chicago. Terminal White's town."

"So you'll—"

"Whatever instrument—computer, machine, sequencer—name it; I'll learn it. Or we'll get somebody."

"AnnMarie plays a drum machine, and—"

"Electronic drums, and she knows how to work delays better than I do," he says and then gets quiet again.

I wish I knew what goes on in his head when he gets quiet like this.

"I don't want to play between shifts," Jonathan says. "I want playing to *be* my shifts. *How* I make my living. To be what I *do*. All the time. I don't give a rat's ass about art. Purity, selling out—those are just excuses masquerading as virtue for people who can't make it. I'm done with ramen noodles."

Jonathan sinks back into his seat. He's staring off someplace.

"So then," I say, "what do we need?"

"For?"

"This electronic body music sound."

Until we get home five hours later, we talk about what he's thinking of doing and exactly what we have to do to pull this off. I have to admit that what he's saying sounds damned good. It'll take a lot of work. But we'll be a step up over Columbus. *He* is *the creative one. Like Sammy was.*

After dropping the last bag on the living room floor in Columbus, I pop the cap off a beer. It's cold and hits the spot, but I'm already thinking about how much we need to get done. *We have to get into that loft before anything changes Tanya's mind—get our crap there. Shift our sound to this electronic body music—*

51

"When are we telling Marsha and Sean?" Jonathan asks, standing in the doorway. "You know. The other band members."

"Soon to be former members," I say. "*After* that last show we have booked."

He nods gravely.

"Now. Amy. Not until we're gone."

"Probably not."

"*Definitely* not."

"But—"

"But what?"

"It's getting to me," he says. "Especially now. With the loft. Having to lie to them. To Amy. I write music, play music to reveal truth. Yet, all I'm doing is lying. I'm a hypocrite. I hate people like me. Self-serving. Selfish."

"Guy, don't bullshit yourself," I say. "You *are* being self-serving. And selfish. You're *leaving them* behind. To go do what *you* say is what *you need* to do."

"Oh, right. Thanks. That makes everything all better."

"You know we have to get out of here. How many times do we have to talk about it? Chicago. Big market. Cabaret Metro. But now that you're going, it's all *poor me. It's so hard to do.*"

He jams a cigarette into an ashtray so hard it flips off the edge of the sofa. "I *hate* this."

"I don't *hate* them, Jonathan," I say. "Try to understand. There are winners, and there are losers. Losers feel so bad about moving on they *don't.* They let opportunities pass by. They cry on the shoulders of all their loser friends. Now, moving on. With me. That takes stones. That makes you a winner."

He purses his lips. I want to reach out, comfort him.

"Amy won't move," I say. "She's already won her game. She's got what she wants. Now she doesn't *want* you to leave. That simple." I nod my head.

He nods.

"The other two don't have what it takes. But you do. So do I. We both do. You're the one who gets out and makes it. With me. In Chicago. Brand-new start."

"Yeah."

"Calm down there, Jonathan. No need to be soooooo excited."

He shrugs. "It's hard."

I know. I've done it before. And not everyone makes it.

Chapter 8

Persistence and Determination
—Scott—

The next morning, the sun oozes through the window above the kitchen sink. Steam rises from a press pot. I watch Jonathan pick up a spoon and stir the black slush. Then he puts the top on and pushes the plunger down.

"Coffee," he says. "Very black."

Fresh from a shower, he's got a gray towel wrapped around his slender waist. His hair looks like blond paint spilled on his head, neck, and shoulders.

"Ahhh," he says. He pours coffee into a cup. "The elixir of life." He picks up another cup from the drying rack. "Want some?"

"Sure," I say.

He pours another cup and sets it down in front of me.

"You'd make a good housewife," I say.

"Nah. I'm a pig. Can't even keep my room clean," he says, sniffing his coffee. "So, what's the plan today?"

"Not going to Logan this afternoon," I say. "I'll call my mom instead. Don't care to hear what anyone there thinks about Chicago."

"He never liked me much."

"Said you were a fag. Long hair, you know. Man does he hate gays. Said he'd kill me if he thought I was queer."

"Hillbilly," he says.

"No," I say. "Trailer trash. Get it right."

I'd left my parent's trailer at seventeen, as soon as I could after Sammy died. I've gone back only once. When my dad had a heart attack and only because my mother asked me to help with his funeral. She'd been on my side. When it mattered. I owed it to her. Once my mother's gone, there'll be nothing that can bring me to Logan or near Appalachia. It's not my home. Not since I've had the choice. It's loaded with trailer trash memories. Both shabby and hard. The stink of living in a double-wide jacked up on cinderblocks: old plastic, mildew, rust, dirt, propane, and septic tanks.

To be fair, my dad didn't drink much. Didn't hit anyone. Not me or my mom at least. He made enough money as a part-time mechanic that we didn't have the usual trailer trash problems. No. The problem was he saw things one way: *his*. Everything was good or bad, right or wrong. Nothing in between. He saw my mother as a nag and me as a failure to be a man. A boy who wouldn't do what he wanted to do with our neighbor's daughters, the chubby, butt-ugly things that ran around the park, wiping their noses on their sleeves. He wanted to deflower them all. I'm sure his heart attack was caused by one of them bending too far over. Probably in Daisy Dukes. A thirteen- or fourteen-year-old.

Mostly though, he hated Sammy. My only actual friend, the only person I ever wanted to spend time with.

Then Sammy died.

I bite my lip.

The doorbell rings.

This early, it could only be Amy. I'm not really awake yet.

Jonathan takes a slug of coffee and then saunters down the hall, the towel wrapped around his waist like a skirt.

The front door groans open.

"Ah," Amy says, "so there you are."

I hear nothing after that, meaning they're kissing. It stays quiet, and I hope they're not going to go at it in the hallway again. Finally I hear the sounds of walking in the hall. As Amy steps into the kitchen, she flashes a plastic smile at me.

"Hi," she says mechanically.

I raise my cup. *Can't wait till you find out Jonathan's leaving you to come with me to Chicago. Nothing you can do about it.* I'm watching that scene play out in my mind: I tell her that straight out and then coldly sip my coffee. She says something proud and then rushes at me, screaming. We have a catfight. Her ex tries to pull us apart. His towel falls off, and—

Fun to think about, but better on Dallas *or* Falcon Crest.

"So," I say. "What's the plan?"

"You said no Logan. Rehearsal isn't until late."

"A few hours to relax then," I say, pushing myself up from the chair. "I'll leave you two alone."

"Hold on," Amy says. "I came here to see you too."

"Oh?" I ask.

"What's going on?" she asks.

"Going on? Nothing," I say.

"Basically," Jonathan says, "we're going to rehearse. We have that gig coming up. Remember?"

"No," Amy says. "I mean, what's going on with you two?"

"Oh, sorry. You mean that we got engaged?" he asks, making an exaggeratedly shocked face.

"Don't be an asshole," Amy says. "Seriously."

"Seriously what?"

"Seriously, what are you two up to? You disappear to Chicago. Your rehearsal schedule gets all funky. One gig? You've been playing out two, three times a month lately."

Jonathan hesitates.

I say nothing.

"Oh," he says. "We're always planning something."

Amy lets out a disgusted hiss.

"Always," he says. "New songs. New arrangements. New places to play: bars, clubs. We're always planning."

"You're so full of shit. Why don't you tell me?"

He bunches his face up.

Rolling my eyes, I brace for a full confession and the shitstorm that'll follow.

"Girl," he says. "We're going to have lunch. Later, we'll rehearse—you know, practice our setlist. Work out kinks. Maybe even try a new tune. Typical evening with White Heat. Nothing more sinister than that."

Curling up her lip uncertainly, Amy moves to the counter.

"Now, I don't know when we're going to be back," he says. "You know how rehearsals go. So why don't we do this: if I get back early, I'll call. You can swing by. But if it's going to be one of those late-night straighten-things-up marathons, just come by tomorrow. Early as you want."

"But you'll call if you get back early?" Amy asks.

"Just told you I would. I'm not lying here."

Something about the way he says that sounds vaguely cautious, as if he can't lie to Amy without giving her a chance to see that he is lying. I half think she picks up on it, but that really doesn't matter. It's too late for her. We're too close to being gone. We've one last gig on Friday. We'll be in Chicago soon after.

Like you always said, Sammy, "Persistence and determination alone are omnipotent."

Chapter 9

This Is the End
—Scott—

"Jonathan," I say, standing on the bumper of the yellow Penske truck. "That's it, right?" I'm holding a pebble-skin black travel case. It's gouged and duct-taped. The logo of White Heat is peeling off and hard to recognize. "I've got the mics right here." Lifting the case over the bass bins and the Marshall amp, I stuff it into a milk crate full of power cables.

Gigs hardly pay enough to cover a rental, so we always go with the cheapest cargo van possible. But tonight we rented a ten-foot moving truck to figure out how much stuff we can take to Chicago. Our gear takes up the three or so feet, with room above. Means we're leaving our beat-to-shit couch and probably all of our furniture behind. *It's all crap anyway. No loss.* All we really have to have is our mattresses, clothes, equipment, stereo, vinyl, and CDs.

New city, new stuff.

"Sean and Marsha are already on their way, right?" Jonathan asks.

"Sure as hell better be."

Standing next to the truck, he's already dressed up as a junkie rock star: long hair, forehead all sweaty, ripped jeans, a tight T-shirt showing off his skinny chest and flat belly, a thick black belt covered in studs, and Dr. Martens with yellow laces. He does like his costumes.

I jump off the bumper and slam the doors shut.

The Main High's a dump, but there and Crazy Mama's are the two places we've played the most. We're practically the house band at Mama's.

I shove the nostalgia out of my head: Randal called earlier today. The loft is ready. Now we have to take possession by June first. We've five days to pack up and move. No time for bullshit.

Tonight's gig is about not burning bridges. White Heat will never play another note after tonight, but we need their demo tape to get restarted, as well as their good references. No matter what we change our band's name to, we'll still be Scott Marshall and Jonathan Starks, with our reputations. We can't escape that. Not yet.

"Amy's not going to be there, right?" I ask.

"Said she had to work on some big project," he says.

One less thing to worry about.

He climbs in through the passenger door. I pull myself up into the cab and fall into the driver's seat.

"Last time," he says, matter-of-factly.

"That it is," I say, jamming the key into the ignition. The chunky plastic fob whacks the dash. The engine turns over, and the truck shudders.

"Let's roll."

The way's familiar. I start us down Neil Avenue, turn right on King Avenue to High Street, and then right again, past the very end of the south campus bars. Crazy Mama's appears on the left. We'll go there one last time for shits and giggles. Now we're driving through the Short North and all the galleries. We hit downtown, go past the Lincoln LaVeque tower, and then hit a rougher part of town: the South Side.

Jonathan's been watching the closed stores and offices pass by. He has a wistful look on his face.

Right then I've the urge to punch that look off his face. *There's no room for doubt. Or regret. Not anymore.*

"When should I announce it's our last show?" he asks.

"Why do it at all?"

"Seems appropriate, don't you think? A sort of eulogy show."

"No. I don't. We'll know. That's enough. If we announce it, do you think that Sean and Marsha'd play?"

"No idea."

"They won't. That I can tell you," I say. "They'll get pissed and refuse.

And then we won't play. One of our most important references goes bye-bye."

"Guess so."

"Come on. We need good recommendations to get started in Chicago. And not playing because we broke up right before a show is *not* a recommendation that will help."

"Yeah. After the show then?"

"Not right after, but after we pack up and get home. Then we'll tell 'em."

"Yeah."

"The loft is ours. We *are* leaving. Hard enough getting that done. Why make it harder?"

"Right. Got it," he says. "We'll know. They won't. And they'll leave like always, and we'll leave and never come back. And yes, yes, I know—it's for a reason. For our ... ascension. Butterflies bursting from cocoons." He taps his foot on the floor of the truck. "I got it. You're right."

I can feel his eyes on my face. I meet his gaze.

"Rock 'n' roll, man," he says.

"It'll be a good show," I say. "A great show. White Heat's last."

I pull the truck up to the back door in the alley behind the Main High and park. The back door's open, and Sean's leaning up against the wall. He flicks away a butt.

"Marsha said she'd be a few minutes late," Sean says. "Got stuck at work."

"Yeah," I say. "Course."

I unlock the back of the truck, and we start unloading. It's great to be playing first tonight. Don't have to deal with someone unloading as we're loading and busting ass to make start time.

First come the big W-bins: two heavy black wooden boxes, each with a fifty-pound bass speaker nailed inside, facing backward. If the top of one were off, it would look like a W inside. They weigh an easy 150 pounds each. We've had these for years, and they are beat to hell, all gouged and scratched and covered with blotches from duct tape and stickers. I take one handle of the top W-bin, and Sean the other. We slide it off.

Jonathan climbs into the truck while Sean and I lug the first W-bin to the door. We carry the next W-bin through the doorway and to a curtain in the back of the Main High. Sean pulls it back, revealing the dinky stage. It's a twenty-foot-wide by ten-foot-deep riser shoved into the back of the room. There's a six-inch step onto the stage. We shuffle across the painted plywood with the W-bin. Light from two white floods pours onto the stage. Against it I can't see into the bar. The jukebox is playing "Sheena is a Punk Rocker." I can hear some shouts. Some laughing. Something hitting a table. I'm guessing the place is decently full.

Sean and I leave the W-bin on the far side, near where he'll be playing bass.

All the monitors here are decent, so we don't have to worry about setting up based on which monitors suck the most or don't work at all. Jonathan will have his keyboard in front of the monitor at center stage. Marsha and Sean each get their own. I can listen to myself in Jonathan's. It's small consolation for the fifty dollars, plus a buck a person with our flyer before ten, and the round of drinks we'll get for playing tonight. Plus "the exposure" we're always reminded of.

The worthless exposure.

Front stage, Jonathan puts down a crate of cables and an armful of mic stands. After Sean and I haul in the second bin, I head back for my Marshall amp. Jonathan sets up the three front mic stands and plugs the mics into the snake. Here a galvanized steel box full of connection slots with a thick cable that leads to the house soundboard. I'm taping cables down.

"Where the hell is Marsha?" I ask. "She still has a drum kit to set up."

Sean shrugs. "Said she'd be here."

"Here," Jonathan says. "Let's start setting her up."

"Let me get my guitar handled. Be right over."

I kneel next to my amp, unlatch the guitar case, and open it.

Picking my Stratocaster up, I take the strap and pull a ring at either end of it around a peg on the body. I hang the guitar on my shoulder. It feels good there. I run one hand up the neck and drag my fingers across the strings with my other, and a memory surges into me of the first time I played this guitar, my first brand-new one, in front of an audience right here. On *this* stage. That show kicked ass. *Too bad you weren't here to see it, Sammy.*

I plug my tuning box into the bottom of the guitar and strum each string, tightening or loosening the pegs as the meter tells me. Then I plug it into my amp and set it in its stand.

Still no Marsha. *She gonna no-show?*

I grab the setlists and tape one on the floor in front of Sean's mic, one in front of where I'll stand, one next to the bass drum for Marsha, and one to the right of Jonathan's stool, sideways, so he can read it sitting down.

"We're done," Jonathan says. "Well, as much as we can be without her. She'll have to do the rest. Wow." He shakes his head. "I'm glad Amy's not coming to our—"

"Jonathan," I say sternly. "Let's get her stool set up. It's right there."

"Oh," he says, alarmed. "Yes. Right."

"Not coming where?" Sean asks.

"Last show," Jonathan says. "Before we, you know. Try out ... new... material. A new sound." He turns to get the stool.

Sean frowns. He turns to me and shrugs.

"Have to ask him after the show. I'll check out the crowd."

I walk offstage and into the bar, hoping she hasn't decided to make this the show she misses. *We need this reference.* Once I can see in the dark again, I look around the room. Most of the tables are full. Even the ones near the stage. Not bad for a Thursday, even though most of these people aren't here for us. They're here to get drunk. Or lucky. We're the accidental soundtrack. But someday they'll all say, "I was there that night." The last time we played here.

Finally Marsha shows up. Even though she's late, she took the time to get dressed up. She's wearing black half boots, torn fishnets, a short black skirt, and a Bundeswehr T-shirt. Like Siouxsie Sioux, her eyes are kohled and her hair is dyed black and tossed around as if she rolled out of bed to get here. *Fake JBF look.* That's her problem. She's not Siouxsie Sioux. She didn't just get laid. She was serving other people their dinners.

"Hey," Marsha says. "Sorry I'm late. But it's no trouble, right?"

"Nope," I say. *Not after tonight.* "We'll have to skip the sound check. What can you do?"

After helping Marsha with the last of her drum kit, the high-hat cymbals and tom-toms, I lock up the truck.

The bartender gives me a wave, and I hold up the setlist. He picks up the phone to call the sound man. This place only has a basic soundboard—four channels—so it's useless for anything but blasting out sound straight ahead and controlling feedback.

Walking up to the bar with a copy of the setlist, I smell the stale beer and cigarettes.

Smells like ex-bands tonight.

Looking back at the stage, I see the band that soon won't be: a Siouxsie Sioux waitress on drums, a hipster waiter patting his bass. And then there is the real talent, with long blond hair hanging around his face, walking his fingers down his keyboard. *The one who's escaping with me. Got that, Amy? With me.*

The sound man taps my shoulder from behind. He's an ex-biker and looks like it with his long hair, beard, barrel chest, and belly to match.

"Let's have it," he says.

I hand him the setlist. "Same as the last few times. Same order. Nothing fancy."

"Yeah," he says, glancing at the sheet. "I remember this. We'll have to wing it without a sound check. Setting up late. Don't come to me if you get wicked feedback." His grin's full of yellowing and crooked teeth.

"We've done it before," I say.

"'Course, man," he says before climbing up a ladder of wood boards nailed to the wall that leads to the sound booth over the bar.

Looking back at the stage, I watch the three of them running through their last preparations: tuning, feeling distances between drums and cymbals, and caressing keys. I imagine the opening of *Apocalypse Now*: the slow-moving helicopter is flying in front of the stage, and following it, huge plumes of fire are bursting up. Not at the edge of a jungle, but across the stage. I hear Jim Morrison singing "this is the end/my only friend, the end." The napalm consumes everything from bass bin to bass bin: the drums, the bass, the guitar, everyone. Afterward, though, I won't be in some hotel room in Saigon, drunk, waiting for a mission like Willard.

I've given myself my mission. *Chicago. With Jonathan. And a band. To get a contract.*

I head to the stage and my Stratocaster. I put it on. It does feel good hanging from my shoulder and leaning on my hip. I switch it and then the amp on. I lightly touch a string. It hums, signaling Marsha to sit behind her drum kit, Sean to pick up his bass, and Jonathan to switch on his keyboard.

The Buzzcocks' "Orgasm Addict" plays on the jukebox as Sean thumps each of his four bass strings.

The weight of the guitar's neck in my hand, and my fingers pinning the strings to the frets, makes it feel like time to play. I give the final look at everyone. Our drummer nods. Our bassist nods. Jonathan takes a deep breath and unfolds his hands above his keyboard.

The lights dim. The jukebox cuts off.

In the sudden quiet, I pick out the opening notes of "Amy's Face" on my guitar. My fingers gather speed across the strings. Simple drumbeats join. Then the bass line fills in the sound.

Strings jump, leap, and shimmer under my fingers. Our music fills the darkness beyond the lights. Right then, Jonathan's fingers fall onto the keys and the song soars away. His voice, sonorous and urgent, erupts, joining the music:

Amy, come dance with me.
The music's almost over.
I know your face,
Familiar as my greatest fear,
As my favorite fantasy
From a thousand lost nights
I'll pretend to not remember.
For tonight you'll be a stranger
Like those thousand times before.
Bodies writhing in the dark.
So won't you dance with me, Amy,
This one last song.
We'll be strangers meeting
That first time,

When everything's unknown,
When every touch
And every thrust
Is like a madness—
A madness of our own
That can't ever end.
And we can daaaaaaaaaaaaaaaaaaaaaaaaaaaaaaaaaaaaaaance.

And they do dance. I can hear them hitting chairs, knocking into tables.

The rest of the set unfolds until, eventually, the music stops. I hear applause. Whistles. Shouts.

For an encore, we play the song *everyone* comes to hear—"The Ritual." The keyboard starts with a throbbing, whirling opening. I hear a few "Oh yeahs!" and whistles. Then I start my precise, relentless line. The bass joins, and then the drums. Tonight there's a charge in the room—an urge to move, dance, and thrash. And they do, until our instruments fall silent. The only sound is their dancing, and then whistles and applause. I switch off my guitar.

There's a crowd of dancers in front of the stage. I see a lot of them pumping their fists. With the lights in his face, Jonathan's still got that otherworldly look: not completely here, not exactly someplace else.

In a moment, he comes back to the here and now.

"Thank you, thank you so much," he says, his hands resting on his keyboard. "Especially since this is such a special night."

"Don't," I blurt. "No! No!"

"Special because what you've just seen is the very last performance of White Heat. Scott and I start anew in Chicago next week. We'll be in a new band with a new name. Then, when we come back, you can say, 'I was there that night.'"

There are shouts, and a few calls for "one more."

"Dumbass," I say, yanking the cord out of my guitar.

Then she emerges from the crowd of dancers right in front of the stage—tall, with wavy dark brown hair to her shoulders, and blue eyes full of pissed-off—Amy.

Chapter 10

Sapphires Aflame

—Jonathan—

I can't look away: Amy's eyes blaze like two sapphires burning.

"So! Jackoff," Amy shouts. "You tell a bunch of fucking strangers."

Without the music from the jukebox, her voice carries through the Main High. The room falls quiet. The crowd from which she just materialized watches us: me standing behind my keyboard on the stage; her seething a few inches lower on the floor. From the very edge of my sight, I catch Scott stepping toward us.

"Oh, no. Not strangers," she says, shaking her head violently, her hair fanning out. "Your *audience*. But me? You asshole!"

"You weren't ... supposed to be here."

"What the hell's that supposed to mean?"

"I was going to tell you. In private. Explain everything."

"What's to explain?" She slams her fist on the keyboard. "You're taking off."

"Why I *have to* go. *Have* to."

"You've already told the whole ga'damned world you're leaving." She throws her hand back at the crowd behind her. "You may as well tell your audience, your precious little audience, why too." Her voice is livid and full of hurt, spittle flying with each word.

"To move where I can get what I need. To get a real chance. So I can stop playing joints like this for twenty bucks and a watered-down drink.

Not even that sometimes. You wouldn't understand. You've already got what you want."

"What the hell are you talking about?"

"Your title. Your career. You're head of a department for a New York ad agency. You're it. You're in. That means you can never leave here. Not for me." I jab my chest with a couple of fingers. "For New York. For Madison Avenue, sure. But *not* for me. And I can't stay here and get what I want."

"You're a dumbass, Jonathan Starks. A true shit-for-brains."

"Tell me you'd pick up and leave your job and come with me to Chicago. Come on. Pack up and be ready to move. Tomorrow. Do it."

She glares.

"See. You *won't* go, and I *can't* stay, and it's fucked up, but that's the way it is."

Her breath heaves.

I watch her from behind my keyboard.

"You're stupid," she says.

"I refuse to wake up one day and find I'm fifty and that all I have to show for it is a few Xeroxed flyers from no-name dives in Columbus, Ohio."

"What am I? Just a lay? A pastime? A steady fuck?"

"That's not what I said."

"Didn't you?" She looks ready to leap onstage. Instead she gives me the Italian salute, bending her right arm into an L and grabbing it inside the elbow with her left hand. She spins and pushes her way through the rapt audience.

"Of course," Scott says. "Your life as performance art. Bowie's got nothing on you. You don't need any Spiders from Mars. You've got Amy."

"Had," I snap.

The night only gets worse. Sean walks out as soon as he closes up his bass's case and picks up its stand. Marsha demands we drop off her drum kit at her house and won't stay. Breaking down with only two of us is a real bitch—especially lugging those W-bins with Scott.

Dropping off Marsha's drum kit, Scott's pissed in that crazy quiet way that makes me nervous, squinting like Blondie from *The Good, the Bad, and the Ugly*. He says nothing on the way back home.

I know I fucked up and burned bridges. Yet what really cuts into me is that Amy didn't deserve that.

But what were you even doing there? You said you'd be working all night on whatever the hell project it was. I needed to talk to you. Alone.

Now that'll never happen.

Chapter 11
One Night at Crazy Mama's
—Jonathan—

The four days since the show at the Main High have been a tumult of packing what we can take, getting rid of what we can't, trying to work a last few shifts to have a couple of bucks for Chicago, and turning in our no-day notice at work. I'm getting too little sleep, feeling excitement and dread, hating what happened at the show, and regretting the way I left things with Amy. All this rumbles around in my mind while I'm alone, sitting at a table in Crazy Mama's the night before the move.

At least I don't have to lie anymore.

I slide a Camel unfiltered out of my pack

"If you're going to kill yourself," I say to the cigarette. "You may as well do it with style. Right?"

I slip it between my lips and ignite my Zippo with a soft click and pop. I feel the heat as I draw a deep breath.

Snapping the lighter shut, I look back at the dancers in the mirrored room next to me. The mirrors make the dozen or so people look like many dozens, all arcing and then flicking their multiplied elbows and knees. They always look down—never directly at each other. That's the only rule to dancing here at Crazy Mama's: be alone. Like the Sisters of Mercy sing, "Life is short and love is always over in the morning"—a line I should have thought of.

Looking at my watch, I see Scott's a half hour late for our last drink at Mama's.

Then fingers alight on my shoulder.

You?

"Amy," I say, looking up at her. "I, um ... Didn't think I'd ever—"

"See me again?" she asks, giving a small pout. She's dyed a shock of her dark brown hair bloodred. It falls across a bright blue eye. Her shirt—open almost to her belly—clings to her like a thin black skin. In her short skirt and ripped fishnet stockings, she looks like a Gothic Venus standing above me. She radiates sexuality like a challenge.

I'm gonna miss you. Like hell.

"Where else would you two go before you leave?" she says.

"I'm sorry about the show—"

"Shh," she says. "Give me a hug."

I stand and wrap myself around her, knowing it's only a tease to drag out the end, which I've been surviving by refusing to think about it. Now, feeling her body pressed into me makes leaving her seem impossible. Tomorrow, though, I'm really gone. For good. We can't ever run into each other, won't ever happen to fall into bed together again, as if it's our first time, when my thumb and forefinger found the tab on her jeans' zipper and pulled it down, tooth by tooth, and nothing but our bodies existed as we tumbled off that edge, free-falling together—the same way it would feel again right now if only I lifted her skirt and slid my hand between her thighs.

It would feel as hot as when I sing "Amy's Face" and "The Ritual" onstage. It's always about you, Amy. Always has been. This is so fucked up.

"You have to go?" she asks.

You never once asked me to stay.

"Little late for that," I say.

She pulls tighter and holds me there. "Okay," she says and then pushes me away. "That's fine."

"Glad you approve." I sit back down at the tiny, round table.

"Do I?" She sits across from me.

"You have to."

"Why do I 'have to'?"

"You won't go. I can't stay."

"I can't—"

70

"You won't."

"You're the one choosing to leave."

"You knew this was always possible."

"So why now? Why—"

"Why what? You think that asking again will change the ending to happily ever after?" I ask, an edge of resentment slipping into my tone. *As if you'll find some fault in my answer—some illogic that, once righted, will keep us together? Let us slip through a crack in reality. Let us escape who we are and everything that means.*

"Well?"

"Because Columbus is a cow town. There are really only three bars in this burg we can play. Cleveland, a couple more; Wheeling, one; Cincy, one or two; Chicago—it's got twenty or thirty. Madison and Milwaukee are close. So's West Bend. And I can't not play."

"Bigger market, bigger exposure, a better chance," she says with a tone of resignation. "It's only that—"

"Don't," I say. I hate her for not even asking me, once, to stay, and then never finding a way out of this for us. So now we're really at the end. "Just ... don't." I look away and at the people dancing, pretending to not want each other.

Her hand falls on my knee. I don't move. Softly, her fingernails scratch the fabric of my jeans. I stare at my cocktail, the slivers of ice floating around the scotch. I should get up. Go dance. But I want her to keep going, to push it—especially now, at the very end. The strokes her fingers make are slow but go farther with each pass, now reaching high up my thigh, and her lips are wet and slightly parted, and she has such an innocent expression.

Everything's a mess, but all I want is to lift up her skirt and find she's wearing crotchless stockings. I'd lay her across the table, spread her open, and bend my mind around her body so it would be like our first night again.

This is so fucked up.

Looking away, I stare at the lonely dancers.

Amy, I can't do this if you don't make me.

Lightly, her finger slips under the fly of my jeans and then slowly presses down the length of the zipper.

"We, um," I say, looking at her so innocent little-girl expression. *Oh, please pull it open. One last time.* "You shouldn't ..."

"You're leaving tomorrow."

"Exactly."

"What more reason do you need?" she asks.

"None."

"I already miss you," she says, holding the tab of the zipper.

"I'm right here." I stare hard into her blazing sapphire eyes.

"But you won't be." She tugs on the tab of my zipper. "Let's go to mine."

I grab her hand. "No."

"Our last time. Alone."

"Not your place. That would be the last—"

Her fingers cover my lips and then grasp my arm, and I let her pull me to my feet and drag me past the bar, into the back room, past the female mannequin dressed in combat fatigues and gas mask, and into the women's bathroom. She slams the door shut and rams the slender bolt home.

"I want you so goddamned much," I whisper.

Pushing me against the sink, she kneels, unbuttons and then unzips my jeans, and pulls them to my ankles.

Someone starts pounding on the door.

Her hand and head start moving backward and forward, the shock of red hair bobbing gently as the realization I'm leaving tomorrow—not planning to, but actually leaving here—pours through my body like ice water. I feel as though I'm tipping over. I push her head away.

She looks up startled.

"It's our last time," I say as I stumble off the sink. "This is a toilet. It stinks."

"You've fantasied about this," she says, hiking her skirt up to her waist, and bending over the sink.

She's wearing crotchless stockings.

"Last time," I mouth, grabbing her hips, my fingers curling around the smooth dip of her waist. Last time I'll feel her. I stroke her hip and the soft skin of her belly. In the polished steel mirror, I stare at Amy's face, those flaming sapphire eyes, her wet lips. *My Gothic Venus*. When she looks back into my reflected eyes, I enter her, watching her gasp.

This is us, lover: getting God.

Watching each other in the mirror, I can't believe any of this is quite real: the narrow, graffiti-covered walls, the Boomtown Rats' "Mary of the Fourth Form" playing from the corner speaker, the angry pounding on the door, Amy mewling. It all grows so loud, and I can't think. I give up trying to control anything, and finally falling to my knees, I kiss the soft flesh on the backs of her legs. I can smell the sex over the stink of the bathroom, and I don't want to move; this will be the last time I'll be able to smell us.

Turning around, she kneels and drapes her arms around me. "I love you, Jonathan."

"Oh, no. Please don't."

"Get a fuckin' room!" a woman's voice shouts from the other side of the door. She pounds harder, and the door shudders. "I gotta piss!"

"You can't go … leave me alone," Amy says.

The ecstasy I was feeling shrivels up. We're kneeling on the filthy floor of the women's toilet—me with my pants around my ankles, her with her skirt rolled up her belly—and it reeks of vomit and piss and dirt, and the music is loud, and someone is beating the hell out of the door, yelling at us.

"Amy, don't do this." Standing, I grab the waist of my jeans and pull them up.

"Do what?"

"Come off it, Amy," I say. I start buttoning my jeans. "This is torture."

"Look at me," she says.

"We can't … I can't. Won't. It's hell."

"Asshole, look at me."

I look. Her expression is frightening: furious, hurt, frantic.

"You're not going to walk out of here," she snarls. "Not like that. No. I'm not going to be left like some groupie whore. Like a—"

"Like a what!?" I shout. "Amy. I'm moving. To Chicago. *Tomorrow*."

"Why?"

"You know *why*. And you couldn't figure a way around it." I reach for the slide lock on the door.

Amy grabs my arm.

"Yeah. I have to go, and you can't find a way to come. Or won't."

Someone is kicking the door.

"I'm busy!" Amy screams.

"You never even asked me to stay. Not once," I say, reaching for the slide lock again.

Amy punches me in the mouth.

I taste blood. As I reach to touch my lip, she tackles me. My head hits the wall, and then my body thuds heavily on the concrete floor. She straddles me, slapping my face. "Fuck you! Fuck you! Fuck you!" she screams. I'm grabbing at her arms, trying to fend them away.

The door crashes open. A pair of thick, strong arms wrap around hers, pinning them to her sides. She lifts off me, howling.

"Amy!" Scott shouts. "Calm down! Now!"

She thrashes against his grip, her skirt still bunched over her waist. He swings her around and pins her body to the wall. "Amy! You done making a fool of yourself?"

A pale-skinned woman with drugstore-red hair steps over me and to the toilet two feet away. "Asshole." She pulls down her pants and squats over the toilet. "Why didn't you ... ahhhh ... I ought to've pissed on you. What are you looking at? Fuckin' perv!"

I roll to my side and push myself up from the floor. Quickly, I step through the door, which hangs askew and won't close completely. A crowd gawks. Several pissed-off women glare at me. Amy and Scott are gone. Gingerly, I touch my lip and then see a crimson stripe of blood on my finger. This is not the way I wanted it—our last time.

Brushing off my jeans, I wade through the gawkers.

In the main room, the stairs are past the bar. I touch my lip with my tongue; it stings.

Scott's head arises from the stairwell, and then his large body, and once whole, he walks over to me. He looks at my swollen lip. "She did a nice job. First day in Chicago. Have fun explaining that one. 'Oh, some ex kicked my ass in the women's toilet.'"

"We—" I say, and then I walk around him, hoping to find her rising from the stairs. *Not the way it should end. Not for us.* I could run down the stairs. Maybe she's waiting for me.

And what?

Scott appears next to me. "Look. I'm not busting your balls for the hell of it. Everything's on the line here. This is way too important. It's everything we've been working toward for the past seven, whatever, years."

"I know," I say, touching my swollen lip. "But it shouldn't have gone down like this."

"You announce you're leaving town, leaving her, in front of an audience after a show. You say good-bye with your pants around your ankles in a women's toilet. This should tell you something. Who does shit like that?"

"Or that ..."

"Or what? That it's wrong leaving her? That you should stay here?"

"That we couldn't find some other way," I say.

"Or maybe this was the only way you could. Doesn't matter. It's done. Now, can we think about tomorrow's move?"

"How bad do I look?"

"Pouty. Not in a good way."

Keith, the owner of Crazy Mama's appears next to us, running his fingers through long jet-black hair. He looks like a cadaver, with gray-white skin and hollowed-out cheeks like a skull's. "Scott, man, you busted the door."

"Lock. I busted the lock."

"The hinges too. The door's all hanging weird and doesn't close right. Now I've got to deal with that shit."

"And?" Scott asks.

"It needs to get fixed. That costs money. You're leaving tomorrow," he says, pushing up his sleeves, revealing tattoos of sinuous black-figure bear claws and Celtic runes along the insides of his arms.

Scott frowns. "Keith. Jesus. We've promoted how many nights here?

We've brought how many people in here to drink your overpriced booze? That last party we played here, you must have cleared three or four grand. Easy."

"But—"

"But what?" Scott is so big and solid; Keith so slight and fragile looking. "We've made this place thousands over the years. It's a five-buck slide lock. A couple of screws. I mean, come on. We've made you boatloads of money. You can take care of this little problem. Fair is fair, right? We've already told you we'll play here when we start touring again. You'll be able to buy a whole new bathroom for what you'll make on that." Scott holds up his hands, offering to hear anything the owner has to say.

The owner shakes his head, turns, and strides back to the bar.

"Let's get our last shot here," he says. "Then, since we've got most of our crap in boxes, I'm thinking, we load up tonight. Except for our mattresses and a change of clothes. We'll be off to Chicago by seven. Get there by one. Then have the rest of the afternoon to unpack. I want to get something out of the way tonight."

"Sounds good," I say, wanting only to get drunk but knowing packing's best.

"Fine. Settled," he says, standing up. "I'll get the shots."

While I'm waiting, I keep almost seeing Amy walk back up the stairs, but I'm disappointed every time.

He returns with two shot glasses, full to the top, and places them neatly on the table without a drop spilling. "You see. Knew Keith'd understand. Didn't even charge us for these." He holds up his glass. "To the future."

"The future."

We tap glasses and drain them. I send my glass spinning in small circles on the table.

"Let's blow this Popsicle stand," he says.

We climb down the steep stairs that split the dance floor from the bar, and as the music fades behind me, I feel that ice-water sensation cascading through my chest and into my belly. The move is real. Happening. Everything's different now.

Chapter 12

Sweet Home Chicago
—Jonathan—

Chicago explodes from the earth in front of us.

As Scott drives us over the crest of the raw steel bridge, I gaze at the city pouring over the plains, the tallest buildings' peaks shrouded in clouds. Lake Michigan stretches out like an ocean to the north, disappearing into the horizon. Like a vast tapestry spread before the city, miles upon miles of houses march in neat squares along streets. As far as I can see, these homes pour over the prairie. The sun pokes through the clouds in a bright splash far to the west.

All this risen from a fire—a second city built upon the ashes of a first. The perfect place to start anew.

"Home," I whisper. *Oh, Amy, I hope this is worth it.*

I take in all the big buildings to put her out of my mind while we make the rest of the drive.

After we reach the building, I find a pay phone to call Tanya. She's not going to be here. Nor is Randal. She's sending AnnMarie instead, and didn't say why, and the abrupt way she cut off the call leaves me feeling ill at ease.

Once I hang up the bulky, black handset of the pay phone, I go around the corner of the Coyote Building and stop to take in the six corners of North, Damen, and Milwaukee Avenues. Across North Avenue, three swarthy middle-aged men wearing baseball caps, T-shirts, and jeans talk in front of an abandoned three-story building with graffiti scrawled all

over it. Next door, a small store displays window signs for *abarrotes,*
plátanos, manzanas, and *productos* Goya. A bald guy, wearing a lip-beard
and black leather vest, walks out of its door carrying a white plastic bag.
A woman in a long black dress appears behind him and shoves her hand
in his back pocket. They both have pallid, effete complexions.

Crossing back under the 'L' tracks, I pull up next to Scott, who's
leaning against the truck a half block west of North Avenue across the
street from an abandoned Russian bathhouse covered in an all-tile facade.

"Tanya said AnnMarie will be by with the keys," I say.

"What about her—or Randal?"

"Don't know. Didn't say. Busy?" I ask, hoping that's the reason.

"Or she's sending AnnMarie to do her dirty work," Scott says. "To tell
us we can't have the loft now. That there's some problem. Or turns out
she needs it for a nursery."

"No. Come on," I say, feeling a prickling of fear. "No. She's not going
to do that."

"She's been a … I don't know. A bit weird since she got knocked up."

"No," I say, shaking my head. "I've known her for … Nah. No."

"So when's AnnMarie going to get here? We'll find out."

"Couple of minutes. She works at the Myopic—that coffeehouse-
bookstore deal. 'Round the corner on Milwaukee." I dip my head toward
the avenue I think is Milwaukee.

"Yeah, Jonathan," Scott says, nodding. "We're here." He's looking at
me the same way he did in the rearview mirror when Rick Astley was
playing and he mouthed the lyrics about how he was never gonna let me
down.

I step back from him and search the avenues for AnnMarie.

"Oh, that's her," I say, relieved, pointing to her rounding the far right
corner.

As she approaches, the details of her face begin emerging: cat-eye
glasses; smooth, pale skin; a softly round jaw—all this framed by a dark
brown bob. In the breeze, AnnMarie's dress plays on her legs.

"So," he asks once she's arrived, "what's up with Tanya? Not like her
to miss out on a huge gift being given."

"Well," AnnMarie says, looking down. "I don't know what to say."

My breath catches.

"Hormones," she says, shrugging. "Roller coaster right now. Never know who she'll be."

"Yeah," I say, giving up a nervous laugh.

Then, she tilts her head, trying to get a better look at me. "Should I ask?" She points at her lip.

"That. Yeah," I say, grimacing. "Long story. Boring."

"Women's bathroom," Scott says. "Jeans down around his ankles."

"Shouldn't we be getting inside?" I ask, turning to the old factory building that holds our new home.

"Yes, we should," AnnMarie says, reaching into her purse and pulling out a set of keys, jingling it in front of me. "Here. Do the honors?"

"Thanks." I snatch the key she holds up, step to the door, and slide it home.

Sorry, Amy. That … everything.

Pushing open the glass door, I step into the dusty entrance; the sound of my steps echoes off the enameled ceiling and walls of lime-sherbet tiles. Boards cover the entrance to the first floor to the right; the stairwell, with troughs worn into the steps, ascends to the left.

"How do you get to the freight elevator again?" Scott asks.

"It's around back," she says. "In the alley."

"Now, there's something that needs to be done from the inside, right?" he asks.

"Loading dock needs unlocking," she says. "Randal showed me."

"I'll get the truck," he says. "See you out back."

AnnMarie and I climb the stairs. Dust and grime cover everything, including the walls. After three flights, we step onto the fourth-floor landing. Here a large gunmetal-gray door of reinforced steel waits. I feel Amy still accusing me of leaving.

Get out of my head, Amy. Different lives now.

I shove the key into the lock, twist it, push down on the latch, and put my shoulder to the door. It scrapes loudly open, stirring up a small cloud of dust from the floor.

Early-afternoon sunlight filters through banks of filth-streaked windows along the north wall, creating twilight in the thirty-five hundred square feet of open space as it spreads over the entire top floor of the abandoned factory in front of me. The walls are raw brick in various earth tones, and wide yellow warning stripes slash the cold, gray concrete floor. A row of six evenly placed concrete pillars, three feet thick, runs lengthwise down the center of the deep rectangular space. Mustiness hangs thick in the air.

"What the hell did they make here, again?" I ask, running a finger along the frame of the door. The black smudge feels gritty.

"Pencils."

"Better than bullets."

"Here," she says. "Let me run down and unlock the loading dock. Take care of the elevator up here. Make sure the inside gate is all the way down and the outside doors are closed." She trots off to the back corner of the loft and pulls open a door.

For a moment, I hear faint steps going down stairs.

I find a bank of switches and sweep them all up with my forearm. From the semidarkness of the twenty-foot-high ceiling, four of the many half-hidden industrial lamps stretching down from the ceiling burst on in a spotty grid.

Screws and chains sprouting from all sorts of odd places, peeling paint, holes, grime-clouded windows, ever more dust, rust, and piles of who knows what suddenly appear.

Shoulda left them off.

Alone in this gaping, filthy space, I feel a panicked dread that coming here was a mammoth mistake.

"What the hell did I get myself into?" I ask, hoping, somehow, Amy can hear and tell me it'll be okay.

It's silent.

Then pounding comes from the elevator.

I run over and pull up on the strap, opening the black jaw-like doors.

"Hey," I call down the shaft.

"Can't get this damned thing to work," Scott yells up.

"Hey up there!" AnnMarie calls up. "Make sure the inside gate's all the way closed. Then close the outside doors all the way or we can't move."

I give the inside gate a yank down, and something clicks, and then I close the outer doors. I hear a low rumbling sound begin. A feeble light from the shaft grows stronger. Finally I see Scott's head rising into the small window in the top door, and when his face comes to a stop, I pull open the doors.

"Love that," he says. He steps into the loft. "Damn. This is a *helluva* mess. Worse than I remember. Filthy. But fine. We knew that, right? So we're good. No complaints get back to Tanya."

"None heard here," AnnMarie says.

He gives her a thumbs-up. "Now, bathroom? I've got to piss like a racehorse."

We follow AnnMarie to the middle of the only windowless wall of the loft, where she pushes open a lone door marked "Women." She flicks a switch, and one fluorescent bulb sputters to nervous light. A bank of ten lockers covers half the wall to our right. Across from them stand two grimy sinks. Beyond those are two stalls with half walls exposing crud-streaked toilet bases, and opposite them I see two showers marked out by a square lip of stone, their heads and fixtures sprouting from the walls, and gray water stains leading to grates in the floor. It smells of neglected public toilet: old urine, strong cleansers, and something even more vile but not quite recognizable.

"I've been listening to your demo tape again," she says.

"Yeah?"

"How fast can we get started?" she asks. "I'm jonesin' to play."

"Need to get set up here," I say. "Clean up. Beds. Gear. Couple or three days, maybe."

"You said we want another singer."

"A woman," Scott says. "Backup with you. If she can run delays and routers, and knows Apple machines and sequencers, that would be a huge bonus."

"A singer-sequencer queen," AnnMarie says. "When do you want to set up an audition?"

"Hell, I don't know," I say, running my fingers through my hair. "End of the week?"

"Guys," Scott says, opening a stall door. "Let's do this outside in a

81

minute. I need to piss here. But before you get too far. We've got to have our shit together so we can come across as professional. We don't even have a phone."

He locks the door behind him, and the sound of gushing liquid striking water pushes us out the door.

In the mottled light of the loft, the amount of work daunts me.

"Damned lot of work," I say.

"I'll be here. Ron will too."

"Where is he?"

She shrugs and then looks around the space, nodding. "Yep. A very lot."

Scott shoves the bathroom door open, shaking his head.

"Shoulda been you, Sammy," he says. "Like we said."

"Sammy? Who's he?" AnnMarie asks.

Freezing midstep, Scott looks at AnnMarie, startled.

"She," I say. "Sammy's that chick you grew up with, right?"

"Sammy, yes. She. Samantha. That was her name. I knew her. Long time ago. When I was fifteen. She's, um … dead now."

"Car crash," I tell AnnMarie.

"Yeah. It was," he says. "But that was years ago." He shakes his head, biting his lower lip. "Hey, more important for us here, *now*: that toilet reeks. So first thing: bleach and disinfectant. Gallons."

"It's two o'clock," she says.

"We need industrial-sized brooms. Mops. Buckets. Soap," I say. "Just to carve some space to put stuff in without sinking ass-deep into dirt. And whatever the hell else. Then get our crap up here. And return the truck in"—I glance at my watch—"three hours."

"There's this giant hardware store over on Milwaukee," she says. "We'll grab supplies there."

"Got the credit card all fired up," Scott says. "But here. Let's get everything onto the loading dock. We'll lock it up there. Then return the truck. Then run to the hardware store. Then we clean this dust bowl up. At least enough for a place to sleep tonight."

Well, Amy, maybe I can do this without you after all.

Chapter 13
Seventy-Five Dollars
—Jonathan—

Early the next morning, the flame from the Zippo illuminates my fingers. They're caked with dust and lined with rivulets of sweat. My nails are black lines at my fingertips.

Scott and I are sitting on the floor, leaning against a column in the middle of the loft with the soft pinks and oranges of dawn poking through the windows. In the middle of the floor, AnnMarie's silhouette bulges from a mattress.

I feel him tapping my arm with the bottle of vodka. I take the bottle and set it on the floor. I've had three slugs and can't think of a fourth. He's finished more than half of it alone and doesn't slur a word. He never slurs no matter how much he drinks.

"We did it," he says. "We're here. So have another swallow or three. Celebrate."

I shake my head, which makes me feel woozier.

"Come on," he says, leaning against me and holding the bottle up to my lips. "This is Chicago. With me. No time to be a lightweight." His hand is on my forearm, and he's looking intently at me again, as if he'll whisper to me how "we both know what's been going on," but I'm too tired to move; my body refuses. So I turn my head away.

My eyes close.

Sleep whelms me.

$$\bullet \ \bullet \ \bullet \ \bullet \ \bullet$$

That evening, the loft is quiet and filled with the golden dusk light of my first day here.

No one else is here, and I'm sitting at my keyboard in the center of the space. I switch on the keyboard. It wakes up; the green and red LCD lights blink. Taking a deep breath, I spread my fingers and slowly drop them to the keys, dabbling out a lazy scale.

After a day of cleaning, I'm anxious to write something, to show off that I'm really here. I keep hearing a hook, but I'm so spent I can't corner it on the keyboard. It annoys me like an itch I can't reach.

Scott opens the door.

"So," I ask, "how'd it go?"

"Got it. Supposed to call them over the weekend for my schedule," he says, throwing his bag on his mattress. "Dark in here."

"Those lightbulbs ain't cheap. Credit card's maxed out," I say. "Like the phone. Stupid expensive in this town. We can't get it until next week. As in Wednesday or Thursday. Of course, we have to call to find out which."

"That about makes sense—call with the phone you don't have yet." He pulls out his wallet and starts counting. "How much cash you've got?"

"'Bout twenty bucks."

"You start tomorrow, right?"

"At 11:00 a.m. Hate lunch shifts," I say. "You know. For some reason I'd thought that after moving here, I wouldn't have to wait tables anymore. At least Le Moloko looks better than Dominato's."

"I'm famished," he says. "I've got fifty-five. Let's try that place on the corner—Friar's Grill. Looks old-school grease pit—cheap."

"Seventy-five bucks. I can see it now: mac 'n' cheese and ramen noodles. Like with Arcade Land."

"Not like with Arcade Land. This is Chicago," he says. "Here there's a real chance. Fresh start. No Sean or Marsha. And no Amy."

That stings; I wrap my arms around myself.

"How much vodka's left?"

"Jesus, how can you think of that?" I ask, grimacing. "I still feel ill."

"You're a lightweight. Where is it?"

"Where you left it this morning." I point at the column where I fell asleep the night before.

He grabs the bottle and takes a large gulp. "Ahhh. Now I'm ready."

"You're insane."

"We're living in an abandoned pencil factory. In Spanish gangland. With a locker room for a bathroom, no kitchen, no phone, and no band. And we've got seventy-five dollars between us."

"We're insane."

"Exactly. But insanity's the only way to get where we're going."

Chapter 14

Music Whore
—Scott—

I roll over again. I'm tired and need to sleep. I spent two weeks busting ass cleaning and fixing the loft, and waiting tables, and then last night, I had to close. I got home around one and have to work lunch today, and then he keeps me up all night breaking in another Amy.

Why did I think it'd be different here. That he'd ... I don't know.

Whatever the hell time it is now, too early, I smell Jonathan's cigarette. That means he's up with Amy Number Two.

To hell with sleeping in.

Opening my eyes, I blink at the hazy light from the windows. I push myself up on my elbows and see him sitting in red boxer shorts at the card table in what we're calling a kitchen—a few feet of wall between the front door and elevator.

He waves.

Throwing off my covers, I get up and walk to the table, adjusting the waistband on my boxers.

"Gotta do something about the noise," I say. "Need to sleep every once in a while, here, man."

"Noise?" he asks, sweeping hair behind his ears.

"'Amy, à la Chicago,'" I say. "Oh, oh, oh, ooooooh. Ooooooh."

"Sorry," he says sheepishly. "I ... That was ... complete surprise. She is."

"You could've dragged the mattress to the other side of the loft. I mean, I had to close, and I'm beat, already lying here. Then I have to try to ignore you two?"

"So," he says, looking like a kid who got caught with his dad's dirty magazines. "You heard?"

"Couldn't help it."

"You enjoy the show?" he asks with a mischievous smile.

"Come off it, Jonathan," I snarl. "Don't fuck with me like that."

"Sorry," he says, lifting his hands. "Bad joke. Sorry."

"Look, if she's going to be over again—"

"She won't." He shakes his head.

"When she comes over again," I say. "Take your mattress to the other side of the loft."

"Seriously. She won't be. It was a freak alignment of the planets. My first and only one-night stand."

"For future reference then. Move the mattress." I step over to our "pantry"—bags of ramen noodles, boxes of mac 'n' cheese and crackers, a can of Cheez Whiz, and a half-empty case of Diet Coke all sitting in a neat line on the floor against the wall. "Triscuits or Wheat Thins?"

"Any *chicharrones*—yummy pork rinds?"

"Nope." I grab the box of Triscuits and the can of Cheez Whiz and then sit at the table.

"She's here," he says.

"Who? Amy Number Two?"

He winces.

I make a star on the cracker with the yellow-orange paste and pop it into my mouth. It's stale and salty.

Then the door to the bathroom opens.

A tall woman steps out and struts toward us, half-naked in one of Jonathan's white button-up work shirts. Her dark hair is cut asymmetrically, pointed at her jaw on one side and up to the lobe of her ear on the other. She looks almost as tall as me and seems she might have a good body under that shapeless shirt. She's attractive yet not beautiful. Not even pretty. Her mouth is a little too wide, cheeks a touch too high, and her jaw a bit too square. She's smiling as though she knows something no one else does.

For a few moments, the only sound is the padding of her bare feet on the concrete floor.

"Nancy," Jonathan says, "Scott."

"I feel like I know you," she says. "I've heard so much about you."

"Likewise," I say. "Well, I've only ever *heard* you."

Her expression doesn't so much as flicker.

Standing, Jonathan offers his chair.

Giving a smile of approval, she accepts and sits. Casually, she picks up Jonathan's pack of cigarettes and taps one out.

"Unfiltered. Mean." She slides it between her too-wide lips.

"If you're going to kill yourself," he says, picking up his Zippo, "you may as well do it with style."

He's got this particular way of lighting one that only he can do. An undetectable flick of his finger pops the lid and then sparks the flint. There's the metallic click, and the flame bursts to life right at the tip of her cigarette.

"You know," she says, letting smoke dribble from the corner of her smile. "That's why I talked to you in the first place."

"My Zippo trick?"

"Uh-huh." She nods.

I don't trust her. Like her even less. She's auditioning, too hard, to be Amy Number Two. *Chicago's supposed to be him and me. In a band. Together. Finally. Us. No Amys.*

"How about we go out for breakfast?" she asks.

"Um," Jonathan says. "Sure." Then he looks at me.

"No Triscuits?" I ask.

"One," she declares, taking the box. "Then we go out for real breakfast." She holds a Triscuit out to me. "Cheez Whiz, mister?"

I slash the Triscuit with a fat stripe of orangey-yellow.

Jonathan watches her chew, looking faintly bewildered.

From his expression, I'm getting the impression that she's not really like Amy after all, and that she's not looking for him to make her life whole. She doesn't *need* him—doesn't need any rescuing.

But you want something. Everybody does.

"You know, Scott," he says, "she sings."

I stiffen.

"Saw her last night at Mad Bar. She's damned good," he says and then looks at her. "In fact, that's the only reason I let you come home with me."

"Best reason *I* can think of," she says. "Now, let's go, boys," she says, standing up. "First, more clothes. I'd get into trouble were I to walk around like this."

He leads her over to his mattress. She slips off his shirt and stretches out, displaying her naked body.

Instead of watching, I fold up the waxed-paper lining of the Triscuits and close the box with a snap.

Once we get dressed, we make the quick walk to Friar's Grill, our corner greasy spoon. Through breakfast, I hold my tongue—even when Nancy waves good-bye and says she'll see us at the auditions.

We step out of the other side of Friar's Grill.

"Jonathan, what are you thinking here?" I ask.

"Huh?"

"Auditions. Her."

"I told Nancy about the audition after I heard her sing. She's great."

"She can't be in the band. Not with you two involved. Won't happen."

"We're not involved. At all."

"What was last night?" I start toward the corner.

"A freak accident," he says, skip-walking to catch up. "I slept with her—with the first woman other than Amy in years."

"One: you're incapable of *only* sleeping with someone. Two: this is *our* band. Not yours and mine and hers. Ours. Yours." I jab his shoulder. "And mine." I poke my chest.

"Whoa, slow up here. What are you talking about?"

"I'm talking about you sleeping with somebody in the band. That if there's a disagreement, it'll be you two against me. Hell, with AnnMarie that's maybe three against one. Or a standoff."

"Stop," he says, waving his hands. "What's this us-against-you stuff? AnnMarie? Really? Nancy has a great voice. That's the only thing that matters. She knows machines and sequencers too. We slept together. Once. My bad."

"She's not coming to the auditions."

"Why?" He stops in the middle of North Avenue. "She's got a great voice. You need to see her onstage. I've already got some ideas for her."

"Exactly!" I say. "You and her, and not me." I glare at him. "I don't care what you do to her in bed. Keep her away from the band."

"You can say no if you want, but you won't. She fits what we're trying to do here perfectly. Fits *why* we came here."

"You're not getting this."

"No, I'm not," he says, twirling around on one foot, hair flaring out. "We knocked boots. That's it. Well, I found out I don't like one-night stands. They leave me cold. There's nothing between us. Except we both want to make great music." He jumps up on the sidewalk and takes off walking.

"I don't want *your* next obsession to be *our* next distraction. Especially at the auditions. Where we give our very first impressions in Chicago."

"My obsession," he says, "is alone. In Columbus. Where I left her. Scott, I didn't even know if I could be with another woman before last night. Ever. Plus, I can't call her and tell her not to show up." He throws up his arms. "I don't have her phone number. Hell, I don't know her last name. Or if Nancy's even her *real* name. If you don't like her singing ... whatever." He pushes the discussion away with the flick of a hand.

"She's not going to be in this band."

"If that's what you want," he says.

"I do."

"Fine."

That means he'll only answer in monosyllables for the next hour—"yeah," "sure," "fine"—like a sulky third grader.

Chapter 15

Lips, Thighs, and Sequencers
—Scott—

AnnMarie's footfalls grow louder as she shows the next woman into the middle of the loft. I won't look up. I've run enough auditions to understand intimidation. It shows this is my band, and that there will be no misunderstanding as to who's in control. A professional-looking headshot of a good-looking woman falls next to my hand. AnnMarie motions the woman to stand in front of the table Jonathan and I are sitting behind. Playing the impenetrable assistant, AnnMarie walks back to the front door to meet anyone arriving for the audition. She then turns to listen.

The woman is tall and skinny in the same way as Jonathan—firm but not bony. She has electric green eyes and long, tightly curled red hair. I'm looking her over as if she were naked—a simple test of how easily someone gets intimidated. If she can't take this, she can't take the stage. Her eyes don't flick away.

Next I look at her headshot again, flipping it over to see her experience. Only modeling. Nothing about singing. I'm not sure what she's thinking. No experience, plus modeling is clearly her priority. Not what I have in mind, but she called and showed up. Only proper to give her a shot.

I hand the headshot to Jonathan, then write "29" on a page of the legal pad in front of me, and circle the number.

"Lynda, right?" I ask.

"Yes," she says, "Lynda Travers."

I write her name down and then tap my pen twice. "So, you don't show any experience on your headshot," I say.

"I've experience, but singing doesn't sell photos so doesn't go on my headshot. Plus what's the use of listing a bunch of bands no one's ever heard of. I could have made them all up. I'll tell you them if you want," she says.

"No need," I say. *Good, gutsy answer.* "Let's see what you've got."

"I think you'll like it," she says, with a flirty look.

She's the type used to getting special treatment by trading on lust and her looks. To that I'm impervious. I write a "No" next to her name, underline it twice, and sit back.

Her singing is quite good but too pop. She'd do well in a girl group. Absolutely not what we're looking for.

Finishing, Lynda stands, breaking out her bright model's smile, full of *so*-white teeth.

"Thank you," I say. "We'll call to let you know if we need to talk more."

"Will you be having callbacks?" she asks.

"Not unless we need them. We'll decide in the next day or two."

"Thank you," she says, and then she catwalks past us, the short skirt and three-inch heels making her long legs even longer.

Jonathan leans over and whispers, "Way too mainstream. What the hell would we do with that?"

"I agree. Totally."

"We haven't seen anybody worth talking to." Shifting in his seat, he runs his fingers through his hair, pulling it into a ponytail and then letting it fall free around his shoulders.

"We've still got a few more to go," I say. "It's not like we haven't been through several rounds of auditions to find someone before."

AnnMarie walks over. "We've got a break," she says. "The next person isn't here for fifteen minutes."

"Good," Jonathan says, standing up to stretch. "I need to move around."

I lift up the top of a plastic cooler and sift through the ice water. I pull out a can of pop, an arc of water following and spilling across the concrete. "A refrigerator and working outlets. Luxuries I'd love."

"Hotplate's not working out so well?" AnnMarie asks.

"The only working outlets are all the hell way over here." I pop the top of the can, and then, out of the corner of my eye, I catch movement in the doorway. Ron's leaning on the door frame, his camera draped around his neck.

"Hey man," I say.

"I'm here to photograph the first meeting of the lineup for Mercurial Visions," Ron says.

"Got room for a poor lost singer?" Nancy asks, stepping around Ron's elbow.

"Just so happens we do," Jonathan says.

"My lucky day." She slides into the loft, wearing a very short skirt, black stockings, and a cryptic smile that makes her look as if she's in on some amusing secret.

"Any luck for you today?" Nancy asks.

"So-so," I say.

"Better than bad," she says. "This'll be fun. No?" She raises her eyebrows, looking directly at me.

I sit bolt upright in my chair and place my hands on the table in front of me. "This isn't for fun. This is extremely serious business," I say.

"Too bad," she says, still smiling. "This could be fun. But I'll do it your way."

"Yes. You will." I ignore Jonathan shifting around in his seat.

She stands up to the mic and closes her eyes.

Crossing my arms, I sit back.

She lolls her head to the right. Her almost-black hair falls across an eye, over a cheek, along her nose, brushing the slit of her lips. She slides her hands, slowly, down and between her legs.

Then she opens her mouth.

Her voice gushes rich and lush as her legs and hands slide along the mic stand as if it were a lover's body. She takes the shaft, rubs herself along it, and then climbs into my imagination; now it's me she's rubbing between her legs. As she crawls through my mind, she's exposing thoughts I don't want found, stroking them until they are swollen and hard: thoughts of what that mouth has done to Jonathan—thoughts that superimpose themselves on her mouth while her lips stroke each sound, as she sucks at the words, her tongue flicking, her head moving forward and back and again, her hair swinging in time with the beat until it erupts into a warm, wet arc of tone, timbre, and melody.

I feel like jumping out of my seat. I need to shake out the images she's putting into my head—I can't let her fondle my mind like this—yet she's pressing the mic stand against her belly, slipping her thigh down its length, sliding it between her legs, up then down; and she lures me back into being that piece of metal between her legs, touching her the way Jonathan did, wishing I could peel away their clothes and see what she saw. All the while, I keep imagining what she did to him while I lay awake that night, listening to them—"Oh, oh, ohhhhh." And then, as I watch her thumb smearing dark cherry-red lipstick along her lower lip, I notice how quiet it is; she's stopped singing. Everyone is looking at me. Jonathan's grinning like an imp.

"Serious enough for you?" she asks.

"Yes," I say. My thoughts are still swollen, and I cannot sit comfortably. "I really need to go to the bathroom." Shoving my hand into my pocket to hide the bulge she's made grow, I stand and hobble off, one leg awkwardly stiff.

Pushing through the bathroom door, I start unzipping and peeling down my jeans. "Fuck you," I say to the bulge in my underwear, slamming open the stall door. "Goddamn you."

Locking the door behind me, I pull down my underwear. My perverse erection leaps free.

"You son of a bitch," I hiss at it. "Damn it! I decide when and who. Not you. This crap doesn't happen—not to me," I say, yet I'm still seeing how she worked the mic, imagining how she must have worked Jonathan with those lips, his slender, tight body getting sucked—

"Fuck this!" I slam the heel of my hand against the metal wall of the stall, and the boom fills the room, echoing around.

I'm sure you heard that, and now you're both so pleased with yourselves.

I grab the swollen piece of my flesh, and I strike it with my fingernail. It stings. "Not," I say, striking it again, "to"—and again—"me."

Finally my body starts obeying and the erection goes limp and shrinks from my palm. I slip it back into my underwear, straighten out my jeans, and zip up.

"Now," I say. "Time to deal with Mercurial Visions."

Nancy's better than I had hoped for. By far the best we've seen. The only one I'd consider hiring.

"But why did you have to sleep with her, Jonathan?" I ask. "Do you like making things more complicated than they should be?"

Leaving the stall, I walk to the door and take a deep breath, preparing to admit that yes, he was right.

It's time to get to business.

I yank the door open and stride to the table. The three of them watch as I cross the floor. Ron has his camera to his eye.

"Well then," Jonathan says with calculated nonchalance. "What do you think?"

I close my eyes and sigh. "Yes. I see what you mean."

"Great," he says. "Do we even want to bother with the others?"

"Of course we do," I say. "We're professional, right? We had them come all the way here. So we let them sing. We might need some of these people again. If only as audience members."

"True," he says.

"So," Nancy says, "I'll bring my equipment along to rehearsal: lips, thighs, and sequencers."

Ron steps back. He vanishes behind pops of brilliant white light.

CHAPTER 16

ANOTHER STUPID
TANYA THING
—JENNIFER—

"Jennifer," our receptionist says on the speaker, **"Mr. Beardsley** again. Line two."

I pick up the phone. "Tell him I'll call him back in fifteen, okay? Thanks." I hang up.

"Okay," I say to Kenny. He's sitting at my desk at Les Femmes. We're looking over his headshots and comps, and deciding what he needs to get his compcard ready. *A lot.*

"How old is this?" I ask, holding up a glossy eight-by-ten.

"Couple of years."

"Looks older," I say, leaning over to him, getting serious. "You're pretty. Everyone says that. You know it. So, yes, pretty boy needs to be here. But you've got this androgynous look, which is really hot right now. This shot looks like it's for a shopping-mall boy band. It's outdated, and it's not your strongest suit—at all."

He rumples his face. At least he's not fragile. A lot of kids tear up when I get after them like this. I've stopped trying to set them straight about how this works, telling them that, unlike in a movie, when I say good-bye, there won't be that last-second call to replace the star who got sick. That's the hope I always see glistening in the tears. I can't stand that.

"The whole idea behind a compcard is to show your range. You are

96

going to need more looks. Here." I reach over to pick up a compcard and hand it to him. "See this? It's for Lynda Travers. She's not just going Irish or cute redhead. Here, intense eyes. Here, a three-quarter shot. More looks, more bookings." I nod to see if he gets it.

He nods back.

"We need more to work with. Has anyone else done recent shots for you?"

"No. I thought Ron was."

"That's kinda what tonight's about. But you can, and need to, arrange stuff on your own. But have the photographer talk to me first. I'll screen out the freeloaders and idiots."

"What tonight's about?"

"I told you when you got here," I say. "Wendy's expecting you to show up at a party with her. Ron's supposed to be there."

"Where at?"

"Some loft in Wicker Park."

"You know who's going to be there?"

"Not really."

He gives a petulant grimace. "Why do I have to go?"

"Wendy said so. Look, I don't want to go either. I hate these parties."

"What parties?"

"Favors for Tanya," I say, sighing. "Look, it's nothing life-changing—unless you don't go. Tanya asked for you, specifically, to show up. We're supposed to check out Ron's new studio, which is in this loft where these friends of Tanya live. They're in a band or something like that."

"A band?" he asks, perking up.

I shrug. "Friends of Tanya."

"Oh. Right. Friends of Tanya," he says, shoulders slumping.

"I know. But it won't kill you to show up."

"What's *with* her and Wendy?"

"Tanya got Wendy into the business—helped her start Les Femmes. In other words, if Tanya says 'come,' Wendy goes. And if Wendy says 'go,' we go."

"Bunch of airhead seventeen-year-old models, and trolls trying to pick them up."

"You've actually met the guys who live there."

"Who?"

"Back in May. Big party at Tanya's place. That guy with long hair. Got introduced in a big way. From Columbus. He and Tanya go way back, I hear."

"Oh. He's cute," Kenny says. "He was with that really big dude."

"Think so."

"They *together* together?" He interlaces the fingers of his hands.

"Don't know. Don't care."

"And they're in a band?"

"That's why they're here, and why Ron has a studio now, and why we're going."

"So maybe it's not just another stupid Tanya thing."

I shush him. "Watch it."

He looks around to see if anyone heard him.

Chapter 17

So Very Pretty
—Scott—

The bon voyage party is pumping. The W-bins fill the loft with a heavy, pounding rhythm. The second keg's been tapped. The whole place smells of spilled beer, cigarettes, and kef. It's mostly Tanya's gang and a couple of people from our straight jobs. Jonathan's parading around wherever. Ron's stalking the whole place with his camera. I follow him by the bursts of light from his flash.

In the far end of the loft, I pour vodka over the ice in my cup and push the bottle back into the ice bucket behind my mattress. This is fun, but it's too soon for a band launch party. We've had only a week of rehearsals. Mercurial Visions is still finding itself and the chemistry between the four of us. We've never performed. Not even for friends. I start back for the lit part of the loft and run into Nancy.

"This is a vanity party," I say to her. "We shouldn't have—"

"Yes, we should," Nancy says. "People are having a blast. They'll put our name with having a blast in their heads."

"Still."

A flash.

I'm blind for a moment. "Thanks, Ron."

"Good shot of a band in their natural habitat," he says. "Want some smoke?"

I shake my head. "Puts me to sleep. I stick with this," I say, holding up my vodka.

"I wouldn't mind," Nancy says.

"What a surprise. I was trying to be polite," Ron says as he leads her away.

They leave, and I notice the redhead model from the auditions is standing two people away. After a moment, she notices me noticing her and steps over.

"You've got a lot of friends."

"Only looks like it," I say. "Mostly friends of friends and co-waitrons. Just moved here."

"I remember that. Moving here. Waiting tables," she says.

I give her a what-can-you-do shrug and eyebrow raise.

"You know, if I had to lose out on the gig, I'm glad it was to Nancy," Lynda says. "She's great."

"You know her?"

"I've seen her perform. Hell, if I'd known I was up against her, I wouldn't have even bothered showing up."

"Then you wouldn't be here."

"Getting to know you?" She gives me her professional smile: wide, white, and welcoming. Her eyes gleam in the light like emeralds.

"You've got really great eyes," I say before I realize I thought it.

"My god. What a lousy line."

"I didn't mean to say that. Sort of popped out. But I did think it. Do. Mean it. They are."

"That's pretty bad too. At least it's cute," she says. "Here. Tell you what. I'll let you take it back."

"All right," I say in spite of myself. *Flirting's only trying to get something for nothing.* "So who do you actually know here?"

"Better. But really, you have to work on your technique."

"Something you could help me with?"

"Now that. Much better. Almost smooth," she says. "The answer's yes. But only if you tell me where you got that cocktail. I don't much like beer."

"Easy. Right here," I say, reaching down behind my mattress and pulling the bottle up from the ice bucket. "Your cup, please."

"Full of beer," she says, holding it out.

"Guess we'll have to fix that." I take the white-plastic cup and dump it into the bucket.

"There's a little beer left. But the vodka's ice cold." I pour her two fingers of it. "Don't have any ice." I hold the cup out to her. "Think Russki."

"Ya Natasha," she says. Taking the cup, she drags her fingers deliberately along mine.

Then Jonathan appears from behind her. He's got on that impish smile of his—cheeks pointing up, brows dipping together, lips bent into a mischievous curve—meaning he's got some surprise or other to unleash. "We shoulda come here years ago."

"You came all the way back here to tell me the obvious?" I ask, the feeling of Lynda's touch fading quickly. "This exact moment?"

"Hey," he says to her. "You were at the audition."

"Lynda," she says.

"Sang something by Yaz. 'Situation.' Yes," he says. "Glad you could make it. But I need to borrow your beau here for a second. A ton of people have been asking when we're going to play—the band. Bon voyage party."

"We never decided," I say. "We're not set up. That's exactly why we needed more time to plan this."

"Here," he says. "Let's do 'Amy's Face.' You and I've pulled that off alone before. Don't need the sequencers. No drums. They know the choruses. Simple. Your Marshall amp, my keyboard, three mics—all into one PA. Ten minutes or less."

"You're right. That'd work."

"I'll grab the wonder twins. Get my keyboard set up. See you in ten." Suddenly he leaps between Lynda and me and pulls us together. A flash bursts.

"Jesus, Ron, where the hell did you come from?" I ask, blinking away spots.

"Trade secret," he says.

"Gotta get things set," Jonathan says, flying back into the party.

"Hey, Lynda," Ron says, sweeping his ponytail back over his shoulder. "We need to set up those new shots for you. I've got time this week."

"Sure," Lynda says. "You finally got a decent studio? Your apartment doesn't cut it."

"Right here," he says. "Got my backdrops, lights, power packs, stands."

"You're shooting here?" Lynda asks.

"Photo studio slash rehearsal space," he says.

"Slash apartment," I say. "Now we work late. No till-dawn bullshit."

"The light at dusk—gorgeous," he says.

"Have you seen Sexy Sequencer Girl?" Jonathan asks, reappearing. "Little Drummer Girl's getting ready."

"Check the bathroom," Ron says. "Can't hold her beer."

Spinning to leave, Jonathan abruptly stops and waves a group of women over. "Scott. Come here. You remember these guys from Tanya's party?"

The first one I don't remember. She's got a bland natural look—no makeup, with long, dirty-blonde hair, and a big chest draped with a long, loose T-shirt. *Gotta be a trendy bisexual artiste type. Wonder if you can use "art fag" for a woman?* She's introduced as Chris.

Next is Wendy, whom I recognize from Tanya's party. She's fierce looking, with short, dark hair that's slicked back like Rudolph Valentino's, and she's poured into a tight, wickedly short scarlet dress. She's an executive type for a talent or modeling agency.

Wendy then leads a tall, slim woman forward. Everything about this woman is long: her legs, her neck, her waist. I recognize her from Tanya's party as well: Charlene. She's like the idea of a model.

"Hey, Ron," Wendy says. "We need new shots for this one." She nods at Charlene. "Looks like we're going to sign an exclusive deal for her in the next couple of weeks. Plus I got my hands on a great wardrobe. Last chance. It's now or never."

"I've got the studio all but set up here. Let me know when," he says, taking a quick shot of the two women.

"When she's the next Linda E. and you sell that shot to the tabloids, I'll need some sugar," Wendy says.

For a woman about to be launched into a serious modeling career, Charlene doesn't look excited or even happy—only blank.

From behind Charlene steps a woman I definitely remember from the party: a slender, slightly built Eurasian woman. Wendy wanted Ron to shoot her too. He called her "exotic looking." She obscures her slightly almond-shaped eyes with the blunt bangs of her espresso-colored hair. The same as at Tanya's party, she merely raises her beer when anyone says "hey," and then stares into the froth as if she hates being here.

I catch Jonathan studying her. He's not checking out her body but rather reading her cutoff shorts, black nylons, sleeveless black shirt, silver necklaces, and large hoop earrings for the particular way she's broken— the special way she needs to be rescued.

He's auditioning her as a replacement Amy. No. That's dead. As of right now. No Amys in Chicago. This is about him and me, alone.

"Lead Singer Man," I say, motioning him to come with me. "We've got a song to play, 'member?" I grab his arm and walk him away from her.

After leaving him to handle the PA and mics, I open my guitar case. My Stratocaster sits nestled in fake yellow fur.

"First audience in Chicago," I tell my guitar, lifting it out. "Make it good."

Standing behind his keyboard, Jonathan's tapping his microphone. I plug my Stratocaster into the Marshall amp. AnnMarie picks up her drumsticks behind the array of flat, black drumheads. Grasping her mic stand, Nancy puts on an expression like she's about to sleep with everyone in the room. Jonathan nods. I stop the CD.

Quiet rolls through the loft.

"I'm sure," Jonathan says into the mic, "everyone knows why they're here. Free booze. A chance to get lucky."

Everyone gazes at him. Whenever he's on a stage, everyone always does. Even the light seems to concentrate on him.

"But," he says, "we've an ulterior motive. That's to thank you for showing up for the launch party of Mercurial Visions. A toast. To you. Thanks for being here."

He lifts his cup high above his head.

"Now we're going to play a song for you—'Amy's Face.'"

His hair flares out as he spins to sit on the stool behind his keyboard. I brace myself, feeling the guitar's weight on my hip. He cracks his knuckles above the keyboard and raises his hands, ready to strike the first chord.

I pick out the opening notes on the strings, breaking the hush. His hands fall; the song takes off into the throbbing notes of the keyboard and the *rat-a-tat* of drums, and then the eyes watching me fade, the faces, the bodies, and, finally, light and dark. There is rhythm, melody and his voice:

"Amy, come dance with me ..."

While he's singing and I'm playing, I know we'll succeed. I can even imagine the dead are still living. But inevitably the song ends.

I hear clapping, and then see the half circle of people around us.

"Thank you," Jonathan says.

Chris, the artist chick in the loose T-shirt, runs up to him before he can leave his stool. "Oh, that's great," she says. "Really. I'm not just saying that. I appreciate how much work it takes to pull something off. Especially something people like. See, I'm a graphic artist."

"That's cool," he says, thickly, as if he's been awoken mid-dream. I'm never sure he knows who he is right after he stops singing.

"Anyway, I wanted you to know I really liked your sound."

"Thanks," he says.

"And ..." she says, "maybe I could show you some stuff. You know. Maybe I could do a cover for you. Or some promo work?"

"Sure. Sounds good," he says.

"Well," I say, "a label contracts covers separately. We have no say in that. We could show your stuff to someone. But we can't guarantee anything. And, well, that hasn't even happened yet. So ..."

"Bring your stuff by," he says. "Whenever. Or better, hang around a rehearsal sometime. Bring your friends."

"Great," she says, her face brightening. "I think Wendy'd come. She'll be dragging her new finds here for Ron to shoot anyway. Charlene. Sure."

"What about that other one. Hoop earrings?" he asks, making a circle at his ear with a couple of fingers. "Jennifer, right?"

"Maybe," Chris says. "I'll ask her."

Knew it. He's trying to replace Amy. Gotta get that dead. Gotta make you understand Chicago's about us.

Several partygoers surround him, all talking about the band.

I leave him with his fans and cruise around the loft for a few minutes before realizing that I've been looking for that redhead, Lynda.

What the hell, Scott? Think band. No need to show off you're straight here. It's my house.

I drain the last of my vodka and start toward my mattress to get a refill.

That's making more sense.

As I get closer, I see a body lying on it. *Lynda. Looking for the vodka—or something else?* She's half curled up, like a baby, with her back to me. The deep shadows cast by the low cinderblock-and-board shelves play tricks with her, making her long hair appear shorn off, and her body boxy. I slink through the darkness—not that I need to sneak. "Brand New Lover" by Dead or Alive masks the sound of my steps, but she planned a surprise, so I plan one too. Kneeling softly, I start, ever-so-slowly, putting my weight on the edge of the mattress.

I lean over to whisper hello. Then the body turns over.

Sammy? But you're dead. I jerk back. *They beat you to death."*

The body sits up from the shadows, and the light reveals a pretty blond boy I vaguely recognize.

"Oh, hey, man," the boy says, "this your place?"

"Um," I say. "Yeah. It is. And so's that." I point at my mattress.

With blond bangs falling across an eye, the moist curve of his mouth, and the smooth edge of his jaw, he's almost beautiful—as if he could be a girl with a little makeup, like Boy George when he sang "Do You Really Want to Hurt Me." His eyes are intense hazel—like Jonathan's. I can't look away.

"Sorry, I was just, sorta, trying this on for size," he says. "Kenny. Kenny Magnum." He sticks out his hand. "You're Scott, right?"

"Yes," I say, finally able to break off the stare. "I am." We shake, and his hand's so warm and smooth. I yank mine away.

Then I remember. "Tanya's party," I say. "You were doing something with Ron. Or Wendy."

"Both. She's my agent. He's a photographer. Doing my headshots, comps—that stuff."

"Okay." I look at him again. *You are really so very pretty.*

"But modeling is only a side gig," Kenny says. "I play guitar. I'm not as good as you. At all. What I really like to do is write songs. And sing. But who knows, right?"

"Right," I say, no longer paying much attention to what he is saying.

Ron's flash goes off, jolting me: I realize I was staring at Kenny again.

"You seen Lynda?" I ask Ron, turning away from Kenny.

"Nope."

"'Scuse me," I say. "Gotta go." I head for the bathroom—the one place I haven't looked for *her*.

I push open the bathroom door right as a large, laughing man pulls it, and I stumble forward. We almost collide.

"Great party!" the man says.

I take a half step back.

"What's the name of your band again?"

"Mercurial Visions."

"Rock 'n' roll, man," he says, holding two fingers up like horns.

I flash my two fingers back at him and then push on by.

In the bathroom, some kid's bent over the sink as if he's going to puke. I see that half-Asian chick Jonathan's trying to make into his next Amy standing in the line for the two stalls. I'm about to tell her, "You know, he's queer," or "He's got a habit," but I think she'd talk and rumors would start. *We're not queer. Not some rock'n'roll cliché.*

Deciding it's better to not start rumors, I step around the line and don't see Lynda anywhere.

The door to the first stall opens, spewing two men, both wiping their noses, getting rid of the VCR—visible coke residue.

I watch the other stall's door, and some boy with platinum-blond hair opens it.

"Fucking kick-ass place, man," he says. The muscles over his jaw grind as his eyes twitch. "Let's dance," he shouts to everyone in the bathroom. He raises his arms over his head and twirls them as he walks out whooping.

Scott, what're you doing in here? It reeks of piss, beer, and puke, and now some guy's puking on the floor next to you. Everyone else is in the loft, drinking and dancing.

When I turn to leave, a hand presses on my chest.

"There you are," Lynda says. "You're a difficult man to find."

"Difficult?"

"See, now it's late," she says. "And I have to work early tomorrow."

"And now …?"

"You have to call me," she says, pushing the bangs from my forehead.

"Yes," I say.

Her head moves toward me, and I feel her lips press mine.

"Don't forget," she says as she steps through the door.

Stupefied, I watch the door close.

What's going on tonight?

CHAPTER 18

LIKE LAVERNE AND SHIRLEY
—JENNIFER—

This party sucks. No surprise.

The loft's big and full of people, but there are only two stalls in the bathroom for everyone, including boys, and now I'm stuck in line and really need to pee. Worse, it sinks like hell and I've lost Charlene, Wendy, and Chris—the only people here I can stand hanging with. I hate this part of my job: coming to these punk-ass parties for friends of Tanya. *Such bullshit.*

"Whatever," I say to myself, digging a cigarette out of my pack.

Of course, the jerkoff in front of me, who's been trying to see through my clothes since I stepped in line, shoves a lighter at my cigarette. I let him light it to avoid getting called a cold bitch and give him a thank-you nod.

"Todd," he says, leaning closer, as if I owed him more for lighting a cigarette.

"Thanks," I mumble, turning my shoulder to him. Now my view is some guy crouching over a sink, hair sticking to his sweaty face. He starts to puke, loses his grip on the sink, and falls to the floor; a thin strand of beer-colored ooze hangs from the corner of his mouth and drizzles across his T-shirt, matting it to his chest. I close my eyes. *Why am I even here?*

That's easy: 'cause I have to be. Now I can't find the people I came with. I'm surrounded by tools and morons. And I really, really need to pee.

The kid on the floor is retching air.

I plug my ears. It's as if I'm trapped in some after-school special. "See kids, this is what happens if you go to parties for pretentious bands in big lofts without an escape plan."

It hurts to hold it; I start shifting back and forth from one leg to the other, and I'm getting more pissed off every second. I never get to see Charlene any more, and here I am, standing in this goddamned line, which is hardly moving.

I toss the butt to the floor and crush its shreds in the grimy liquid that has pooled there.

I hate this stupid place.

One of the stalls opens up, and the cigarette-lighter-idiot-boy goes in, so finally I'm next.

After I pee, I'm getting gone. Anywhere but home. Sucks I'm the only one who still lives at home with the Ps. I'm nineteen already. With a real job. Living with the parents pisses me off. And yeah, Charlene, I'm talking to you—leaving me at home.

We'd planned to move in together last October. Two best friends. Living in the city like Laverne and Shirley. We used to talk about how we'd decorate the place; we'd find spreads in magazines we'd make it look like. But she met Richard that summer, and she moved in with him instead.

I know. You love him. Your career is taking off. I'm happy for that. But I'm stuck at home. I never even get to see you anymore. It's like you died.

A stall door opens, and I run in and barely get my pants down in time. *Finally.*

After I leave the stall, I find the puking boy has passed out, his face in a puddle of vomit, spilled beer, and cigarette butts.

"Oh, that's it," I say. "I'm done. Gone."

The music gets louder again as the bathroom door opens.

"Jennifer!" Wendy shouts over the music.

I step around the line and over the body of the passed-out boy. "I've got to get out of here." I slide past her.

In the loft, the music throbs in my body, and it's dark, crowded, and smoky.

"You don't want to leave, do you?" she asks.

"Yes. Absolutely." I say. "I need to get some fresh air. Where's Charlene?"

"Having fun. Like you should be. Mingling," she says. "Go talk to the singer, Jonathan."

"Why? He's just another one of Tanya's idiot friends."

"Chris tells me he wants you, specifically, to come with her to rehearsals," Wendy says.

"Oh, that's worse. And I *have* a boyfriend."

"So what," she says. "You're not married."

"I don't do that."

"Why not?"

"Because I don't. Because he doesn't. Because ..." I curl my lip. "No. I can't. Not like you."

"And what do you mean by that?" Wendy asks, her eyes stern.

"I didn't mean—"

"I'm just fucking with you." Wendy hugs me. "Learn. There's nothing like having options. Novelty. Keeps things exciting."

"I'm going to visit Martin tomorrow," I say.

"Martin? All the hell way up in Michigan?"

"I need to get away."

"When did you decide this?"

"Right now. I'll drive up today. Later this afternoon. Be back tomorrow. Sunday. Late. Don't worry."

"Girl," Wendy says, "I'm not your mom here, okay. But small towns. They aren't Mayberry. Welcome wagons, Aunt Bee, Opie, and Barney. He might not—"

"He keeps saying he wants to see me more."

"So see him more. With advance notice. Plans."

"You don't know him," I say. "Not like I do."

"Look, do what makes you happy. But"—Wendy bites her lip—"what if he's out of town? Or having some party with those clods he hangs out with? You want to show up for that?"

"So I'll turn around and come back. Nice, long drive. I'll be getting away from Chicago."

Then Wendy gets this strange look on her face like the one my mom gets when she thinks I'm up to something. "You're not going to stay there, are you? As in forgetting to ever come back—accidentally living with him?"

"No," I say defensively.

"I know things didn't work out with Charlene. But he lives in a town with the population of the building I live in."

"So?"

"You're a city girl, Jennifer. Small towns are like living with a nosy extended family. Everyone will be all up in your business. You won't be able to fart without the whole town knowing. Plus you're marked. Modeling agency plus city girl equals wild thing—freak. The women won't talk to you, thinking you'll steal their husbands or seduce their sons. And the men? They think *Penthouse Forum* is real and you're like some wild fantasy come to life: parties, wild sex, coke, one-night-stands. And they'll think you've got some wild, freaky friends that you'll hook them up with for a three-way."

"Martin's not like that," I say.

"Okay. You're right. I don't know him. So I can't say. Sorry. Remember: I'm not telling you what to do here. I'm only asking you to think before you make any big decisions. There are a couple girls looking for roommates in our office."

"Oh, no," I say, shaking my head emphatically. "No chance. Terri's a bitch. Katie's a complete moron. I'm surprised she can figure out how to breathe."

Wendy laughs. "Not the sharpest tool in the shed."

"I'm only going to visit. One night."

Chris swaggers up to us, her hands wrapped around her belt, thumbs up. "They want to see my work."

"Congrats," Wendy says.

"I have to swing by the next rehearsal and show them my portfolio. And we're all invited." Chris looks directly at me. "Jonathan. He wanted me to make sure you, in particular, get invited."

"So I heard," I say.

"He *is* sexy, girl," she says.

"Take him. All yours," I say. "Where's Charlene?"

"Had to take off. Richard's leaving on a trip—needed something," Chris says. "I don't know."

I fade into the background until we leave, keeping quiet on the drive to Wendy's place, thinking about Michigan, wondering whether or not I *am* planning on forgetting to come back, like in a summer romance movie. I eventually come to the conclusion that I'm not sure.

CHAPTER 19
TOO THIN TO FEEL
—JENNIFER—

I should've listened to Wendy.

Instead I took off as soon as I woke up. *No call—too early,* I told myself. Surprising him sounded like more fun anyway.

Looking back, I can't believe I missed it. It's so obvious: Nearly everyone living in Shelbyville works a few minutes away in Holland or Saugatuck, taking stories back with them. Holland is pretty but uptight and boring—it's where all the Chicago yacht owners sail for a weekend getaway; the stories from there are of being looked down at, insulted, and sneered at. Saugatuck, though, is the gay getaway—Provincetown for Chicago—and Martin and his friends love telling stories about what they've seen there when catering to the hotels and parties; the more outrageous the tale, the better: the trannies asking, "Have you ever sucked a woman's cock?"; glimpses of an orgy in the flickering light of a bonfire burning out of sight from the road in the woods; old men and pretty boys petting in the tall grass; naked men wrestling in the mud after a rain; all the used condoms in the motel rooms they cleaned; and boat trips full of men kissing—and blowing kisses at them.

Whenever Martin's friends would sit around his apartment, drinking beers, swapping these stories, I would have to ignore them, because I knew they'd end up talking about how they wanted to go down and "beat the fuck out of a couple of faggots."

So obvious.

Once in Shelbyville, I turn down Maple Street, two blocks from his parents' house. Seeing his black Camaro in the driveway, I know he is home, so I park my car down the street and sneak along the sidewalk, past the main house, and then up the driveway to his apartment. Coming up to the door, I stop and peek through the window and see Martin reaching for a box of cereal. He is naked, his hair is matted into odd clumps, and his bed is a mess.

"A breakfast surprise," I whisper. Carefully, I try the door. It's unlocked, the way it always is in a movie. I pull it open.

"Hey, sleepyhead," I say.

He jerks around and stares at me, confused for a moment.

"What?" he asks. "What are you doing here?" He looks scared.

"Nice to see you too," I say.

A blond man steps out of the bathroom, naked and flushed. "What's the matter, baby?" he asks, reaching out to stroke Martin's hair. "You look like you've seen a ghost."

Then the blond sees me and looks at Martin and then back at me.

"Oh god," the blond says to me. "Such bad timing. I'm so sorry."

I cease thinking.

Then I start contracting, my body thinning to a line. I am too thin to see, too thin to hear, too thin to feel.

Like in a horror movie, the next thing I remember is waking up on Wendy's couch, but she refuses to let me wallow. Nope, we're going out so I don't have time to think about what happened. A lot of her job is managing the million personal disasters that happen to the models, clients, and photographers on every casting and shoot over every breakup, cheating lover caught, or day rate leaked. I've seen it work so many times, so I let her handle mine, and tonight that means Smart Bar.

She turns on *Savage* by Eurythmics to set the mood, and we clink rum sours together. "To us."

"Where the hell is Charlene?" I ask. "She's always out with us on nights like this."

"Left her a message." She gives a quick shrug, as if it's nothing to think about, and then grabs a bottle from her nightstand. Before I realize what she's doing, she's already sprayed me with one, two, three quick mists of perfume. So tonight I'll smell like someone else. Later I'll wash it off and be back to being plain old Jennifer—me.

She drives us to Smart Bar and snags great parking on Racine, behind Metro. Turning the corner from the alley between the Gingerman and Cabaret Metro, I see Smart Bar's simple black sign of two women in white outline. Underneath it we enter a long black tunnel. In the shuddering fluorescent light, bright graffiti murals of dancers shimmy at us as we walk toward the cover window. A heavy rhythm pounds from below. The woman behind the arched ticket window waves us past the line of people paying the cover charge. Wendy pecks the bouncer guarding the stairs on the cheek, and he lifts the rope. We've never shown our IDs or paid a cover charge here. All we ever have to do is smile and say hi, and the ropes go up as if we are in some commercial for couture jeans; as the brand's logo floats across the screen, the voice-over announces that "for girls like these, the ropes always rise."

As we walk down the staircase enclosed with a chain-link fence, the rhythm from a dark soundtrack throbs through me; this is a place where vampire-white skin is the norm and suntans are shunned. With each step, the pulsing in my chest and legs grows stronger. At the bottom of the stair, darkness spills out before us and the Sisters of Mercy's "Temple of Love" welcomes me back to where everyone knows life is short and love is always over in the morning. Here everything is understandable, normal, and predictable.

First we say hello to the bartenders and what regulars are there as we go from the side bar to the main, where we find a good seat along the curve by the women's restroom.

Sitting down, I light a cigarette and watch the smoke twist up one of the tight columns of light that shoot down from the ceiling in a long row down the whole length of the bar, splashing off the black lacquer, casting an eerie, glowing light.

Not long after getting our drinks, Wendy nudges me on the shoulder.

"Look out," Wendy says, flicking her head toward a tall blond boy with tightly styled hair, pressed jeans, and a polo shirt. "Suburbanite invader looking for a wild time in the big city. In under five minutes, they'll be here, trying to score."

While the blond boy looks back at her from the far end of the bar, a man in a Cubs jacket hands him a full beer. The blond nudges the other man's arm and nods at us. The boys start walking over.

Oh, here we go.

"Let's at least get a drink for having to put up with them." She finishes her drink as the blond and his friend come up to us. She shakes the cubes around her empty glass before setting it on the bar.

"So can I get you a refill?" the blond asks.

"Jack and Coke."

"Strong."

"I like strong," she says.

I see the blond raising his eyebrows to his friend.

This isn't Porky's, dipshits.

I finish my beer and let them buy me another. *This really isn't worth a free beer, but they won't leave without calling us stuck-up bitches or frigid.*

"Mike," the blond says, pointing to himself. "And Adam."

"Justine," Wendy says. "And Melissa."

Whenever Wendy's dealing with uninvited guys trying to pick us up—every time we go out—she always gives these names. If someone gets the reference to *The Alexandria Quartet*, or the Marquis de Sade, that means he might actually be worth talking to. No one ever has.

So we nod coldly at whatever they say, sending out *not-interested* signals hard and fast.

Still, Adam offers to buy another round.

Then Jonathan appears from behind the two boys.

I catch my breath.

"Hey, Jennifer. How'd you like the party?" Jonathan asks, pulling his hair from his face. He's sweaty, as if he's been dancing.

"*Justine* and I," Wendy says, "were talking about that earlier."

"Justine?" He looks lost for a moment. "I'm terrible with names. You'll forgive me, won't you?"

"I have to go to the bathroom," I say, standing up.

"Sure," Jonathan says. "Maybe I'll see you later. Make sure you come by rehearsal next Tuesday. Your friend Chris knows about it."

I walk into the salon of the bathroom. Staring into a mirror, I pull out my lipstick and start tracing my lips. *That's one person I didn't want to see.* I purse my lips at myself and then blot them. *He'll be waiting out there. With Wendy. He's exactly the type.*

"Why do I have to deal with these people?" I ask my mirror-self. "Moron." That comes out louder than I expected.

The women at the other three mirrors glance at me, one still holding her sponge applicator over a cheek.

Even more bullshit I don't need to deal with. First a queer ex-boyfriend, and now a musician stalker. I'm going to tell him, right now, that I don't give a rat's ass about him, his band, or his loft. I'm not going to come to his rehearsal Tuesday—or ever.

I snap the cap back onto the lipstick and march back into the darkness.

Wendy's alone, smirking.

I stop and look around. "Where is he?" I stomp my foot.

Wendy looks at me and bursts into laughter.

"My god," she says after catching her breath, "you should have been here. Oh, Jesus. You should have seen the expression on their faces when they figured out they were in way too deep."

"Where the hell is he?" I ask.

"He who? That blond?"

"Jonathan."

"Hell, I don't know," Wendy says.

"Oh, that's just great."

"What do you care?"

"He probably thinks I'm some sort of a cock tease," I say.

"So what? Who cares what he thinks? What anyone thinks? We're here to have fun, right?"

"Yeah," I say. "But still."

"Still what? Let him think what he wants."

"But I'm not like that," I say. "I don't care what anyone thinks of me. Who I really am. And I am not a cock tease. I'm not a bitch either." I look around. "I'm going to find him."

"And say what?" Wendy asks. "'Oh, you misunderstood; I'm only *pretending* to get free drinks'? Sit your ass down. Forget about him. Think about what we're here for. We're on a mission. Of fun."

"Yeah," I say, sitting back down. *What* can *I say?*

I slump onto the bar. Still, it pisses me off that he has the wrong idea. I am who I am, not anything else. Now Chris is going to be working with him.

"Fucking wonderful," I say to my beer.

CHAPTER 20
THAT RING
—JENNIFER—

"Jen," my mother says through the door to my room with that annoying trace of a French accent she tries so hard not to lose. "Are you staying for dinner?"

"Already ate," I say, sitting on the edge of my bed, dragging my toes through a pile of clothes next to the stack of magazines Charlene and I used to read to find pictures of the apartments we liked. Some are hanging on the walls, along with band posters and shots from the kind of life we would lead when we lived together. But Charlene's living a different life, without me.

I should probably take them down, right?

But it's too late today. Chris will get here soon to take me to a rehearsal at that band's loft—for "moral support," she said. I don't want to go, but it's better than sitting around here. I drag myself up from bed, grab my lipstick, and then purse my lips at the mirror. I run the oxblood color around my lips.

Looking at the mess in my room, I see a necklace sticking out from under a magazine, an *Illinois Entertainer*. I lift the edge and see a jumble of jewelry, including some rings.

Wearing a ring will keep mister keyboard player from getting all hot and bothered.

I scoop up several and pick through them, trying on the ones might work, first one at a time, and then in pairs, and twice in triplets. Disgusted with them all, I toss those rings back under the magazine. Pushing a napkin aside, I untangle several more from a chain necklace with an ankh pendant.

Off falls the ring I bought for Billy—a simple white-gold band. It was a token of what I had thought had been love. He was twenty when we met at Smart Bar; I was sixteen; he took me everywhere—to clubs, to parties, to dinners—and everywhere, he knew people. He introduced me, and I loved it—being a club-girl Cinderella; I thought I loved him too. Everything I've ever read and all the shows I've ever seen have made clear that a token of love makes the couple stronger. But the day I gave him this token of my feelings—the ring: a simple, white-gold band that cost me every penny I had then—he looked scared, not happy.

The next morning, holding the ring between his thumb and forefinger, he told me that he was too old, I was too young, and that I was better off without him. He said that he'd "struggled with this realization" and he was "... only thinking of you. You could do so much better."

"Consolations like the spit in a rapist's hand," I whisper.

The moment he gave me back the ring, I wished I had been born short, fat, and ugly. Then men wouldn't only want my body. They'd care about who I am, not what I look like. The one thing I have, my looks, is a curse that has always returned to hurt me. I've told Wendy this is why I can't trade on my looks. She says that "it's the only way to get revenge on all the assholes—turn the hurt into cash."

But then I'd be a hypocrite. *Or something worse.*

That ring lies on the floor, a reminder that men want my body and the right to brag they had it, and nothing more. Tonight, though, I slip the band onto my ring finger and hold up my hand. Now, I look married. *Definitely not interested. Definitely not available.*

Hearing the doorbell, I shove my lipstick and lighter into the pockets of my jeans.

"Jen," my mother calls, "Chris is here."

"Coming." I rush to the door and slip through, shutting it behind me before anyone can see in.

Chris follows my mother into the living room. My mother is short, slender, and French-looking, with her long, thin nose; short-cropped sandy-blonde hair; and high cheeks. She eats little to keep her figure, trying to avoid becoming thick like her peasant mother in the Vosges. She hated everything about living in the countryside. She's pushed me to get an education and learn to speak good French—to do everything to escape being lower class. That's why she married my father, an ex-diplomatic attaché from Saigon—to be sophisticated, upper class; to escape. But that route ended years ago in an angry divorce. I've heard nothing from my father in years.

Her second husband, my stepfather, works for UPS, delivering packages, and the only thing French about him is his last name: Gaultier. My mom fights a constant war to keep what part of her upper-class status she feels she has left after divorcing her attaché. Her obsession with France and a high-class life is annoying. She always talks about how wonderful Paris is—how much better it is than Chicago.

Sometimes I want to yell that we're blue-collar suburbanites in Chicago. She'd never hear me, though. All she really wants is a slender figure, her memories of what was, and dreams of what could have been.

When I took Spanish rather than French in high school, she hardly said a word. I think that was when she stopped really trying with me.

As soon as I say hello to Chris, I say good-bye to my mother and start leading Chris back to the front door.

"It was nice seeing you again, Mrs. Gaultier," Chris says.

"What time are you going to be home?"

"Not too late," I say. "I'll see you tonight."

"Your father will be home late."

"I'll be quiet."

My mother smiles stiffly and goes into the kitchen.

"You heard anything from Charlene?" Chris asks.

"No. It's like she moved to another planet." I pet my cat, Sarabeth, on the head. "Let's get out of here."

As soon as we get outside, Chris says, "I was up all night putting my portfolio together. I know they're going to love it. It's … Yeah. This is gonna be very cool."

"It'll be great. A real break," I say. I should feel happy for her, but I can't; I'm annoyed that Charlene left me stranded at home by marrying that guy and has hardly bothered calling. Now I'm envious of Chris having this chance to do something she really wants.

I hate everything about tonight: another shitty scene in Jennifer's life.

"You know," Chris says, getting into her Maverick, "I think the singer has a crush on you."

"Oh, please."

"Just saying."

"I'm staying single," I say, slamming the door shut. "They only want what's between your legs. For camouflage, for an accessory, or for another notch in their belt."

"I don't know," Chris says. "At least he's got something going on. He's not full of it like most of the creeps who hit on you. Plus he's kinda sexy—moves like a cat, all slinky and smooth. The hair."

I ignore her.

Chris pulls out of the driveway and starts toward North Avenue. It's about a half hour to drive from Lombard to Wicker Park, and I really don't want to talk about this the whole way, so I turn up the volume on Depeche Mode's new single, "Strangelove."

She's quiet while I stare out the window at one of Chicago's low-rent 'burbs. I see all-the-same-looking small houses with the all-the-same-looking lawns and carports, except for the occasional stop 'n' rob or boarded-up house with an overgrown lawn.

"You can be his friend," Chris finally says. "For me. Let me get in good with them, and then forget about it. Only for tonight."

I sigh. I don't have the energy to explain why I don't want to.

"He talks enough," Chris says. "You can probably just nod and smile every once in a while. He'll have the conversation for the both of you. Who knows. You might even like him."

"I don't want to like anyone."

"Girl. Not *like* like. I mean *like* hanging around. *Like* as in *friend* like."

"I don't feel friendly right now."

I twist Billy's ring round on my finger and then hold my hand up to see how it looks.

"My god," Chris says. "That ring."

I close my hand and cover it.

"You never wear that."

"I guess."

"Why now?"

"I look taken," I say.

"Well, perfect," she says. "Now you can be nice to him no problem."

"Can I see your stuff?" I ask, leaning into the backseat and grabbing the paint-speckled brown portfolio. I spend the rest of the ride looking through Chris's drawings and sketches. They impress me as usual, and that makes tonight even worse; I feel envious—and then guilty because of what I feel. She's my friend. I can't be envious that she has a talent. But I'd trade my body, my eyes, and my face for half of what she has.

We talk about her work the rest of the way to Wicker Park.

"Rock-star parking," Chris says, pulling up to the curb directly in front of the door to the loft. I watch her jump out of the car and then stretch over the seat to take the portfolio from me. I open the door slowly and step out, sighing, knowing tonight's going to suck.

"Hurry up," she says, holding open the glass door of the building.

First I need a cigarette to help me put on the right face as I walk into the loft, letting everyone, Jonathan especially, know how totally not interested I am.

I light up, take a deep drag, and then follow Chris up the worn stairs.

Isn't this supposed to be fun—hanging out with a band at rehearsal? Especially in an edgy loft?

These things always look great on MTV. Most people would kill to get invited, but I did nothing; and here I am, hating it.

On the fourth floor, a large, gunmetal-gray door protects me from going in. *I can still leave. Go to Mad Bar or Holiday or Artful Dodger.*

Chris reaches around me to pull on the metal handle, and the door opens with a metallic groan. "They said just come on in."

"Course they did."

Chris walks in first.

Ron's sitting on the floor, leaning back on a column, his camera resting on his knees. He looks over, and his camera is up and flashes before I take my second step. Closer to the middle is the band. Nancy, who always seems to be smiling about something, strokes her mic stand with a leg. AnnMarie waves her drumsticks at us from behind the array of polygonal black electronic drumheads. Jonathan turns on his stool. He smiles.

Next to him, the guitarist Scott stands, holding the neck of his guitar so he looks like an oversize, muscular number 4. He glances at me and then at Jonathan, shaking his head. With a sour look, he turns away.

What's his problem?

"Grab a piece of the floor," Jonathan says. "We're about to start." He points to Chris's portfolio. "Hang on to that. We want you to give a listen first." He walks his fingers along the keys before flicking his hair back over his shoulders.

I feel a nudge on my leg. Ron holds out a beer.

"By the way, guys," Jonathan says. "The Sound Kitchen called today. They want us to play Thursday after next."

"There we go!" Nancy says.

AnnMarie raps out a drumroll.

Ron snaps several shots.

"Nine days, folks," Scott says. "So we've got a hell of a lot of work to do. We need a solid forty-minute set. Right now we've got, what ... four songs down well enough. This is our first gig. The tape we gave them was from Columbus. We've gotta be better than that old thing. We want to knock 'em on their asses."

"Aye, aye, Bossman," Nancy says. "What's first?"

"'Sammy's Face.' We'll limber up on that."

"You mean 'Amy's Face'?" Nancy asks.

"Yes," Scott snaps.

"Who's this Sammy guy?" Nancy asks, her smile crooked.

"Samantha," AnnMarie says. "Old girlfriend. Got, um, killed. Car crash."

"Oh," Nancy says. "Sorry."

"Long time ago," Scott says. "Another life. Let's get on to now—the show we've got coming up."

Listening, I'm impressed in spite of wanting to find out they've got no real talent, like so many of Tanya's hangers-on. I enjoy watching them so much that I don't even notice the time pass; it's after midnight when they wrap.

"Overall, damned good," Bossman Scott says. "But we still need to get tighter. And nail down 'So Long, So Wrong.' Tomorrow, then. Everyone can make it, right?"

"An hour later," Jonathan says. "La Moloko."

"Nine o'clock then," Bossman says. "Chris, your portfolio." He shakes his head. "I'm wiped. Can you swing by tomorrow. Early? Eight, eight thirtyish?"

Chris's shoulders fall. "Sure. Sure. That's … fine."

"Probably better," Jonathan says, jumping up and stretching. "You know the sound better now. You've heard what we're trying to do. It'll give you some ideas, right?"

"Yeah," she says. "You're right. I've already got some ideas I was thinking about. So yes. See you tomorrow." She's smiling again.

They start turning gear off, and Ron takes a couple of photos. I dislodge a cigarette from the bottom of my pack and slip it between my lips, and suddenly, a Zippo bursts into a flame at its tip. I step back, surprised anyone could sneak up on me like that. I nod a thank-you to Jonathan as I exhale.

"*De nada*," he says, slipping the Zippo into the lighter pocket of his jeans like a gun into its holster.

Now I see what Chris was saying; he is sorta sexy, with intense eyes of some color I can't pin down. *But I ain't doing boyfriend again. Not ever.*

"So, Melissa, eh?"

"No," I say. "That was—"

"I like Melissa. The tragic lover in *The Alexandria Quartet*."

"But … Wait. You recognized that?"

"With Justine? Of course."

"Nobody gets that."

"I'm not nobody," he says, and gives a laugh. "Those morons didn't belong there. Gotta scare them away somehow."

I want to tell him I'm not really who he saw that night. *But what's the difference between acting like it and being it?*

"Nice ring," he says.

"Ring?"

He holds up his left hand, points to the ring finger, and then strokes it with his thumb and forefinger.

I hide my hand. "That. It's nothing. From a long time ago."

He nods as if he actually understands what happened with Billy and this ring.

"Gonna swing by tomorrow?" he asks as AnnMarie strolls over.

"No," I say. "Plans."

"Tearing up the town are we?"

"No. We always go to Neo on Wednesdays."

He looks to AnnMarie for help.

"Goth-industrial club," she tells him. "Lots of concrete, mirrors. Ladies' night Wednesdays."

"Ahhhh," he says. "Free booze."

"Good music," I say.

"Good reason to avoid hearing us play the same song ten times in a row. Perhaps you'll stop by some other time. Might actually get to talk to you."

So you can try to slip off my panties? No chance.

As I walk toward Chris, the phone rings.

"Jonathan," Bossman Scott calls out a moments later, phone in hand, with the same sour look he had earlier. "For you."

He runs toward the phone, leaping, and sliding the last part in his sock feet.

Everything's wrong tonight, as it has been since I drove to Michigan. Especially Jonathan—he's leaning against the wall, making beckoning gestures at the phone, as if he expects whoever it is to crawl out of it.

Nope. Never coming back here.

CHAPTER 21
UN-NORMAL
—JENNIFER—

The Wednesday mob at Neo is relievingly normal.

In the smoky semidarkness, someone jostles my stool, trying to squeeze through the people crowding the raised concrete bar area. It's railed off like a balcony, overlooking the empty dance floor, though it's too early for any dancers. Wendy's sitting next to me on a stool, facing away from the bar, talking to a very pretty young girl with dark hair. *Work or pleasure? Can't tell: Music's too loud.*

My fingers tap out the solid rhythm on the concrete bar, which feels cool against my forearms. As usual, people are checking each other out in the mirror behind the bar as they drink. Chris will be by later. Charlene won't. But that's gotten normal.

This is what I need—for things to be what I expect. Because while Neo and Wendy feel right, I still feel wrong, as if I can't feel straight anymore.

Using the reflection in the mirror behind the bar, I examine my face, turning my head slowly to one side and then to the other, checking for something that might have changed. I'm not sure what to look for, but I don't see anything wrong: my lips, my eyes, my hair, the way I'm holding my glass, the way I sip. *Normal.* Next to my reflection, Wendy runs her palm across the girl's shoulder and down her arm. The girl looks down uncomfortably. I want to tell her, "Don't worry; Wendy'll take care of you—if you let her."

Realizing how normal everything is, my shoulders go slack and fall, releasing the tension that's been stuck there since Michigan. I lean back on my stool, feeling very okay with all the normal around. *I'm fine. Past week's been a blip.*

Then I feel a finger tapping my shoulder.

I turn.

Jonathan's standing there. "What's up?" he asks.

"I thought," I say, feeling the evening suddenly turning weird. "You had rehearsal."

"We did. We're done. Now I'm here. So's Chris. Someplace."

Why are you here? Things were finally starting to feel right.

"AnnMarie and Chris are right. Neo's cool. Like it."

I take a drink.

"Tell me. What do you think of 'So Long, So Wrong'? I mean *really* think—not just fluff-this-guy-off 'okay, good' sort of thing."

"Well … It *is* good."

"Thank you," he says, "but can you tell me what you like about it? What not?"

"I don't know," I say, suspicious of the question. *Why do you think I care enough to have an opinion other than 'good'?*

"You're not a musician, right?"

"No."

"I hear Ron talk about—"

"I'm an executive assistant slash assistant project manager at Les Femmes."

"Chris mentioned massages?"

"Used to. Well," I say, sighing—I hate explaining this. "I didn't have my license. But I worked at Wild Hair under licensed supervision."

"Sorta like residency?" he half-asks, as if he's not expecting an answer.

Then he looks closely at me, with eyes that seem to be almost every color in turn. "How old are you?" he asks, offering me a Camel straight.

I shake my head and slip a Winston out from my own pack. "Nineteen."

"Ah, that makes sense."

"What makes sense?"

"You know, I've never met an ex-masseuse before—licensed or not."

He lights both our cigarettes with a noisy, flashing flick of his Zippo. "Did you have to massage fat people?"

"Sometimes." *Don't even try. I don't get picked up. Ever.*

"Manipulating flab. Ugh."

"You think of something that's not so bad."

"How about really hairy guys?"

"That," I say, smiling in spite of myself, "does suck. There was this guy. Always came in on Tuesdays at 6:00 p.m.—my night. Always wanted a 'supervised' massage 'cause 'it's cheaper.' Hated touching him. His back was covered in monkey hair. And he was such a pussy, whining, 'Oh, you're pulling my hair.'"

He puts a fingertip on my shoulder. "You know what? I have to go. My friend is out of the bathroom," he says. "Well, my ex from Ohio."

As if I care.

"Might get a bit miffed if I spend the night talking to you. But," he says, putting a finger across his lips as if considering something. "I really do want your opinion of 'So Long, So Wrong.' I want to hear what a real listener thinks of it. How about Friday? We're going to be doing a lot of work on it then."

"I don't know anything about music," I say, shaking my head, "So I don't—"

"Exactly. Around eight? That'll give us a couple of minutes to talk before the rest of the band arrives."

Why do you think I'll show up at all? Arrogant—

Then this strikingly good-looking brunette with a streak of red in her hair walks up in a micromini, her tight shirt tied up to show off a flat, pierced belly. She looks me over with bright sapphire-blue eyes. Her expression is so intimidating that I pull back.

"Amy," he says, "this is my friend Jennifer. Jennifer, Amy."

Instead of saying anything or nodding hello, she curls her lips at me as if challenging me to a fight. Her eyes flare like gems aflame.

I look away and then watch as he takes this Amy woman to meet Wendy.

As Amy arrives, Wendy steps back, which is about impossible. No one intimidates Wendy; she's *always* the boss.

After a moment, he and Amy slip off into the crowd, her hand possessively gripping his ass.

What is your game? No, I don't care.

Next I see Wendy has her arm around the young girl.

Now this I understand.

I take another drink.

Normal.

But feeling normal doesn't last long.

• • • • •

The next day, when I happen to walk past my mom watching TV, I hear "It's four thirty in Chicagoland, and topping the news tonight is the tragic death of nineteen-year-old model Charlene Pollard." The screen fills with a grave-looking blonde behind a blue-and-white news desk, holding a sheet of paper.

The picture switches from her talking to a street scene outside a luxury high-rise apartment building, with an ambulance, two fire trucks, and several police cars blocking traffic off, all their lights flashing. Several people in uniforms gather around a black-shrouded shape on the sidewalk. Two other groups of uniformed men keep onlookers away. The caption reads, "Live from Dearborn Parkway."

"Yes, Christy, this is where it happened, outside of the Dearborn Towers, the exclusive luxury residence here on the Gold Coast. At about four twelve this afternoon, nine-one-one calls started coming in, reporting a falling woman. Charlene Pollard was pronounced dead at the scene, after having fallen twenty-three stories from the penthouse."

"Jennifer," my mother says. "No."

"You were going to be my roommate," I say to the black-shrouded shape on the sidewalk. "Remember? Best friends. Together."

"In the living room," the reporter continued, "there were signs of a second person and at least one empty bottle of alcohol. So the Chicago police are treating this as a homicide. Her live-in boyfriend, Richard

Barthes, the owner of the apartment, is wanted for questioning in her death."

I don't remember anything else the TV or my mother said. All I remember about that whole night is that I cried and that I felt hate—real, burning hate—for the first time. I wanted Richard Barthes to pay.

Chapter 22

Tempt Me
—Jonathan—

Staring at some new lyrics on a sheet of paper, I'm still trying to get a handle on yesterday.

I'd been here almost a month when she called the day before yesterday. She said she'd driven here for a couple of meetings, which would be over in a day, and since she was "in Chicago anyway …"

I invited her over.

Which was a mistake.

Before the call, we weren't supposed to see each other again—ever. I'd dealt with never seeing her by knowing *never again*, and losing the protection of *never again* has been treacherous. For the first time since I left Columbus, I allowed myself to imagine what would happen *when*, not *if*, I saw her: how we'd tease and torture each other, building the excitement until we couldn't stand it, and then it would be like our first time again, but even more, because it was never supposed to be possible. She breathed life into these thoughts when she agreed to come over, and they've hobbled me; I've not been able to finish the new song for our first gig in Chicago because I can't think of anything but her.

Then last night, she showed up here in the flesh, and my head wasn't at rehearsal. I kept tripping over songs I've been playing for years. Amy was there, watching, and I couldn't help staring at her, anticipating all the things we'd do once we were alone. We couldn't finish working on the newest songs we need for the full set.

After an hour and a half, Scott turned off his guitar.

"This is pointless," he said. "Everyone. Go home. Think about songs we can cover ... something ...I don't know."

Pointing at Amy, Scott looked at me. "Your brain is over there, between her legs," he scolded. "Figure out what's important here—her snatch. Or your band!"

That ripped it.

Amy jumped up and started marching at him, full of pissed off, her finger out, wagging. I had to step between them and lead Amy to the back of the loft, telling her we were going out, just her and me. We bummed a ride with Chris to Neo. We talked about her portfolio on the way over. She's very good. Amy made a few very smart suggestions. In spite of the flare-up, I could not take my mind from how great it'd be when we got home again.

Yet when we did get home, all we did was go straight to bed, take off our clothes, and ...

And what? Have sex? Sure—all fleshy, moist, and full of semen.

But it wasn't fierce like it once was. Not even enjoyable.

With nothing left to say, we rolled over and slept. I woke up not knowing who she is, only that she isn't who she used to be, so we can never be what we once were. It's as if what we had been never really was. Worse, I can't wash away knowing this, so once she leaves again, everything, including my memories of us, will be completely gone.

She should have stayed away—simply kept living in Columbus as a dream.

Not only has she putrefied what we were and who we could be, but I also haven't been able to finish the new song for tonight's rehearsal—the song we have to have for the full forty-minute set that we have to have *tonight*, so we can rehearse it enough before we play it live.

We don't want to get stuck playing covers, but this song simply refuses to work.

"What 'cha doin'?" Amy asks from on the mattress. So far she's only gotten her panties on.

"Trying to finish a song," I say, crouching over the page on the keyboard.

"'Trying to finish a song,'" she says. "Hmm."

I tap my pen, rereading lyrics that don't work. Reworking the weak melody is pointless without the words to give it shape.

"Not exactly exciting. Well, not for me."

I stare harder at the last few lines. They sound like bad high school poetry, and I resent her for that. I scribble them out, just as I'd like to scribble last night out. I want her to go back—not to Columbus, exactly, but to the way she was before she came.

"Let's do something," Amy says.

"Like what?" I say.

"Show me around. Grab some lunch at a cool dive you know. Show me where to score some clothes. Or a twelve-inch single. I don't care. Anything. The stiffs at the meetings went to Marshall Field's and fucking Applebee's. Oh, and T.G.I. Friday's. Clone food. This's your town. Show it off."

"Scott and Nancy said they're heading over to Reckless Records later. Great stuff there. Like Magnolia Thunderpussy. You could still catch them at hers. I'll give them a call and tell them to wait."

"Oh, now that's an idea—an afternoon with Scott. Trying to get one of us killed?"

"I told you when you called I'd have to get some work done."

"Don't you want to show me how great Chicago is?"

"Yes. But later. I have to get *this* done *now*. Like in *two* hours."

"Don't you want to tempt me?"

"Tempt you?"

"Yes. Tempt me. With the fruit of the tree of Chicago."

"An apple? That's New York's gig."

"You're not being any fun."

I try rereading the lyrics, humming to drown her out. But she's lodged "tempt me" in my brain. *Tempt you? As I remember you, yes—in fact, I'd have no choice. For whoever you are now? No chance.*

At the sound of her bare feet padding across the floor toward me, I look up. The soft, late-afternoon light caresses her, highlighting and shading the extravagant curves of her body. She's put on her let's-get-nasty expression. It's like a scene from a straight-to-video porno—the lonely, impossibly hot mom walking in on her son's piano teacher to offer lessons of her own.

"Come on, mister," she says. "Tempt me."

I can't force myself to want her. Even to finish this song.

"Sin with me." Amy stands inches away. The sunlight brightens the reds and blues of the butterfly tattoo on her left breast.

Once, lifetimes ago, I'd been able to make out only that she had a tattoo through a gossamer hunter-green top. That night, I'd so wanted to know what she hid, see it, and perhaps touch it. But now I simply don't care.

"Tempt me, Jon," she says, bending down, placing her hands on my shoulders. "Make me fall. All the way to Chicago."

I can feel the warm skin of her thighs pressing on my knees.

"Amy—"

"I'm staying here to be with you," she says, her lips grazing mine.

"Yes," I say, reaching up to roll a lock of her hair between my fingers. "You are."

"So if you won't tempt *me*, then I'll have to tempt *you*—with different fruit," she says, straddling my leg. "Sorry. No cherry left. That's been picked."

Oh, Amy. Don't be like this. I close my eyes. *Can't you be the Amy I knew, and not this triple-X cliché? This, I can't do.*

"Scott needs me to have this song ready before rehearsal tonight," I say.

"Always Scott's needs. What about your needs?" She tries to kiss me.

I twist to the side and jab my fingers on the lyrics. "Right now," I say, "*I* need to get *this* done."

"You're only looking for an excuse. You don't want to tempt me with Chicago. I might find I love it. But that's not in your plans, is it? No. Use me, sure. Then send me home. Wham! Bam! Thankya, ma'am. No wonder you were such a lousy lay. Who are you anymore?"

"Who am I?" I spring up from my stool.

Slipping off my leg backward, Amy loses her balance and tumbles to the floor. "Yeah, asshole," she says, glaring at me. "Who *are* you?"

"Me? Who are *you*? Acting like some softcore bimbette."

She rolls over and stands up, facing the widows, and brushes her ass off toward me. "Fucking asshole."

"You, Amy—whoever. You didn't even try," I say. "You never even fucking asked me to stay."

"Would you have?"

"Not the point. You should have asked. At least *tried* to make me stay. Done something. But—"

"But what? Would you have given up your band? And Scott. Wanting to get his hands all over you?"

"Oh, this again," I say. "My god, give that a rest."

"He so wants to fuck you."

"Look, woman. You! You didn't ask me not to go. Not once. *You* never tried. *You* couldn't figure out how to keep it working. You—who taught me how to keep on living." I grab my head. "I loved you so much. *You* let me walk right out of your life. Like I was *nothing*."

"Yes. I did," she says. "Yes. Because I love you. Because you wouldn't stay. Because you couldn't. I knew it."

"No!" I yell, leaping up and rushing to her. "Bullshit."

She snarls. Her sapphire-blue eyes blaze.

"*Bullshit*. No. *You* couldn't figure it out. Didn't even try. 'Cause ads matter more than me."

"And music doesn't matter more than me?"

I clap my hands an inch from her nose and hold them there, twitching, feeling heat flooding my face.

"Gonna hit me now?"

"Leave," I say, straining not to yell. My body shakes.

"That's not really what you want," she says, leaning forward, taking the tips of my fingers into her mouth.

I jerk my hands back, march over to her clothes, and grab her skirt. "Get dressed. And get gone. Stay in Ohio." I whip the skirt at her.

Letting it strike her bare breasts, she stomps up to me.

"You," she says, "are *such* an asshole." She cocks her hand back to smack me. "Whoever the hell you are."

I catch her wrist. "Do us both a favor and get out."

With her free hand, she grabs my crotch. I jerk in pain. She pushes her face into mine. "I'll leave when I'm goddamned ready," she says, and she bites my lower lip. I wince but can't pull away. Holding my lip in her teeth, she unbuttons my pants, reaches in, and starts stroking. When I grow hard into her hand, she lets go of my lip.

I close my eyes and kiss her.

Amy, I miss you so very much.

A tear dribbles from my cheek. *I hope that burns you like it burns me.*

Chapter 23

Dreamerz
—Jonathan—

Forty-five minutes later, I lie, eyes closed, breathing in the smell of us, together. Amy's body feels limp with sleep and warm against me.

This I remember. You're still Amy. My Amy.

Her, us, now—it's perfect. I don't want this to ever end.

Then I remember that song I couldn't finish. I look at the clock: almost six thirty.

"Shit," I hiss. *Everyone'll be here in a half hour.*

Gently, I pull my arm out from under her and quietly roll away. Lightly placing the sheet over her shoulders, I look at the shape she makes in bed.

"I'm not going back to Ohio," I whisper at her. "Even if you still *are* there."

Looking at the steady rise and fall of her chest, it hits me. *It's what you were saying: "Tempt me, sin with me, make me fall."*

"How I could I have missed that?" I whisper, walking to the keyboard. *Moron.*

Naked and standing on wobbly legs, I scribble down those lines, and then several more that start flowing into my mind. They hint of a killer melodic line and how to rework the chorus and the bass line.

"Come on, Jonathan," I chide myself. "This is so obvious. Where's your head been?"

I write "Sin with Me" across the top of the page.

The sound of the keys sliding into the door wrests me from the new song. I leap toward the bed, crawl in next to Amy, and pull the sheet over myself right as the door swings open. I pretend to sleep. Scott's boots thud loudly across the floor along with another pair of shoes. Plastic bags crinkle, and something thunks down on the table.

Following that, there's a hush, and then whispers, quiet treads of boot and shoe, my keyboard's stool sliding a few inches, papers shuffling.

Then there are only the sounds of faraway traffic.

"So," Scott says quietly. "Pleasure *after* business. With her, that's a shock."

"I like them together," Nancy says. "She's his *recurring* brief habit. Nice twist."

I take this as the excuse to fake waking up, so I stir, roll over, and open my eyes. I wave. Nancy, smiling as always, waves back.

Scott waves his meaty hand at the new song. "Good stuff," he says.

"We need to rework the bass line and chorus with everyone. Easy fixes," I say, reaching for my jeans. I extract my boxers.

"Still. We need to nail it down by next Thursday," he says. "Seven days."

Under the sheets, I slip on my boxers. Slinking out of bed, I lay the sheets over Amy's shoulders again.

"What was that about recurring … whatever?" I ask Nancy.

"Brief habit," Nancy says. "A habit that's interesting because it's new, and brief because it's discarded before it gets stale. And it's replaced by a fresh new one. Now, you've worked out a nifty trick—same habit, briefly, again and again and again. It always feels new; never gets stale. Frederick would be proud."

"Sorry to break up philosophy hour," Scott says, "but you might want to get your habit dressed before everyone else gets here."

• • • • •

Rehearsal goes very well in spite of Amy watching; tonight I have a new song to focus on. We work out the kinks quickly and have "Sin with Me" ready to go in a couple of hours. After three hours, Amy's still content to listen and drink. Looks like she's finally having fun. Before running through our set one last time, we break, and that's when Randal shows up. He's alone *again*. Scott asks him why Tanya hasn't come around lately.

Randal says nothing; he only shakes his head as though he's trying to get something out of it, and he then takes off without a word, leaving an odd feeling hanging around us.

Deciding break's over with that, we run through our set, which sounds almost good enough, and Scott gives a few last notes.

It's the usual crew of late—the band, Ron, Wendy, Chris, and Jennifer—plus Amy. Everyone's milling around, talking, getting restless to go someplace when Ron holds up his camera, and asks Wendy, "When's Charlene going to get over here to do the shoot? I'm all set up."

She glares at him. Chris looks shocked; Jennifer, mortified.

"Shit. Kenny," he says, "I mean Kenny."

"That son of a bitch," Jennifer spits out. "He should die for what he did. Threw her off the balcony. Goddamn him!"

Amy leans over to me. "What's this about?"

"A model. You never met her," Scott says. "It was on the news. 'Bout a week ago. Fell from—"

"No," says Jennifer. "She did *not* fall. She got murdered. Her boyfriend pushed her off a twenty-three-story balcony. Pushed *my* friend off. Made her fall. Twenty-three stories. Goddamn him!"

"Okay. Pushed," Scott says. "Anyway, she was here at our first party and was supposed to do a shoot here."

"It's pretty fucked up," I say, and immediately I regret my shallow words.

"We are ... were ... best friends," Jennifer says. "Almost roommates. We were supposed to be roommates! That fucker!" Her face wrinkles up as if she's going to cry.

With a camera up to his eye, Ron seems unsure if he should take shots of this or not. He doesn't.

No one speaks until Wendy says, "Let's get gone."

She, Jennifer, and Chris leave.

"Wonder what happened," Scott says once the door closes behind them. "I mean, people don't get thrown off a twenty-whatever-story balcony for nothing."

"Cops're still trying to talk to the boyfriend," Nancy says. "Read he's some sort of international business dude."

"So, you knew her, this model?" Amy asks.

"Not really," Scott says. "Only met her a couple of times. Once here. At our first party."

"I'd been hoping to catch her at a rehearsal," Ron says. "Set up a session. But I never got a hold of her. Now that I've got things ready, I can't get a hold of Kenny. Let's hope he hasn't gotten himself shot or something." He laughs. "Curse of the North Avenue loft."

"Oh, come on, man," I say. "That's ill."

"Let's go out," Amy says. "Check out a club, bar—whatever. Get away from the curse."

"I dunno," Scott says.

"Club Dreamerz," AnnMarie says. "It's like a four-minute walk. Nothing else like it in town."

Scott's doubt crumbles quickly, and in a few minutes, we're down the stairs and out the door.

While we walk along Milwaukee, Amy's the only one talking—about how the neighborhood is using pop art and punk images to make itself over as cool, and how it's starting to show up in some advertising in New York: images from and inspired by Keith Haring, Basquiat, Warhol, the Sex Pistols, and Lichtenstein.

"Love it," she says. "Sells a lot of pants."

We arrive at Club Dreamerz—one storefront among blocks of them, with a hand-painted sign above the door. Inside, carved-up and graffiti-covered booths sit empty along the one wall under twenty-foot-high stamped-tin ceilings. Across from the booths is an art nouveau bar filled with people wearing black leather jackets bearing band logos painted in white, and boots or thick-soled shoes, the men with plaid flannel shirts tied around their waists like skirts, the women in black dresses. Piercing and rings glint in the darkness as the music howls from the dance floor in back.

"Yes," Amy says, grabbing my arm. "This is fucking awesome. They got this nailed. It's, like, perfect."

After ordering a round of Jägermeister shots, we toast and drain the thick, sweet liquor, and then head back through a short hallway, passing bathrooms with doors hanging off-kilter, to the dance floor, which is in a moody, boxlike room with walls covered in graffiti names, obscenities, and black-figure scrawls. Huge bass bins crouch in the corners; midrange and treble speakers cling to the walls above. In the far corner, I can see a patio through a doorway that looks though another doorway. In the middle of the empty dance floor, Amy starts tossing her arms out and flicking her legs, keeping her head lowered long enough for her dark hair to fall straight down, obscuring her face, before she tosses her head around and her hair bursts out into a fan.

I join her.

Thrashing at the angry music that has vocals like snarls, I try losing myself in the music, exploding into motion; but thinking about Amy takes up too much room in my head, crowding out the music. The rhythm fails to sink in, and I can't make my body match the music.

After two songs, I give up and walk out onto the patio, alone.

Spitting sparks, an 'L' train clamors above the far end of the patio, drowning out the sound of the music. Look down at the patio, I notice it's paved with headstones: "William Hunter 1952–1978"; "Maureen McCormick 1958–1978: Beloved daughter of …"; "Laura Smith 1956–1977: Too soon taken"; "Genevieve C. Tolbert 1950–1985: Daughter, sister …"; "Jeannine Martin 1957–1978: Lying in the Arms of God …" *Are these mistakes? A patio paved in damaged memorials—did they get these at a closeout sale for the dead? Or maybe it's littered with the owner's memories carved in stone.*

I wonder what'll they put on Charlene's headstone. *"Life lived too pretty"*?

I join AnnMarie, Nancy, and Scott at a picnic table. Several bottles of beer crowd the center. Snagging one, I drink. It feels cold and good.

"So," AnnMarie says, "that's Amy."

"So it is."

"I can see her giving you a fat lip."

"Forgot you knew that." I light a cigarette.

"I can't believe she's in my house again," Scott says. "Thought those days were over."

"Our house," I say, remembering Amy telling me, "He so wants to fuck you."

Scott pops his lips. "Our house. Yes. Still. Thought those days were over."

"Why?"

"Because we're here," he says, pointing down. "And she is there." He points off into the distance.

"Jealous?" I ask.

"Why the *fuck* would I be *jealous*?" He drains his bottle. "She's a problem. Always has been."

"What *problem*?"

"You haven't been able to get your brain out from between her legs the whole time she's been here."

I rap my bottle on the table, running my tongue along the inside of my teeth.

"Hell, in Columbus, you couldn't keep your dick out of her long enough to bother rehearsing."

"You know—"

"Look what happened. Opening for Warren Zevon. Lost between her legs. And then here. Two days ago. We have our first show coming up. Zero time to waste. You practically stared at her crotch the whole rehearsal. It was pointless. Had to call it a night early."

"Oh, like tonight? 'Sin with Me?' Two hours. New song. Done."

"She got your dick wet."

"Don't," I say, shaking my head. "No. Don't talk about her like that."

"Oh, really now," he says. "Don't talk about her—"

"Boys," Nancy says, "you're both handsome."

Scott gives her a feral look.

I toss down my cigarette and crush it out across the name "Eileen S. Bobbitts" carved into a headstone.

Then I feel an arm sliding down my chest, and then lips pressing against my neck. I look up at Amy's face.

Scott leaves.

Amy pushes me over enough to sit down and drapes her arms around my shoulders. "You're going to get so boring here without me around."

"What's going to make me so dull? Me being here? Or that you're not?" I ask.

"Either. Both."

"And neither is going to change, right?"

She gives me a sour look and moves to the other side with Nancy, who raises her eyebrows at AnnMarie, her grin much less playful than usual.

"So," AnnMarie says. "What do you do?"

"He hasn't said? Guess he wants to forget everything," Amy says. "I'm the head of a design group for Kolby, Green, and Michelson."

"The New York ad agency," AnnMarie says. "Impressive."

"I like it."

"Don't they have an office in Chicago?"

"Yep," Amy says. "I've thought about moving here. But it'd be a horizontal change into a bigger group—a demotion, really. Right now I'm the head of my area. I report directly to the creative director in New York. Here, I'd have to report to the Chicago director. But it's tempting. Bigger market—all that stuff. Same reasons Jonathan abandoned Columbus. And me."

"I didn't *abandon* anyone," I explain plainly. "Nor did I *abandon* Columbus. I *came* here to get what is only *available* here."

Amy swirls the last of the beer in her bottle, takes a swig, and puts it down.

"Um," she says. "I still live in Columbus. You don't. You picked up and moved. With that wannabe boyfriend of yours."

"Please, girl," I say. "Let's drop that delusion of yours already. That's *you* being jealous."

Amy laughs hilariously. "Oh, it's the blind leading the blind."

"You know," I say, "this really isn't fun anymore."

"How can it be? You're here. I'm still there. That's not right."

"*You* chose to stay."

"*You* chose to leave." Her eyes glow like burning sapphires. "This is only Chicago, Jon. I'll be in New York soon—a year or two, I think. If this current project goes well, sooner."

I shrug.

"Really?"

"Yeah. What does that mean to me?"

"What does New York matter to a musician? Are you actually asking me that question?"

"You're going. Not me."

"You could. With me."

I shake my head and feel AnnMarie and Nancy watching, rapt. "No. I can't."

"Sure you can," she said. "Buy a ticket home to Columbus. Live with me. You've got almost nothing here—"

"Nothing?"

"A mattress. Clothes. You can ship the keyboard. Hell, I can buy you a new one."

"Oh, no, no, no." I'm shaking my head vigorously. "Not … no. Mercurial Visions doesn't fold up and fit into a portmanteau."

"There are plenty of drummers and backup singers."

"You came here to trip me up, didn't you?" I ask. "You want me to fuck this all up."

Her head shakes as her eyes grow narrow. "I did *not* come here for *you. I* came on *business.*"

"*You* called."

"I want you."

"See."

"See what!" She slams her fist down. "What? That I want you? That you want me? That it's stupid we're apart!" She's shouting now.

Everyone's watching now.

"That's not my fault," I say.

"You left!"

"*You* couldn't figure a way out of this. *You* couldn't solve the problem—a problem I'd never have had—"

"You motherfucker."

"Why are you here?"

"Making a mistake."

"Then leave," I say, standing.

She turns to stand but then stops. "Oh, no. No. I see it now." She bows her head. "God, why did I think you'd stay …"

Unable to take a breath, I wait for her say something.

"You're *in love* with that skinny little thing," Amy says, raising her head. "Actually in love with her."

"What are you talking about? Who?"

"How could you, *ever, ever* love *anyone* else." Amy swipes two bottles off the table at me.

Jerking my hands up, I block one bottle from my face; it shatters on a headstone. The other hits my chest and drains into my lap. I leap up, rivulets of beer snaking down my legs.

"How *could* you?" she yells, jabbing two fingers into my chest so hard she pushes backward.

"I *don't* love anyone. No one else. No one. Not even *you* anymore." I turn away and march across the headstones to the doorway, where Scott steps silently out of my way.

"Fucking asshole!" Amy screams after me.

A beer bottle shatters on the doorway beside my head. I feel the splatter of cold beer hitting my face and slivers of glass deflecting off my jacket.

I walk straight through the bar as a bouncer rushes past me toward the patio.

Chapter 24
Just Walk Away
—Jonathan—

Each step on my way home from Dreamerz becomes an exclamation point of anger at her, at myself, and at life and the shitty choices it keeps giving me.

An 'L' train screeches overhead as cars snarl along the street beside me. I need to keep moving to avoid any chance she might catch up to me; but I can't run. That would burn up my anger and rot my resolve to cast out all my memories of her, to grind to death every feeling I might have ever had for her, and to strangle the very *idea* of love in my heart. *Kill it. Dead.*

"Kill it. Dead," I tell the night. "Kill it all. Dead. All dead."

Once in the loft, I search for anything of Amy's. I'll leave her no excuse to even call me. *Kill it all.*

After finding only a last lipstick, I make another sweep of the space. I need to keep angry, focused on what makes me angry, 'cause I know this final ending will hurt worse than when I left Columbus. There are no fantasies left. No hopes. *What we'd been is beyond dead.*

As I pass near the door, I hear a hesitant knock.

I consider walking past without answering it, but I stop instead. I open the door, stone-faced.

Amy stands in the fractured light of the hallway, biting her lip, her hair mussed, knees scraped, eyes red, and cheeks streaked with mascara. "They threw me out."

I nod.

"I'm sorry. I was wrong. It's all a mess and—"

"No," I say, shaking my head. "It's past that."

"Please. I'm drunk. I can't drive six hours right now. I don't know where else to go. I'll leave first thing in the morning. Please let me get some sleep. Two hours. Anything." Her chin starts shuddering, and tears fill her eyes. One spills down her cheek. "Please."

Closing my eyes, I sigh. "Couch."

"Thank you."

I walk to the couch and pat it without looking back. "When I get up—"

"I'll be gone. I know. Yes."

In the bathroom, I reek of beer; my soaked shirt and pants cling to my skin. Peeling everything off, I act out what I'll say if she comes to me during the night, trying to make things right with her thighs.

"That's it. No more. I should've known better. I should've never taken your call—never said yes when you asked to come."

I examine how I look as I say these words: hard. As I need to be.

"I should've known better. Should never've taken that call. Never said yes. When you asked to come. Never shoulda trusted you again. You came here to destroy. To trip me up. Make me fall."

"Oh, no, not me."

"Just go. You can't fix it now. Only break it more. You're better in dreams—a memory to fondle. See, sometimes it's best to just walk away."

I keep repeating these lines to myself in the mirror until they sound as impervious as I feel. Then I hear a melody weaving itself around my anger, hardening around lyrics I'm saving for her. Humming the melody, I rush to my keyboard and write my thoughts down as lyrics while the wound's still bleeding. The words exhausted, I turn on the keyboard and plug in my headphones. Rereading the lyrics, I hum the melody playing in my mind and make my fingers repeat it, and I keep reworking it until Scott opens the door. I notice the time: nearly three hours since I left Dreamerz. I watch him walk in and then stop at the hunched silhouette of Amy on the couch.

He points his thumb at her, shrugging his shoulders like "What gives?"

"Too drunk to drive. Letting her crash till morning."

"Going to bed," he says, and then he walks off into the shadows at the far end of the loft.

I rework the music and the lyrics until I have to shake myself awake every few moments. Turning off the keyboard, I lay my head down and close my eyes.

There is only the sound of the traffic below.

• • • • •

The sun's begun seeping between the buildings of Chicago, probing the loft with a soft, pink-orange light, when I wake slumped over the keyboard, my back stiff as stone. I drag myself to my mattress and collapse. I haven't the will to even take off my shoes.

When the sound of Scott talking wakes me again, the loft is full of bright, clear light pouring through the windows.

Suddenly I remember Le Moloko. I shoot up in bed, trying to clear the haze from my mind. *What day is it? Friday. Right. It's Friday. I work lunch Friday. Today. Okay. What time is it? Where's the clock?*

The clock reads ten fifteen.

Twenty-five minutes to make it to work.

I toss the covers off and stand up. My back's killing me. I look over at the couch.

It's empty.

"Didn't say good-bye," I mumble. *Why would you?*

Scott hangs up the phone.

"Who's that?" I ask.

"Got called in to cover a shift. Hell, they know I've got a double tomorrow. I need a day off soon."

"Did you see her leave?" I ask.

"Nope. Gone when I got up."

Stretching out my back, I remember my new song and walk to the keyboard. I turn the sheet so I can read the lyrics. Along the edge, Amy wrote a note:

Jon—

It's all a mess.

I'm sorry it's like this. I'm like this. We're like this.

I don't know how to fix anything. I don't think you do either.

Farewell, my love,

Amy

Below she drew a heart with a sad face in the center.

We finally did it. Killed it dead. It hurts. Like I've never felt before.

I let out a weary sigh. I can't think about this anymore.

"Time we just walk away," I whisper.

"Hey," Scott says. "That a new song on your keyboard? What are you calling it?"

"Just Walk Away."

After I get back from working lunch, Scott leaves to grab a bite to eat before rehearsal, leaving me alone with "Just Walk Away," which has harried me since I woke up. Sipping bitter instant coffee, I try to reread the lyrics but keep looking at Amy's note.

Helluva mess is right. No fixing it. Not anymore.

I copy the lyrics onto a new page and fold up the copy with her note. I kiss it, and the realization of what we've finally done makes me want to rip it up—to burn it—but it's the last thing of Amy's I'll ever have. I slip the note into my back pocket.

After rereading the freshly copied lyrics, I change nothing and write "'Just Walk Away'" in big letters across the top.

That done, I switch on the keyboard and tap out what I can remember of the melody from last night. It flickers back. My fingers gambol over the keys, and the melody, free from my memory, starts slowly dancing around the loft. Then it demands more, and my left hand joins the music.

A darker thread comes to life—the true sound of the words. With this the song congeals. I feel the music now; it's as if I were still standing in the bathroom, watching myself glare back from the mirror.

I realize Scott has returned only after he's taken his Stratocaster off the stand, slung it over his shoulder, and started playing along. For the first time, I start singing the lyrics. Now I hear how the rhythm will work. Then comes the sound of the chorus.

We keep repeating "Just Walk Away" until it feels hard and real.

Suddenly he stops playing. "Hang on. Listen. Somebody's at the door."

Silence rolls around the loft as my fingers slide off the keyboard. I watch him opening the door. The other two members of the band, Nancy and AnnMarie, push in, followed by Lynda, her curly red hair flowing back over her shoulders.

"Jesus, guys," Nancy says, her smile slightly wider than usual. "We've been out there forever. Couldn't you hear us pounding on the door? I understand getting into your work, but, um, we're part of the band too. How about letting us in on it?"

"Damn good, no?" Scott asks.

"So we're working on that first, right?" she asks.

"We've got a show a week from today," he says. "Eight days. Including tonight."

"I want to work on that song to start off," I say, "even if to only sketch out the chorus and drums." I need to get it out of my head. I can't live that moment much longer.

"Fine," he says. "If it doesn't work quickly, we need to move on."

Right then, Ron arrives with a twelve-pack, his camera slapping his chest. Scott pulls a bottle of vodka from the fridge, pours two fingers into a glass, and drops in a few ice cubes. He tips in some soda and gives the cocktail to Lynda.

"So. You remember how much I like beer."

"How could I forget? You're going to help with my technique because of it."

The door groans open again, revealing Randal, Aryan blond and lithe, in his usual boldly striped shirt and skinny, straight-legged jeans.

"Would you look at what the cat dragged in," Scott says.

Stepping in, he looks around approvingly. "Well, well, well. You *are* fixing the place up after all." He shakes Scott's hand.

"So what brings you here tonight?"

"Well, it is my building," he says. "More important, I understand there'll be some free music."

"Sit your ass down on the couch. Ron's got beverages."

"Where the hell have you and Tanya been?"

"Long story," he says. "Total buzzkill. Later."

"Drummer Girl," I say, "listen to this." I play the melody, humming the rhythm, marking the time with the nod of my head. "See what I'm getting at?"

"Sure," she says, taking out her sticks.

Nancy slinks over to her mic and machines.

"Nancy," I say, "I don't have the sound of the chorus down quite yet." I hold the lyric sheet out to her. "Read it. You two do something with it. You'll understand better when you hear it."

In a half hour, everything is in its place: drums, chorus, and melody. By midnight we've decided to use "Just Walk Away" at the Sound Kitchen to finish our set.

• • • • •

In the three days before our first performance as Mercurial Visions, I lose myself in my mindless job at Le Moloko, writing and mailing the press release for the show, and tightening up the songs on the setlist. All the while, I avoid being around people as much as possible; I don't go out for drinks, and I eat my meals alone, at the loft. Not because I'll run into Amy in the bars as I would have in Columbus, but because I won't. I had to go through leaving her once already. This time is worse; we broke something I hadn't realized I'd counted on when I moved here: that she *could* be here—that *we* could be. Somehow.

Now that's gone too. This—the finality—I can't confront yet.

I go to my keyboard and play the whole set through again and again, determined to be amazing at the show, as if by playing well I can make everything right.

How? That's impossible to explain, even to myself.

Chapter 25
Coffee to Make You Sleep
—Jonathan—

On the day of Mercurial Vision's first gig in Chicago, Scott has to work lunch, which leaves me with all the packing.

Early in the afternoon, I test each mic, every cable, and my keyboard before packing it away. After writing out setlists for everyone, I call Ron to confirm the time he'll be over with his hearse. I have everything ready long before anyone's due to arrive, so I stand in the window, looking south at the Loop. Memories of Amy slip through my mind. They slide past in a montage. I feel panicked as these fragments of her and who we were pile around me.

I run to the box that holds my keyboard, kneel in front of it, and pull apart my careful packing. I quickly set it up and start playing "Just Walk Away," turning the volume up to push these thoughts away. Eventually I slip away from the memories and unanswerable questions, and I'm alone again. I start playing songs I've heard recently on the radio, first "Need You Tonight," and then "Sweet Child O' Mine," "Faith," and "Never Gonna Give You Up," which I stop playing as soon as I recognize. I immediately switch to "Red, Red Wine" to wash that song from my mind, along with Scott's eyes looking at me in the mirror.

Right then Scott arrives home from work.

I feel off kilter, yet I keep that to myself and hope to settle down before our first show as Mercurial Visions.

After we snag gyros and fries at Friar's Grill, AnnMarie arrives.

Within minutes, Nancy follows, and then Ron shows up with his black '73 Cadillac hearse. Once we load it up, I ride shotgun, and we go about ten minutes in silence.

"You're awfully quiet," he says.

"Yeah. I get like this before a show sometimes."

"Heard about the drama at Dreamerz," he says. "I was upstairs watching some shitty band."

"Didn't miss much." It's not as if he'd understand how much I've lost. "Mostly just sucked."

"She's out of her mind," he says.

"No. She's not. Not really." Then I sigh, stuck, as always; I've never been able to explain her or us in a way that made much sense. "Scott'll tell you she is. But he's wrong. The crazy—that's all part of the ... of a ... game. It's not real. Might look real. *Needs* to look real. But it's play. Make-believe. Real lover, make-believe drama—passion squared." This is as close as I'll ever come to explaining her or us.

"Right," he says, letting his voice drop off to silence.

What I need to tell him, tell someone, is that tonight, for the first time in I cannot remember how long, I've no lover, even imagined, for whom to play "Amy's Face," "The Ritual," or "Just Walk Away."

What's the point in playing with no one to sing for?

We turn the corner onto Division Street and, in a couple of blocks, pull into the alley behind the Sound Kitchen. Arriving first, I head in to let the manager know we're here. The storefront bar has booths along one long wall. People sit in only one: three guys and a blonde with high hair. They talk, oblivious to everything around them. All along the opposite wall is an old-time Chicago bar, heavy with deco-shaped slabs of wood, rounded billowy mirrors, and liquor bottles lining glass shelves. High stools run the whole length of the bar; five are occupied. Square Formica tables with chairs fill the area past the bar, and tucked in back, at the far end, a shallow, square stage sits empty in the darkness. A slender alley runs alongside it—the way to the bathrooms.

I hate setups like this—people walking in front of us all night to piss.

"It's a start," I remind myself. "In Chi-town."

At the end of the bar, I find the manager hunched over a liquor order.

He's fortyish with hair touched by gray and a paunch, and he's dressed in jeans and a button-up shirt. Looking up, he tells me we're to play first, which means we have plenty of time to set up. Tearing down is another matter—we have twenty minutes. We can park along Division. The pay—"fifty bucks and one round of drinks: draft or well liquor." He goes back to checking his order.

We spend the next thirty-five minutes setting up in the twilight and deep shadows of a single yellow spotlight. We run a quick sound check. Scott plays with the six stage lights, finally deciding to leave them all most of the way up. With the half hour we have left, we grab a table near the stage and get drinks. We have to pay for these; the free ones come *after* we play.

This leaves me time to wonder for whom I'll be singing—not the audience, but the one I'm trying to convince I sincerely feel what I'm singing.

Then Chris arrives with Wendy and Jennifer. They walk over.

Jennifer's showing up pleases me unexpectedly well.

"Make sure you sit up front at one of these tables," Scott says, pointing to the four right in front of the stage. "Nothing's worse than playing to empty seats."

Aside from the three of them, there are only thirteen people in the place, including the bartender and manager.

Drawing circles on the tabletop with her finger, Jennifer has a distracted look in her eyes, as if there's some other place she'd rather be. This makes me feel as though I should apologize that she's here to watch us, or for her friend getting thrown off a balcony, or for what Amy said at Dreamerz. And then I remember how wounded Amy looked when she accused me of loving Jennifer, and how that accusation has burned up the last chance Amy and I will ever have; and now I think Jennifer should apologize for that. *Or I don't know what.*

I tell Scott I'm going to recheck my equipment.

Onstage, pretending to check my keyboard over, I see Lynda walking to the table. A few moments later, Kenny arrives, though I don't recognize him until he gets to the stage and hellos Scott; I thought he was a girl.

Fifteen whole people. Hell of a first time out. A lot like Ohio.

After spending the next few minutes trying to remember what it was like to play before Amy, I realize can't. Then Nancy, Scott, and AnnMarie step up onstage. I feel completely naked here. I see our friends at the table. I see Jennifer.

Well, Jennifer, you're the closest thing to Amy I have tonight—the altar upon which we were sacrificed. Tonight I'll perform for you. Only hope you understand. It's all true. Every word.

Feeling the thread of excitement that stretches from my belly down through the backs of my legs, I crack my knuckles and then look over the gap in front of the stage for dancing, and the tiny audience, with everyone we know sitting at the first two tables—the only people who care that we're onstage. Nodding, I check the setlist, and then after I check where Jennifer's sitting one last time, I notice a guy with long blond hair, tow-white eyebrows, and a red beard standing almost next to the stage as if he'd suddenly materialized there.

Where the hell'd you come from?

Right then, the stage lights come up.

I spread my fingers and drop them onto the keys. Music flies out over the audience; layers of drums, guitar, and voices follow, flowing around me.

I begin to sing, the world fading away until only Jennifer, I, and the music exist. Now I'm untouchable, infinite—beyond any care—as I'd been with Amy when we devoured each other, piece by piece. For song after song, this delight holds, but then the final note of our closing song, "Just Walk Away," slips from my fingers. As it continues thrumming in my body, I hear clapping and blink away the flash from a camera. I wish I could keep playing, never stopping, forever.

The stage lights fall; I can see that even the bartender is clapping. The man with the three-color hair raises his hand up, extending his pinky and forefinger.

I don't do this to please you; I do it to have a reason to wake up, to keep from wrapping my belt around that chandelier. To keep breathing. Amy, you showed me that.

That stings.

The manager has walked over, and I overhear him talking to Scott.

"Impressive," the manager says. "Truly. Look, a band canceled the Saturday after next. Would you be interested in filling in?"

"Absolutely," Scott says.

"Meet me after you've broken down. We'll talk," the manager says.

I start breaking down the keyboard and mics and pack them in their scuffed-up road boxes. As we clear the stage, the next band is lugging in their own boxes and crates, piling them near the entrance. A tall, lanky guy with bad skin and blond dreadlocks says, "Great sound, man. Too bad the crowd sucks." He keeps walking a crate in.

"Thanks. Better than when we started," I say, carrying my keyboard case out into the dark, stuffy alley.

Once we finish packing up the hearse, Scott and I head back in to talk to the manager.

"Nine days. Saturday," the manager says. "Midnight. Right before Acumen Nation. You'll need to make some fliers. Here are the names of all the bands. Put 'Free before 10:00 p.m. with this flier. Five dollars after' on it."

"Great. We'll be here."

"Now, it's fifty bucks, plus a buck a person you get in here before ten with your flier. So make sure you put your name across the bottom."

"All right—fliers with our name at the bottom," Scott says. "Lots."

"The fifty bucks for tonight," he says, handing Scott a white envelope. They shake.

"By the way," the manager says, "get a new demo tape. You sound completely different. Hell of a lot better. Go to Soundworks over on Lincoln. They'll cut you a deal if you can record at night. I know Mike over there. Tell him I told you to call."

"Mike at Soundworks," Scott says. "Will do. And thanks."

See, this is why I moved here. Amy was always the audience to my thoughts. Now I'm left talking to myself.

Cabbing it back to the loft, I realize I work the night of the gig, so I'll have to give up my best shift. That'll cost me about a week's worth of rent.

What's a few more days of gyros and ramen noodles? This's why I moved here. It's rough. See what I mean, Jennifer?

Her name jars me.

What are you doing in my head?

No. I shake my head. *I only played for you because ... because you're the last thing Amy spoke of before we finally died. Your name came off her tongue. I heard it.*

I bat away these thoughts with my hand and then stare out the window at the passing three-flats until the cab drops me off in front of the loft. I stare up at the fourth-floor lights.

"Jonathan," I say. "Stop thinking."

We're buried under the headstones at Dreamerz. Done. You moved; she didn't. Now you have to make it worth it. Starting tonight. We had a good show. Got invited back—on our first outing.

"So put on a happy face." *Maybe I'll believe it.*

I jaunt up the four flights of stairs, taking them by twos, and pull open the door. Scott's stepping out of the freight elevator with a crate of wires in his hands. Kenny follows with mic stands. AnnMarie drags her drum crates out, and then Nancy emerges with her Apple and MIDI sequencers. The only people that we invited who bothered to show up—Lynda, Wendy, Chris, and Jennifer—crouch next to the stereo. Someone slips in the Revolting Cocks' *Beers, Steers, and Queers*, filling the loft with a solid industrial throb. Ron's camera flashes.

Twenty minutes later, all the gear sits at the center of the loft, ready for our next rehearsal.

I slump to the floor and lean against my keyboard case.

Her smile in place, Nancy puts her hand on my shoulder. "Good show, front man."

"Yeah, but where was everyone?" I ask. "Everyone else who'd promised to come? All the waitrons who said, 'Sure, I'll be there.' Just like in Ohio. Nothing but talk. I thought they'd ... I don't know. Be different here."

"People are people," Scott says, "wherever they are."

"They're always going to each other's damned plays, their improv and dance performances, but for us—"

"Chill out."

"If it's the same everywhere, why did we bother coming? Giving up so—"

"Hey. Smoke a cigarette before you have a stroke."

Nancy takes the cigarette from her mouth and puts it between my lips. "Deep breath. Nicotine relaxation."

I inhale deeply, closing my eyes.

"It was Thursday after all," Nancy says, looking even more amused than usual. "No one could find it. They were all too hungover. Or they had to work. Or they were getting laid, watching reruns of *The Love Boat*, giving themselves enemas ..."

"Okay," I say, blowing out the smoke. "Yes. We had a good show. Frustrated's all. I should know better. I do. But you guys did." I wave my palm at the five of them. "Look. Really. Thank you. For being there. I appreciate it. *We* appreciate it. This toast's for you. All five of you."

"That's better," Wendy says. "Flakes are part of life, like cold sores."

"Cold sores," I say, scoffing. "You never know which lips to not kiss. Oh, here." I get up and step over to the turntable. "I picked up a new twelve-inch single. 'East West,' by Armageddon Dildos. It's giving me some ideas." I slip the disk from the cover and lower the tone arm, and the danceable industrial rhythm pours out. From there the party simply flows on.

Eventually I find myself talking to Jennifer, alone, and she's smiling and laughing, which makes her look very pretty—perhaps even forgivable. *You didn't know what Amy would think. Hell, I didn't.*

"By the way," I say, "you never told me what you thought of 'So Long, So Wrong.'"

"I don't really know. I mean, I like it."

"That's good. At least."

She furrows her brow. "It's better than a lot of stuff. What I'm hearing on the radio," she says. "Better than your earlier stuff too."

"Even better."

"It's thicker. Like you've added sauce." She grins sheepishly.

"Added sauce? First time I ever heard that," I say.

Then Chris tells Jennifer they need to take off.

Walking them over to the door, I feel relieved she's going.

"Thank you both for showing up." Then I remember the fliers for the new show.

"Hang on. Chris, we're going to need fliers for the next show. Can you help with that?"

"Oh, sure," she says.

"I'll call tomorrow with the details."

As they walk down the stairs, I wave at them through the doorway.

I get back to the party, but now everyone starts taking off except Lynda. That's fine by me, as what energy I have left is crumbling into exhaustion. Once I've said the last good-bye, I stroll to my mattress and pass Lynda pressing Scott up against a column, her red hair cascading over his shoulders.

First time I've ever seen Scott allowing that. Night's getting odder by the moment.

After crawling under my covers, I try to sleep, but the purrs and heavy breaths of the two lovers keep pulling me back to being completely awake whenever I get close to sleeping. I try putting the pillow over my head, but it feels claustrophobic. Then the rustling of sheets, her gasps of air and his grunts, and the thuds of the mattress being pounded make the empty space in my bed far too lonely; this drives me out of bed, back into clothes, and out into the street.

I don't know where I'm going, exactly—only away until I'm so exhausted I know I can sleep. Then I remember seeing this place—Uncle J's Diner—about a twenty-minute walk down North Avenue at Ashland, and decide to get something to eat there.

North Avenue is desolate at 4:00 a.m. When the rare car does appear, it creeps along, the driver examining the dissipated hookers exhibiting themselves alongside the dark, lonely avenue, finding a reason to do what a black Maverick is now: slowing to a stop next to a woman in a short red dress, who leans down to the window. In a moment, she tosses away her cigarette, opens the door, and climbs in. The Maverick pulls away.

Most of the buildings are empty and in disrepair. The few occupied storefronts I pass wait for the morning in darkness, with hand-painted wooden signs and displays of sun-bleached merchandise behind smutty windows.

As I pass the corrugated-tin gate of a junkyard, a dog's bark rips apart the silence.

I jerk away.

"Fucking asshole dog," I shout, flipping off the tin gate.

Now very aware of how alone I am, walking late at night in Spanish gangland, on a deserted street full of darkened windows and boarded-up doorways, alone with the hookers and johns, I try to relax and convince myself that Ashland and that diner's gotta be right around here, and that it's still open.

Two blocks farther down. I see the glow from a sign that could be for the diner. I walk more quickly. I tell myself to not look back, no matter what I hear.

As the sign for Uncle J's Diner grows larger and more distinct, the tangle of the last few days—of the arguments, of Amy leaving and Jennifer appearing, of Scott being with Lynda, of straight jobs and being broke, and of how long we've to go and how long we've already been going—all mixes with weariness and the surrounding desolation, making me want only to curl up and sleep right here. When I arrive at the steps to Uncle J's Diner, I turn to head back to the loft but realize that's worse, with my empty mattress, and Lynda and Scott probably still going at it.

Light assaults my eyes when I step through the door of the diner. The thick odors of frying bacon, frying eggs, frying potatoes, deep-fat fryers, and hanging smoke envelop me; I've lost what little appetite I might have had, but I take the last open booth across from the half-full counter. Picking up the plastic-coated menu, I glance over the choices: "2 × 2," "2 × 4," "pigs in a blanket," "waffles: plain, strawberry, and pecan," "hash and eggs."

Revolting.

Then a stoop-shouldered, pudgy woman, with her graying hair pulled back and tucked under a net, comes up to the table, order pad in hand.

"Cup of coffee. Black. Buttered white toast. That's it."

The coffee arrives first.

I watch steam rise from the cup for a couple of moments.

"Oh, that's brilliant, Jon. Coffee to help you sleep."

Looking around, I half-wonder what everyone else is doing here at this hour of the morning with their ashtrays overflowing with butts.

Some are alone; a few sit in pairs, whispering. Most everyone's glancing around. *As if anyone would care what you're talking about.*

I need to stop thinking—to think of nothing until I'm too *tired* to think, and I can't possibly stay awake, no matter what I hear.

Yet Jennifer keeps peeking into my thoughts, which makes me feel like I'm teetering on the brink of getting back together with Amy again. I catch my breath.

Don't take this wrong, Jennifer, but what are you doing in my head?

My toast arrives, the plate thumping solidly on the table. I pick up the knife and smear the soft pat of butter on the browned white bread. I salt it and take a large bite. It's crisp and soft at once.

You're what—nineteen? A teenager.

I wash down the toast with water.

What? Amy redux, Jonathan?

Alone in this booth right now, I've no real answer.

I pick up a triangle of toast and take another two bites.

Don't think so. But I don't know so.

I tear off another bite, and as I chew, the ponderous smell of grease, the sick feeling in my belly, and depth of my exhaustion all congeal at once, and I feel so deeply tired—too tired to chew. Leaving most of the toast and untouched coffee on the table, I toss a five on the counter next to the cash register.

Looking down the long, dark corridor of North Avenue, I dread the long walk back. I want simply to be home and to crawl under my covers and pass out. Since there's no chance of getting a cab all the hell way out here at this hour, I force a foot to take the first step. As the sounds of my steps are consumed by the empty night, it's hard to tell the difference between what I'm seeing and what I'm imagining.

I must wonder if this has all been a mirage.

Chapter 26
Before They Vanish
—Jonathan—

A week's passed since we played Sound Kitchen, and well, not much has happened.

I work tonight. Wednesdays are decent money, but I'm feeling anxious about needing to get something done today. *Other than wait tables.*

I grab a pen and start sketching out ideas for songs I've had floating around my head, but whenever I try to pin a few phrases down, they squirm away, leaving only ugly, uninteresting globs of words. Giving up on words, I dabble at the keyboard; my playing sounds ragged and half-dead, and finally, in disgust, I sit on the couch, glancing through an *Interview*, reading the comments from the lead singer of some band I've never heard of as he stares back from his enormous picture.

"Pretentious prick," I tell the photo. "You've nothing to say. At all. Never do. Other than 'Buy our new CD. It's this. It's that.' Bullshit."

Annoyed, I toss the *Interview* to the floor and lie down, my feet dangling off the armrest of the couch. I'm imagining a someday, long from now—the day I go into the magazine's office and give my interview:

> **Interview**—*It's been said that your songs come from your own relationships—your lovers.*
> **Starks**—*Lovers? No. Only one, ever. Amy. But ...*
> **Interview**—*But?*
> **Starks**—*You could say we were several lovers. So, yes, in a sense, my lover-s.*

Interview—*In a sense?*

Starks—*We were always only really Amy and me. But we played games. We pretended to have affairs—to be having affairs—when we were together. See, that's "Amy's Face." What it's about—playing at being many lovers for each other.*

Interview—*And so when will you get back—*

Starks—*Never. That's dead. And gone.*

Interview—*I see. And so now, you're looking for—*

Starks—*Oh, no. Not that. No. I can only take losing a lover—a lover like that—once. I'm eschewing lovers.*

Interview—*For?*

Starks—*Ever. At least for now. Can you get my smirk in here?*

I point where I'm imagining the printed version of the magazine is, indicating where I'd like a smile to show.

Starks—*Here. Me smiling right here. See, I know I can't be alone forever. Not and stay alive. But I don't want to talk about that anymore. Ask me something else.*

Interview—*Well, how are things now that you've moved to Chicago?*

Starks—*I don't know. Really. I don't.*

Interview—*You just had your first concert.*

Starks—*And nothing. Scanned all the papers, rags, everything. No write-ups. Only a couple of listings in "about town" sections. It's a lot like Ohio. I've been wondering if coming here was so smart.*

Interview—*Really?*

I shrug.

Starks—*I gave up so much. Gotten nothing.*

Interview—*You mean, of course, Amy?*

Starks—*Always comes back to her, doesn't it? That's boring.*

I stand up, ending the interview.

"That was almost fun," I say, kicking the *Interview* across the floor. I still have an hour to kill before I leave for work, and I'm getting impatient.

I flip through a couple of magazines lying next to the couch, which I've looked through several times already, and I fling each one away so it hits the floor with a slap. Tossing my hands up in exasperation, I walk to the table and rifle through my work bag. Seeing my apron, I realize I forgot to wash it, and it smells like old restaurant. I toss it to the table and then find what I'd been looking in the bag for in the first place: *Balthazar*, the second book of *The Alexandria Quartet.*

First, though, I'm rinsing out the obvious spots on my apron, but two don't want to come out, so I have to scrub at them; but I get it too wet, and I curse under my breath. *Hate this crap.* So I roll it up in a towel and squeeze all the moisture out as best as I can, and then I notice how late it's gotten.

"Time to make the doughnuts," I say, shaking my head. "Bullshit."

A couple of minutes later, I'm buttoning up my starched blue work shirt when a knock at the loft's door interrupts.

"Oh, what the hell, now?" I say to myself. Then I shout at the door, "Look, I'm late. You'll have to wait."

Fastening the last button on my way across the loft, I'm ready for my shift now. I pull open the door.

Randal gives a quick wave with a rolled-up newspaper.

"Come on in," I say. "Scott's not here, and I have to fly. You're welcome to hang out."

"What gives, man?" he says.

"Umm ... I work?"

"Obviously you haven't seen it."

"Seen what?"

"The *Reader.* Just came out today," he says, unfolding the one he's holding to the music section. "Right there." He points to an article:

Mercurial Visions
See Them Before They Vanish
G. Beaubien

Press releases are hype. They're supposed to be, supposed to excite people about something, but most of the time, the copywriter is blowing hot air, and even the time spent seeing how full of BS he is isn't worth it. But the copywriter of Mercurial Visions' press release is the lead singer, and for once, every word was spot on; nothing was exaggerated. If anything, he was modest.

Simply put, this band rocks. All-original songs that avoid merely parroting postpunk or trying to sound "alternative"; their sound rides waves from the mellifluous to pounding dance anthems, from heartache to venom and regret. And Jonathan Starks—PR man, keyboard player, lead singer—sets them aloft, chased by Nancy Mauer's richly sensual voice, which seems to have, finally, found a true home. The guitarist, Scott Marshall, knows he's not Eddie Van Halen or Michael Schenker; nor does he even try to be, understanding guitars don't *have* to be played fast and loud, or be the center of attention.

You will want to dance, pound your fists on the table, and sink into the luscious riffs, all in turn. "Just Walk Away," their closing song, is a sure club single—one that will be on a radio near you soon.

And this was their first show—*ever.*

No insult to the Sound Kitchen—I've lost
many a great evening there—but what is this
band doing playing there? Cabaret Metro is
where they belong.

Mercurial Visions is at Sound Kitchen
one more night—next Saturday at midnight.

"Ho-ly shit," I say.

Randal raises his hand, and I roll out my palm for his low-five.

"Party. Here. Tonight," I say, and then I remember I'm late for work. "Crap," I say. "I've gotta get gone, but Scott's gonna get back soon. You two get the party going. I'll get out of there as soon as I can. Then we can really party. Can you call the girls?"

"Sure."

"All the girls. That means Tanya this time."

"She's not in Chicago anymore," he says.

"'Scuse me?"

"She was having a rough pregnancy," he says. "A week ago, she lost the baby. Moved back to Columbus. Don't know for how long. Told ya last time—buzzkill."

"I, uh," I say. "Shit."

"It happened. Nothing you can do," he says. "I'll call everyone. We'll party. Now, I didn't come over only to show you this." He waves the *Reader* at me. "Now that Tanya's not here running the family's Chicago properties anymore, I am. And I'm not really family. So they started looking over the books. And they want to start collecting rent on this space."

"Rent?"

"They wanted fifteen hundred a month."

"Jesus!"

"Hang on. I pointed out that isn't market value for this neighborhood. I showed them articles about the drive-by shootings. The Party People and Latin Kings' turf battle is practically next door. So, bottom line, I got them to accept a grand a month. For, I'm guessing, a year or so."

"A thousand dollars."

He nods his head.

"Whoa, that's …"

"Not right now. You've got a few weeks. And I'm the one who reports to them, sooo …"

"A grand a month."

"I've got your back. Don't worry. Now, get to work. I'll make sure we have a party here for you when you get home."

Tossing my bag over my shoulder, I walk out into the street feeling as if nothing is real anymore: not the cars, not the 'L' tracks overhead, not even the city.

Chapter 27
Beaters
—Jonathan—

The days before we play our second gig at the Sound Kitchen have been an alternating succession of afternoons and evenings waiting tables at Le Moloko and rehearsing our set until late, tightening the four songs we'll lay down at Soundworks. Mornings are always slept through. Not once have we talked about our new rent or how we're going to pay for the recording session at Soundworks, as if our best strategy is to ignore everything and hope it all walks away on its own. I'm too tired to try to look at it head on, other than knowing that Scott and I will have to take on extra shifts whenever we can.

Then, yesterday, Nancy came in with the whole deposit for Soundworks. That means we can record, but getting the physical recording—that'll take more money.

Chris did a good job on the flyer, using a couple of choice quotes from the *Reader*. She took some to Smart Bar and Neo with Jennifer, giving them out to all of their friends. We hit all the bars we know with stacks of them. I took fliers to work and got a couple of vague promises, but I'm not getting my hopes up about the waitrons.

The Friday before the show rolls around. That afternoon Ron's here, and I'm getting into my starched work shirt for my shift while he sets up for a paid shoot for a new sushi joint. He's taken over a chunk of the south wall, near the windows, which he's washed off again. The sunlight's pouring in onto a card table. Two large lamps on stands blare light onto the tabletop, erasing the shadows. He holds a light meter next to a plate and then moves one of the lamps a few inches away.

The money from this will help with the electric bill. Still, I hope he's gone when I get home. I need sleep: I have to close tonight *and* work brunch tomorrow *and* then get to the show.

It's past midnight when I drag myself up the four flights of stairs after work. Ron's cleared out, so it's quiet. Plus I can sleep in now: I was able to trade my brunch shift tomorrow for one Sunday. I'll have to work a double Sunday, but better sucking on the floor than sucking onstage.

I wake up the afternoon of the show with the sun pouring through the windows. I try to squeeze out a little more sleep by pulling a sock over my eyes. I'm too anxious to actually sleep, but I lie there anyway, until the sound of AnnMarie arriving makes that impossible. I drag myself from bed.

That evening, AnnMarie, Scott, and I are packing all the equipment onto the elevator when Nancy and Ron get here, and then we haul everything through the back hallway to the loading dock, and finally into the hearse. The damned W-bins barely fit.

It's one of those nasty midsummer days in Chicago: hot, hazy, and humid. I have to shower to cool down, but by the time I'm done drying my legs off, my face is already covered in sweat again. In the hearse, the AC feels like heaven.

We park in the alley behind the Sound Kitchen and unload while the opening band plays. I can taste the sweat dribbling down my face. It stings my eyes, so I go in to rinse my face off in the bathroom sink. On the way back, I linger to check out the crowd and stay cool in the AC. The place is full, but I recognize no one—not even Chris, and it's her posters that got people here.

"Manager thinks it's gonna be another twenty minutes before we can set up," Scott tells me. "This time we can't even *buy* drinks until after we play. 'Long way to the top, getting ripped off 'n' under-paid.'"

I can't worry about that or who did or didn't show; I've got bigger problems, just like last time: I've no one to perform for. Not Jennifer—she couldn't be bothered to show up tonight. So I go over the setlist in my mind, imagining the opening notes and how each song has felt when I've performed it before, hoping this'll be good enough to pull me though the show.

The opening band finishes up, and the jukebox kicks back on with "Terminal Joy" by Terminal White.

"Time to roll," Scott says.

When the back door opens up, disgorging the opening band's members, equipment in hand, I'm sweating like hell. I pick up a crate, and we start lugging the gear in. I repeatedly wipe my face off with a towel. Once everything's onstage, I wipe my face off again and assemble my keyboard and mic. By the time we finish the sound check, the only person I've recognized is Lynda, but she—I cannot sing to her. Wouldn't feel right. At all. Yet I'm naked up here again, without someone to live the truth I'm singing, but then I remember that cryptic chick, Michele. She's not here either, but she wasn't supposed to be, and that matters, somehow. So, with her in mind, I start the show, and we play a tight set.

After our second encore, the whole bar is clapping and whistling.

Thanks for listening, Michele—and not asking any questions.

After we break down for the next band—Acumen Nation—we haul our gear back out to the alley and repack the hearse.

"Guys," Scott says, "let's celebrate at Smart Bar after we drop off the equipment. Kenny can get us all in free tonight. Good AC too."

I'm so not in the mood.

Completely drained and annoyed at so many things, I climb inside the hearse. I keep silent, and so does Ron, until we've made a few turns.

"Eight," I say. "We only had eight fliers—even after that great write-up in the *Reader*. Eight whole bucks."

"Full house."

"For who?"

"Who cares?" he says. "They all saw you. They had a great time. They'll be the ones who show up next time."

"Always gonna be next time. Never this time."

"Dunno what to say."

"Nothing," I say, and then I scoff at myself. "You're right. It was a good show. The new material went over great. So … It's good. Next time is better than never, right?"

When we pull through the intersection of North, Damen, and Milwaukee, I see Chris leaning up against the wall next to the door to the loft, and beside her is Jennifer. I'm not sure if I'm pleased or pissed. We pull around the building and into the back alley, where we stop under the door of the loading dock.

The two walk down the alley. Chris, as always, is in her plain, loose T-shirt, beat-up jeans and no makeup. Jennifer is in cutoff jean shorts, fishnet stockings, and a sleeveless black shirt, with oxblood lipstick and all those earrings.

"So," Chris says. "How was the show?"

"Good," I say. "Actually, very good. Too bad you didn't see it."

"Her car died," she says. "By the time I could come get her, you guys had already started. So ... headed here."

I hear the loading-dock doors being unbarred and pushed open.

"Well," I say, motioning my hand at the hearse, "gotta get this ..." I look up at the doorway. "Why don't you guys head up?"

It's cooled down some, so unloading the gear doesn't suck quite as much as loading it. After lifting the cases, W-bins, and crates onto the loading dock, we haul them down the narrow hallway and into the elevator; and then, on the fourth floor, we unload the elevator, lugging everything back to the center of the loft. It takes a couple of trips.

"Now," Scott says. "To Smart Bar."

"I've gotta bail," I say. "I'm beat. Have to work a double tomorrow. Brunch. Bright and early. Have a cocktail or three for me."

"Lightweight," Nancy says, grabbing Kenny's arm and leading the way out into the night.

In a few moments, only Chris, Jennifer, and I are left.

"Jennifer and I are going to be heading home soon. About an hour or so. We can take you back when we leave."

"I don't know ..." I say. "It's—"

"Look. Here," she says, handing Jennifer some keys. "I'll hitch a ride there. Come pick me up whenever you're ready."

"You sure?" Jennifer asks.

"You're the one who had the shitty day. Stay. Mellow out."

She looks down at the handful of keys.

"I can *always* grab a cab back here if it sucks."

"Okay," she says with a shrug. "Sure."

Once Chris leaves, I step over to the couch, still wondering at Jennifer being here at all.

She follows me, casually.

Sitting on the couch, I scooch over. As she turns to join me, the oversize hoop earrings in each ear flare out, and the light catches the dozen or so small hoop earrings in her left ear, which I have a sudden urge to nibble on, followed by her ear, and then her neck, and then—

"Car trouble, eh?" I ask, hoping she can't read on my face what I was thinking of doing.

"Yeah. Starter, generator, battery. Don't know this time. Happens. She's a beater. But she gets me where I'm going. Most of the time."

"Hear ya. Had one in Ohio. Ages ago."

We nod in agreement, sharing our understanding of what beaters are like, but eventually our heads stop bobbing. Then it's so quiet and we're sitting so close, and it feels like the loft is pushing us together, as if it wanted her to miss the show so we'd be here, alone, together, just like that Friday, years ago, when everything seemed to conspire to get me to show up at a party I'd decided to skip: my running out of cigarettes and having to go to buy another pack, giving me the chance to change my mind and show up at the party after all—the party where Amy was.

Changing my life.

Here Jennifer is—alone, so very close. I want to reach out and touch her. Change my life again.

Wait. Wait. Wait. She's not Amy. No one is Amy. This is so—

"Do you like living here?" she asks.

The sound of her voice scatters these thoughts.

"I mean," she says, "for parties, rehearsals—sure. But living here? It's so much ... emptiness."

"Well, we have ideas, to, you know, fill it up," I say, quickly gathering myself together to not say anything straight-up stupid. "But right now. No money."

"Like what? Pretend you have the money."

"Well, in back," I say, reaching my hand out toward the far end.

"We're going to build raised bedrooms." I stand up, showing her how high. "About seven feet up. With a sitting area between to separate them. Right there, at the head of a wide staircase"—I walk over to the middle of the loft, where I imagine this being, and sweep my hands up to show the expanse of the staircase I hold in my mind—"There'll be a balcony running the whole width of the room." I motion both hands out toward one wall and then the opposite wall.

"Brocade drapes. Blocking off each bedroom's entrance, for soundproofing. Sliding doors too. Drapes on all the windows." I point to the banks of windows on each wall. "Heavy, dark bastards so we can sleep right through the middle of the day. There, a real kitchen with a tiled floor." I indicate the card table and the rows of boxes, cans, and bags of ramen noodles on the floor. "Then a living area there, where you are, full of couches. A theater of couches with a projection TV. And right there"—I point to a large space on the windowless wall between the front door and our makeshift kitchen—"I want a concert-size poster of Joy Division's 'Love Will Tear Us Apart.'"

She's staring where the imaginary poster hangs.

"You know what one I'm talking about?"

"Um," she says, shaking her head.

"From the single. Black background, with the angel lying on the ground, a wing open, one arm thrown to the side, her other hand covering her eyes because she cannot bear to see what's in front of her."

"Sounds dramatic and awesome, like something I'd see in *Details* or *Interview*," she says. "But it's not bullshit. You're actually here, doing something about it. Which is a major change from all the talkers."

"I've been lucky," I say. "A friend of ours—her family owns this building. So it's not like I'm a rock 'n' roll star, here, swimming in money. We wait tables to pay for this."

She looks around again, with an expression like she's reassessing the place. I'm not so sure I like being judged like that—for being honest.

"So that's what I want," I say. "What about you? What do you want? From life?"

"I don't know." She lolls her head to the side, pouting in a vague, I-don't-like-to-talk-about-it way. "Get my own place, first of all."

"Still with the parents, eh?"

She looks down and barely nods, and I remember about her friend Charlene, who was thrown from her apartment's balcony; they were supposed to be roommates.

"So, you think it'll really be like in *Details*?" I ask.

"Oh, um," she says, looking surprised I'm here. "Yes. Well, depends."

"On?"

"If you can do it. If you do, like you said, yes. If you end up like a talker"—she shakes her head—"no."

"My, honesty. Brutal and right out there"

"Prefer lies?"

I shake my head. "Just don't hear it often. Unadorned. Unspun. It's a compliment."

She smiles.

"That, and," she says, "it's going to sound insane, but I want to be happy like the people in magazine adverts, doing whatever it is they've done that makes them that way."

She holds her hand up to stop whatever I might have started to say.

"Yes, I know. They're selling something. Beer. Jeans. Whatever. But that's not what I'm talking about. I want to feel the way they look. Laugh the way they appear. I want to be happy like that."

"They're in ads."

"I know that. I do work at a modeling agency. I make my living doing this."

"Then you know it's only an idea of what happy looks like, cooked up on Madison Avenue."

"That's not what I'm talking about. I'm talking about what they're pretending to be. I want to really be what they pretend to be: not pretend happy, forcing a smile to sell jeans, but real happy—without the jeans."

"What makes you think that kind of happy is real at all?"

"You," she says.

I sit back.

"You look like them when you play. I've seen it. It's like you are what they're pretending to be."

175

"Do I?" I place two fingers to my lips. "I've never seen myself playing so I ... Okay."

"And, here," she says, pointing into the loft. "Like in a magazine ad. But I'm here. It's real. I feel happy about it. Do I look happy?"

"You know, I think you just might."

Her smile breaks wide.

"Oh yes," I say, nodding. "Now you definitely do."

"See," she says, "just like in magazines. My car died, and I missed your show, but I'm smiling. Happy."

"Yes you are," I say.

She takes my right hand and turns it palm up.

"Do your hands ever get sore from playing?" she asks.

"Sometimes," I say. "Especially when I can't get a song to work."

"Are they sore now?"

"Actually, tonight went really well."

"Oh," she says, laying my hand down.

"I mean, yes, tonight went well, but there's a song I'm working on I can't get right, so yes, my hand is a little sore."

"Have you ever had a hand massage?"

"Can't say I have."

She picks my hand back up, drives her thumbs deeply into the flesh of my palm, and then intertwines her fingers with mine, pushing my hand backward over my wrist and then pulling it forward, quickly, three times in a row. Then she curls two fingers, pinches my forefinger between them, and pulls them down its length, dragging all tension out from the tip of that finger, and then the next finger, and the next. I stay as silent as she. Then she gives my other hand this bliss. My eyes close to slits as I watch her work. She's intent and very serious, as if nothing else exists but our hands.

You should see yourself now. You look happy. Imagine it's the same way as when I'm playing.

Then she wraps both hands around my forearm near the elbow and, gripping tightly, draws them down to and over my wrist and hand, and then finally off the tips of my fingers, dragging all stiffness out; and then she does the same to my other arm.

This feels unreal.

Proudly, she looks at me.

"That was like heaven," I say. "Do you like doing that?"

"I don't like getting paid for it, if that's what you mean. I like giving it away."

She dips her head, and her body lists forward, and we kiss.

Chapter 28

Ought Not
—Jonathan—

"Now," she whispers, her lips grazing mine in the shape of that syllable. She pulls back a couple of inches and looks at my face. "I want to do your back. Turn around."

I turn and feel her kneeling on one leg into the cushions of the couch, extending the other to the floor, straddling me across the lowest part of my back. The warmth of her legs spreads along mine. As her hands slide over my shirt, prodding, pushing, and rubbing my shoulders and back, my body melts. I sigh. Her hands move to my neck, and I feel her flesh on mine and how snugly she's drawn herself against me—I feel warmth from her spread legs against my back.

Something Amy would do. Tempting me. Teasing me.

I turn and slide two fingers under the waistband of her jeans, grasping the button. Her belly's so smooth and soft.

She presses her hands into the cushion right behind her, and leans, slightly, back.

My mind's full with the thunder of my pulse.

Wait. Jennifer: Amy saved my life. And you're—

I pull my fingers from under her waistband.

"That was," I say. "Magnificent. Really."

"If I had some oil"—her eyebrows rise—"I could really ..."

She kisses me, her tongue flicking through my lips.

No. Not like this. Not pretending it's Amy.

178

I pull back. "Chris," I say. "Doesn't she need to get picked up?"

"What?"

"Chris. She's at Smart Bar. Don't you need to pick her up?"

"I ..."

"If she cabs it back here now ... you know. She might ..."

"Uh," she says, shrinking away.

"We can do something Monday. Better, right?"

"What?" she asks, shaking her head.

"Ron's shooting here tomorrow, and I work later. But Monday I'm off; we have rehearsal, but it's not going to go late. We'll have time to relax. No rushing around. No one to pick up. Better, right?"

Looking bewildered, she nods.

"You two said you wanted to go home early tonight. Plus that awesome massage all but put me to sleep. Happens to people all the time, right?"

"Yeah. All the time. Sure. You're right," she says, leaping up from the couch and almost tipping over.

I catch her arm.

"So we'll see each other the day after tomorrow," I say. "Rehearsal'll start at six, six thirty. Won't last too long. Come by at seven, eight. Or earlier. Listen for a bit. Then everyone's gone."

She regards me warily, but eventually, she says, "Okay."

As we walk to the door, the thought I've made a horrid mistake convulses inside. We stand silently in the hallway, looking at the floor for a moment.

"We'll talk. The day after tomorrow," I say, definitively.

"Yeah. Sure."

Then she disappears down the stairs.

"You sure, Jonathan?" I ask myself.

I close the door.

"You *sure* that was right?" *Not that it matters: needle in, damage done.*

But staying true to an ex-lover ... no. I shake my head. *She's not the same shape as the hole Amy left, anyway. But neither was Nancy. So why her and not Jennifer?*

"Because sometimes I feel guilty about Nancy," I whisper.

• • • • •

The next morning, the smells of eggs cooking wake me up. I toss off the sock covering my eyes and prop myself up on my elbows. Scott's sitting at the table, writing. Lynda's at the stove, scraping scrambled eggs onto a plate, wearing only one of his work shirts, her hair flaming red in the morning light pouring through the windows. She notices I'm up.

"Morning," she says. Scott glances over, nods, and then continues writing.

I wave a couple of fingers back.

"Eggs? Coffee?" she asks.

I nod, and then, after throwing the covers off, I adjust the waistband on my boxers and amble over.

"Look," Scott says as I scrape the last of the eggs onto a plate. "I've got to put down the deposit for next Tuesday. Then head to work. Lynda's staying for a shoot with Ron."

"Cool," I say, shoveling in a mouthful of eggs.

"Here's a list of what we need Tuesday. All you need to do is call Soundworks to make sure they've got everything we need. The recording engineer said to call around four."

"I have to be at work at four," I say.

"I'll already be on the floor. You can be a few minutes late."

And get stuck in that crap station next to the kitchen. "All right."

"Go over it. Make sure I've got everything before you call."

"Sure."

"When I get back from work, you'll have to tell me what happened last night."

"Nothing to tell," I say.

"Nothing?"

"Yep," I say. "Said she had to go pick up Chris after about a half hour."

"Not what I was expecting to hear," he says, looking almost pleased now.

"Expecting?"

"Well, you … alone … with girl. No Amy."

"No," I say, shaking my head. "You got it wrong."

"What part? She is a girl, isn't she?"

I scoff. "Yes. But no. I'm not looking for a substitute."

Scott raises his eyebrows and then picks up his coffee.

"Think about it," I say. "Who have you known me to be with? Ever."

"Well, Amy. And Nancy."

I nod. "Except for Nancy. I don't know how to explain her. And still feel weird about it sometimes. So, yeah. Only Amy. That's killed dead." I purse my lips. "Now. Just don't want it. Nothing." I shake my head.

"I—" Scott starts.

"Let's not talk about this."

"Okay," he says, nodding, his expression skeptical yet pleased.

Then he drains his coffee. "Look, I've got to get rolling. Deposit's due soon. See ya tonight. Late. You"—he bends down and kisses Lynda—"I'll call later."

She pats his thigh, and he leaves the table.

"This band's gotta start paying *us* soon." Scott opens the door and disappears into the stairwell.

"What time's Ron coming over?" I ask. *I dig that he's using the space. It's very boho, like I imagined it would be like living here.*

"What time is it?" she asks.

"Eleven fifty."

"Wow. I gotta get ready. He'll be here in about an hour. Scott said you had some extra towels. Soap ..."

"Everything's in the bathroom. Towels are in the first locker."

As I watch her walk into the bathroom, I'm surprised at Scott. *A woman? In your life? Won't it "only get messy and interfere with" your success? But she's busy succeeding herself. Right. So she'll be around just enough: a night in bed and breakfast afterward every once in a while—maybe two or three days in a row. Maybe. Won't ask for any more than that.*

It feels stuffy in here, so I open the windows on the south wall, letting a warm breeze gush in. The faint sounds of Lynda showering mix with the street noises.

So, Jon-boy. There's no one. Not after last night. Welcome to lonely.

• • • • •

The next evening, I'm rereading *Mount Olive* by Lawrence Durrell, waiting for everyone to show up for rehearsal. I'm avoiding thinking about last night; I cringe whenever I do.

A knock at the door jerks me from prewar Alexandria.

Nancy or AnnMarie arriving early. Scott's still not home, so I trudge to the door, push down on the handle's tab, and pull the heavy steel door open.

Jennifer stands in waning sunlight.

For a moment, I'm not actually sure I believe what I'm seeing.

She has this inscrutable expression: nearly amused, a bit smug, but heavy with a challenge that I do everything *exactly* right.

"Oh, yes," I say, sweeping my arm into the loft for her to follow. "Please. Come in."

Inside we stand in the quiet. Unsure what I'm feeling, I point at the stereo. "What do you want to listen to?"

"What've you got?"

"Oh, lots and lots o' stuff," I say, leading her to our CD and vinyl collections. "Here," I say, picking up a CD of The Cure's *Mixed Up*. "I was about to put this on."

"Oh, yeah. I listen to that all the time. But I think I saw something," she reaches down and picks up Soho's *Goddess*. "I like 'Hippychick.' Wanna hear the rest."

"We'll get you hooked right up." I slip it in.

Right as "Hippychick" starts, Scott gets back home.

"Hey man," he says, dropping his bag by the door. "Everyone's going to be here any minute. Let's get set up."

"Sorry," I say to her.

She shrugs. "Worked late. What can you do?"

"Want to help?" I ask.

"Why not."

Since we only break all the way down and pack up if we're playing out, there's not much to do except turn on the equipment and hook up the mics. Most people don't care about anything more than the on switch and the volume nob, but she asks about organizing the cables and connections. While I'm showing her how we run the mics to the PA, AnnMarie arrives.

"Looking to roadie?" AnnMarie asks, dressed in a short skirt and heels, which, as usual, aren't quite sexy on her.

"Nah. Checking out how you run your sound."

"Learn anything?" she asks.

"Yeah," Jennifer says. "Clever solution for your mics, running that simple PA. I like it."

AnnMarie runs a quick check of her drum machines and mic. By then Scott's changed out of his waitron uniform, plugged in his Stratocaster, set it on its stand, and poured himself a vodka on rocks. Then Nancy arrives smiling at her inside joke, as usual. A couple of minutes later, Ron gets back and moves the last of his light stands off to the side.

"Okay, guys," Scott says, picking up his guitar. "Four songs. Perfectly. Exactly like we're going to lay them down."

For the next couple hours, we run through the songs we're recording on our demo, getting each one sounding tight. By then it's almost ten thirty. Scott gives a last couple of notes on "Just Walk Away" while I lean on the keyboard. I'm having trouble believing Jennifer's bothered to stay. Not only are rehearsals boring—same song, over and over; notes; this tweak; that change; repeat; and then on to the next song, and the next— but also because of what happened, or rather *didn't* happen, last night.

"That's it," he says.

"Ron and I are heading to Exit for Bondage-A-Gogo," Nancy says. "Anyone else?"

Ron holds up a pair of handcuffs.

"No thanks," AnnMarie says. "I hate having to be unlocked to go pee."

"Meeting Lynda at hers," Scott says.

"Not I," I say. "Beat. Work early."

"No thanks," Jennifer says, remaining on the couch.

In a few minutes, it's quiet and we're alone. Again. I feel the loft pushing me toward her. Everything is telling me it's okay—that I'm free. And need someone.

Reaching down, I take her hands and lift her from the couch. She reaches her arms around my neck and leans forward to kiss me.

Need this.

I run my fingers down her sleek back, feeling her small, firm breasts pressed into my chest. I nuzzle her ear, which is pierced with a dozen earrings in a row. Each hoop flicks off my tongue in turn, from her lobe up, until I've sampled every one. They taste so much better than loneliness.

I'm betraying no one.

Her hand finds the top button of my jeans and tugs on it, pulling it open; then she opens the next and the next. I slip my fingers into the waistband of her jeans, sliding them across her soft, smooth skin until I can feel the fly of her jeans. This time I unbutton and I unzip it. Sitting down, she pulls her shirt over her head, leaving only a sheer black bra. Reaching behind her, I ease apart the clasp; it falls away, leaving her half naked.

And oh, so different.

Then Jennifer lays out on the couch. I grasp the waist of her jeans, and she pushes her hips up, letting me pull them over them, and then her thighs, revealing a tattoo of a black panther crouching high on her right thigh, its tail flicking the edge of her black panties. With the jeans finally at her feet, she kicks them off. Then I slip my fingers under the waistband of her panties. She thrusts her hips up again and I slide the soft, silky black fabric down her smooth legs. I kiss her panther from tail to nose.

She pulls at my shirt, and I take it off as she peels down my jeans. I sit to kick them off, and then I lie atop her; she's so smooth, so warm, and so firm. Then she wraps her legs around my waist and pulls me down, and it all goes so softly, so easily.

So different. Why did you keep this from me, Amy? Because I can simply love her. Not turn her into music?

Chapter 29

The Future Sound of Ourselves
—Scott—

Through the thick plate-glass window separating the sound room from the studio, I watch Jonathan. Eyes closed, he presses the headphones to an ear, listening intently to the playback of the instrument tracks for "Just Walk Away" we laid down earlier. He weaves his head back and forth, waiting for the right moment to sing. The swish of his hair keeps time.

This is the last of his vocal tracks. After this, we've only the backing vocals to record.

He starts singing into the large mic. *He sounds better than I imagined, Sammy.*

"You guys're damned tight," Mike says. He's the sound engineer and looks about seventeen. At first I couldn't take him seriously. I got over my doubts, though, once I saw how quickly and sharply he handled the banks of black boxes and patch cables on the control board, knowing exactly how to make what we suggested happen. He's pulling the rolling one-inch reel-to-reel deck alongside him.

"Keep it up like this," he says, "and we can start talking mix tonight."

"I've got the time."

On an overstuffed white leather couch below the window, AnnMarie and Nancy sit with Jennifer. *Why are you even here?*

On the other side of the window, Jonathan still sways as if in a trance.

A moment later, he begins singing again, right on time.

When the song finishes, the reel-to-reel starts whirring back to the beginning of the song.

"Backing vocals, right?" Mike asks.

"Last of them," I say.

Nancy and AnnMarie stand up.

"*B* and *C* mics again," Mike says to himself as he leans over the wide, segmented board, pulling out patch cords and plugging them into new slots, and then checking various levels.

Jonathan hangs his headphones over the back of a chair in the soundproof room. He picks his way through the jungle of mic stands, wires, travel boxes, and drums, and past his keyboard and a rack filled with small percussion instruments, and pushes open the thick, sealed door.

"Nancy," the sound engineer says, holding out a pair of headphones to her. "Plug them in next to the others. The *B* slot. AnnMarie, use his. Move them to the *C* slot."

"Guys. Last track, last song," I say. "We've been kicking ass so far. Let's kill on this." I watch AnnMarie adjusting her mic in the sound room. I get a sensation that feels like a million ants crawling over me. It's that same feeling of destiny I had sixteen years ago. Finally, after all those years and all the shit we've taken, this is it. *We'll make it. Soon.*

"Okay," the sound engineer says, leaning over to a mic sticking up from the control board and pressing the red *talk* button. "Let's have a few seconds of quiet. Then I need you to sing for a couple, exactly like you would normally. Let me set my levels. Then we're live."

They give thumbs up.

I catch a glimpse of Jennifer laying her head on Jonathan's shoulder. *Not here. That's simply not professional.*

The music begins again, and I watch them lean close to the mic, and in time with Jonathan's vocals, they start singing, layering their voices on top of his. They sound better than they ever have. I listen to the sound of our future selves.

"That's a wrap," the sound engineer says as the reel-to-reel whirs, rewinding. "We've still got about twenty minutes. Do you want to talk about your mix?"

"Yeah, there're a couple of three things I'd like to bounce off of you," Jonathan says. "Like this idea for some echo effects in 'Just Walk Away,' when Nancy sings that line right after," he says. Then he sings: "It's safer this way ... Remember the silence ... and walk away ..." He molds his singing with his hands. "Right there."

"Echo's easy. You'll have to show me exactly. But before we go on," Mike says, "I've been cooped up in here since ten this morning. Can we move this to Lounge Ax for a beer or two?"

"Sure," Jonathan says.

After Mike boxes the tape of our session, writing "Mercurial Visions" and the date across the top, he slides it onto a slot on a wall of shelves and then grabs his lighter and smokes. With that, he leads us along the hardwood floors of the quiet white hallway, down the long stairwell, and out into the noise of Lincoln Avenue. Even at a quarter after one in the morning, traffic clogs the two working lanes. We dart between the slow-moving cars, and the sound of live music grows clearer.

Here Jennifer turns from being merely annoying to being an actual problem.

A bouncer is checking IDs outside the door of Lounge Ax.

Jennifer tells Jonathan she doesn't have an ID, so he asks Mike if "there's someplace we can go where they don't card?"

"You've gotta be shitting me," I say, shaking my head.

"It's cool," Mike says. "Happens all the time."

Jonathan gives a no-big-deal shrug and nod at Mike.

"No. It's really not okay," I tell Jonathan. "Not at all."

"What's the—"

"Problem? *We're* supposed to be *working*. And now we're accommodating *her*?"

"Jonathan," Jennifer says, "I'll go home. No problem."

"Yes, problem. Him. Making a big deal of nothing."

"You see Lynda here?" I ask him. "Ron?"

"You want to do this thing?" Mike asks. "We need to ..." He motions to the door.

"Or are we spending the twenty minutes I put the money up for here, on the sidewalk, squabbling?" Nancy asks.

I clench my jaw. "I cannot believe this," I say under my breath.

Walking to the bouncer, I turn and take my wallet out. Then I lift my ID and hold it out to him. "I've got mine. But I'm actually over twenty-one."

The bouncer ignores my ID and looks to Mike.

He nods, and then they shake hands.

The bouncer waves us all in without a word.

"Sure," I say under my breath, walking past the zebra-striped stools along the bar. "No problem. Come right along. What the hell." I jam my ID back into my wallet.

Chapter 30

Peephole
—Scott—

"So," Nancy says, ushering me into the living room of her new apartment the next evening. "What do you think?"

"Cozy." The room is done over in leather and dark wood. One whole wall is floor-to-ceiling bookcases, stuffed with books, like some tony men's club. I half expect a butler to appear from of the hall with cocktails on a silver tray. "*Madam.*"

"That and, well," she says from the large bay window. She waves for me to join her. Once I get there, she points out the window at the trees and open space of Wicker Park. "My front lawn."

"Impressive," I say. "Frankly, I thought you invited me over to help move heavy furniture around."

"No. I paid people for that."

I nod. First she fronts half the deposit for recording the EP, then she's buying an apartment and furnishing it like a Gold Coast mogul. She's got no job she's ever talked about. It's like she's some trust fund kid or secretly works as a day trader or is the legendary Madam X, the ecstasy queenpin. That must be what she's always smiling about.

"Paid people," I say. "Right. With the millions from your Swiss bank accounts. Which comes from—"

"What was last night about?" Nancy asks. "The sidewalk drama."

"Jennifer."

"No kidding."

"Okay. Remember Amy?"

"Uh-huh."

"Psycho, hurling-bottles, fucking-in-the-middle-of-the-day Amy?"

"Yes, Scott, I know who."

"No, you don't. You saw her a couple of times. I basically lived with her, off and on. She was an absolute obsession with him. I'd even thought he'd stay in Ohio for her. She's like a black hole he almost didn't escape."

"And since she's not in Chicago ..." She moves her hand, palm up, in small circles to push the idea along.

"Jennifer's a replacement Amy."

"Um, Scott," Nancy says, "they're a *bit* different. Slightly. As in, from different planets."

"He's not."

"You lost me there."

"Love like his is deadly," I say.

Her smile droops to incredulity.

"I've seen it," I say, looking down. "Sometimes someone does end up dead." I refuse to think about that, and look at the leather-bound books in the bookcase. "I'll ... No. Wrong. *We'll* have to keep him focused."

Nancy has left me in the bay window and now runs her hand along the back of a chestnut-brown leather couch. She offers it to me to sit on. I shake my head.

"She's a cancer. I know because it's the only way Jonathan seems to be able to relate to women—to *a* woman. Other than you, it's been Amy and only Amy for as long as I've ever known him. But it's been off and on, and off and on, and off. He's bipolar with her. And he will be with Jennifer."

I stare through the doubt in Nancy's eyes.

"I had to shepherd him that whole time. For years. I kept bringing him back to music when he got lost in her thighs. Ignoring their manic fuckfests—wherever, whenever—listening to their fights, hoping I don't find one of them dead afterward, or sprawled naked in the middle of the floor, sweaty, his spunk all over her." I close my eyes, and wipe my hand down my face to strip that image from my mind.

"Frankly," she says, "I think he needs to get laid to write. 'Just Walk Away,' our best new song, came from schtupping his obsession."

"Breaking up with her," I correct.

"They had to be schtupping to break up."

"Yeah." I turn my back to her.

"Hey," she says, "I'm not choosing sides here."

"You need to get that Jennifer's only another body for him to plug himself into to bring his obsession to life. Goddamned Frankenstein's monster."

"He is … who he is. We're married to him. For better *and* for worse."

"Sure," I say, tapping the end table with my thumb.

"Don't worry about what you can't change. Think about what you can." Her smile leaps back. "Let's get a cocktail."

She snatches up her keys, and I follow the trail of her perfume into the warm evening.

That didn't go well. I need someone on *my* side in this. AnnMarie's all cozy with them. Ron thinks they're "so photogenic." Lynda—well, it doesn't matter what she thinks. What matters is turning this around. *Starting tonight.*

When we push open the door to Rainbo Club, a former burlesque hall, only six people sit at the bar that wraps voluptuously around a small half-moon stage covered with liquor bottles. The long row of booths across from the bar are empty.

Nancy pulls up a stool at the bar and orders two pints.

I add two shots.

"You trying to get me drunk?"

"It was your idea to get a cocktail."

"I see—trying to take advantage of me." Her smile turns mischievous. "What do you take me for? Some common whore? Tsk, tsk."

"Common whore?" I *rat-a-tat* my fingers on the bar. "Hardly."

"So you *do* think I'm a whore?"

"Uncommon *woman*," I say as the barmaid sets out the drinks in front of us.

Nancy picks up her shot. "To *Nights of Cabiria*."

After draining the shot, I spin the glass on the bar. "Nights of who?"

"Fellini." A hint of disappointment flits through her smile. "Not important."

I feel as if I lost something here. I'm unsure what, but I want it back.

"You might be right," I say, picking up my pint, "to think about what I can change."

"Yes?"

"Amy—complete obsession. Jennifer—probable obsession. You— one night. How's that? How were you safe and the other two not?" I take a long pull of my pint. "He's never picked a woman up. Ever. Then there's you. Because of a lighter trick? And that's okay for him. What am I missing here?"

Pausing in thought, she turns her pint around on the bar. "I can't speak for him, of course." She takes a long drink. "But for what it's worth, the night I met our front man ... It was right. I can't put it any other way. The planets, the moon, the music, the lighting, the cocktails, the audience.

"Before that," she says, her forefinger up, touching her lips thoughtfully. "I think he had it right with Amy. Hold on; let me finish." She holds a hand up to stifle anything I might have said. "Most people only like the thrill of the new, the wow, the 'how interesting this person is,' and when it's new, you want to gobble your lover down: every particle of them—every fiber, every memory and thought. Finally, you want to disintegrate into them. To own and be owned. But then, the thrill fades, and most people get indigestion or this whole 'seeing each other all the time' thing goes flaccid, and you wonder who the hell this is and 'why is he here all the time?'

"Jonathan and Amy found a neat trick: never *let* it get stale. They were always falling in love or breaking up, always living out the most thrilling, hottest parts—a love affair cast away before it moldered, but lived over and over again. That's too emotionally exhausting for me, thank you— having constantly to be that high, raw, and shimmering all the time. It's better, I guess, than everyone else who wakes up one day and realizes she doesn't feel it anymore, but there he is. What do you do then? No thanks for that either. I like boring."

"You? Boring?" I scoff.

"You're right, 'boring' isn't the right word. More like assignation apoptosis," she says, "knowing that when the morning comes, the love's over. Lovers really aren't all that.

"That night, after I sang"—she taps her finger on her lip—"must have been in the right mood from the show. I don't really know. But I saw him do that thing with his Zippo and looked at him. There it was—the moment. The idea of sleeping with him—I had to. And that was that. It was over in the morning. But it pissed you off. For weeks. Oh, yes"—she nods—"don't make that mock innocent surprised face."

"I don't want him to be sleeping with someone in the band," I say.

"We weren't in a band then, and we don't sleep together now."

"It wasn't so clear then." I grunt and take a drink. "Now you're, what ... celibate?"

"No, not celibate. Out of the market. Celibacy is AnnMarie's gig."

"AnnMarie?"

Nancy gives a noncommittal half shrug.

"Hey, Scott," Kenny says from behind us. I turn and see his friendly, flirty smile. It sends a pulse through my chest—a thrill. Like with Sammy. Jonathan once. I look away. I hate that sensation.

"Hey, Nancy," he says.

"Hey you," she says.

"So," he says, extending his hand to her, "how did the recording session go?"

"Got some great stuff," I say.

"When're you mixing?"

"When we get the money. A week or so, I hope."

"You mind?" Kenny asks, pointing at an empty seat next to me.

"Grab it." I call the barmaid over, order another round of shots, and a beer for Kenny, and we talk shop: our recording, his band and songwriting, where to play. All the while, he slips in flirty glances and smiles at us both. It irritates me more whenever it's with Nancy.

You can't sleep with someone in the band. The same one Jonathan slept with.

I shake my head. *Always hated queer games like this.*

"What are you disagreeing with there in your head?" he asks, putting a finger on my hand.

It burns. I take my hand away, shaking my head.

"Nothing," I say.

"Okay," Kenny says with a smirk. "As long as it's nothing."

His expression of knowing more than what's being said unsettles me. I take a drink.

"Hey," he says. "I have to go."

"Oh?" I ask.

"Have got to get up in"—Kenny pulls back a sleeve to find his watch—"too few hours."

"Where're you headed?"

"Evergreen. Next to the park. Eight, nine blocks."

"You're practically next door to me," Nancy says. "Let's go together."

I shrug and drain my pint of beer.

You remind me so much of Jonathan. That thought sends a cascade of excitement through me. It's too strong. I stand up and take off toward the exit. Walking dissipates the panicky feeling, but I need to get out. I feel trapped, as though I'm back in the trailer park, hiding with Sammy.

Stop it. You're dead.

Pulling up next to the door, I wait for them. There I notice a blacked-out bay window filled with bondage Barbie dolls and a masked Marquis de Ken, whip in hand, standing in the midst of them. Kenny arrives with Nancy, stepping up right beside me.

"That way," Kenny says, rolling his hand, thumb out, toward the bondage scene.

"Dom or submissive?" Nancy asks.

"Where I live, actually," Kenny says. "But either. Both really. Barbie, Ken, GI Joe, whoever—I don't care." Kenny then looks at Nancy, raises an eyebrow, glances at me, purses his lips, and winks. "Sometimes at the same time."

Turning quickly, I push my way out the door and into the night.

Finally outside, I relax in the warm night air, yet what I felt in the Rainbo Club clings to me like hot tar. I want to scrape it off, this vague sense of dread that reminds me of things I saw growing up and that never should have happened, like Sammy getting killed and the need to run from it.

I follow the two of them but keep quiet while they talk about the neighborhood.

"I'm over here," Kenny says after a few blocks. "Were you serious? About rehearsal?"

"Sure," Nancy says. "Stop by tomorrow about six."

"Will do," Kenny says, walking into the shadows of Evergreen Street.

Once we reach the park, she turns right, and I watch her walk the last few doors to her new place. She waves bye, and I continue along Damen Avenue, looking into the park. The streetlights cast the leaves of the nearby trees in dark summer greens, and beyond that lies deep blackness, obscuring everything.

Approaching the intersection of North, Damen, and Milwaukee Avenues, I hope Jonathan's working late. I could use the time alone.

Nobody deserved to die. It happened anyway. That's what Jonathan refuses to see.

Crossing Damen, I pass the fenced off no-man's-land between the legs of the 'L,' a deserted alleyway of gravel and garbage. As I emerge from under the tracks, I see no lights on in the loft.

He is working late. Good.

After unlocking and opening the street-level door, I step into the darkness. Behind me the door swings closed, muffling the sounds of the street. The building is silent except for my steps as I climb the four flights of stairs. On our landing, I stand still and listen: nothing. *Good.* I unlock the strapped steel door and slowly push it open in respect of the stillness. Closing the door as softly as I opened it, I let the stillness wrap around me. The murmur of the street four stories below sounds very distant.

Weak shafts of light from the windows provide the only light, and I strain to see into the deep shadows for movement.

Nothing. Good.

"Oh, Jonathan," I whisper into the silent darkness. *I've worked so hard trying to keep you safe and to keep the band going. For both of our sakes.*

A sense of nearly remembering some horrid crime surges up inside me, as if I did something unforgivable but can't quite remember what. As if what I felt at Rainbo Club was a peephole and if I dared looked through it, I'd see what I don't remember: my unforgivable crime.

The sensation grows so strong, so quickly, like in Rainbo Club.

Bolting away from the sensation again, I rush away from the windows and the light.

I don't want Kenny around here anymore. He can't flirt with me like that. It's wrong.

In time, my eyes grow accustomed to the darkness, and I can now make out the shape of Jennifer's head atop Jonathan's chest, their bodies covered in sheets.

"Jonathan," I whisper. "She'll kill you. She won't mean to. But you'll be dead anyway. This time, I won't let it happen."

Chapter 31

Dime a Dozen
—Scott—

When I arrive home from work, I find Jonathan and Jennifer showing Lynda and a friend around the loft. *Lousy night for dropping by. It was a very rough night at work. I can't wait to get out of these clothes.*

At the restaurant, only fifteen minutes ago, I picked up all of tonight's checks and charge receipts from the hostess stand, and then slipped behind the heavy wine-red curtain next to the bar and opened the office door. The manager sat at a paper-cluttered desk pushed into the corner. His thin, somber face made him look much older than thirty-two, as if the restaurant had sucked those years out of him, feeding on his life. I dropped my check presenter full of receipts onto the table opposite the desk and untied my long black apron, dumping it alongside the check presenter.

"Slow night," the manager said.

"Decent money, though." Sitting, I took out my checks, and started adding them up.

"Got your request off for next Friday," the manager said.

"Cool." I pulled out my cash and unfolded it. Ordered by denomination, each bill faced the same direction.

"I can cover it," he said, turning around in his chair to face me. "This week. But you've been making too many schedule requests."

"I'm sorry?"

"You need to be here when we need you scheduled."

197

"Hang on. I'm always on time. Never ask to be cut early. Do my job. No one has ever complained about me—ever. I always come in to cover lunch shifts when you need me. So I don't think it's too much to ask for an occasional night off so I can play out. It's not like I call in sick because I'm hungover, like Robert, or want to go to some party, like Christy or Robin."

"I don't have the people to always be able to cover all your shift requests. Especially on Thursdays, Fridays, or Saturdays—our busy nights."

"*Sometimes* I need weekend nights. I always give you *at least* a week's notice. Month if I can. Plus everybody's always complaining about not having enough shifts. Me? Never. I have a goal in life."

"People're complaining you're *always* getting the nights you want off."

"What can I say? They bitch about not having enough money. I'm giving them the chance to make money. On prime, big-money nights. What do they want? To get paid for breathing?"

"I don't know if I can give you all your requests off," the manager said.

I pegged my eyes on his. "I need you to understand. My music is more important to me than any *one* job. If I can't get the time off I need here, I'll have to go somewhere I can."

"That a threat?" the manager asked, leaning forward, bracing his hands on the armrests.

"No threat," I said. "A fact. But I will tell you that I will always be here when you schedule me. On time. And I'll do a hell of a lot better job than anyone else. If that is not good enough, don't know what more I can do."

He leaned back in his chair. "Like I said, I can cover you this time."

"Should I be looking for another job?" I asked, sitting bolt upright, my eyes still on his, deadpan.

He looked away. "I can't guarantee I can give you off every request."

"In that case," I said, "I *can* guarantee I won't be here."

"Don't talk to me like that."

"Why not?"

"Lose that attitude, Scott. Now."

"No," I said. "That was my last shift."

"What?"

"Like I said, I no longer work here." I pick up the pile of cash, and continue counting. Without another word, I give him the cash I owe, the credit card receipts, and the bank. He silently runs the numbers on a calculator, counts the cash, and gives me a stiff nod when he finishes.

I left the office and marched directly for the door, ignoring everything and everyone here. My skin tingled with the same sense of sure success I'd felt at Soundworks.

This is my next step.

In the loft, when the four of them start back to the front, I pull Jonathan aside with a jerk of my head.

"We've a situation," I say. "Follow me."

I sit on my mattress.

"Do you guys need anyone at Le Moloko?" I ask Jonathan, kicking off my shoes, my voice as quiet and calm as I feel.

"Why?"

"I quit."

"What?"

"Manager forced my hand." I start pulling off my white work shirt, which is flecked with small stains and reeks of restaurant. "Said he can't give me time off for gigs. That this was the last time." I unfasten my pants. "Complete bullshit," I say, pulling them off and tossing them into the pile with my shirt.

"No shit," he says, running his fingers through his hair, and scooping it away from his face. "Don't know. I'll have to ask."

"As much as it pisses me off to lose the money from there," I say, "nothing's going to get in the way of Mercurial Visions."

"Sure, right."

"Persistence and determination alone are omnipotent," I say, mostly to myself. *Sammy would've approved.*

He curls a lock of his hair around his fingers, nodding.

"You take care of those that take care of you." I grab the top pair of jeans from a neatly folded pile and step into them. "Total bullshit."

"No doubt."

"Only took me a week to get this job. Even if it takes me that long again, I'll get some work done around here. Drop our demo off at some more bars. Maybe even Wax Trax! Something." I shove my arms into a striped shirt. "Hell. It'll probably work out better this way. So thank you, asshole." I throw my hand up in the direction of where I used to work.

"Just so you know, I've got around a hundred 'n' fifty bucks."

"I've eighty-five. Don't worry about it. Waiting jobs are a dime a dozen. Won't take more than a few days. It was worse in Columbus."

Chapter 32

Roommates
—Scott—

Slumping into the couch, I stare across the gaping emptiness of the loft, listening to the two of them showering together.

Six weeks have passed since I quit. No job yet.

September's rent was due nine days ago. We have less than half of it.

Randal said he can cover for a few weeks. That means back rent will pile up as long as I'm bringing nothing in. Even Randal can only go so far.

"They own this building to make money, after all. And Tanya isn't here anymore." He's reminded us of this more than once.

Last week I even called the Tenants Union to see if they could help. They told me that since we're living semilegally in a commercial building, there's nothing we could do but "hope you won't get evicted."

Then we've still got the bills from Con Ed, Ameritech, and Keyspan. There's nothing to hope for from them. They'll simply cut off the electric, phone, and gas.

We can't go begging Nancy. We've already mooched off her for the recording and mix, and the way things look, we'll have to hit her up for the cost to press the CDs. She even asked us to sign a letter of intent stating that her money is a loan and that she will be preferred when—if—we start making any money.

I get it girl. It's business.

But even food is pinched thin now. We've gotten to the point of eating only what Jonathan can snag from his restaurant, a rare two-dollar

Maxwell Street Polish from Friar's Grill, and whatever we can find in the discount bins at Jewel—mostly packages of broken ramen noodles and dented cans of vegetables and Chef Boyardee.

That and Jennifer's charity dinners out—like tonight.

I scoff at my life. *I hate that I still have no job. Stupid.*

I feel like breaking something. Instead I get on the floor and crank out a hundred furious push-ups. I'm about to start a hundred more when Jennifer steps out of the bathroom, a faded red towel wrapped around her slender waist. By their mattress near the back of the loft in the twilight, she pulls a pair of black tights from one of the cinder-block-and-board shelves they share. She lets the towel fall away.

I look away.

Her. Feeding us. Poisonous.

Finished dressing, she strolls over.

"So," she says, "where do you want to go?"

"Up to you. You're the one with the money."

"Someplace close? I've a shoot to be at later tonight."

"Sure."

"Busy Bee?"

"Why not," I say.

"It'll work out. I've confidence in you guys."

"Yeah." *Think you have to tell me what I already know? That I need a cheerleader?* I rattle my tongue back and forth between my teeth, holding back.

"So," Jonathan says, appearing from the bathroom and walking over, a towel wrapped around his waist like a skirt, his long hair matted to his head and neck. "What're we doing?"

"Busy Bee," she says, laying her head on his shoulder.

"Pierogis and kielbasa. Perfect," he says, stroking her hair tenderly. *Poisonous.*

While he finishes dressing, I stare out at Chicago, trying not to think about how sour things have turned with Nancy subsidizing our CD. Jennifer feeding us. All because that asshole wouldn't give me the few days off I needed. *Long way to the top.* I snort in disgust. *Fucked up.*

Elbows locked, Jennifer and Jonathan meet me at the door.

"So," he says, "nice, hearty, peasant food."

With that I open the door and we climb down the stairs.

On North Ave, passing under the 'L' tracks, we turn right, go by the entrance to the North Avenue 'L' station, and open the door to the Busy Bee. We take a table in the back room.

As we eat, I avoid watching them brush fingers, nudge shoulders, and shoot each other sly, knowing looks. Her especially. It's as if she's baiting me. As she does every night, forcing me to listen to their bodies rubbing against each other, their grunts and moans growing louder and louder. Sometimes they go at it in the afternoons too—a few yards away, covered only by sheets, as I'm practicing my guitar.

Is she teasing me? Tricking me into imagining what she's doing to him?

That feeling of almost remembering something unforgivable bubbles up inside again, making the room feel too small. I look away and hold the table edge so tightly my knuckles turn white, and the hideous feeling lets up, and I can breathe normally. Afterward, I direct my full attention to each bite I take, ignoring everything else.

When we finish and she stands to take the bill up to the cashier, I resent her.

"Thank you," I say, unable to meet her eyes.

Once she leaves for the shoot she's working on, Jonathan and I walk to the loft in silence. I can tell he wants to say something but is holding back. I can see it in his tight lips and how he avoids looking at me even as we climb the stairs and step into the loft.

I lie down on the couch and close my eyes, trying not to think about breakfast and whatever it was I could nearly remember.

He starts playing an almost familiar melody.

I try to place it, but recognition slips away as soon as I think I know it.

"I've been thinking," he says.

"About?"

"We need about fifteen hundred in less than three weeks."

"I know," I say, pinching the bridge of my nose. "I've been out looking for a job every day. There isn't shit right now. Slays me. People're always hiring. Except now."

"Yep. I see you trying," he says. "And you shouldn't take a crappy one just to have some money that won't ever be enough. Maybe we'd make rent, but then, you'd have to quit again."

"*And?*" I ask, not in the mood for guessing games.

"I was just thinking that Jennifer basically lives here—"

"Stop," I say, sitting up. "No. Just no."

"Why not?" he asks, continuing to play that almost-familiar melody.

"Because this is our space. Our work. Our band. Ours. Yours and mine."

"Which we're going to lose soon."

"I'll borrow the money. I've already thought about that."

"From whom? Everyone around here's broke. Randal's not, but he's already covering our asses. Or are you planning on mortgaging the band to Nancy?"

"No," I say, shaking my head. "I know that. We already owe her too much. But Jennifer paying rent here? Being an equal? No. Not acceptable. That's inviting the devil in."

"The devil? That's my lover you're talking about."

"I'm trying to protect you," I say.

"Protect me? From what? Her?"

Yes.

"Like from Amy?"

"Yes," I say. "Exactly."

"Amy saved my life, man. You have no idea."

I don't want you to die. Almost remembering something unforgivable surges up again. Standing, I shake my head as the walls start pushing in on me.

"No. Forget it," I say. I start pacing in a small circle to keep from remembering. "Didn't mean that. Came out. Not happy about the way things are happening is all."

"Look at it this way. She can, for all intents and purposes, live here. For free. Or," Jonathan says, abruptly stopping the melody. "We can give her the keys and she can start paying *some* rent."

"That," I say, slashing my hands down, "makes all the difference in the world. She's not our roommate now. And I won't have her deciding what *we* do with *our* place. Period."

"She won't. She loves the plans we have. She told me she wouldn't change a thing."

"What!" I yell. "You've already told her she could move in?"

"No," he says calmly, picking up that almost familiar melody as if it had been hanging in the air, waiting for this moment. "I've told her about our plans. She thinks they're great. Loves them. That's it. Sure, yes, we've talked about living together. *Someday*. In the future. I have *not* invited her to move in here. Wouldn't. Not without talking to you first. Which I'm doing right now. Which I also think is a very good idea *right* now. She starts letting herself in. We end up having more money to pay our grand a month in rent. And we can stop having to mooch off Nancy to get the remix done. Another fifteen hundred we don't have to pay her back for. Plus we need to get discs pressed, and sent out. Hundreds there. Shit, we might even be able to afford noodles that aren't broken into little bits."

"This is," I say, shaking my head, "the wrong way."

"Quite frankly, she's going to be basically living here anyway. Right now she feels out of place. Like a guest who's overstayed her welcome. She's my *lover*. I'm not suggesting she sign the lease. Keys for cash. A lot simpler. A *hell* of a lot better. For *everybody*."

"I don't," I say, and then drum my fingers on the armrest. The fabric makes more dust than sound. "Know."

"We've talked about live-in lovers before. In Columbus," he says. "Like we agreed then. She won't be on the lease. If it doesn't work, she's gone. Conversation over."

How did we get here? This is worse than with Amy.

"We knew it was going to happen. Only now we need the money."

This is punishment. For what, I don't remember.

"It's helpful. For all of us."

I sigh. "I don't know what to say."

"*Yes* would be good."

I look around at all the equipment, everything we've built. Everything we *are* building.

The black widow moves in. So take the money, Scott. Then get her gone. While you have time to stop her.

"What are you thinking?" he asks.

I shake my head, waving a finger at him.

"Truth is, Scott"—he strikes a dramatic chord on the keyboard—"she *already* lives here."

A sense that I'm about to make a horrendous mistake wells up and grows so strong. I grab my head.

"This was going to happen sooner or later." He plays a soothing melody. "And sooner happens to be better."

"This place," I say, examining my palms, "is still ours." Dropping my hands, I drill him with my eyes. "Yours and mine. Not yours, mine, and hers." I shake my head gravely. "I won't allow that to change."

"I don't want that to change either. I won't let that happen."

"Comes down to her or me. Her or the band." I hold his eyes with my stare. "She goes."

"Always." He crashes out a heavy final note, letting it hang in the air.

Chapter 33

The Weight of Survival
—Scott—

Worse than Jennifer getting her own keys and officially moving in is that it has taken me nearly a month to find a job, so she has had to pay my part of the rent. Twice.

I've picked up whatever extra shifts I can to pay her back for September and October, while saving up for November.

There's no chance I'm going to keep owing her money. While living on her charity, I can't say a word about what a slob she is or how she's always inviting friends over to hang out while I'm busting ass to get the band up and running. Between her friends and Ron's photo shoots and rehearsals, I've hardly been able to find any time to be alone and think.

One night it started shaping up that I might have some time alone. Lynda had landed the lead in a low-budget indie film and was in California for who knows how long. After wrapping up rehearsal earlier, everyone took off, including the roommates.

The last to leave, Kenny invited me to meet some friends out at Holiday. It sounded like a pack of students from Columbia College. I supposed they were mostly those half-queer artists he brings by rehearsal on occasion. This made me wonder again if he actually likes boys or is dabbling in being bi. Being bi is so trendy in those artsy crowds—as if an artist isn't real if he isn't queer or at least swings both ways—as if a straight artist is either too closeted or has no struggle inside worth expressing. Either way, the idea is that breeders can't create real art. Can't perform either. *I've heard that crap too many times.*

Such horseshit. If you're queer, you're queer. It's not an affectation. A badge. A magic hat to wear in order to create.

I'll hate him if he turns out to be one of these artfags.

So I told him I was too tired and finally got my time alone.

Tonight I'm feeling revived riding the North Avenue bus home. After two and a half weeks of working every shift I could, I've earned a decent chunk of the money I owe Jennifer. As the bus approaches my stop, Book of Love's new single "Pretty Boys and Pretty Girls" is still running through my mind: "Sex is dangerous," she sings. "I don't take my chances."

"Well, neither do I," I whisper, stepping off the bus near the loft and heading straight to the bodega on the corner of Damen Avenue for a little reward. I push open the door with cutout letters reading "Happy Halloween" taped above a witch and worm my way around the center aisle of the cramped little store. I hold my bag in front of me to avoid knocking some little box or bottle from the jam-packed shelves. Finally reaching the bulletproof Plexiglas fortress behind which all the booze is secured and the cashier hides, I ask for a bottle of Absolut. The somber, dull-eyed man turns silently, pulls the clear, bullet-shaped bottle off the shelf, and sets it on the counter on his side of the clear wall. Only after I push the cash into the deep, curved slot under the Plexiglas does the man put the bottle, and then my change, into the revolving cylinder, finally turning the opening toward me.

Putting the bottle in my bag and slipping its strap over my shoulder, I feel the weight of survival.

This'll be a nice anecdote for an interview, showing how far we'd fallen and how we had the perseverance to claw our way back up. *The straight boy fighting. The straight boy winning.*

Guiding the bag back out the tight aisle, I leave, my head high. *Fighting. Tooth and nail. Every step of the way.*

Walking to the loft, money in my pocket, I let myself resume plotting the work we've still got ahead of us.

First, we need to wrap up our demo mix. Second, there's pressing as many CDs as we can afford on a single run. Third, we have to get those

CDs to radio and club DJs. Especially the one Kenny knows at the station out of Northwestern, WNUR. Fourth are the labels. Fifth, with all that exposure, we need to start selling the CD at all the independent record stores like Reckless Records and Wax Trax! Eventually getting it into stores in Milwaukee, Gary, West Bend, and even Columbus. Sixth, with that money, we'll be able to afford more and sell them at shows. Those profits are all ours. Seventh, we need that backdrop for the stage Chris designed—a large black sheet displaying a man's torso in silver, arms raised, reaching beyond the edge, like an overexposed black-and-white negative. Eventually we can put it on T-shirts and sell them at shows. Even put it on posters or wall hangings.

Climbing the four flights of stairs, I hear music dribbling down the stairwell, which means the roommates are here. Opening the steel-strapped door, I see instead Jennifer and her boss Wendy sitting on the couch with only the front bank of lights on.

"Where's Jonathan?" I ask on my way to the kitchen table.

"Has to close tonight," Jennifer says. "Someone called in sick."

Grunting in acknowledgment, I take the bottle of vodka out of my bag and place it in the center of the table.

Nice to see it here.

I can't stand being in my uniform, so I head to my mattress in the darkness at the far corner of the loft. There I pull the wad of cash from my pocket and unfold it atop my mattress. I lift an edge of the mattress and retrieve a thick envelope from under it. From that I take out a stack of bills and count out $240, all in twenties, adding five more twenties from what I earned tonight. Then I fold the top flap under the bottom and give it a satisfied pat.

That done, I start stripping. After pulling on jeans and a shirt, I slip the envelope into my back pocket and then return to the light.

"So," I say, "who wants a celebratory cocktail?"

"Celebrating what?" Jennifer asks.

"Surviving. Life knocked us down. And we picked ourselves back up. Now, we can raise a drink to that." Turning over three highball glasses on the table, I ask, "Who's having what?"

"What's to have?" Wendy asks, slicking back a stray lock of her dark hair.

"We have vodka and whatever's in the fridge. Diet Coke. Juice, I think. Ice, of course. I have mine on the rocks. No martinis. We never have vermouth."

"The same," Wendy says.

"Why not," Jennifer says. "I'll have mine with Diet Coke."

"One vodka, rocks, and one skinny black bitch it is," I say, pouring our drinks.

"Sorry," I say, handing Wendy her glass. "No olives. No lemons to twist."

"What sort of bar is this?" she asks.

"One that barely paid rent." I hand my roommate her glass. "Speaking of which." I take the envelope from my back pocket.

"What I owe you for September's rent," I say, handing it to her. "October's will come once I have enough for November's. A couple of weeks."

"That's not important," she says, ignoring the envelope.

"Yes it is," I say, and then I shake it at her. "Take it."

"But—"

"I pay my own way."

"It's no big deal. Really ..." she says, staring at the envelope. "You guys have to mix the songs—"

"This is rent money. For the loft. It's what I owe you. We'll deal with money for the band. Jonathan and I."

She looks at her friend, who nods and mouths "yes."

Wendy gets that who pays for what *does* matter. A lot. *It's about ownership and say.*

Jennifer takes the money. "Thanks."

"Count them. There are seventeen twenties there."

"I trust—"

"Don't trust. Count."

Sighing, she counts out all seventeen bills.

"Everything's correct. We both see it. No doubts later," I say, and then I pick up my glass. "To making it."

210

After we drink, I turn to sit with them, and they slide over to give me space on our only sofa.

"Snug," Wendy says.

"We want to get another one. Or two," Jennifer says. "Right now we need the money to mix our CD."

Our CD?

"So," Jennifer says, "he isn't sure when we can."

"*I*," I say, thumping my thumb on my chest, "want to mix our CD in two or three weeks. But until *I* see how much money *I* make these next couple of weeks, Jonathan and *I* can't make that decision."

"We going back to Soundworks?"

"Jonathan and I are, yes. Us. Alone."

"I don't mind hanging out. Like before."

"To be frank," I say, "I'm not worried about you. It's Jonathan. Studio time is very expensive for us now. Ask Wendy. We'll barely be able to afford the two hours we need. Can't waste a minute. He cannot be distracted."

Wariness bunches up Jennifer's brow.

"Thinks you'll distract him," Wendy says flatly.

I nod.

"He can't even think about you. He has to be there, concentrating one hundred percent. There must be music and nothing else. At all. I need him like that. We *all*"—I include Jennifer, Wendy, and myself in a large circle I draw with my finger—"need him like that."

Giving an annoyed pout, she looks into her glass.

"You want it to be the best it can be, right?" I ask.

"Yes, Scott," she says, lighting a cigarette. "Of course I do."

"It's not you. Not even Nancy and AnnMarie—band members—are coming. They laid the tracks. But too many people making too many suggestions." I shake my head at the idea.

"Yeah." She exhales a cloud of smoke, and I have to sit back to avoid it billowing into my face.

"You don't let boyfriends or girlfriends on a shoot, or backstage at a runway show, right?" I ask.

"No," she says. "I wouldn't. Just thought I could …"

"Could what? How many of your girls think that they would suddenly

211

start calling the shots, directing people around their *glamorous* life, just because they get a headshot and go on a couple of comp shoots?"

She nods. "No kidding."

"They're surprised that their so-called *dreams* don't simply happen. They get bent."

Wendy smiles wryly.

"'Aren't we trying to live our dreams?' All resentful. 'Don't we believe in ourselves?' Have hope. Aren't we trying like the Little Engine That Could?"

"Been eavesdropping backstage?" Wendy asks.

"Don't need to go backstage," I say, "I hear it all the time in restaurants. I have to walk away before I say anything. Those aren't *dreams*. Those are *fantasies*."

"That's what we traffic in," Wendy says. "All sorts of illusions."

"They suffer from still believing in that feel-good-about-yourself faith parents and marketers sell to us kids growing up," I say. "But the ant never moved that rubber tree plant. A bird ate him. Takes more than high hopes. It takes work and more work, and sacrifice, and single-minded determination. Nothing can get in your way. Nothing."

Silently, Wendy nods, a knowing expression on her face

"Jonathan's gotta concentrate. One hundred percent. Worrying about you being bored, or what your opinion is, or whatever. They're distractions, so he can't be his best. That's a problem." I nod. "For all of us. Including you." Between me and her, I make a small circle with two fingers. "You live here now. The band's gotta start making money. That's the whole point of what we're doing."

"I get it," Jennifer says. "You're right. I won't go."

"We're only going to be gone a couple of hours. You'll be the first person to hear how it goes."

She takes a drink.

"Oh, and this should interest you, Wendy. Ron's shooting here that night. Some of that new talent you sent him. Why don't you do some comps, Jennifer? You'll be here anyway."

Jennifer makes a sour face.

"Sure," Wendy says. "You'll be right here. Your own house."

"I don't know."

"You'll have fun. I know you will. I did. Getting all glammed up like those chicks you send out on thousand-dollar-a-day jobs."

"I don't want—"

"Yes, you do. Really. You do."

"But it's just me."

"It's just them too. Charlene was who she was, no matter what she looked like on film."

• • • • •

The next afternoon, I stuff a vinegar fry into my mouth. It's been months since we've had the money to get carryout from the Northside back at the loft, and I'm enjoying the hell out of this. Jonathan's eating but brooding. *Right before we mix the four songs.*

"Jennifer said she didn't want to come along tonight," Jonathan finally says.

"Oh?" I ask before swallowing.

"Said she decided it would be better if she didn't tag along. Wouldn't talk about it. I'm thinking maybe you told her she couldn't go."

A fry burns the roof of my mouth. I take a big, cold gulp of beer. "Nope. We talked about the session, yes. But I did *not* tell her not to go. Ask Wendy. She was sitting right there."

"What's there to talk about?"

"Well,"—I blow on a fry—"why Nancy and AnnMarie weren't going."

"She asked?"

"Yeah."

"About Nancy and AnnMarie?"

"It came up."

"Just happened to come up," he says, pursing his lips, his fingers ticking back and forth quickly twice.

"Basically, yes."

Looking down, he shakes his head.

I sigh. Laying my hands flat on the table beside my food, I start an explanation I shouldn't have to make at all. "I get home last night. She's here with Wendy. I've finally got the money to pay her back for September. So I suggest drinks."

"What's this to do with—"

"Hold on," I say, my finger held up at his face. "It does. If you'll let me." His brow furrows.

"So after we toast, Wendy brings up the mix. Something we can now do, since I have money." I sweep the palm of my hand before him. *See, the cocktails.* "Jennifer talks about how we're going to *Soundworks*, and how *we* need money to press copies of it. Fine. She *was* there last time, right? Then Wendy points out that Ron will be shooting here tonight. That he's doing comps for some new talent, that it's in Jennifer's house, that it would be a great way for her to get her own comps, et cetera. She's not sure. We're mixing at the same time. That is when I tell her that it won't be a problem. That Nancy and AnnMarie aren't going. That fewer people turns out being better."

He grunts.

"Really. Think about it. She'll have to sit around doing nothing for two hours. Not exactly what I call a good time."

"I want her opinions."

"Her opinions?"

"Yeah," he says. "If she likes this, or doesn't like that, and why."

"She's not creating our sound." I shake my head. "No."

"That's not what I meant. But she's the type of person who'd buy it, so ..."

"So nothing. A camel is a horse designed by a committee," I say. "Anyone more than you, me, and the sound man is a committee."

"But she might have good ideas."

"Are we gonna run a focus group to figure out what sounds best? Jonathan, this sound is ninety percent *you*. What's going on in *your* head. Me, the girls? We take those ideas and fill them out. You and only you know what it sounds like in your head. Not me. Not Nancy. Not AnnMarie. And certainly not Jennifer."

He makes a sour face.

"What if she makes a suggestion and you don't like it? So you say no. Is your mind going to be on the music or on her hurt feelings?"

"That won't happen."

"It's happening right now. We're not even mixing."

"Whatever," he says in that deadpan way of his that means he won't talk about it anymore.

"You want those?" I point at his fries.

He pushes the aluminum container at me.

"She'll do her comps. Ron's shooting a couple of other chicks while we're mixing." I snag a fry. "That will give her something to do. Not only tonight but maybe in the future as well. The main point is that she decided, herself, on her own, not to come."

He grunts.

Chapter 34
Laughing Like Children
—Scott—

A month after we finish the mix of our debut four-song EP, we've scrounged the money to get 250 CDs pressed without having to sponge from Nancy. It's stripped to the bare minimum: only a jewel case, a CD with a simple black-and-white label Chris designed, and an all-text back cover bearing the track listing:

1. The Ritual
2. Amy's Face
3. Just Walk Away
4. Sin with Me

Kenny took a copy to a radio DJ friend of his, who liked it and said he was going to play it. Tonight. Nothing we've done has ever gotten airplay in a major market—not even on a college station, where Kenny's DJ friend works: WNUR.

We're all here in the loft, waiting to hear it: Mercurial Visions, lovers, and friends. I'm sitting on the floor, my back against a column. AnnMarie's with Jennifer and Nancy on the couch. Kenny's getting a cocktail. Ron has his camera ready to catch our expressions. Everyone is here except for Jonathan. He has to work and will probably miss the first time a song of ours ever gets real airplay.

We've been listening for our song to come on the radio for about two hours when the door opens, letting in a gust of cold, wet, late-November air.

"The door," I yell, curling up. "Close."

"Not much of a party," Randal says, sauntering over.

"Waiting to hear it, man," I say.

"Ah, explains the lecture hall feel. Have a notepad for me?"

"L21ST" by Cabaret Voltaire wraps up, and everyone gets quiet, leaning a bit closer to the speakers.

Let's hear it. Come on.

"And now," the DJ says, "a new single, right here from Chicago. Off the new EP single *Some Have to Dance, Some Have to Kill,* here is 'The Devil Does Drugs' by My Life with the Thrill Kill Kult."

"Crap," I say. "You think he'll keep his promise, Kenny?"

"I guess." He shrugs. "He should. I don't know him that well."

Great.

Something hammers the door, and then it pushes open. Another gust of cold, wet air bursts in.

"Have they played it yet?" Jonathan asks, jumping through the doorway.

"Close the door!"

"Well, has he?" he asks, pushing the door closed with his shoulder.

"No," AnnMarie says.

"So I *didn't* miss it," Jonathan says, tossing his bag next to the door. "Awesome."

"He's got an hour left," Kenny calls over to him.

Jonathan gets a drink while a safe-sex public service announcement plays. It ends.

We hush, listening for the next song ...

"Love Will Tear Us Apart" begins.

"Shit," I say.

"Oh, yeah," Jonathan says. "Love that song. Last time I was over at Reckless Records, I saw the concert poster of 'Love Will Tear Us Apart.' Huge. Three by five foot. Awesome."

Oh, please. Not this again.

"The first money I actually make from this band, that's where it's going," he says, pointing to a large blank space on the wall near the black doors of the elevator. "Dry mount it. Bam. Right there."

"Your way of telling Jennifer something?" I ask.

"No. A Reminder," he says, reaching down to lay his hand on Jennifer's shoulder.

"Of what?" Jennifer asks.

"What makes it worth it. Makes it worth singing about."

"Being torn apart," she says, "makes us worth it?"

"You're being too literal."

"What do you mean 'literal'?" she asks, slumping back into the couch, looking annoyed.

Good. Tear them apart.

"Meaning love is rupture. It tears you from your before life. Remakes you time and again."

She grunts and pulls away from his hand.

"That makes for great lyrics," he says.

She looks askance at him. "What? We're a song?"

He shakes his head. "Still, too literal. I'm talking the *drama* of *falling* in love. *Out* of love. *Being* in love. That drama makes for good lyrics."

"So I really am a song to you."

He purses his lips, and cracks his knuckles, raising a hand, pointing, as if he's about to start a lecture. Yet he stays silent.

They look at each other.

"Well," I say. "Is she only a song?"

Thrusting an open palm at me, he gives me a *what-the-fuck* look.

"No," he says. "*She* is not. But there is drama in all relationships, *ours* included. And *that* drama *can be* a song: the before versus the together; the expectations, both met and not; the always choosing to be with her every day, every hour, and every moment, all while knowing she can change her mind like that." He snaps his fingers. "Or you might change your mind and not even know why. Drama. Especially when you don't like each other for a moment. After you've both changed. It's dramatic, 'cause the stakes couldn't be higher."

"So don't take the risks," Nancy says. "Just have sex. Simple, clean, *and* with only the passion you care to give. Or not. It's only sex. Hell, you can even make money at it."

"No drama there," he says. "No risk. Well, there's time, disappointment, embarrassment, maybe a nasty case of something. Ack, these sound like lyrics for a ditty in a safe sex PSA."

"So," I say. "Amy was only for the drama—not the sex?"

He gives me an ugly stare, flaring his nostrils.

I'm saving your life here, moron.

"Neither one," Jonathan says. "You *never* got that."

"Oh?" I ask. "So what don't I get about Amy?"

"Nothing to get anymore." He lights a cigarette. "No point in explaining what's gone."

"I see," I say, nodding gravely.

Jonathan offers his cigarette to Jennifer.

She waves it off and then lights one up for herself.

Good job, girl.

"So basically," I say, "you're saying drama's the reason to have a lover. It's not that you love her. You love the *drama* of loving her."

Jonathan shakes his head violently, his hair flying around.

"I don't think that's what he's saying," Nancy says. "Not really. He's only saying one must write about the unique drama of a particular relationship. *That's* what makes it interesting. See, poets have been trying to put into words what it *feels* like to be *in love* for millennia. They think the particular way they feel *love* is unique, and so special that the world needs to understand. Yet read enough love poems and they all start to sound the same."

"Sort of," Jonathan says.

"Poetry," I scoff. "Like Romeo and Juliet killing themselves. Madame Butterfly. Emma Bovary. Anna Karenina. All end the same way."

"Exactly, the drama," Jonathan says. "Not the naked emotion, spread on an examining table. That's the same old song."

"Every one of those is a suicide," Nancy said.

"Proof. Love's dangerous," I say. "It kills. Don't get suckered by it."

"The real swindle," Jonathan says, "is believing you're above it all. Sneering at all the grinning dupes, proud of being miserable *all* of the time. But the people who grin are happy—at least *some* of the time."

"And end up dead," I say.

"Or feel like you want to die," he says. "But I get to smile."

"In other words," Nancy says, "it's better to love and win glorious feelings, though checkered by pain, than take rank with those poor spirits who neither enjoy nor suffer much because they live in the gray twilight that knows neither love nor loss. With apologies to Teddy."

"Dead's worse."

"Emotionally dead?" he asks. "Sure. That *is* worse."

"Scott," Nancy says, "I've gotta agree with him. There's magic to it. But magic comes with risk. Danger. Highs and lows. Take Ron here. You've seen how many naked women through that camera of yours? Does it thrill you like it did when you were fifteen?"

"Not hardly," Ron says. "It's still sweet looking at naked girls. But it's nothing like the first *Playboy*. Or that sophomore in high school, Laura. First real tits I ever saw. Nothing's like that now. Course, how could I get a shoot done if I were gaping at a chick's tits like a fifteen-year-old the whole time?"

"Can't fall under the spell anymore," Nancy says. "Too bad."

"Not everyone *wants* to fall under the spell," AnnMarie says. "And not because you see naked ass all the time. It can be because you're not interested."

"Then you don't have to worry about getting hurt," I say.

"You can go through the motions, not caring or even understanding why anyone cares," AnnMarie says, "and still get wounded."

"Like in some sad European movie?" I ask. "Where the heroine sacrifices her virtue to the evil count to save her true love? Or the family castle?"

"No," AnnMarie says. "Like getting pregnant the only time you've ever had sex because that's what your boyfriend wanted, even if you didn't understand why he wanted it. Because you gave up the child for adoption. Because the child gets killed in a parking lot, shopping for his fake mom's birthday when he runs out in front of a car. I mean hurt like that."

"You're a mother?"

"Was," AnnMarie says. "Malcolm's dead."

"Guys," Kenny calls out, leaning toward a speaker. "You're on."

All heads turn to the speakers: our music flows out.

Now it feels as if millions of ants are crawling over my skin. I feel I'm exactly where I must be at exactly this moment and that I will be rewarded for all my persistence and determination.

Destiny. Jonathan, you must feel the same way I do. Please. Sammy did.

"That was 'Just Walk Away,'" the DJ says, "by Chicago's own Mercurial Visions. Wicked new sound, right? Let me know what you think by calling the listener line. And if you want to check out the rest of their music, they'll be at Avalon December second, the Friday after next, at eleven. Belmont and Sheffield. Be there to support noncorporate music. You know I'll be there. And now—"

I pump my fist. "Hell yeah!"

The photographer shoots and shoots, the no-longer mom claps, the lovers kiss, the groupie-roadie whoops, the landlord shoves hands forward, thumbs up, and the sequencer queen grabs my hands and pulls me up. We start dancing. Everyone joins in. We whirl around until we're dizzy and laughing like children.

Chapter 35

Joie de Vivre
—Scott—

Feeling Lynda trace slow, curving lines across my back, I lie on my side, away from the light seeping through the drapes in her bedroom.

I need to leave. Shoulda known better than to have come here last night.

After our show at Avalon two weeks back, this guy came up onstage. He was dressed too well for our normal crowd, in a skinny suit, no tie, like some New York or London hipster, and started talking to Jonathan. Fans always want to talk to the singer.

Now, we didn't have much time to clear the stage for the next act, but I let that go at first and started packing up.

But you keep talking, which is annoying, 'cause that means I'll have to pack your crap as well. Or drag you from your adoring fan. I'm not your personal roadie over here.

AnnMarie and Nancy were almost done, and I'd started on his gear, when Jonathan yanked on my shoulder from behind.

"Scott," he said. "This is Vic. He's from Wax Trax! Ministry and RevCo's label." Jonathan nodded his head with this "uh-huh, exactly" expression.

I extended my hand. We shook.

"The new songs are great," Vic said. "I've been following you for a while. Caught 'Just Walk Away' on NUR a couple of weeks ago. Had to come out and give the rest of your stuff a listen."

Okay …?

"I'd like to talk about what Wax Trax! can do for you."

Shit!

"Now, I'm heading to London for a few days, so here," he said, handing me his business card. It had "Artists and Repertoire" below his name.

"When I get back into town in a couple of weeks, let's meet. Talk business."

After all these years.

This morning is that couple of weeks later, and today we're meeting him—in less than three hours.

So why the hell am I lying around in bed with Lynda? To prove I like girls? Everyone knows, Scott, so get your stupid ass out of bed.

"What 'cha thinking about?" Lynda asks.

"Nothing. Band business. Have to be taking off."

"Why?" she asks, wrapping an arm around my waist. "We never spend a lazy morning together."

"Today isn't the day to start."

She smacks my ass, leaving a pleasant sting.

"Get me my cigarettes?" she asks.

I reach over to the nightstand, grab the pack and lighter, and hand them to her over my back.

"Let's have sex all day," she says. "Forget everything else."

"Love to," I say. "Not today though."

"You don't really *have* to go," she says, sliding her hand down my belly, pushing her fingers through my pubic hair.

"Yes, actually. I do." *I remember Russ Meyer: "An orgasm is fifteen seconds. A movie is forever." Like our music.*

"Be late." She wraps her fingers, loosely, around my growing erection.

"No, I can't," I say, grasping her hand.

"You don't have to leave *right this second*." She rubs her leg over mine.

"Yes," I say, nodding. "Right this second." I pull her hand away from me and then give my erection a sharp crack with my fingernail.

I stand and pick up my clothes.

"I'm going to be busy the next few days," she says.

"Too bad," I say, not caring that much: I have Wax Trax! waiting for me.

I lean down to kiss her anyway as she lies tossed across the bed.

As I step into the dreary late morning, a clammy wind blows on my face. I shiver and turn my collar up. It's usually a ten-minute walk, but I start speed walking, wondering if Jonathan's gotten ready or is at least out of bed. I don't want to have to roust him from our roommate's arms.

Not on the morning of the most important meeting of our life.

Nearing the Northside Bar & Grill, I can see the first floor of the Coyote Building—a long, narrow triangle with floor-to-ceiling windows. It was probably a prime space once, but now it's decrepit, with wires and long strips of paint dangling from the high ceiling. Dust covers the floor and counters like gray frost. But with the number of new restaurants, coffee shops, and galleries opening around here, I imagine it'll get rehabbed soon, like the rest of the 'hood. Once we sign this deal, maybe *we* should take it over and use it to sell Mercurial Visions paraphernalia: T-shirts, CDs, posters, and even custom gear. We could make it look sweet.

Make cash when we're not performing.

Turning down an alley parallel to North Avenue, I cut through the parking lot next to the Northside and arrive at our building.

As I open the door, I unexpectedly hear the sound of Jonathan's keyboard playing a song I don't recognize.

Climbing up, I keep listening, yet still it escapes me.

Is Kenny rehearsing something? Without telling me?

As I round the second-floor landing, I hear Jonathan singing.

I take each step softly so I can listen. At the fourth floor, I stand, my ear to the steel door. The song is completely new: not only passionate and sensual but upbeat as well.

When the song fades to silence, I unlock the door and walk in.

In a long, baggy black shirt, Jennifer sits on the floor next to a small cassette recorder, a mic in hand. Jonathan waves me over.

"Jen," he says. "Rewind it. Play it for him."

"I heard it. I was at the door listening."

"Well?" he asks, standing up behind the keyboard, spreading his arms. He's naked but for boxers.

"Impressive. I—"

"No," he says. "This ... no. This is the best I've ever written. This," he says, walking around the keyboard to tap his finger on the recorder. "This is what we should be taking to the meeting. Fuck. I wish we had a four-track. I'd call the other two. We'd lay it all down right now. I've got it all. Here." He taps his forehead. "Goddamn, why didn't we buy that four-track from whatever his name was when we had the chance? *Shit.*"

"Relax, man," I tell him.

He spins on a heel. "Is it rewound yet?"

"Yes," she says, pushing a button.

"Listen," he says. "Listen. I want to bring this today. Hold on. Hold on. Okay ... here." He drops to his knees, pointing the speaker toward me, slapping out a rhythm on the bare flesh of his thigh.

I can hear it all, exactly how the song will unfold, and hate that we don't have it for the meeting. It breaks completely with who we were before Chicago and pushes deeply into the sound we've been moving toward. With work, it will make "Just Walk Away" sound like a B-side. Again I feel my skin prickle with the feeling of a million crawling ants— that rush like destiny.

"So?" he asks.

"That's it," I say. "That is *it.*"

"'Joie de Vivre.'" He jumps up and spins, hair flaring outward. "Yes!" He drops to his knees and kisses Jennifer. "Play it again." She starts rewinding the tape.

"Hold on," I say. "We've only got, crap, less than an hour to make it to the meeting."

"Change it. We only need a day to get this punched out." He drums his thighs as "Joie de Vivre" starts again. "Or we'll just bring this tape. I'll explain everything."

"Hang on, man," I say, shaking my head. "The sound on that sucks. It's completely unprofessional. And we're pros. Not a bunch of high school dropouts with a couple of guitars and a drum kit."

"Listen to that," he says. "Listen. This is *it.*"

"Yes, it is," I say. "But ... no."

"We only need a day," he says, staring wildly at me. "Two, tops."

"We're going with what we've got. This already *is* our chance. We're taking it."

"Goddamn it," he says, pulling a fist up to his lips.

"They came to us. They want us, with what we have."

"And I want to knock them on their asses. This will do it."

"They *already* want us. We have nothing to prove. But canceling on an hour's notice makes us look totally unreliable. Completely unprofessional. Even if they thought this would sell a million—"

"It will."

"They'd never trust us. Chance gone. That's not happening."

He closes his eyes and tips his head back.

"I know," I say. "Really. But remember: they came to us. They *already* want us. It's a question of going in for the kill. In"—I look at my watch—"fifty-one minutes. Don't worry. This song'll get made. But we're not going to half-ass it. We want it to be right. Professional. All the way."

"Yeah, yeah, yeah," he says. "Probably right. But damn it ..." He sweeps out his arms. "It's so *good. So* much better."

Jennifer stands and wraps herself around him. His hand makes long strokes up and down her back.

"Now," I say, "we've really got to kick to get out of here. And we both look like shit."

"Yeah. Looks like Lynda's servicing you well," Jonathan says.

She slaps him on the belly. "Servicing?"

"Well ..."

She slaps his belly again. "Servicing? Is that right?"

Looking innocent, he reaches out to touch her face.

She steps back. "Go take your shower," she says, walking back toward their mattress. "Just wait and see if you get *service.*"

"Jen," he says, "I wasn't talking about you."

"You've got a meeting." She crawls under the covers. "I think this station's now *self* service."

He starts walking back to the mattresses.

"We've gotta get going," I say.

"You shower first. I'll be there in a couple of minutes."

"You're shitting me," I say as he walks back to her, his hair lashing back and forth. "You're doing this right *now*?"

In the bathroom, I rip back the shower curtain. "This, I cannot believe." Turning on the water, I shake my head. "If you're not in here by the time I get out, I'm dragging your ass in here. I don't care what you're doing."

I quickly shower and begin drying my hair.

He's still not here.

Wrapping a towel around my waist, I storm out of the bathroom, and then I see him atop her, his hips furiously pumping between her wide-spread knees.

"Jesus fucking-ass Christ," I blurt, and I turn back to the bathroom. "I mean ... *what* the *fuck*?"

Raking the brush through my hair, I glare into the mirror.

"Oh, that's right. You can't think. The scent of her pussy makes you an imbecile." Rapping the brush on the metal counter, I take several deep breaths. "I'm going alone. At least I'll be there. On time. I'll tell them you're sick ... or something."

Chapter 36

Not Even in the Movies
—Scott—

He saunters in naked and flushed from sex, still partially erect.

I stare at it for a moment and then look into the sink.

"Well, we're back to full-service," he says, sounding very pleased with himself.

"Simply unreal," I say, lifting an arm to run my deodorant underneath. "I just—"

"The most important meeting of our goddamned life is in less than a half hour, and you're balling Jennifer. Please. Explain that to me." I lift my other arm. "No, don't. I'll lose my mind."

"Shower only takes three minutes. Nothing. We're fine."

"No, we're not," I say, setting the deodorant down. "She's more important to you than we are."

"We late?"

"You're not getting this."

"Are we late?"

"Jonathan," I say, looking at his reflection in the mirror. "Just ..." *I don't even know what to say. That I shouldn't have to worry if you're going to get off in time for us to meet our record label.*

"What's more important to you?" I ask. "Getting off or getting a contract? No, don't answer," I say, holding my palm out to stop his reply. "You just showed me."

I walk away.

Twenty minutes later, Jennifer's dropped us off at 2449 North Lincoln Avenue.

It doesn't look like much: a two-story, white-and-lime-green storefront with a Wax Trax! record store on the street level. A big sign in the window reads "We Pay Cash for Your Vinyl." I check the address again.

"Yep. This is where it should be," I say. "So where do we go? Do we have to buy a record to get in?"

"Over here," Jonathan says, pointing to "2449" over a single glass door to the right of the record store.

"Sure. Why not?"

We walk up the narrow staircase to the second floor. It hardly seems like the center of industrial club music. It's a walk-up apartment over a used record store.

At the top of the stairs, we open the door.

The room's walls are covered with album, EP, and single covers; tour and album release posters; and lacquered and mounted records and CDs from everyone I can think of: Ministry, Revolting Cocks, Lard, Pailhead, Front 242, My Life with the Thrill Kill Cult, 1000 Homo DJ's, KMFDM, PIG, Meat Beat Manifesto, Front Line Assembly, Young Gods, Coil, Chris and Cosey, In the Nursery, Controlled Bleeding, A Split Second, Luc Van Acker, Laibach, and the Genetic Terrorists. It's a Goth-industrial temple.

Finally.

I catch myself staring. *Stop that. They came to us. We have what they want. And they'll have to pay for it.*

Jonathan's gazing at the paraphernalia, so I approach the reception desk.

From behind the large desk, a college kid with platinum-blond hair looks up. "Can I help you?"

"Scott Marshall. From Mercurial Visions. We have a meet—"

"Yes, a meeting with Doug and Vic," he says. "Let me tell them you're here." He picks up the phone.

Don't go acting all tough and untouchable, so superior. You're a fucking intern, working for nothing merely to get close to the bands on the wall. I am one of those bands.

"They're expecting you," he says. "Go right on in." He nods toward a door to the right of his desk.

"Jonathan," I say, "let's go."

I pull him into the office. Here too the walls are covered with band posters, logos, and discs. It looks like a record company office should, except it's small and was probably a dining room once.

"Hello," Vic, the A&R guy from Avalon, says, reaching out to shake my hand. He's dressed in another European-cut suit without a tie.

"This is Doug, the executive producer, owner, overseer of everything." He indicates the man sitting behind a large desk covered with stacks of papers and files. "Doug, this is Scott Marshall."

The owner looks to be in his early fifties, but he's trim, unlike most management types, and is not dressed in the corporate drag of khakis and button-down shirt, or sack suit. He looks more downtown hipster, in a bold-print shirt, with a shock of brown hair hanging over his forehead.

The owner reaches his hand out, and we shake.

It's a good, firm shake, which I like.

"He said you were a big guy," the owner says. "He's right."

You queer? 'Cause there will be no favor-for-a-favor bullshit with my band.

"So you must be Jonathan, what was it, Starks?"

"That's me," he says. He shakes the owner's and A&R guy's hands.

"Have a seat," the owner says. "Now, let's talk. Vic here has been telling me about you guys for a while, and he gave me that single you pressed yourself. That takes some stones. Confidence is good. I have to say I like the sound. And I think a lot of other people will—"

"That's old stuff," Jonathan says, reaching for his back pocket.

You did not bring that goddamned tape.

"Jonathan," I say. "Listen to the man here. We're talking recording deal here."

"He's right," the owner says, looking concerned. "But what do you mean 'old stuff'? Have you changed your sound?"

The A&R guy glares at Jonathan, annoyed.

"No," I say, grabbing Jonathan's hand, and squeezing hard enough to make him wince. "We have *not* changed our sound. He's got some ideas he'd like to *talk* about."

"Good to hear. We can't have a band changing every five minutes. What would there be to market? A brand-new old band?"

"Evolution," I say. "Slow change over time. New ideas to keep things fresh. To keep putting out material people want. That, yes."

The owner looks satisfied, and the A&R guy relaxes, and Jonathan jerks his hand free but puts it behind him.

"So," the owner says, "as I was saying, we like your sound, both Vic and I, and I think we can really do something for you. Now, we need to find out what you think you need, and then we'll tell you what we think we can provide."

Then Jonathan whips out that fucking cassette he and Jennifer made a couple of hours ago.

"Here," he says, holding the tape out to the owner. "This is what you can do for us. Make this song. Get it into DJs' hands."

You dumbass!

"Jonathan," I say, wanting to yank the cassette out of his hand and beat him with it. *This is our chance—the opportunity. You're fucking it up.* "You can play that for them live. Once we've orchestrated it."

"Do you have a cassette player?" Jonathan urgently asks. "Best thing I've ever written. Scott even thinks so."

Don't! I'm screaming inside. *Don't do this.*

The owner and the A&R guy both look at me, baffled.

"Yes," I say. "I did say that. I do think that—with some work—it will be the best we've ever done."

"Better than 'Just Walk Away'?" the A&R guy asks.

"Hell yeah," Jonathan says. "It makes that sound like a B-side reject."

I restrain myself from physically closing his mouth.

"Vic," the owners says, "bring that player over."

I don't believe I'm watching this—everything we've worked years to get, evaporating.

"May I?" the A&R guy asks, holding out his hand.

Jonathan hands over the cassette and then pulls his chair up to the desk.

I feel my breath coming hard and fast. *This is not how you do it: This is how you completely fuck things up.* I want to punch him so hard he can't breathe.

But the A&R guy pushes the button on the tape player.

I hear the music I'd heard when I was climbing the stairs not even two hours ago.

Jonathan starts rapping out a rhythm on the desk. He looks fierce, like he might explode if anything touches him. I close my eyes. At the right moments, he sings a chorus that exists only in his brain.

I'll be damned if it doesn't sound good, that crappy little cassette tape, with this hands rapping out a beat on a desk and him singing imagined choruses. I peek.

The owner and the A&R guy are both digging it.

When the song ends, Jonathan lifts his hands and grins like an imp.

"See what you mean, man," the owner says, nodding. "That would make a killer single. Especially with your backup vocals and loops."

It's impossible that they haven't kicked us out. We should be dead in the water. Now they're stoked to make a single from that crappy junior-high recording.

Shit like this doesn't happen. It simply can't—not even in the movies.

Chapter 37

Original Wave Night: Bumps
—Scott—

"Call everyone," Jonathan says, running to the back of the loft, hands up, thumb, forefinger and pinky out.

"Yes, girl. Yes!" he calls out, leaping onto his mattress where Jennifer's sitting.

I rip off my leather jacket, throw it against the wall, grab the phone, and start dialing. I dial Nancy's number first, but after three rings, her machine picks up, and I have to leave a message, which sucks. Then I call AnnMarie's, and it's the same, and I'm beginning to think no one gives a shit that we've got a contract now.

I call the Myopic. Finally I get to tell AnnMarie the news and hear the same excitement I feel. But I tease her and won't tell her the details. I do let her know she has to be here for a party at eight.

Love that. Delivering the news that confirms this is what happens with persistence and determination. Like you said, Sammy.

I dial Lynda's number next, finally having something serious to show off to her. Of course, a machine picks up.

"Lynda. Scott. If you're there, pick up. I've got news. Lynda?"

Drumming my fingers on the table next to the phone, I'm about to tell her to show up at the party when I hear the phone being picked up.

'Bout time.

"Hold on," a man says, "she'll be right there."

Who the fuck's that?

233

I hear the receiver hitting a table, and then some indistinguishable noises. Moments pass.

"Scott?" Lynda asks.

"Yeah. It's me."

"Sorry, I was in the shower. What's up?"

"In the shower?"

"Well, I needed one," she says. "Especially after last night."

"Yeah?"

"Oh, him. He's the photographer. He's picking me up."

"Right. I see," I say. "Well ... we ... got offered a record deal. We're having a party. Tonight."

"Congratulations! Really! That's wonderful," she says, sounding genuinely excited. "But, damn. I can't tonight. I'm going to be busy."

Then I hear the mouthpiece being covered.

"Stop," she hisses. Then, muffled, she says, "I'm on the phone."

"Sorry." Her voice comes back again, clearly. "Lou's being a dumbass. So what are you up to Saturday?"

"This Saturday?"

"Yeah. We'll celebrate then. Goddamn it, Lou. Wait," she hisses.

I hang up.

Why'd you have to go and fuck things up like that?

I call Kenny next. I need to hear someone be excited, hear admiration for sticking to it through all the bullshit, and he doesn't disappoint. He is so excited, as if he's the one signing the deal. I enjoy simply listening to his voice and being admired. *Like I admired you, Sammy, for trying to get away.*

Even better, once people start showing up, I get to tell the story of the cassette tape and nearly getting kicked out of the office, over and over. Every time, Kenny watches rapt, waiting for me to get us out of the mess yet again, and a high comes on, as if nothing that had happened before can touch me. *I'm free.*

Minutes ago, Jonathan got home from work, grabbed a cocktail, and finally joined the party, still dressed like a waitron.

"Guy," I say, pointing at his shirt. "Gonna change? Not like you're getting tips here."

He shrugs.

"Just think," I say. "Soon we won't have to wear restaurant rags ever again."

"'Bout goddamned time." He raises his glass. We toast.

"Next stop—Berlin. Original Wave Night," I say.

Grabbing coats, we pile out, tromping down the stairs and into cars.

Wendy and I are sitting in the backseat of Jennifer's car when she leans over to me. "Heard Ron mention blow."

"Said he's gonna look for it," I say.

"He going to share?" she asks.

"Didn't say. Not exactly," I say.

"In that case, he'll share," she says, putting her hand on my thigh, moistening her lips and smiling.

As high as I felt a few minutes ago, Wendy's obvious flirting reminds me of the call to Lynda. *Her photographer. Bullshit. Can't have Lynda thinking I sit around waiting for her.*

Wendy's hand warms my leg, and her plump tits gorge the fabric of the tight green dress that wraps her body. *Ooo, hold on here. Telling Lynda I fucked someone she works for'd be sweet. Bonus: she'd have to wonder if I could influence Wendy to take jobs away from her.*

Let's do it.

"Hey," Jonathan says from the passenger seat. "What are you two conspiring about back there?"

"Party favors," I say.

"Oh, you kids," he says.

"I need to talk to Ron," I say to Wendy, "right after we get in."

"I have a feeling we're going to have *too* much fun tonight," Wendy says, slipping her hand around to the inside of my knee.

I drape my arm around her shoulder. *Too bad you're not here, Lynda. To see it happen.*

We park on Belmont near Sheffield, and the four of us walk past the Belmont 'L' station, joining everyone else in front of Berlin's blacked-out windows. Inside the door, Berlin opens up into a dark world of chandeliers and cartoon-character cutouts hanging from the ceiling and on the walls. In a dialogue balloon directly overhead, Donald Duck says, "Miss Duck, if you're nasty." Behind the big bar opposite the dance floor, black-and-white monitors show Max Schreck in *Nosferatu*. On the boxes overlooking the dance floor, two boys dance together to the thick, erotic rhythms like pole dancers at a strip club. On the main floor, reflected in the wall of mirrors, most of the rest of the boys dance with boys; a few dance with some of the girls. The rest of the girls dance with other girls. They're all pretty, young, and dressed like it in tight T-shirts and jeans or short skirts with boots, or colorful print shirts, skinny pants, and chunky-soled shoes.

I tug Ron's elbow. "How things looking for party favors?"

He shakes his head. "Don't see anyone I know here," he says, flopping his hand over—limp wristed, little finger raised. "This is Kenny's neck of the woods. Hang on." He waves Kenny over. "Can you score some cola?"

"Kylie Minogue tapes?" Kenny asks. "Sure. I saw someone. I'll need some cash."

We peel off some twenties. Cash in hand, Kenny slips off into the crowd. Wendy looks at me expectantly. I raise my eyebrows and give her a quick nod.

After we order shots, Wendy leans into me to watch the dancers bumping thighs and grinding groins.

You see, Jonathan. I'm not waiting for Lynda. No one dies if you don't really care.

Kenny reappears. "I know the DJ. Says he's going to play 'Just Walk Away' later."

"Choice," I say.

He leans close to me. "Got good shit," he whispers. "Ain't cheap. Could only get two quarters each."

"We'll have to deal."

He squeezes two snow-sealed quarter grams into my palm. I stuff them and my driver's license into my front pocket and grasp Wendy's elbow and move toward the bathrooms. We walk around the DJ booth, through the back corridor, and into the men's bathroom. The door to one stall hangs open, but one of the three boys standing at the trough urinal glares at Wendy.

"I'll bump first," I say. "Give it to you outside."

She leaves.

Closing the stall door behind me, I take the rectangular blue snow seal and my driver's license out. After carefully opening the waxy paper envelope, revealing the seal watermarks and chunks of white, I chop the chunks to loose powder and scoop a small mound onto the corner of my license. Then I flush the toilet with my foot as I inhale noisily, getting everything inside my nostril. My sinuses tingle.

Kenny's right. It's good shit.

I dig another bump out with the corner and inhale it quickly as the water drains. Folding the snow seal up, I turn to leave, first wiping any VCR from my nose. I step out of the stall and leave the boys' room right as I feel numbness spreading through my sinuses.

Wendy's waiting, and she grins as I slip my driver's license and the snow seal into her warm hand. She vanishes into the women's.

Tipping my head back, I feel *the fall*—a fresh numbness dropping down the back of my throat. I'm racing standing still. My mind speeds through everything I want to do right now: dance and feel Wendy's body against mine, and then take her home and prove to everyone Lynda isn't all that. And I want to be in the studio recording, to hear our songs on every radio station, to have people recognize them, to recognize me, to see our CD in shops, to play Metro, to play New York, and I feel like God right now and know all these things will happen, inevitably, and I need to do something—walk or spin or dance—anything other than stand and wait for her.

I feel my license and the snow seal pressing into my palm, and I slip them into my pocket. Wendy's sniffing hard. Then "Just Walk Away" starts playing, and I grab her hand, and we push ourselves onto the dance floor, squeezing through bodies, and begin grinding to the music.

Here, on the dance floor, is proof that things are already happening. My music is enveloping me, inspiring strangers, commanding them to dance. I need to float above the crowd and yell "I made this!"

This must be how that desert sky god felt on the seventh day. 'Cept I'm no fairy tale. I'm right here, right now, living this.

We keep dancing until I feel the itchy, demanding need for another bump, and we walk off the dance floor to the back corridor, and the bathrooms, and another inhalation of feeling like a god. And then there is more dancing, and the night is spinning into a fantastic, throbbing paradise.

After I don't know how long, I have only one nearly empty snow seal left—enough for one last bump—and my hands are trembling. I ask Kenny if he can get more, and he says he's already been looking but everyone's gone. Wendy asks for more. I hand her what's left, saying that's the last of it, and want to get out of here soon. She spins away into the crowd.

Now the need for another bump turns vicious, taking over my thoughts. I'm crashing. We'll both be zombies soon. Closing my eyes, I try to still my trembling body and relax my tensing jaw. My mind keeps flicking from Wendy, to a corner of my license rounded with a bump of white, to wanting to leave and get the hell away from here and everyone else.

I run into Ron and Nancy by the bar and tell them we should leave. *Like now.*

Right then, Jonathan and Jennifer walk by, and I grab them, saying we're leaving, but Wendy's still missing. They say they haven't seen her either, but they tell me not to worry. It's something she does.

"Be back," I say. "A minute."

Wandering through the crowd, I hunt for her, concentrating my jittery thoughts on finding her dark, slicked-back hair. Turning the corner of the corridor behind the DJ booth, I see her pushing a woman up against the wall, her hands on the woman's hips.

They're kissing deeply.

An arm's length away, I stare at them, aware of the sick feeling, deep in my gut, of things gone completely wrong.

The woman notices me staring and stops kissing Wendy, nodding my way.

Wendy peels back from her and then follows her eyes to me.

"Hi. This is my friend Maureen," Wendy says. "We go way back."

"Yes," I say. "I can ... um ... see that."

The woman strokes Wendy, peering at me like a cat defending its kill.

"She told me she knows where to score more party favors," Wendy says, leaning back into the woman's long body.

The woman nods.

"Okay," I say. "But everyone's ready to head out."

"Where are you heading?" Wendy asks.

"Home," I say. "The loft."

Wendy whispers to the chick.

"We can meet you there," Wendy says.

"You both?"

Wendy nods slowly, biting her lip suggestively.

"How long?" I ask, not sure that I believe her.

"I don't know," Wendy says, with a shrug. "An hour or so."

She looks up to Maureen, who nods.

"Why don't I come with?" I ask.

"No," the other woman says, shaking her head. "It's late. She wouldn't like a boy there at this hour."

"We'll meet you," Wendy says.

Looking the two over, I try to find a clear thought—something firm I can trust in my twitchy, nervous haze.

Then the chick slides her hand down Wendy's chest, and runs her thumb over her nipples once, twice, until they rise through the thin fabric of her dress.

Staring at Wendy's hardening nipples, I understand things more clearly.

"Okay," I say. "I'll leave the bottom door unlocked. Just knock. I'll be there."

"See you in an hour or so," Wendy says.

Jennifer drives us back to the loft, and once inside, she and Jonathan run to their mattress.

Leaving the lights off, I put on *Floodland* by the Sisters of Mercy only loud enough so I don't have to listen to them, and I then throw myself down on the couch to wait. I think of Wendy and that woman and start turning their bodies over in my mind, the different hair colors and shapes, imagining how different the flesh of each one would feel.

Suddenly I notice my eyes have closed, and I force them open again, refusing to fall asleep before they can arrive. *Floodland* is long over, but now I think I hear whispering and giggling, and that pisses me off even more, so I put on a new CD: *I See Good Spirits and I See Bad Spirits*, by My Life With the Thrill Kill Kult.

Fitfully, I keep shifting, first sitting with feet on the ground, then with my legs over the armrest, then lying down, and then back to sitting up.

Then the thought of being duped blasts away all fog in my head.

You've been played, Scott. Dipshit. How could I fall for that crap?

I curl up, furious with myself. I want to cover my head in aggravation. Sleeping would be better. I'm so tired but so very awake. Jitters force me to pace around for a few minutes. As I sit back down, anxious exhaustion settles in.

It's been well over an hour. So yes, I'm screwed.

Fidgety, I get up and pace again. That takes too much energy, so I fall down onto the couch. *Stupid waste of time, to prove that Lynda doesn't matter. Who cares?*

I snort in derision at myself.

Thinking takes too much effort now. I lie out along the couch. As I fade in and out of consciousness, my earlier sense of being admired and of succeeding at last succumbs to humiliation.

So sorry, Sammy. None of this was supposed to happen—not without you.

CHAPTER 38

MANNEQUIN
—JENNIFER—

We're sleeping in after last night at Berlin.

Well, he's asleep. I'm looking at his face, his eyes softly closed, lips quietly resting together, a ray of light falling across his cheek. I trace the curve of that cheek with my finger's shadow and feel like the heroine of a teen romance novel. I should be thinking of how we'll always be together and how lucky I am. Instead I'm thinking about the sex, feeling as if I had wings. *But that's strictly adult reading.*

"I want to rip you to pieces and swallow you all," I whisper. "I love you so."

Leaning down, I hold my lip barely over his, and let his warm breath stroke my face.

Do you gaze at me like this when I'm asleep? Do you feel anything like this? Or feel anything at all? The teen heroine realizes she can't know, even if you say yes, and she gets scared. Then she tries to wake you to find out if she can see the love in your eyes.

Quickly I kiss his cheek where the slice of light falls across it, and he stirs but stays asleep. *The teen heroine's still alone, wondering what you feel.*

I comb the hair away from his brow with my fingers and delicately tuck it behind his ear. He shifts again, more this time, but still refuses to wake. *The teen heroine's worried that this is a sign. She's unsure what to do.* Rolling my fingers through the ray of light, I make the shadows jump over his face.

Adult novels are more exciting. So I run my fingers, lightly, across his cheek and then down his neck, down his shoulder, through the blond hair on his chest to his belly, and then over his hip, feeling my fingers rise and fall with the contours of his body.

"Hi," he says.

"Hey," I say, looking into his eyes. *Does she see the love there?*

He pulls his fingers delicately down my cheeks.

When I'm here with you, you're thinking of me, right?

He's staring at my body now.

Or do you think of your music? Some song of yours?

He sits up.

"Little boys' room," he says. "Be back." He kisses me and then pushes himself off the mattress.

"Pffft." *Not exactly romantic. Or sexy.*

As I watch him walking across the floor, a feeling of déjà vu hits. I can't place the moment. *A movie? An ad?* The scene is of someone's lover walking, naked, through a raw space dramatically lit with the same shafts of light, cutting through twilight.

It looked perfect. I *am* sure I envied that I wasn't part of it.

This time it *is* me. I'm watching *my* lover in *my* place. I'm the one to wonder about and to be envied.

I'm enjoying being her. She's so unlike any of the awful girls Ron had me pretend to be in the shots he took for Wendy, which she put in a talent book at Les Femmes.

Then Jonathan *insisted* on framing and displaying three of the shots. I look at the eight-by-tens.

Who'd want to be any of those women? I hate them.

One has me glancing over my shoulder as if I'm a carefree flirt, in a sheer top I'd never even look at on a sales rack. One has me lying down on our couch, sipping a glass of water I pretended was a cocktail; I'm looking up, dramatically, as if I'm a Ewing girl about to drop a bomb on *Dallas.* The last is of me in suburban corporate drag, standing authoritatively in front of one of our brick walls.

I'm none any of those women. I don't wear those clothes. I don't flirt like that. I don't drink cocktails while plotting to take something over. I'm sure as hell no corporate clone. These are softcore stills of image porn—illusions.

If Ron were here now, he could take shots of who I really am; but we're both naked, and that's creepy—as it is here most of the time now. With all these people in the loft all the time, it's as if I'm living on the set of a TV show that peeks in on my life: *"Look! Jennifer's on top of him. Hear what she sounds like. See what she looks like when she wakes up with him. Here's what Jennifer looks like the morning after sex."*

Suddenly I get it. *Jonathan's showing me off, like everyone else. I'm a prop to you. That's why you put those photos on the wall: "Lookit! This is who I fuck, everyone. Aren't you jealous?"*

Somewhere inside me, a sick feeling splits wide open. *He's using me, like everyone else.*

Right then he steps out of the bathroom.

I pull the sheets over myself. He walks over, nude, showing the studio audience how hot he is, how cool we are. *"See, we walk around naked. Look at us strutting. Don't you want to be us?"*

I am not *an exhibition.*

"Jonathan," I say.

"Yes?" He stands next to me.

"Why ..." I need to be sure to say this right, so he can't slip away by twisting my words all around.

He kneels in front of me. "Why ... what?"

"Why do you have those photos of me hanging on the wall there? Like trophies?"

"It's something you did. You look good. Ron has people come in. Maybe they'll see you and—"

"You *are* showing me off. Like I'm a piece of—"

"I'm showing off what you *did*. That looks good. Maybe you'll make some money. I'm only trying to help out here."

I purse my lips. *I doubt that.*

"Hey, if you don't like them, I'll take them down. No big deal. But I like them most when you're not here." He sits beside me. "They let me look at you."

"I don't look like that."

243

"Well, actually, you do. That *is* you. But you're not *her*, or *her*, or *her*. Gotcha. I know exactly what you mean. Everyone has this idea about the long-haired guy who plays and sings. They think I'm having orgies and shooting black tar, or downing a bottle of Bourbon a day—like I live some low-end version of an MTV rock star's life.

"That goes for you too." He shakes his head. "The rock star's girl. You're that in people's minds, even in your own clothes. In spite of working in an office."

He points at the photo of me in the corporate wife's dress. "That's you." I shake my head.

"Yes, it is. That's your face. It's your body. Ron took that photo of *you*. But not really you. I'm a waiter. I only play a rock star onstage. You're Jennifer. Loft-living urban homesteader and assistant producer. You only play suburban corporate droid in black-and-white prints."

That had helped for a while. But things only got worse when they should have gotten better, starting with Wax Trax! finally releasing Mercurial Visions' EP a few weeks later.

This was supposed to be like the triumphant scene at the end of the movie—everyone rooting for them, at the edges of their seats, and then—yes, they *do* make it!

But all this has done is make me wish that they never met that A&R guy or recorded "Joie de Vivre," and that no one had heard of Mercurial Visions.

Before all this, we were only dreaming about what might happen. No one knew us except when they played out. Then, Jonathan was only my boyfriend. Now that he's a rising rock star, I've turned into the rising rock star's lover.

I don't like getting pushed around like this.

Sure, when Wendy got me out of Wild Hair Salon's School of Massage Therapy—that softcore whorehouse—and gave me a *real* job at Les Femmes, I went from almost-masseuse to executive assistant, and now to assistant producer. I chose those promotions.

This new crap is happening *to* me, and things keep getting weirder and weirder.

Les Femmes was strange enough before—full of pretty boys and pretty girls, the talent, plus their managers, the photographers, the producers, the scouts, and the advertising people, all playing this twisted popularity game. Sure, I *had* to play, but as the boss's assistant, I could to stay mostly apart, touching it only when I had to, as if it were a deck of Community Chest or Chance cards. But then my photos went into circulation, and I'm talent now, getting examined, picked over, and discarded, people flashing cash in my face that I'll never get. *"Just smile, girl. Smile."* So now I'm supposed to play *in* the game. *I won't. I hate it. And I won't pretend to be those softcore illusions.*

Worse, "Joie de Vivre" gets this killer review in the *Tribune*—one I wish had never gotten written.

Joys of Love, Loss and Clubs

M. Isbister
Chicago Tribune Electronic Music Critic
1/18/89

Mercurial Visions "Joie de Vivre" Wax Trax! 4-song EP Five Stars
Releases are rated on a scale of one to five stars
A debut release can be killed by misperceptions, especially when it comes from a label known for its hard-driving industrial bent. If it's Wax Trax! and the band's from Chicago, it's going to be Al Jourgensen, with an assortment of other musicians: Ministry, Revolting Cocks, 1000 Homo DJs, and now this one.
So it will play out like this: In the store, a disc from a band you think you've heard of catches your eye. It looks good in the rack. You think "Why not?" pick it up, flip it over, and see Wax Trax!. Then you either

245

put it back because you hate industrial, or you plunk down your money for something you know you'll like, because you like Al and his projects. Later the CD tray closes and you press the play button, or the stylus lowers, and then ... something you never even imagined flows from the speakers—something you really, really like and never knew you did.

This is what the debut EP "Joie de Vivre" by Chicago's Mercurial Visions sounds like when you first hear it. Each track is utterly danceable—the first and last irresistibly so. More European club music than gritty Chicago industrial, the title track makes you need to dance to this passionate ode to a lover, to the lovers' physical rapture. Jonathan Stark's skills as a wordsmith excel here with lines that jump up and grab you, lines you wish you had thought to say to your ex before she walked away that last time, lines he sings with such emotional intensity you can feel her body next to yours. And there is not a dram of sugar—just beat and energy that will hook even the jaded.

This is no one-hit disc. The next track, "Just Walk Away," follows up physical embrace with kicking loose from someone you should never have slept with in the first place. It's a good-feeling song about feeling bad. Again the beat sinks into your body and makes it want to move, in anger or relief, for "sometimes it's best when it's over," as Mr. Starks reminds us.

By now you realize this is not Wax Trax! as usual. This band sounds like they left Chicago's industrial streets for a long stay in Belgium, with a stopover in Ibiza. It's Front 242's electronic body music to move to, with a dollop of postpunk attitude, another of industrial might, and ample poetry of the flesh.

The third track, "Amy's Face," reaffirms this is not a rehash of some other band but rather something new, real, and important. If you've gone to a dance club—and if you're reading this, you have—you know the scene: A stranger. Throbbing beats. Sweat. As the evening grows late, a face you've seen a thousand times before looks fresh, as if you're seeing it for the first time, but this time you know how it will end.

It's love in the rhythm zone.

Full of pummeling rhythms, the final cut is "The Ritual," *the* club ode to the potent lust—the desires that make us go out, stay up late, drink too much, and dance where it's safe to live as you want—out loud. It's a world where anything is always possible—a haven where the only rule is rhythm, and dance is the only work.

For those who passed it by, consider this opportunity knocking a second time. Keep your ears open and your body limber for that song from the band from Wax Trax! that doesn't sound like Al.

I should feel great and be shouting "Hurray!" 'cause dreams *are* happening.

But I liked dreaming better.

Now strangers think they know all these intimate things about me. They think they know we've broken up because the song says "sometimes it's best to just walk away." They think we later play sex games where he picks me up in a club, pretending I'm a one-night stand. Those are songs about *another* woman. Only in "Joie de Vivre" does he sing about me. It's impossible to explain to everyone.

At work, when any of the new kids find out that I'm with the singer from Mercurial Visions, first it's "wow," and then it turns to getting the EP and how they've danced to the songs. Inevitably it moves on to asking how things *really* are. If it's true what he says in his songs.

I don't know this person. Why is she asking me that? I mean, who *is* she?

It's like being poked to see if I'm real—if we're real. As if everyone's hoping she'll hear "it's only a song" so she can say, "Hah! I knew it. Nothing's *really* like that."

It *is* real, but only for us. *Mostly him and Amy.*

It's so frustrating. Especially since I have no place to escape anymore. Since "Joie de Vivre" and the review came out, it's been like a parade here in the loft, with people coming and going and hanging out, and the calls. I can't go and lock myself in my room here; there are no rooms. I'm trapped in the open, exposed. *"Here I am, everyone. You've seen me in photos. You've read about me. You've heard about me."*

Jonathan's been no help. Now that things have gotten extra weird, he's extra busy. We hardly ever get time to talk. Time to be alone? Only when we're in bed, and sometimes not even then; if he works late, I go to bed alone. Basically, I'm on my own in this overcrowded loft, reading about him and his band, and listening to songs about his exes, and one about us having sex.

Then, tonight, freakishly, I'm completely alone. A night when I need someone to talk to, no one's here. The roommate's gone. Jonathan's working until late. There's no rehearsal. No shoot. The last time this happened was before they recorded "Joie de Vivre."

Sitting here on the couch, I feel as though I'm going slightly crazy.

I stomp my foot.

"Do I have to move back home to feel normal?" I ask the empty loft.

There aren't even strangers traipsing around here to give me an answer.

This silence unsettles me; I finally get my wish to be alone, and the place feels more like the setup for a scare in a slasher flick than a home. I don't like this. It's *too* alone—nothing but emptiness and hushed sounds of the streets. I turn to look out the windows, and I can make out an 'L' train rumbling on its tracks, full of people who can't see that I'm alone here in this big, deserted place, about to become the next victim of some masked villain they'll later scare themselves with in theaters.

Getting up from the couch, I turn on the tube. We only get four channels out here—can't afford cable yet. As I flip between them, I catch a glimpse of her name: *Charlene Pollard.*

I flip back a station to see Charlene's photo and name superimposed over a police station.

"... boyfriend was questioned by police today, and was released without charges," the disembodied voice says. "Richard Barthes voluntarily surrendered at O'Hare International Airport earlier this afternoon. He has been out of the country for several months, in Indonesia for business, and this is his first trip back to the US since before Ms. Pollard fell to her death.

"Asked to comment"—the scene cuts to a fat cop behind a lectern—"Sergeant Luckac, the lead officer for the case, says that both of the glasses with alcohol in them had only Ms. Pollard's fingerprints on them: two sets—one from her right and one from her left hand. Right now, her fall appears to be an accident. She had been drinking alone and apparently lost her balance on the balcony—"

I switch off the TV and stand, staring at the black screen.

"No," I say. "That's insane. They're lying. Charlene was going to move in with me. She had a career. You're wrong. She didn't slip. She was murdered. Her asshole boyfriend paid someone. Come on, Charlene; tell me this is wrong. You didn't really slip and fall. You weren't just drunk. It's too stupid."

I stare at some bits of yellow paint stuck in a groove in the floor.

Fucking nothing's real—not her slipping because she was drunk, and not those mannequins of me posing in photos. Even this loft is fake—borrowed, empty, and full of people I don't even know. How is this a home?

Finally it becomes so clear: "Joie de Vivre" isn't real, either. *It's a con too. Jonathan, you lied when you said you wrote it about our love when you were watching me sleep; it's sex—like the other smut you sing. All your songs are about lovers. I'm only the centerfold of your porno EP.*

So—do you think of me when we're together? Or Amy?

"Do you still want her?" I shout into the emptiness. "Or am I subbing for her?"

Closing my eyes, I cringe.

Did you even write it about me at all? Or did I happen to be the body in your bed at the right time?

"It's an ode to fucking," I tell myself. "*Who* never mattered. It's a lie, like everything else here. This place, us, everything—pure bullshit.

"You're not gonna make a fool of me," I say, shaking my head violently. "Not like that closet queer Martin. Not this time. Not a chance."

I march to the mattress and look at everything in our—not *our* anymore—*his* bedroom.

It's not even a bedroom. It's a mattress on the floor.

"Fake, fake, fake," I say, pointing at the mattress, the shelves made of cinder blocks and boards, the cardboard box "drawers."

"Lucky you, Jennifer. Haven't moved much here yet."

Some clothes, a few tapes, and my red leather jewelry box.

My satchel and a garbage bag'll work fine to get myself gone.

I start yanking my clothes off the cinder block shelves. After I clear them, I take a deep breath, holding up my hands.

"Slow down," I tell myself. "Careful. Take nothing of his. Leave no reason for him to call."

Rummaging through the pile on the mattress, I pick up his long-sleeved shirt I used to wear around the loft when it got cool at night.

Folding it carefully, I lay it back on an empty shelf.

Can't say I trashed your stuff.

Next I search the apartment, grabbing all my CDs and magazines. *Anything I forget is gone forever.*

I've dumped the last of my stuff onto the mattress when the sound of the door opening makes me freeze.

I refuse to look. If it's Scott, he'll probably help. If it's Jonathan ... I shake my head.

Throwing open my satchel, I start stuffing my clothes in.

"Hey, lover," I hear Jonathan say over the *thunk-thunk* of his bus-driver shoes.

I keep shoving clothes into the satchel until it overflows with sleeves and tails.

"Wanna go to Bondage-A-Gogo over at Exit?" he asks. "Nancy popped in at work and said Ron and Scott both want to go."

The satchel's overfull, but I try stuffing more into it. Pissed that nothing more will fit, I clench my fists. My body shakes. Listening to him walking over to the mattress, I close my eyes. *Why won't you—please— leave me alone?*

"What's, um ..." he asks. "What's going on?"

I know he's staring at me from across the mattress.

Good. I finally have your attention.

"I'm leaving."

"What?"

I hope you're seeing the real me right now. The one who can't be conned. The one who won't change her mind.

I feel the mattress sag as he kneels on the bed. He touches my shoulder.

Pulling away from his fingers, I grab another handful of clothes and try to stuff them into the satchel, and they won't fit, and I feel tears of frustration and anger building up, about to burst, but I refuse and punch the satchel.

"Fucking thing!" I shout.

CHAPTER 39

MISTRESS MAYHEM
—JENNIFER—

It so doesn't feel like it's already 1989. Almost Valentine's Day. Not that anyone could tell. Back home, we'd have a cupid or two up, or a heart. Something. It's the same thing with Christmas; no decorations here. No tree. No wreath even. Jonathan's not that interested in that. I doubt Scott is either. I think he hates his family.

I shouldn't care that much. But wouldn't it be nice—

Jennifer, stop being your mother.

My water's come to a boil and I'm breaking a handful of spaghetti in half when the front door opens.

"You've got almost perfect timing, Jonathan," I say to the roiling water as I drop in the pasta.

Then I hear Kenny's voice, and then Scott's, followed by Jonathan's. I roll my eyes. No one was supposed to be here tonight but us.

Dinner alone—poof, like everything else in our TV-set life.

"Oh, it's *so* warm in here," Kenny says. He strips off a full-length leather duster and reveals he's wearing a skin-tight black PVC shirt with long sleeves, and chaps that expose his butt entirely. He's wearing cowboy boots.

"Every day is Halloween," I say to myself, half hearing the song in my head.

"Hi, Jen," Jonathan calls. "Look who I ran into on the way up." He walks around them to give me a kiss.

"You get those chocolate-covered espresso beans from Myopic by any chance?" I ask, trying to look around Jonathan at Kenny.

"Oh, sorry. No. Ran into them." He throws his thumb over his shoulder.

Finding myself gawking, I look at Jonathan.

"The outfit, right?" Jonathan asks. "It's for some Valentine's Day party." He turns. "What was that party called again? House of ..."

"Whacks," Kenny says. "Like 'whack your ass.' 'Whacked out.'"

"Right," I say, not sure if this is *Candid Camera* or for real.

"You want to come?" he asks.

"Me? I mean," I say, shaking my head. He's half naked.

"It's fun. PVC, leather, or discipline-chic required. Or you can wear an evening gown. Your boy there'll have to do black tie. Unless you're hiding something I don't know." He winks, giving me a mock shocked face.

"What?" I'm still waiting for one of them to laugh and point to the camera.

"Fetish party," Kenny says. "All the kinky people go: dominants, submissives, sadists, masochists. Thirty-five bucks gets you in the door."

You're serious, aren't you?

"Free drinks. Free canapés. And all sorts of *fun* people. You can find about anything you want. But you have to go in gear: leather, PVC, dog collars, and ball gags. At least formalwear. For those who *only* want to watch."

"Oh, no. That's ... No." I shake my head.

"How about you?" he asks, looking at Jonathan flirtatiously.

"No thanks. I've got all the kink I can handle." He blows a kiss to me. "You got a six-shooter with that outfit?"

"Ten-gallon hat?" I ask.

"I'm not doing western. Not straight western anyway." He growls playfully at me. "And I don't have a six-shooter; it's a forty-five automatic."

"A forty-five? Automatic?" I ask.

"Colt. Big, *brawny* thing." He says this like he's talking about a boyfriend.

"Why?" Scott asks.

"Oh, long story: When I asked for deposit money on my apartment, my mother found out where it was and about flipped. You know—gangs,

253

drive-by shootings—the usual sketchy neighborhood stuff they like to show on the news to scare the pee out of everyone. So after she talked to my father, they agreed to give me the money only if I promised to take protection. So the forty-five." He shrugs. "I took it. Makes my roommates nervous. But they secretly like it being there. I tell them to imagine some crackhead coming through the window, out of his head, ready to rape and kill, and *boom*! his innards're on the wall. Feels like safety."

"No thanks," Scott says. "I do *not* like guns. Too many bad things can happen."

Kenny dismissively shakes his head. "Nah. It can be a hoot. Blow off steam. You pretend the target is whatever you hate, and *blam, blam, blam*. I used to shoot guns with my dad when I was a kid. I mean, it's there. It's got bullets in a clip, which I only put in when I go to target practice. Which is about never. I only took it for the cash, anyway."

"Mercenary," Scott says.

"Sure you don't want to come along?" he asks Scott. "Got a dog collar I can loan you."

"Not this time."

"Kinky chicks. The kind you don't bring home to mother," he says, imitating Rick James. "Do things to you didn't even know could be done."

"Sounds like fun," Scott says. "But ..."

"Oh, Little Red Ride Me Good." He puts his hands on his hips. "Must stay true. You don't have to *do* anything. Watch. It can be fun: trolls and chickens; conservative Miss Accountant turning into Mistress Mayhem, May I Have Another; over-the-top porn; free *cock*-tails."

Scott shakes his head.

"Next time," Kenny says, putting his duster back on.

"Aren't you going to freeze?" I ask.

"No," he says. "Too hot for that." He swings his arm around in a wide circle and then thrusts out his hip right as a finger lands on it. "*Sssssssss.*" He grins.

What? Am I his mother? What's next, nagging them about getting cherubs and hearts up on the wall or having an Easter egg hunt? Please, woman. It's like those suburban clones Ron made me dress up as are taking me over.

CHAPTER 40
BOOK OF LOVE
—JENNIFER—

A breeze gently tugs at the envelope in my hand. While it feels good to get outside and away from the loft, I'm not liking doing it as a gofer.

At Milan Does Chicagoland, I was the boss. I sent interns to do this kinda work. With this tour, I'm the chimp, running errands and fetching.

Lifting my face to the sun, which has broken through the clouds, I try letting the warmth cheer me up.

Only five months ago, I was packing to move back home. *In time for Christmas, even.*

I'd been so frustrated with my life. Then, after the news report on Charlene, I really needed someone to talk to, and of course, he wasn't around. As usual. That tore it. I began to see how fake everything in my life was. I was leaving. I stuffed my things into my satchel until I couldn't fit anything more.

Right then, as if on cue, he came home. He got so earnest and all concerned, asking me what was wrong.

If that satchel had been bigger, I might not be here right now, doing this bullshit scut work.

Instead, everything flooded out: "Joie de Vivre" was only about sex, the band was a lie, the loft was like being on TV, he was fake and never had time for us, his songs were fake, and Charlene didn't slip and fall, but she had to have been murdered. And this sounded like nonsense when I heard myself saying it.

255

He asked me to slow down and start at the beginning, which was "Joie de Vivre," and I told him it wasn't about us; it was about him and any woman. The next minute, I was listening to him play a smutty song and "Joie" side by side, and then somehow, I ended up on the wrong side of real; I had to prove *I* wasn't being fake to *him*.

It's all been so ridiculous and embarrassing.

Of course, then he'd made me smile, talking about my clothes and stuff; he was going to do the picking and let me do the putting. I kinda hated him for that, but I loved him more.

Now I'm a gofer. I shoulda stayed pissed.

Pushing open the door to the Addison 'L' station, I let out a disgusted hiss. *And come on, Charlene—falling? Drunk? That's too stupid to be real.*

After that night of weirdness had come more: the holidays. For the first time I can remember, I didn't have a tree for Christmas. Visiting the parents wasn't any better. Sure, they had a tree, but their place didn't feel like home anymore.

For New Year's, we'd been planning this huge party at the loft, but Jonathan and Scott had taken so much time off for the band that they couldn't get New Year's Eve off.

At first getting left on my own for New Year's really annoyed me, but I got to thinking I could party with the girls like I had before I lived in a big-city loft and had a rising–rock star boyfriend.

New Year's Eve started almost normal. We met at Wendy's place like usual. Of course she looked as if she'd stepped right off a page in *Cosmo*: a body-hugging black dress, with red-tipped frills along her cleavage and the hem of her skirt; fishnets; whore-red pumps. Chris showed up in her usual baggy clothes that hide her large breasts and hips, as if it would be bad for a guy to be attracted to her physically in any way. She wants men to lust only after her talent.

We were missing only Charlene.

After we had a toast for her, they gave me shit for not coming out with them anymore.

I had to admit that they were right: It had been ages since we'd all been together for a night out. When I lived at home, all I could think about was going out and getting away from home.

I really did miss doing nothing but messing around with these guys. So this New Year's Eve, I got to hang with them.

But we had to get to Neo before it got full; we had to have seats at the bar.

"Everyone bundled up?" Wendy asked. "Single digits. Windy."

I tucked in my scarf and pulled my hat down over my ears. My gloves slid on last. We looked like Eskimo bunnies for the dash to the car.

"Let's go," Wendy said, opening the front door of her building.

A blast of frigid air hit us.

"Holy fuck!" Chris said.

"Out, out, out," Wendy said.

We run-walked down the sidewalk and around the corner of the building to her car. The wind cut straight through my hat and scarf. It felt like I had ice crystals inside my nostrils. Wendy unlocked her door as I ran around to the passenger side. The snow was more like ice; I nearly slipped twice. Wendy got in and unlocked the back door for Chris right as the wind picked up. I ducked my face into my scarf, to which clung bits of ice grown from my breath.

"Hurry up! Hurry up!" I stomped my feet.

Wendy lifted the lock of the front door, and I scrambled onto the hard plastic of the seat and slammed the door closed. It's a freezer in there, but at least there's no wind.

"Heater," Chris said. "Hurry."

Stiff as a board, my whole body shivered. As the car started warming up, cold air poured out from the vents. I blocked mine with my hand as plumes of our breath frosted the windshield.

"Give it a minute. Heats up quick," Wendy said.

Finally warmed up, we started on the road, and Chris complained she hadn't met anyone worth dating in ages, and Wendy didn't make it better, saying Chris only liked to date "poser artfags." Which is true. Her last lover, whatever-it-was-friend, Fey. No last name. It broke Chris up when they split, but he was such a freak—not really a boy, not a girl. He was worse than Kenny by about a hundred times.

This brought up me and Jonathan, and then the accumulation of all the things I'd wanted to tell someone but had never had the chance to:

that Scott pushes Jonathan around; not directly, but in his attitude, as if he's *the* boss; and that Scott makes no secret of not liking me and I suspect he's trying to get us to break up, all sneaky like, because everything's "for the band" and the band's so damned important. Plus Scott knows I have to worry about sounding like I'm a jealous control-freak girlfriend. It's like he's jamming me between himself, Jonathan, and the band, and I'm sure he's going to make Jonathan do something he doesn't want to. "For the band." I wriggled my fingers in quotation marks.

"He's jealous," Wendy said, and then she went off about his being queer, but I told her, "You'd think after Martin, I'd see it," and Chris agreed with me. Wendy simply shrugged, shaking her head.

By then we'd turned from Fullerton onto Clark at the building with the glazed white-tile corner that looked like a castle turret. We snagged a spot right after I said, "Parking karma," making quotation marks with the first two fingers of both hands.

We run-walked again, almost jumping into the alley leading to Neo to get out of the wind, and didn't slow up until we got to the door, passing the armless mannequin of a woman and the slideshow of Gothic images on the brick wall: the skulls, crucifixes, mausoleums, and dramatically made-up mourners. There we pulled open Neo's tin-encased door, and music poured into the alley. Kissing the bouncers as they waved us in, Wendy led us past the cashier's window and up the stairs to the poured-concrete bar. We grabbed three stools and ordered beers and shots.

This felt more like home with family than either my parents' house or the loft.

It's also the last time I can remember feeling really good.

Since then I've been able to keep my head together by telling myself that everything that's wrong is only the stress of the gigs, the constant rehearsing, and the worst of it—finding out that having a recording contract *doesn't* mean you make any money.

Scott dropped that bomb one rehearsal after a meeting with Wax Trax! about a full-length CD. He'd also asked about getting the royalties and was told, basically, that that might not ever happen.

I could almost hear the plans we'd made shattering on the concrete floor. No one could believe it.

Then Scott explained how this worked: "Sure. We *will* get our cut of the *profits*. That's the key word: 'profits.'"

That means that the EP has to earn enough money to pay back the advance money the label "loaned us against earnings" for the recording sessions and mixing sessions. No expense was spared of course—"only the best for our artists." Once it's out, the sales have to pay the cover artist, the layout professionals, and for the insert's printing costs, the jewel cases, and pressing. Then there's also the sales force going out to get the CD into the stores, the distributor, shipping, and of course company overhead, including the salaries of accountants and management. Basically, if the disc sells well, it might break even. If it goes gold, it could mean some profits, which we would split 50–50 with Wax Trax!, and then the royalties that actually get paid would then have to go pay Nancy back first, and then to cover the band's costs, and then, if there are a few bucks left, we would then split that four ways.

Tours sponsored by the record company play out the same way. The band busts their asses, and the company gets paid for rent on the spaces, security, promotions, sales, and whatever else they can think of first. What's left over *then* gets split between the band and the company. The same holds true with merchandise.

As for gigs at nightclubs and bars, Wax Trax! can't be bothered with them; the money's not worth the effort. That's no different from before the band had a deal; once the costs are paid off, Nancy will get paid, and then what's left gets split.

In other words, don't quit your day job.

Scott summed up what everybody was thinking when he pretended to grab a waist in front of him, and thrust his pelvis at the imaginary ass, saying, "Bend over. I'll drive."

Right after that rude news, a huge, expensive fashion show, for which Wendy was one of the financial backers, started—*Milan does Chicagoland: Italian Windy City*—and that was murder. There were all these jerk-off producers, driving me nuts with a million pointless questions, showing me which models they *might* want and those they *did* want, and telling me they needed this there at whatever time, demanding to know "why's Cindy working for Alexander now, and me on Wednesday?" and to "make sure my name is spelled right"; and my pager was going off all the time, even when at night when I was trying to sleep; and I was constantly beat, dragging my ass up the stairs. All I ever wanted to do is nothing, but it seemed like there was another rehearsal or shoot every night.

I had no clue what they were rehearsing for. The EP was out. There was no recording coming up, and no gigs. Jonathan had a few new ideas, but what's the point if you're getting screwed?

When I asked, Scott gave me an earful about not having to front the money for the recording, mixing, or production and said that they get wholesale prices on our own CDs, which they can sell themselves, and that they need to be prepared, and he kept lecturing me, and I tuned him out.

A week later, things got better. For a night.

I'm on my way home after walking for some time, knowing my life as TV show would continue: I'd open the door, and the place would be full of people, and they'd be loud and stay until late.

I need someplace to get some peace. Like in a real home.

I sigh, pushing the key into the lock and opening the door.

"Yep," I say, seeing Scott, Jonathan, AnnMarie, and Nancy. "Gang's all here."

I turn to skate to Northside, have dinner, a beer or three, and wait for them to leave.

"Hang on," Scott says as he hangs up the phone.

"Guys," he says, raising his thick arms. "It's official. We're opening for Book of Love. At Metro."

I stop and turn back. He's got on an expression I've never seen before: actual joy.

"Cabaret Metro?" Jonathan asks. "Our Metro? On Clark Street?"

He nods.

Whoops erupt, even from me.

The buzz of playing Metro lasts one night.

The next day, Scott's back to being Mister Business, the Bossman. The whole band is here again when I get home, sitting at our table, planning how they are going to take advantage of this. They don't even notice me. And I'm the only one who has actual experience running large shows.

"Hey guys," I say. "You do know that I produce shoots and shows all the time. Part of what I do for a living. Moving people around different locations, taking care of sets, the seating, making sure the right clothes arrive—"

"This is a bit different," Bossman says. "We know who and what every time, but we don't have the hundreds of thousands of dollars to spend every night on craft services and assistants. We've got to run with the minimum people, and on a shoestring."

"That doesn't matter," I say.

"Matters everything. It's *our* money. And we don't have much."

I look at him, and he at me. Neither of us blinks.

That he dismissed me so quickly pisses me off, but I've never actually risked my own money. So I listen.

It boils down to the fact that the only way we'll actually make any money, without being a top-ten pop act, is direct merchandise sales and self-managed tours, which we'll have to take all the risk for. It'll be all our money down to rent the venues, our money to promote, print up shirts, make wall hangings, buy the CDs wholesale, rent the van, and pay for gas, hotels, and food for our tour, starting with Cabaret Metro and ending wherever we can afford to go on a Midwest tour.

Scott calls it "a great opportunity" and then divides up the work between them to find out costs for a truck, gas, hotel rooms, food, insurance, and whatever else he thought they needed.

I'd sat on the couch, eavesdropping. *Prick.*

That meeting ignites five weeks of chaos: phone calls, more meetings, and grabbing meals at ten at night and frequently at two in the morning. When they aren't working at their restaurants, they're rehearsing, signing agreements, booking venues and hotels and a van, trying to get deals on printing T-shirts and backdrops, and buying their own CDs from Wax Trax!, putting down deposits using cash advances and exhausting one credit card after another.

Me? I've been left doing chimp work: fetching things, making calls strictly to find out contact names. Stuff I've always delegated.

Like my having to go pick up the paperwork for Metro today. *Fetch, girl, fetch!*

261

The train pulls into the Lake Street station, and I make the long transfer to the O'Hare line, the folder flapping as I march through the tunnel, slipping around the buskers and other riders.

It's not as if I've had any chance to talk with Jonathan. Mostly he's consumed with the tour, working his next restaurant shift, or sleeping. When I do get time with Jonathan, he's only partially there. I get it; I really do. But I *need* to talk to him, at least once in a while. I get lonely, in spite of always being around people, or his body lying next to mine.

My train comes almost as soon as soon as I step onto the platform. *Lucky with the trains.*

Then, about five days before Metro, the tour comes together, leaving us dead broke and with six credit cards maxed out. We had to ask Randal if he could take only half the rent. Scott decided we shouldn't take any more money from Nancy, because we still owed her for the recording sessions, and anyway, she'd already hinted her bank was closing.

We haven't been busted like this even after Scott quit his job. We never had debt then.

In the press releases and promotional material, Jonathan's billing it as the "Micherigan Tour" after Lakes Michigan and Erie: Cabaret Metro in Chicago; the Oriental Theater in Milwaukee; Merlyn's in Madison, Wisconsin; Jane's Tavern in West Lafayette, Indiana; Radio Radio in Indianapolis; the Lighthouse in Cincinnati; Jackie Lee's Night Club in Akron, Ohio; the Newport Music Hall in Columbus; and, finally, Frankie's Inner City in Toledo, Ohio. It spans nine cities in ten days; they'll be staying in seven hotels, and Jonathan's mother's and Tanya's houses in Columbus. Boxes full of T-shirts, CDs, and silk-screened wall hangings have all arrived and sit in stacks against the wall. Because of minimum orders, it's more than we can possibly take with us on the road.

Between the hearse, Kenny's car, and a van, they have room for six people: Ron's working as a roadie and photographing the tour in addition to tossing in his hearse. Kenny's the other roadie, and sales boy for the merchandise, as well as driving his own car.

"This is our shot. Let's not blow it," Scott said this afternoon, right before sending me out to fetch the paperwork for Metro. "Don't forget to grab gyros on the way back."

Yep, that's me: gofer-chimp-ATM.

While Scott not taking me seriously and having me fetching things for them while asking me to pay for most everything annoys the hell out of me, what really pisses me off is that Jonathan never even *asked* me to help out—not in any significant way. I do production work all the time. I do it for a *living*.

Trying to not be too tempted to "accidentally" lose these papers I'm fetching for them, I turn to the window and watch the train emerge from the underground tunnel, rise up to the elevated tracks, and pass through all the buildings. I imagine it would suck to live in one of the apartments flanking the tracks. *Trains, 24-7. How do you sleep?*

From the North Avenue stop, it's a quick walk to Friar's Grill. I pay for the gyros and fries. *Walking ATM.*

Back at the loft, I set out each of the tin containers on our table. Scott sits next to me. I lay the folder next to his elbow. He nods.

Can't say thank you? Even for lunch?

We unwrap the foil from around the gyros, and steam bursts out with the smell of spiced lamb and garlic. They tear into the shards of seasoned lamb and pita, a stream of white sauce dribbling down each of their chins. Hungry and tired as well, I bite into my gyro; it's fatty, hot and full of garlic, cumin, yogurt, tahini, and dill.

A couple of minutes later, I'm full and put down what's left of my gyro. Scott's already done, having torn out big bites. My lover's still working on his, and once he swallows the last inch of it, he sucks the juice off his fingers.

"So," I say, "when do I get to see you guys?"

"We'll be back June second," Scott says.

"I mean in concert."

"Well," he says, "I don't … know."

I ugly up a frown at him.

"At Metro, we need someone to sell the merchandise. Kenny can't get the night off, so …"

"But—"

"Look," he says. "We've got roughly seventeen thousand dollars in credit card debt. Every time we take a breath, those bastards pile on interest. We're all taking two weeks off work. We're completely broke. If we don't sell this merchandise"—he waves his hand at the stacks of boxes—"we're screwed. No rent money, no food money, and we'll be working for MasterCard and Visa for the rest of our lives. Yes, we'll make something from Metro, but it's punk. We're the opening act. They expect us to be grateful to even step onstage. Sales of merchandise is the only way we'll make any money. We've already gotten the first of six credit card bills. Over nine hundred in minimum payments. Randal's already holding off the Harmen Company for the other half of rent for this month. We need cash now simply to make sure we have a home to come back to next month."

I look at Jonathan.

He raises his eyebrows.

"We really need you to come through," Scott says, "with many hundreds of dollars in sales. A thousand. Two, even. Help us keep this roof over *all* of our heads."

I sigh. *Same as it ever was.*

Bossman Scott stuffs three fries into his mouth.

"How about on the road," I say. "Kenny will be selling—"

"Jennifer," Bossman says, "this is not about you. Another person means more food and another hotel room. Another car means more gas. In other words, spending more money we don't have. Can't do it. Not for anyone."

Jonathan's frowning as if he's looking at photos from a car crash.

"I'll pay for myself. *My* own hotel room."

"Okay. Well then, I'll let you make the choice," Scott says, holding up a hand, fingers spread. "Because of the extra expenses, do we?" He pinches his thumb. "Lose electricity?" He pinches his forefinger. "Gas." He pinches his middle finger. "Telephone." He pinches his ring finger. "Or is it Visa you'd like to avoid?" He pinches his pinky. "MasterCard? Or were you thinking that this place is too big?"

"Scott," Jonathan says, holding a hand up. "Got it."

"Sure I get it," I say, crossing my arms. "Jennifer: everyone's walking automatic teller machine."

"'Scuse me?" Scott snaps.

"When did it become my responsibility to pay for everything here?" Jonathan starts.

"I have to pay for electricity, gas, telephone, all the credit cards, rent? When did you two concoct this plan?"

Jonathan shakes his head at me.

"I never said that," Scott says imperiously.

"You told me that if *I* want to spend *my own* money to see you, *I* have to choose what *not* to pay. Where's you paying for anything?"

"What the hell do you mean?" Scott demands.

"That I'm paying for way more than half of living here, and you treat me like a genital disease: it felt good getting me, but you hate having me around."

"Jennifer," Jonathan says, reaching over to touch my arm. "That's not—"

"The fuck it isn't," I say, yanking my arm away. "I'm keeping this place afloat. And I want some say in what I do."

"See!" Scott shouts, jumping up, thrusting his finger at me. "That is exactly why I should never have let you move in."

CHAPTER 41
THE BETTER THINGS GO
—JENNIFER—

The stage lights go black. The audience roars.

I bite my lip and then look at the backstage pass again: a white fabric sticker on my shirt with "Cabaret Metro" in slashing blue letters at the top of a blue square, and *Book of Love* stamped there in smeared black ink.

God-damn rocks. Mercurial Visions just opened for Book of Love. At Metro.

"Joie! Joie! Joie!" the audience starts chanting, stomping their feet, whistling, and clapping.

My song.

"Joie! Joie! Joie!" The noise gets louder and louder.

From the blacked-out stage, the first notes sound. Cheers explode. The lights blaze.

"Where there's love," Jonathan sings, "there are ghosts."

My body is on fire. I grab onto a box edge to keep from floating over the stage and then out over the audience. They'd look up and wonder, "How can she do that?!"

When the music stops, the lights fall dark and the cheers grow so loud, like thunder. As loud as if I were onstage, bowing.

A moment later, Scott comes around a corner from the stage, pumping his fist in the air; his torn-up jeans, tight black shirt, and black boots make him look exactly like the rock star he is right now.

Popping out from behind a scrim, Ron kneels, his camera flashing rapidly three times at Scott.

I push myself between some travel boxes. Scott shouldn't see me; he wants me at the table, selling T-shirts and CDs. But there's no way I'm missing being backstage at Metro for this moment. *Not after all I've done.*

Smiling wider than usual, Nancy appears next, the slit in the long, slinky black dress flying open, exposing her long legs. The camera continues its hail of flashes. Flipping up two fingers like horns, AnnMarie appears next in a short black dress, which here transforms her to sexy. When Jonathan rounds the corner, he shambles off stage, his long shirt flying open, the sweat pouring down his chest, glistening in the camera's flashes.

Stepping out from between the boxes, I hug Jonathan. We kiss.

Flashing, Ron's camera captures us here, backstage at Metro; it's a shot of the real me.

Soaked with sweat, Jonathan smells like he's just had sex.

A big man with long dark hair taps him on the shoulder. "You need to get your equipment gone. Ya got ten minutes."

Book of Love's roadies are rolling boxes toward the stage.

"Whoa," Scott says. "Jennifer. What're you doing here?"

"Chris has got the stand," I say. "We were dead."

"Now's the rush. People are"—he shakes his head—"I ... Christ!" He gives a curt wave of his hand.

"I deserve the whole five minutes I've been back here," I say, but he's already turned his back to me.

"Yes, you do," Jonathan says. "But could you go down and help Chris now? Can't talk. Gotta get everything gone." He turns to talk to some backstage hand who is pulling at his shoulder.

"I was *already* leaving," I say to his back.

I walk through the backstage to the stairs, remembering all the times I've been out there in the audience, watching, and wanting so much to be onstage, with everyone watching *me*, holding *my* fists in the air—and now I'm off to sell CDs.

After my last fight with Scott, I didn't think I'd be here tonight. I imagined that I wouldn't be living in the loft any longer either. But

Jonathan smoothed things over. He's like the devil with that silver tongue of his. Scott agreed to let things said in anger go. I agreed to be the smiling salesgirl, but without apologizing for wanting more say in things. That I let lie. *For now.*

A lot of people look like they're leaving, and the stairs are getting crowded. It takes me a couple of minutes to get to the bottom. There's a mob of people at our little fold-out card table, and Chris is answering questions like mad, holding a T-shirt out to one person and taking his money while three others hold CDs up, cash in hand, and I shove my way through the crowd to our table and start taking money from the people wagging their hands at Chris, and people are pushing and asking "how much is this?" and "how much is that?," ignoring the signs that tell them, and asking me to hold the wall hanging up, and I catch some guy trying to walk off with a CD. I grab it back, but I can't do anything else, not even call a bouncer, 'cause I'm back gathering tens and twenties, and counting out singles, and I'm not sure if everyone I think has paid really has, but we've run out of CDs on display, so I reach into a box underneath and pull a tall stack out, and someone's trying to get a discount for buying one of each thing, and Chris grabs some change from the stack of bills in her lap, and then more and more, and then she stuffs it into her pocket, but I need change now, and three people try to buy shirts at once, and *damn* it's busy. But after a few minutes, it's down to two people deep, and then only one person, and then it's empty around the table.

"Thank god you got back," Chris says. "I was going nuts."

"Sorry. I planned to come back earlier. But Scott got into this hissy fit. Didn't expect any rush. I mean, Book of Love's playing right now. Who leaves?"

"There'll probably be a couple of people now and then. Almost no one was here when Mercurial Visions was playing."

Taking a deep breath, I roll the wall hangings back up and straighten CDs out, and then I start refolding T-shirts. We could only afford medium and large. Short, skinny people'll get stuck looking like they're in their parents' clothes. Everything looks as good as it's going to get on our meagre sales stand. Behind us are the sample T-shirts hanging on a folding screen—one showing the front, "Mercurial Visions: Live," and one the back, "Micherigan Tour '89"—and a silkscreened wall hanging open. Next to us is the large booth for Book of Love, its display packed with four different T-shirt designs, many different buttons, and official programs. Two people sit inside, looking bored, as "I Touch Roses" fills the hall around us.

Three girls step out of the bathroom, dressed in tight jeans, thick-soled shoes, and hoop earrings, their cutoff shirts showing belly piercings. They giggle as they walk up the stairs leading to the concert. Now the only people here are working: us, the Book of Love salespeople, and the two chicks taking tickets at a large black stand sitting dead center of the hall. One of them is Vero, whom I sort of know from hanging out here, and I wave hey. The vaulted eighteen-foot-high ceilings make the lobby feel empty.

"I sold about, what, twenty-some T-shirts and thirty, forty CDs. I don't know how many hangings," Chris says, moving her hand over the CD-covered table. "Plus what you sold. Close to a grand, I think. More, maybe."

"Should make Scott happy," I say. Then I grin at Chris. "Hey. You want to go up and catch some of the show?"

"Me? Oh, yeah," Chris says.

"Make sure you're back before the encore, okay?"

"Sure," Chris says, loping toward the stairs up to the concert hall. "I'll be back before they finish."

"Get me a beer," I yell, but the music is pounding and she's already started up the stairs. I sit down in the folding chair and run a finger along the open wall hanging Chris created—the image of a man's torso stretching up, reaching off the fabric and into space, in silver on a black background, like a photo negative. You'd think it would be enough for him to get free art. *But expecting her to sit here for free too? She deserves some fun.* I stick my tongue out at Scott.

Along the bottom, the words "It's safer this way/Remember ..." run in matching silver tones.

Should have used a line from "Joie." We will, once we have the money.

The money.

I sit bolt upright.

Chris has all the money. I've got no change. If she loses it? Shit!

Leaping out of the chair, I take two steps toward the stairs before remembering the merchandise I'm babysitting. I stop.

"Or are you getting me a beer?" I ask out loud.

"No," I answer myself. *Didn't hear me. Definitely not.*

"Goddamn it!" I hiss. "How could you forget the money?"

Idiot intern move. Ex-intern on any of my shoots. Now I gotta get this solved.

The two at the Book of Love stand look bored. I consider asking them to watch my stuff for about two seconds. *Even more stupid than forgetting in the first place.*

Hanging next to the red velvet ropes cordoning off the outside doors are the two ticket takers, including Vero. She's always been cool. *Better than losing all that money.*

"Hey, Vero," I say to her. "Could you watch our stand for a couple of minutes? Chris took off with the change. Need to go grab her."

There's no one in the lobby right now. Veronica looks at the other ticket taker.

You need to say yes. Please.

The other ticket taker shrugs. Veronica shrugs.

"But," Veronica says as she comes over to the card table. "It'll cost. A smoke." She sticks her hand out.

I slap the rest of the pack into her palm and then take off, running up the half flight of stairs to a landing where the stairs split: one flight to the left, one to the right.

"Which one? Which one? Come on!"

I jog up the left flight. *Please be right.*

At the back of the main floor, I stop. I glance over the people crowding the back bar and don't see her. I slide between people toward the stage, scanning faces as I go. Lights blaze and change color, transforming all the faces I see to howling demons and then, quickly, into screaming human fans. Then "Tubular Bells" crashes through my body. It's sinister, so loud and disorienting—as if I'll see Linda Blair floating above the audience, her head turning in circles.

All that goddamned money. Scott's waiting for something like this to happen.

"Where the hell are you, Chris?" I shout into the music.

I squeeze into the audience, sliding toward the stage, the bodies more tightly packed with each person I pass.

Dodging flying elbows, thrashing heads, and lit cigarettes waving around my face, I get so close to the stage there's no space to go forward, and no one will move.

"Where are you, Chris?"

This is the perfect time for Bossman to walk into the lobby.

I tilt my head back. "Oh, come on," I yell. "Where—"

Keep your head, girl. Think shoot gone bad. Calm, cool, and collected.

I take a deep breath.

We hate standing in the back, right? We always try to get up front. Not center stage if it's too packed. So which side?

I look at the right of the stage and then the left. *Useless. Can't see shit.*

Whaddya expect, girl?

It's fifty-fifty. Standing here's worse than choosing wrong.

Taking off to the right, I search every face around me as each suddenly glows red, blue, and then white, and then falls to an outline, and then blazes red again as the stage lights change. About twenty feet from the stage edge, I can't push any farther. I strain to recognize her face.

Nothing.

Fine. She's not here. The other side now.

I turn back to fight my way across the undulating mass of bodies.

Come on, Chris. Where are you? Stay someplace I can see you. Don't lose that money. Don't be downstairs, Scott.

Someone grabs my arm.

I turn, saying "Scott, I—"

Chris stares at me, eyes wide open.

Leaning close, I shout, "The money!"

"Oh, crap." I don't hear her but only see her lips move. She reaches into her pocket and hands me a wad of bills. "Sorry," she mouths.

Shoving the money deep into my front pocket, I push my way back through the dazzling, color-changing faces. I'm sure someone has been turned away, because Vero has no money. I take the stairs two at a time, turn on the landing, and hurl myself down the final flight, and as I round the corner, I see no one guarding the table.

"Shit!"

I jump to the floor and start running to the table. *Please. Nothing's missing. Nothing's—*

There he is, standing a yard away, hands on his hips: Jonathan. "Watching the show?"

"I—"

He waves his hand at the table, shaking his head. "I'm counting on you. We all are."

"Hold on, here," I say, looking around for Veronica.

"What? You were up catching more of the show."

I shake my head, and then find Veronica's standing at the ticket stand, talking with the other ticket taker. I wave her over.

She strolls to the table.

I won't look at him until he understands that's *not* what happened. *Not even close.*

"Did anyone come while I was gone?" I ask her.

"No. Quiet," Veronica says. "No one'll be here until the show's over."

"*Didn't* leave it alone," I say to his stern frown. "*Chris* wanted to see some of the show. She kept the change. Accidentally. I had to go get it. Vero was here the whole time."

His frown softens. Then he purses his lips, nodding.

Veronica picks up a CD. "Cool." She turns it over, reading the song list. "Can I have one? For covering you here."

"Well ..." I say, hating that he's waiting as if this is a test of how committed I am. I sigh.

"Come on," Veronica says. "They only cost you guys a buck. Least you can do after all the times I let you in free."

I want to give it to her. I *owe* her.

"They're not mine," is all I can come up with to say.

"A buck?"

"You weren't here. I mean ..."

"I needed a light," Veronica says. She scoffs.

I look to Jonathan. He raises an eyebrow.

I nod. "Sure. Yes. Take it."

"Thanks," Veronica says, walking back to the ticket stand.

"Don't. I know. Stupid to forget the money in the first place. Stupid to leave. To have gone backstage. I've fired people for less than this," I say, sitting down in the chair. "I'll pay for the CD to keep the receipts in balance."

"No," Jonathan says. "Not that. Nothing bad happened. *Could* have. Think if someone stole stuff."

"I did. And, now it turns out it's a good thing I'm not going on tour. You don't have to worry about me surprising you backstage. Or forgetting the change, or giving away a CD." I pick one up and run my finger across the title: "Joie de Vivre."

"This is your future too," he says, sweeping his hand over the table.

"Our future. Yes. I know. But I had to get the change."

"How did it get forgotten? This is—"

"*Don't* scold me." I put the CD back down. "I and Chris, *both*, are here because we want this to work. We *both* gave up our nights to work here, *for free*. Chris even gave you artwork. That you're selling. *For free*."

"But—"

"But what? Scott won't approve? Of Chris catching a couple of songs in exchange for all her free labor?"

"Now, hold up."

"No, you wait a moment, here. No one gives and gives and gives, for nothing—not even those girls who are so desperate to be on the cover of a magazine. We give them things. Little things. They cost us nothing but mean a lot. Shows we're not raping them for their time. I want to feel the same here."

He's silent but so wants to say something; his teeth are tapping together.

"So far," I say, "we've sold twenty some T-shirts and thirty, forty CDs. I'm guessing. Not sure about the hangings, but we've moved more than a few. We've pulled in close to a grand, I'm thinking."

He nods and almost smiles but keeps silent.

"I'll pay for the one I gave Vero."

He shakes his head. "No. I'll just tell him I gave it away as a promo to a club owner. Easier."

Why, thank you soooo much. My smile twists into the tone I think this in.

I see Chris walking down the stairs and hope he doesn't says anything to her.

A roar erupts above us. Book of Love has finished. Next will be the encore, and then the flood of people leaving.

"Let me hurry up and finish loading our stuff. I'll be here as soon as I can to help. Then we're meeting at Exit to celebrate." He smiles for the first time.

"Sure," I say without enthusiasm.

He turns and jogs to the stairs leading to the stage.

Everything's gotten so fucked up since Mercurial Visions put out that EP. It's only getting worse the better things go for them.

I don't want this—their success.

CHAPTER 42
EXIT
—JENNIFER—

After we park on North Avenue, the three of us walk past the Old Town Ale House to Wells and then past the Second City theater and across the street to Exit. Chris and I hello the bouncer, who's slouching on his stool outside the door. He waves us in with a fistful of dollars, shifting on his stool to open the door. Jonathan follows us into the front bar. Music pounds through the room. A lot of the guys have on black leather jackets, jeans, and boots; the chicks mostly wear either short black skirts with fishnet stockings and granny shoes or long, flowing black dresses, going for the vampiress look.

People crowd the glossy black bar of welded-together machine parts: chains, gears, shafts, and metal plates. Small video screens stuck between bottles behind the bar repeatedly show the bloodiest scenes from *Evil Dead II* in slow motion. We push our way along the bar and find AnnMarie and Ron drinking beers at the very end.

"The others're in back, dancing," Ron says as his camera flashes at us.

Grabbing my hand, Jonathan leads us through the passage at the rear of the room, past the bathrooms and cigarette machine, and into the back room. It's like the Colosseum; rows of bench seats all around the sides of the room look down into a dance pit covered with a dome-like iron cage. A chainsaw hangs from the very top. We lean over the waist-high wall surrounding the pit and watch the swarm of jerking and twitching bodies.

"Stainless Steel Providers" comes on; Jonathan starts pulling me down the stairs into the pit. Twisting my hand away, I wave him on without me. He bounds down the stairs, and I lean on the wall to watch him dance, my forearms on the cage. Scott's easy to see; he's big, like a gladiator, using his size and arms to hack out space for himself to dance in. Nancy's almost next to him, but she's like a hooker working a room; she gives a lusty move with this person, then another with the next person, and another with the next, and the next. Long hair flailing, Jonathan dances alone in this crowd, moving as if he's with an invisible lover.

Once the mood of the songs changes too much, the three of them climb out of the pit: the gladiator, the whore, and the lover, his skin glistening with sweat.

"Shots to celebrate," Scott says, leading us back through the passageway to the front bar.

The bartender lines up seven shot glasses. I squeeze myself in right behind Jonathan. As the bartender finishes pouring each shot, one of us grabs it.

"To Metro," Bossman says. "To finally cracking the big time."

The shots drained, glasses clatter to the bar, upside down. Another round gets poured. Vodka still burning in my throat, I shake my head.

"Don't be a lightweight," Chris says, grabbing her shot.

"Bad luck if you don't," Jonathan says, handing me the shot.

"To finally making a few bucks," Scott toasts.

I sip it, feel queasy, and set the rest of the shot down.

"By the way, how much did we make tonight?" Scott asks.

"Sold seventy-odd shirts and about ninety CDs," I say. "Probably forty of the hangings. Definitely over two grand. Haven't counted exactly."

"And that's as the opening act," Jonathan says.

"That about covers the van and gas for the tour," Scott says. "Maybe even some of the food. Still have to cover the hotels. And the merchandise. Those goddamned credit cards: the interest. Then rent on the loft." He pegs me with his gaze. "This is no game."

"Yeah. I got it," I say. "The first six times."

"*Reeeally* now?" he asks.

"I produce shows all the time. I run shoots, manage people and money. A hundred times bigger than this. I made sure the booth was handled.

Then I went back so I could catch you guys onstage. For the *encore*. Feel what that's like—"

"Ho, now," he says. "Feel what that's like? To be onstage? In the band? You're not. Ron doesn't strut about onstage, bowing. The applause is for *us*. *We* four. Who *play*. Who *practice*. Who give everything up. Like watching concerts—"

"Look, *Bossman*," I say, "don't you *dare* scold me. I'm not some groupie intern. *You* don't pay me. *I* pay for *your* electricity, gas, telephone, and most of your food. I never see my lover. I live in a TV show, with strangers traipsing around *my* house. At all hours. For *your* band."

"*My* band? Is that all this is to you?"

"Hey, hey," Jonathan says. "We're supposed to be celebrating."

"Mercurial Visions wouldn't even be playing Metro without me. I bankrolled your home slash rehearsing studio, your food, your electricity—all that. Without me, you'd be living in some South Side shithole, playing the corner bar for fifty bucks and a free drink, pretending you have a chance."

"Look, bitch," Scott says, "we *didn't* need you. We certainly don't need you now."

"Don't need me? Really?" I ask, yanking the thick stack money out of the bag and shaking it at him.

Uncertain, his eyes shoot back and forth between the money and me.

"Well, then. Here's what you don't need me for," I throw the stack of bills at him.

The stack bursts in midair. Bills flitter all over the bar, falling on tables, the floor, and people's heads and arms.

"You cunt!" Scott shouts, leaping up to chase down all the bills.

Nancy, AnnMarie, and Ron scramble to snatch up the bills before anyone else does. Jonathan stands there, his mouth gaping.

I storm away and out the door. I don't know if Chris is following me. *Don't give a rat's ass.*

Near North Ave, Chris catches up to me, and we walk in silence to my car. I cannot speak. I'm beyond furious at Jonathan. I want to hear how Scott looked scrambling around for his money, but I turn on the radio instead. Chris silently stares out a window until I drop her off at her car. At the loft, I walk to the mattress and start undressing while Scott's bitchy, condescending speech, his calling me a cunt, and the expression on his face when I hurled the money at him play over and over again in my mind. I stomp to the bathroom. Leaning over the sink, I yank open the water faucet and start splashing my face.

"And you said nothing," I scold Jonathan as if he were in the mirror. "You stood there, mouth hanging open. Didn't even leave the bar. You two deserve each other."

I stare at the water dripping from my nose and chin. "At least I know where I stand: nowhere."

I'm around to pay for dinner. Drive 'em around. Be available to fuck.

"Inspiration?" I shake my head.

"Bullshit," I say to my reflection. "Not this girl."

The soap scrubs up into a thick, white froth.

"This is it."

I rinse the lather from my face.

"I'm not doing this anymore."

After blotting my face dry, I toss the towel into the corner and yank open the door to step back into the silent loft.

Jonathan's standing right by the doorway, which gives me a jolt.

"The money went everywhere," he says. "No idea how much we lost. What the hell's going on?"

"Jesus fucking-ass Christ! Are you stupid? I pay rent. I pay your bills. Pay *his* bills. Pay the *band's* bills. I *am* part of this. I'm your lover. Supposedly. Not some groupie whore or starry-eyed intern he can order around. Come on!"

"Of course," he says. "I see it. I do. Have."

"What the hell, John-boy?"

"I'm working my ass off to—"

"Be a rock 'n' roll star. 'Money for nothing and chicks for free.'"

"Wrong. So I don't wake up some sorry-ass fifty-year-old waiter who could've been. Without this band, without my music, I'm nothing but a fucking waiter. But now that can change; it's there. Right there. An inch away. Years of work. All I need is that one last inch."

"Inch? More like a thousand miles. This rock-star thing?" I shake my head. "You make no money. We're in debt. If we're lucky, this tour will let us pay rent. You still wait tables!"

"I have a *chance*."

"Is this what it's going to be like from now on?"

"Wendy. She loses her job, who'd she be? Can you imagine Chris *not* painting? Charlene? She had that something—before she fell." He takes a breath. "You? What? Going to clubs? Being an assistant whatever? What if your life isn't a twenty-four-hour photo spread? What if you actually *were* on a TV show?"

"What's this shit? Do *not* change the subject."

"At Exit. Just now. You said you lived on TV. Like always—comparing yourself, or what you're doing, to this show or that movie or some character in whatever. As if you're only real if you've seen it on TV."

"My god," I say. "This isn't even about music. Or money. This is a game for you. You *like* pushing us to the brink. Pushing us to almost break up, and then we get to make up. From suffering to 'we're in love' again. Teeter-tottering from one extreme to the other."

"Oh, now who's the one changing the subject here?"

"No. I won't do this anymore."

"Won't do what?"

"I need a smoke," I say.

"What won't you do?"

"This," I say, waving my hand around at the equipment, boxes of merchandise, this TV studio I'm living in.

"It's a bitch," he says, lighting a cigarette and giving it to me. "I know. I've been killing myself like this for years."

"For what? Interviews? Groupies? Your picture on the cover of a magazine? To see yourself on MTV? You wanna look at yourself from the outside?"

"Freedom."

"Oh, come off it. That's so late-night infomercial," I say, blowing out a thick cloud of smoke at him.

"I'm deadly serious," he says, waving away the smoke. "When we make enough money for me to quit my straight job and hire people to tend the stands and lug our shit around, I'm free to concentrate on music.

To simply play, and write, and perform. To make people feel things they might never have before. Or have forgotten feeling. Or thought they'd never feel again."

"I'm not even in that future. What? You need to be free of me?"

I smack his face so hard my hand stings.

"You're free, then. Enjoy it."

CHAPTER 43
C-TOWN
—JENNIFER—

I step onto the skinny sidewalk between the asphalt of the parking lot and the tall fences of rough, wooden slats enclosing all the patios behind the apartment building. I'm supposed to look for a painted ceramic plaque reading "Home Sweet Home." That would be his mom's place.

This is hardly what I expected to be doing a week after throwing the money at Scott and then basically being told I was not part of Jonathan's future plans. He looked so stunned when I smacked him. I was a little surprised myself; that was more Scarlett O'Hara than I knew I had in me.

But after a moment, his expression got so serious and mischievous; I'd never seen anything like that on him—or anyone. It was as if he'd realized he had something devilish to do.

Then he grabbed my hand and pulled us to the mattress. I tried to pull away, but he wouldn't let go. His breath was hot against my cheek.

I'd been so angry, but now I was starting to feel scared, especially when I felt his hand slide between my legs and start up the inside of my thigh. I squeezed my legs closed, pinning his hand.

"Stop it," I said. "Now." I grabbed his wrist and tried to wrench his hand from between my legs.

That imp's grin of his spread across his face. He looked me right in the eyes. I saw his lips start to move. He was mouthing something about being able to do anything he wanted to me.

I'd never been scared like this. His eyes grew so intense.

All at once, he froze. His eyes grew wide, his mouth shaped as if he were saying "Oh."

Then he went slack, sat up, and tried to pull his hand from between my legs.

"I, um," he said, "deserved that smack. I thought you meant ... That you wanted me to—No ..." He shook his head. "It did sting. Does."

Wary, and with my heart still racing, I let go of his wrist and relaxed my legs slightly. He took his hand back and placed it on his lap.

"Well. Jennifer." He said my name so carefully, enunciating each syllable. "I wanted to tell you something earlier. Think you might ... like it."

Better be good.

"June third. Come see us perform. Columbus. I'm staying at my mom's. Just you and I. She'll feed us. Scott doesn't need to know." He nodded his head, looking down at his hands. "Just show up. It's only a six-hour drive."

That night's been impossible to forget. Especially since he left early the next day, and we never had the chance to talk about it anymore. Now, a week later, I'm walking round the noses of cars, looking for a plaque on his mom's door. I'm still trying to sort out what happened, and I hope that being so far from the loft will help me. Instead this whole trip feels like a scene in a movie where the heroine uncovers an insurmountable truth—like this is some kind of ending.

I find the door with the plaque. Grasping the latch, I take a deep breath.

"Okay, girl." I open the gate.

The patio is poured concrete, strips of dirt along three of the sides, filled in with a garden of crabgrass and dandelions. I walk up to the sliding-glass doors and see a gap in the drapes. Before knocking, I turn my head sideways to peek through it. I can't see anything.

I knock.

A chair scrapes. Shoes tap on Formica. The drapes part behind the glass doors. A young chick looks at me. She has red-orange hair with a bright-white streak hanging off to the side, Egyptian cat-eye makeup, a short black skirt, and an *Alien Sex Fiends* T-shirt. She must be his sister Lisa.

Sliding the door open, she turns. "Lover boy," she calls, "your woman is here."

"Thanks for the intro," I say under my breath.

Then she pulls the drapes completely back for me.

Jonathan appears from a hallway and gives me a hug.

Feels good. Hope that's a sign there's no secret to uncover here.

He releases me, and then I notice the smells of frying bacon and freshly cut onion, and then the sounds of sizzling and the steady thunk of a knife on wood. Hunched over a counter, a woman's chopping onions. *His mom.*

"Let's get your stuff up to the room," he says, taking the bag and my hand. "Come on." He pulls me behind him around the corner and up a flight of stairs to a short hallway. There he leads me through one of the three doorways and into a small room with a couch, a desk, and some boxes piled along one wall.

"My mother thinks I should sleep on the couch downstairs and you should sleep here. In my old bedroom. You know—I should be a gentleman. She won't force the issue." He drops the bag on the bed and pulls me to him. "Oh, I've missed you," he says, and then he kisses me. "Let's make love. Right now."

"Oh, no," I say, shaking my head.

"Dinner won't be ready for a while."

"Come on," I say.

"Why not?"

"Your mother."

"She's busy making clam chowder. It won't be ready for an hour. At *least*," he says. "And you're all I've been thinking about since I left."

"I just got out of the car. I'm whipped. What about your mother and your sister?"

"What about them?" he asks, pretending confusion. "Want me to let them know not to disturb us?"

"Don't be stupid."

"Anything for you," he says, his hand slipping down my cheek and along my neck, finally grazing a breast.

I grab his hand, and hold it there for a second.

"No," I say, yanking his hand away. "I can't. Later."

"I'll hold you to that promise," he says and then kisses my forehead. "So. Let's meet Mom then." He pulls me to my feet.

"I just got here."

"If we don't go down, what do you think she'll be imagining we're doing up here, alone? The hanky you're not pankying. She's got a *filthy* mind. All prudes do."

I let him lead me down the stairs and into the kitchen. His mother's stirring in a deep pot.

"Mom," he says.

She turns.

"Jennifer," he says, looking at me. "Jennifer, Mom."

I shake her hand. His mother is as short as he had described, but she's younger looking than I had imagined.

"I've heard a lot about you," Mrs. Starks says.

"Me too," I say.

Then there is only the sound of sizzling.

I stand awkwardly. *Why aren't you saying anything, Jonathan—giving the needed comic relief at this point of the meet-the-parents scene?*

Mrs. Starks smiles pleasantly. "Dear," she says, "could you get the soup tureen?"

I step out of his way and all the way into the living room, where I sit down.

Joining me quickly, he stands next to the couch, laying his hand on my neck.

"So," Lisa says, appearing in the doorway, twisting the shock of white hair around her finger. "When're we going to Crazy Mama's?"

"I figure we'll leave around ten thirty," he says.

"Tonight?" I ask.

"Yep," he says. "We know the owner, and we promised we'd play a gig for him the next time we got back to town. We owe it to him. He always let us play there, even when no one else did. Scott called about an hour ago and said everything's set for a short, unannounced gig. Just a half hour. Cool crowd. Then we'll get to party. Have some fun."

"I'll get to see you guys play twice," I say. "Where is he, anyway?"

"Scott? At Tanya's. With everyone else."

Then his mother comes into the room.

I straighten up quickly. She sits across from us.

"So," I say. "How's it been—the tour I mean?"

"Like I was telling Mom—exhausting. After a show, we pack up the equipment and merchandise. Most of the time before 2:00 a.m. Try to be in bed by three. Up by seven. Hope no one swiped the van. Hit the local diner for breakfast right as the sun's coming up. Stock up on Jolt Cola and Tums. On the road again. Grab Gurber King, McRonald's, Wenchy's, or whatever for lunch on the road. Get wherever we are going. Then we have to find the hotel. Always a pain in the butt. By that time, your brain is cooked: too little sleep, too many hours on the road. Add lousy directions. We got lost in Indianapolis for over three hours."

I feel my eyes glaze over. *I don't need the blow-by-blow. Just tell me how the shows went.*

"Check in. Shower. Nap. Find food. Nap. Get ready for the show. Find out how to get wherever we're playing. Get there. Set up. Play. Break down. Load the gear back on. Head back to the hotel. Crash. Next city. Next."

"Yeah, but," I say, "how have things been *going*?"

"Well. We sold out in Milwaukee and Madison, and almost in West Lafayette and Indianapolis. Good showing in Cincy. Sold out in Akron. The ticket sales have more than covered the guarantees for the venues, the gas, and hotels even. With the CD and T-shirt sales, we're looking at making money—not petty cash. If we keep up like we have here and in Toledo, we'll clear over ten grand. We can pay rent; put a solid dent in the credit card bills."

I humph. Thought we'd actually make money.

"Oh, hey," he says. "I completely forgot. We got a blurb in the *Chicago Tribune*." He jumps up and runs into the kitchen, stranding me with his mother and sister for another awkward scene in this romantic comedy we're playing out.

"Here," he says, holding a page up, with a ballpoint-blue circle around one paragraph. "I know; the review is about Book of Love. But he writes about us. Right here," he says, pointing to the circled words.

The opening act, local club faves Mercurial Visions, held up well next to the popularity of Book of Love. Mercurial Visions' club sound is harder but still synth-pop enough to appeal to the whole crowd, who danced and even knew lyrics to "Joie de Vivre" and "Just Walk Away." Then, lucky for Book of Love fans, a lot of the up-front crowd left as soon as Mercurial Visions finished—the best kind of compliment for an opening act; these people didn't come for the headliners.

CHAPTER 44

CRAZY MAMA'S
—JENNIFER—

"This is the exit," Jonathan says on the way to Crazy Mama's.

I guide us off the freeway and onto Lane Avenue. Soon we're passing along the edge of The Ohio State University. On one side are square, brick projects-like dorms. On the other side are shabby two-story houses with sagging porches, until we turn onto High Street and I can finally see the campus itself. Even at night, it looks like a photo from a college brochure: wide lawns full of trees, and big, imposing brick-and-stone buildings with pointy towers, gables, and columns.

Across from that, I see bars, one after the other, as if there's nothing to do here but study or drink.

Jonathan points to a neon sign for The North Berg, with an arrow pointing downstairs, below Donato's Pizza, and tells me, "That's where it all began one twisted night oh, so many years ago. Playing euchre. We needed a fourth, and Scott volunteered."

After we pass blocks full of bars, restaurants and stores completely take over. Even this late, students fill the sidewalks, most carrying backpacks or wearing OSU clothes in scarlet and gray.

Then Jonathan points to an old theater marquee that reads, in large black letters, "Sat 6/3 Mercurial Visions."

"Tomorrow night," he says.

Then the bars take back the street, this time on both sides. People stand in lines to get to places like Papa Joe's, Travel Agency, Rock 'n'

Roll Palace, and Mean Mister Mustard's. Cars cram the street here, and people are crossing willy-nilly, not caring if the light is red or not, or even if they're at an intersection at all. We crawl along in the traffic. Right after we creep past South Berg, the sign for Crazy Mama's hangs out over the sidewalk.

After that sign, the bars, and all street life, simply stop; there is only a strip mall across Seventh Avenue, and blocks of two- and three-story buildings with hardly anyone on the sidewalks. It's like someone turned off the fun.

He tells me to turn left on Seventh Avenue and then left again into an alley behind Crazy Mama's, and to snag a space near a black doorway. I carefully fit the car between Ron's hearse and a green Dumpster. It's a tight fit; we can't open the doors all the way, so we have to squeeze out.

After walking through an alley that reeks of piss, puke, and rotting garbage, we turn onto High Street and come to a wood door, painted all black, and nailed to it is a thick wooden cutout of a blonde woman's head wearing angular sunglasses and smoking a cigarette in a long holder.

Jonathan strokes the painted blonde hair, his fingers flipping off the curled ends, gazing at it as if it's an ex-girlfriend. "Been a long time."

"It's the same," his sister says. "Nothing changes in this town."

He pulls open the door and holds it for us. We climb steep stairs in a skinny stairwell lit only with reflections from round mirrors scattered over the black walls. As I step into the bar, music pumps from a mirror-encased dance floor. To the left, a room crammed with small round tables full of people drinking, smoking, and talking, and the bar itself is crowded two people deep. It's small, dark, smoky, loud, and full of freaks.

Cooler than I expected. Even with all his ghosts lurking about.

Stepping around me, he leads us past the bar to an open doorway at the far end. There a tall, skinny man with long black hair steps in front of Jonathan.

"Keith," Jonathan says. "Didn't I say we'd be back?"

They hug.

"Good on your word, man," he says, sweeping his arm, blackened with tattoos, around the full bar. "Look what your goddamned name does to this place. Shit. I call a couple people and wham, half the damned town shows up. Like the old days."

"Like the old days." Jonathan looks very pleased.

The owner then leads us to the end of the bar and though a doorway into a back room where Scott's setting up mics; the keyboard case is pushed against the wall behind him. Kenny is sorting through cables with Nancy. AnnMarie is setting up about half the drums she normally uses. Ron is freezing moments with sharp blasts of his camera's flash. Overlooking this all from a glass case is a mannequin of a woman in combat fatigues and a gas mask.

"Want me to set up your gear?" I ask. "You can hang out, catch up."

"Sure. Great," he says. "I'll be around if you need me." He turns to talk to the owner.

There: the act of kindness that shows the hero and heroine are moving in the right direction in spite of the difficulties. Every happy ending needs this hint a wink to the audience that everything'll be okay.

His sister follows me to the corner of the room that they're using for a stage tonight. We step between the four small tables arranged to keep the space in front of the band free. She watches as I set up the stand near the center of the area blocked off by the tables. Then I open the heavy black case, which feels relievingly familiar, as does catching Scott watching me.

My expression sours.

Lisa follows my eyes. "Oh, him? Enema. Definitely."

Lifting the keyboard from the case, I carefully set it on the stand.

"Now, could you hand me his stool?" I ask Lisa.

I'm sure Bossman's still watching, so I keep ignoring him as I unfold the stool and sit on it to adjust the height of the keyboard and the mic the way Jonathan likes. That done, I step around the keyboard and plug the cables into the snake, and then I turn the keyboard on; all the while, Ron snatches shots.

The way Lisa keeps looking around the room gives me the heebies—like the chick in a horror movie who notices that something's wrong right before the slasher pops out of wherever.

Scott steps out from behind a clump of partiers. "Everything good to go?"

I nod.

Amy appears from behind him.

I freeze.

She puts her arm on his shoulder, leaning her breasts onto his arm. Her nipples show through her sheer black blouse. Her red micromini clings so smoothly to her hips I know she can't be wearing anything underneath. Sex radiates from her violently.

"I didn't know you guys were going to be here," she says, sounding so very innocent.

He steps back and looks her over. "Obviously."

"Jonathan here?"

He gives her a cold stare.

"*I* haven't seen him," she replies.

"I imagine that's on purpose," he says.

Amy looks at me for the first time with her bright blue eyes. "His taste in women hasn't improved."

"Nor has talking with you." He walks away.

The ex. I expected this, right?

Raising her eyebrow, Amy gives me a wicked grin, turns, and struts away, her glossy, red high-heeled boots making her ass pump voluptuously, as if she is a centerfold come to life.

Ron's camera captures its swells and waves.

I'm shaking. Not sure if I'm more pissed at her or at Scott for leaving me alone with her. I take a deep breath.

Course you just had to tell me how she gave you a fat lip in that bathroom. Right there.

All at once, this bar feels as if it has been transported into a David Lynch movie where something horrible has already begun to happen and I can do nothing stop it—only watch it unfold.

All this needs is a midget to step out of that bathroom and start speaking backward.

I go look for Jonathan. Sliding my way through the growing crowd and back into the main room, I almost worry I'll find a severed ear or see Scott inhaling from a gas tank and whimpering "Mommy."

Jonathan's not at the bar. He's not sitting at any of the tables around here.

I push my way onto the mirrored dance floor. He's not dancing either. *Okay. This place isn't that big. Where else is there?*

I glance down a skinny hallway at the edge of the dance floor. From a hidden doorway, Jonathan's head flies back; he's laughing. I take a step into the hallway, reach out, and tap his shoulder.

"Hey," he says, still laughing with the DJ who's sitting inside the little DJ booth there. "What's up?"

"Amy's here."

"I heard. So I'm hiding. Don't really want to run into her."

"You will."

"Probably." Smirking, he shakes his head.

That smirk disturbs me. It's part of this nightmare I can't escape from. Part of how it will happen. By secretly looking forward to meeting her, he'll find out he wants her again, as if this whole night's another Jonathan and Amy duet.

I won't watch this.

"Jonathan," I say. "Don't let that happen."

"It's a half-hour set."

"No. Her. Don't meet her."

"What?"

"Don't. You can't talk to her."

"Not planning on it," he says, stroking my shoulder. "Believe me. She's the last person I want to see. She gets out of line. We'll kick her ass out." He tosses his thumb over his shoulder like an ump ejecting a player on WGN.

"She made her choice. So've I." The smirk's left, replaced by a real smile.

Come on, Jen, don't be so pitiful; you're not the girl the audience wants to get killed first because she's so useless. You're the resourceful one—the one who survives. The one audience roots for. She's the bitch who gets killed in the most horrible way. The one the audience wants to see get what she deserves.

"Everything set?"

"Yeah," I say, and I tear a cigarette out of my pack. His Zippo's out and lit before I can find my lighter.

He doesn't see how wrong being here is; how wrong *here* is. Leaving him joking with the DJ, I push my way through bodies to the back room and realize how treacherous any place gorged with someone's past can be.

I have to figure out how to get out of here in one piece. It's tricky, 'cause Lynch never lets anyone escape unscathed.

By the time I get to the keyboard, I've decided that I need to get us both out of here as soon as the gig is over.

Someone grabs my elbow.

I jerk my arm away.

Scott looks at me in surprise.

Yeah. Something bad's definitely going to happen tonight.

Then Nancy and AnnMarie emerge from the crowd and join us at the instruments.

"Go grab Jonathan," Scott says. "It's time we get this done so we can start partying for real."

On my way back to the DJ booth, I find his sister talking to a bunch of people, and tell her we're about to start.

Tonight's soundtrack: Amy theme-music. Old time favorites like "Amy's Face" and "The Ritual." At least there's "Just Walk Away" and "Joie."

Jonathan's still talking to the DJ. I tell him everyone's waiting, and he asks the DJ to stop the music at the end of the song after next. I take off.

In the back room, I start squeezing through the crowd to the corner where we're set up. As I get around the last couple of bodies and am about to step through the ring of tables, I see her—Amy—standing alone in front of the keyboard. Opposite her, Scott adjusts the way his Stratocaster lies across his body. To the sides, Nancy and AnnMarie adjust their mics.

It's the O.K. Corral. For once I'm rooting for Scott.

I feel a hand pulling my shoulder.

"Don't need this," Jonathan whispers into my ear, nodding at Amy.

Letting go, he steps between the tables and around her to his keyboard. The music stops playing. The whole room goes suddenly quiet.

I try to step back, but the crowd pushes forward.

"Hey, Jon-boy," Amy says. "How've you been?"

"Wonderful," he says after a moment without turning around.

Is this a Mercurial Visions or a Jonathan-and-his-ex show?

"I'm going to New York. Like I told you. Wanna come?"

Pursing his lips, he shakes his head. "No thanks."

"She that good in bed?"

He looks down and starts to turn away.

"You can really make the big time there. Get you away from your queer guitarist roomy. And this sad little girl."

"You made your choice," he says. "When I left."

"I couldn't go then," Amy says. "Now I can take you. Think of it. New York City. Us. The games. The songs you'll write."

Without so much as glancing back, he walks away from her.

As he gets to the keyboard, the crowd surges forward, shoving me, stumbling, between the tables and directly at Amy. I must either grab her or crash into the keyboard.

I catch myself on her shoulder.

She turns her head, snarling, "What the—"

Immediately an ugly expression flashes across her face, and she shifts her weight. Leaving her right leg extended, she swings her shoulder back around, leading with her elbow. It catches me in the back of the neck, and shoves me forward, over her leg. Falling forward, I have nothing left to grab. I get out a quick screech as my hands slam into the keyboard, full force, knocking it from the stand. I land across the legs of the stand, which gives way under me. My hands barely cover my face before hitting Jonathan's knees.

"Told you she can't keep up with me," Amy says. "No one can."

The camera keeps flashing. Then I see Scott ripping off his guitar. His chest strains the buttons on his shirt. He's frightening; it's like watching Bruce Banner erupting into the Hulk. He leaps at Amy.

"You're fucking out of here!" he yells, grabbing her jaw and lifting her to her tiptoes.

"Go! Now!" he roars.

The camera keeps flashing.

In the charged silence, I freeze. My hands and chest hurt; I'm not clear about what just happened.

Then voices cry out: "Catfight! Catfight! Catfight!"

Jonathan's helping me up, but I stumble and want to sit down.

Scott lets Amy's face go.

"Lover boy to the rescue," she says to his face. "Fucked him yet?"

"You!" Scott bellows at her. "Get out of here!" His face is red; bands of muscle and tendons spring from his neck in a picture of rage.

"Jonathan. You're so stupid." She looks more sad and hurt than angry. "So stupid." Amy shakes her head.

The cadaverous owner appears with two bouncers, who turn her around and start walking her away.

Scott glares at me. "What the fuck!"

He looks at Jonathan. "Told you you shouldn't let her come." He points at me. "This is *exactly* why! She's a menace!"

Chin shuddering, I shoulder people out of my way as angry, frustrated tears dribble over my cheeks. As I leave the back room, I see her being walked down the stairs. Stopping, I drop my head and steady myself on a table. All I hear is my heart's pounding and my heaving, raspy breath.

"Wasn't your fault," Lisa says, appearing beside me. "Everybody saw her trip you."

I stare at my fingers, spread out on the table. I hurt in so many places. There's an ugly scrape on my right hand. Someone touches my shoulder.

"Whaddaya want!" I shout, squeezing my eyes closed.

"To make sure you're okay," Jonathan says.

"No. Not okay. Not okay at all."

"We'll take off right after we get done. Twenty, thirty minutes."

"No," I say, shaking my head. "Just … go."

The camera flashes, relentlessly.

"We'll leave. Really, I—"

"Play," I say, pushing him away. "Go …" I turn my back to him. It hurts in so many places on my body. I hate this place. Coming here tonight was such a mistake.

"I'm getting you a drink," Lisa says. Her shock of white hair dangles across an eye.

I shake my head, waving her off.

"She's gonna be outside anyway," she says. "You're stuck. Have a drink."

I can't believe how much the scrape on my hand stings.

"Come on," Lisa says, taking my arm as she cuts a path to the bar.

I let her pull me along. *I can't care anymore. Don't want to.*

Then the DJ's voice booms through the sound system, "Back from Chicago for a private thank-you show for supporting them way back, when you knew them as *White Heat,* it's *Mercurial Visions.*"

The keyboard strikes the opening chord of "Just Walk Away."

Amy theme music. She's here even after she gets kicked out.

I sip the beer his sister bought me, paying no attention to anyone and trying to ignore the music, but the lyrics still creep in.

"Yes," I say under my breath. "You're right. Walking away *can* be better."

Next come more ex-lover theme songs—"Amy's Face," "The Ritual," "Sin with Me"—until this bar is stuffed with the sounds of his ex-lovers.

At last I hear "Joie."

The whole bar whoops so loudly.

Once the DJ starts filling in for the sound of applause and cheering, people bump into me as they return to the tables. Someone is standing next to me for too long, and it pisses me off, so I look up to tell her off—

"Hey there," Tanya says. "You'll have to catch me up on Wendy and let me know how Les Femmes is doing."

"What?"

"Oh, Jonathan. Glad I caught you," she says as he walks over to us; she then looks back to me. "Let's talk later, okay?" She pats my shoulder and turns to talk to him.

This night gets weirder with every moment.

When Jonathan finally has time to talk to me, I say nothing, and I stay quiet when he introduces me to a parade of old friends.

So many places on my body hurt. I'm tired. I want to go home.

CHAPTER 45

CONCERT-SIZED
—JENNIFER—

The early afternoon sun is harsh as I drive down I-90, straight for Chicago. My thumbs tap the steering wheel in time to Celebrity Skin's cover of "SOS" as Toledo recedes, beat by beat. Twenty minutes ago, I dropped Jonathan off at their hotel and gave him a last good-bye kiss. He tried to talk me into hanging out and catching the show since I missed the one at the Newport Music Hall. I would've liked actually being able to see them once, but four hours is too long a drive after a show starting at eleven, and there's no room in the inn for me. Not that I bothered asking. I knew it was impossible, and he didn't offer anyway.

Woulda been nice if you'd at least asked me. But why would you have?

This whole trip's been a train wreck. Starting with Crazy Mama's.

After the scene in the back room with his ex, we ended up staying longer than he said we would. I hated every minute of it. By the time we got to his mom's place, it was very late.

I was beat, but I couldn't sleep.

So I was lying with my back to him, and he was petting me, sighing, trying to get me to talk and let him convince me things are okay.

I won't, because things are *not* okay. I won't let him put makeup on the scene at Crazy Mama's. Or let him pretend, in that way only Jonathan can believe, that "it's just like new, even better than before."

Hell, that sounds like a line from a song. One you'll write back in Chicago about this.

Maybe I should dictate it and get liner credits for writing a song. Not just a dedication, like on the *Joie de Vivre* EP: "For Jennifer, who helped make this happen." I snort a laugh.

"What?" Jonathan asks.

"Inside joke. You wouldn't get it."

"Try me."

I curl up.

Eventually he rolls away, finally leaving me alone. Not that I'll be able to sleep. Scenes from tonight keep playing in my head like highlights of Crazy Mama's worst moments. After the better part of an hour, I sit up in bed, trying to stop this loop from playing.

"What?" he asks.

"Nothing."

I'm too pissed at myself to say anything. Things got out of control.

When I'm on the job, managing shoots or a show, I handle spats and fights backstage, onstage, wherever, all the time. I'm the calming influence, the voice of reason. But here, in my own life, I've been tricked into playing the dupe for the jealous lunatic—the idiot who can't control herself because of a boy. I've been turned into the problem that pushes along the plot of this rock 'n' roll miniseries we're living in.

Tonight was only the next twist in the plot after Exit. It broke things further. The next step in the plot is obvious; we're done. *But I want the happy ending, not the logical one.*

It's as though Scott's hijacked the script. He's turned me into a walking menace who falls into the keyboard and almost trashes the show, nearly wrecking Jonathan's equipment. I could've ruined the Newport Music Hall show and ruined the tour. Made us lose money. But that wasn't my fault. It was hers. Yet Scott's got *me* standing in Jonathan's way, and not Amy. I'm the one Scott's been able to push in the way of their making it, turning me into an obstacle to overcome.

But why does Scott get to write the script? What happened to the story Jonathan and I were living? Or was there ever our story? Was there only his or Scott's, with me as a subplot—a red herring?

Jonathan sits up. In the darkness, I can barely see the outline of his face.

Need to be back in Chicago.

"Sorry," I say.

"For what?"

For not being a part of your goals. Or part of what you need.

"For Amy tripping you?"

"No."

"Try to see the bright side here." He turns on the lamp. "We'll get in the papers. Extra publicity." His expression says I shouldn't take him *too* seriously.

Those gonna be lines in a new song about "how everything happens for a reason/and the reason is success"? Even love and jealousy?

"I don't want my picture in the paper," I say. "Don't let Ron give them a photo of me."

"Okay," he says. "I'll make sure."

"I don't want to be in that story." *But you'll twist me up in your next song anyway. I'll be whoever you make me for the audience, including the devil Scott's turned me into. What would one photo matter? Or a hundred?*

"You know," I say, tossing off the sheet, "it's fine. Let him publish one. It'll be the same as another line in the song." I walk to the window.

"A line? In what song?"

I pull back the curtain. "Oh, come on, Jonathan."

"Come on what?"

"Will it be like 'Just Walk Away'? But 'it's better with a fall'?"

"Better with a fall?"

It turns out I'm looking onto a yard in front of the building, across from a row of buildings facing this one.

"You know. Trip. *Fall.* Crash."

"Okay. You fell."

"The song about tonight. Perhaps to go with the photo of the catfight for the cover of the single. Chris will make it look great."

"Um … Kinda lost me there."

"The song you'll write. Like you always do. About your women."

"My women?"

The lamps mounted on the buildings throw a pale yellow light over the yard, which is crisscrossed with sidewalks connecting all of the buildings to each other.

"Your music: a highlight reel of your bed."

"Oh, come on now," he says.

I hear him pulling back his sheets.

"We've already been through this, remember?"

"You write songs about what happens in your bed. Or doesn't."

"I write what I know."

"You know nothing about Scott?" I watch a cat dart from its hiding place under a bush.

"He's not—"

"Your lover? Why don't you sleep with him? Get it over with. Then you can write about him." I can't tell, but the cat might have caught something. The lights cast odd shadows, so it's hard to see clearly.

"Look," he says. "I know tonight was messed up."

I feel him step up next to me.

"But how's this suddenly about me? I didn't trip you. Amy did."

"You'd've loved to take her into that bathroom again and gotten yourself another fat lip."

"Where the hell did that come—"

I face him. "You accused her of abandoning you. Like I'm just filling in until you get her to Chicago."

Jonathan's expression drains of concern and hardens into a frown. He'll get all quiet now.

Because I'm right and you can't stand it. You truly love only her. Even she couldn't defeat music.

In the silence of his old bedroom, I'd wondered what my old bedroom looked like back home. Mom did say she'd straightened it up.

Now that I'm driving back to Chicago, I've decided not to care about that.

I try to distract myself by taking in the countryside, but Lake Erie has flown away behind me, and it's monotonous here: corn and soybeans in neat rows, an occasional barn, some cows here and there. So I'm stuck watching the road unfurl in front of me, and then, taking advantage of the monotony, what happened at the Newport Music Hall bubbles up in my mind again.

Jonathan had left early with Kenny to meet up with the rest of the band.

I'd simply wanted to sit in the audience and watch the show. Then, on the drive down with Jonathan's sister, she'd begged me into going backstage before the show begins.

When we got there, the opening act, Willie Phoenix and the Shadow Lords, was setting up under the Mercurial Visions banner hanging at the back of the stage, the eight-foot-tall version of the wall hanging with a torso, arms raised, reaching beyond its edge, looking like an overexposed black-and-white print.

I didn't want to go backstage and have to deal with Scott, but Lisa had already talked to whoever she knew and scored two backstage passes. We flashed them to the bouncer, and he let us go backstage. I had such a bad feeling about this. After a couple of false turns, we found them. Jonathan was sitting back on a stool, combing out his hair. AnnMarie was looking at herself in a mirror. Behind them, Scott swished ice around in a glass. Sitting quietly in a corner, Nancy had *Lolita* propped open on her knees, and Ron was taking photographs of everything. *Looks about the same as in the loft. Only more cramped.*

Then, from behind me, a man barked out, "Who's Jennifer?"

I turned. A bouncer filled half the passageway.

Nervous, I raised my hand. *What the hell happened now?*

"The guy at the stand wants to talk to you," the bouncer said, throwing his thumb toward the front; then he left.

Feeling Scott glaring at me, I looked to Jonathan and shrugged in uncertainty.

"No clue," he said, shaking his head.

As I turned to leave, a short, wiry man appeared in the doorway right next to me, looking like a Jamaican leprechaun with long dreadlocks and a pointy smile, his white teeth nearly glowing against ebony skin.

Jonathan introduced him as Willie Phoenix and talked about watching him down at the Distillery, listening to "Knockin' on Heaven's Door," "My Apartment," and "Misunderstanding."

I left him reminiscing and got out. On the way, I was wondering what could be wrong: *The keyboard doesn't work now? Is the stand broken? Or did Amy get the police to show up?*

In the lobby, Kenny was standing next to the card table.

No police lights. That's good.

Then he explained to me he's never gotten to see Mercurial Visions, and since I was there, it might be his only chance, so he was wondering if I would mind covering the sales table.

Of course: Scott's little friend gives up his car, takes off work, and has missed six shows, so he deserves to see them tonight. More than the "menace." If I tell his little half-queer friend no—

"Sure," I said, pulling out the chair behind the table. *At least I get to listen.*

This time I made sure I got the change.

Around South Bend, the view gets more varied and includes signs for Notre Dame. *Not that I can really see it.* Then it's back to farmland.

Staring along the lanes of the freeway, I try to remember what it was like at the loft before the tour, before they put out that first CD, back when I could believe I mattered more to him than his music; when I came home as his lover, not as another song he hasn't written yet.

The sun still shines brightly in spite of dark clouds gathering to the West, near Chicago. The next sign tells me "Chicago 91 miles." That means I'll get there before four. So for the next hour and a half to two hours, it's me, the road, and my music. I wish I had "Born to be Wild," "Frankenstein," or some Zeppelin. Then I'd be in a '70s road movie, near the end, when she makes it home after all her crazy adventures. Of course, something could be going on that the driver doesn't know but that the audience knows, 'cause we're watching, like in *The Hitcher.*

We're all thinking: Look out! Look out!

See, though, I *am* watching out. *Don't worry. I can handle anything after Martin—even Kenny and Scott in bed together, with Ron documenting away.*

The only thing that could surprise me would be if Scott moved out.

I laugh. *That's about stupid, Jennifer. Shit like that doesn't happen even in movies. Not even* Pretty Woman, *and that was more than I could believe. It's fine for fairy tales, but we live in Chicagoland, not Never Never Land.*

Of course, when it looks the worst, there's always something that saves the couple—a little detail mentioned earlier, like a trinket caught in a shot, or a comment by one of the characters that's forgotten until the last minute and which turns out to be a secret desire, or some thoughtful gesture that stops the split, and saves what they both want, even if they don't know it yet.

Like climbing up a fire escape with a rose in your mouth to surprise the woman you can't really lose.

Or a poster of "Love Will Tear Us Apart." Concert-sized. The white-stone angel covering her eyes on a flat black background. Like you imagined it in the loft one day.

That day will be today.

There's no time to dry mount it, but I can stop by Reckless Records on the way back to the loft and then hang it up like a regular poster.

Close enough.

In the distance, a thunderhead blackens the skies over Chicago.

Storm'll have blown over by the time I get to Reckless Records. Or should have.

CHAPTER 46

THE ANGEL
—JENNIFER—

The storm was blowing full force when I made it to Reckless Records yesterday. So I had the poster wrapped up tightly, and with a run to and then from the car, I got it home safely and put it up last night. It looked good on the wall: three feet by five feet, black background, with a black-and-white photo of a lying angel, one arm akimbo across a wing, her other arm laying its hand across her eyes in grief. "LOVE WILL TEAR US APART" was printed in white across the top, and "JOY DIVISION" across the bottom.

All day today at Les Femmes, the pretty young girls complaining that they aren't getting glamorous jobs and aren't millionaire supermodels like Linda E. annoyed me more than usual, and it's later than I expected when I climb our four flights of stairs, beat. Since I don't know when Jonathan's getting back home today, I'm relieved I have the poster up already. That also gave me time to get to my old salon, *Viva!*, for one last nudge—another moment I remember: that he loved the first massage I gave him. *Should be good for a line or two in a song about weathering a storm between lovers.*

Pulling open the heavy gray door, I see the equipment piled in the center of the loft. It's so quiet I can't be sure if they're asleep or have gone out.

Closing the door carefully behind me, I walk lightly to the table and quietly set down the bag from *Viva!* I sneak a squeeze bottle, a flask of

303

oil, and a small bottle of scent out of the bag with hardly a sound. I pour some of the oil into the squeeze bottle and drizzle in a touch of the opium scent he mentioned he likes so much, and then I swish the squeeze bottle around. *For a massage. After being on the road that long, you'll love it.*

I slip off my shoes and tiptoe over to the mattress, where I find him sleeping with a T-shirt over his eyes.

To stack the cards more in my favor, I make this scene R-rated: I strip off my shirt and my bra, and dab some of the sweet-smelling oil near each nipple. Then I kneel down next to the mattress. Carefully drawing back the sheet, I look at his body—at his chest rising and falling steadily. I peel the T-shirt off his face. He stirs, moving a hand over his eyes; his other arm falls off to the side as if reaching for me. He looks like the angel from "Love Will Tear Us Apart."

Bending over, I sweep my hair back and kiss him lightly on his lips, on his chin, on his chest, on one nipple, and then on the other; I feel him wake up. I gaze at his fluttering eyes. He nods, gives me a weak smile, and then looks around the edge of the mattress.

"Hi," I say, holding the squeeze bottle behind my back.

"Hey," he says, reaching for his cigarettes.

"How are you?"

"Beat. To death. Need some more sleep."

"I've got a surprise for you," I say.

He grunts, lighting up.

"Did you like the poster?"

"Yeah," he says, shrugging. "Thanks."

It's not exactly the reaction I was expecting. That poster's something he's been dreaming about. I put it exactly where he told me he wanted it. It's the wish, granted, that reveals the deep love for each other, the hidden strength of the two, that keeps them together.

You did just wake up, though. It's the scare before the kiss. The audience needs the suspense.

"That's the one that you've been talking about, right?"

"Yeah. It is." He looks down at his hands. "Looks good. Really."

I'm half-naked here. I smell like opium. I've granted the wish.

"What's the matter?" I ask, sitting back on my heels.

Shouldn't we be kissing now as the shot pulls back, showing us together, revealing that, yes, we will be together?

"I'm ... just tired. Very tired."

"Maybe I should let you sleep."

"Probably," he says, taking another drag of his cigarette. He falls back onto the pillow, throwing his arm across his eyes.

The wind rattles the panes, first stronger and then softer, but never stopping. I glance out the window at the ugly gray weather; dark clouds are pushing the sky down, making everything feel as if it's trapped in a small box.

This is plenty of suspense.

As he turns away to snuff out his cigarette, I kneel to the mattress.

"I've got a surprise," I say.

"Yeah. So you said."

"You have to turn all the way over."

He sits still.

I motion for him to turn over, and he only stares at me blankly.

"Here," I say, leaning toward him. I hold my perfumed breasts out to him. "Smell."

In the twilight, I watch his eyes shifting from my face to my breasts, and back again. He lifts himself, quickly sniffs, then falls back to the pillow. He nods.

The panes rattle loudly as a cool gust runs over the floor, blowing across us.

"What's wrong?" I ask.

"This isn't working."

"What?" I shake my head.

"This," he says, motioning his hand between us a couple of times and then around the darkened loft. "All of it."

"I don't understand, Jonathan."

"It's not working. With you. Living here. Us."

"What are you saying?" I stare intensely at him, watch his lips move.

"You have to ... move out." He looks away. "I'm sorry. I'm really so sorry. But we have to take some time off. Rethink things."

"What? Jonathan, we ... this is supposed to be us smoothing everything out ... I got the poster—"

"Thank you," he says. "But I can't do this any longer. I can't. I've tried. But—"

Unwilling to watch, the angel from "Love Will Tear Us Apart" keeps her eyes covered.

Chapter 47
Falls Like Dirty Snow
—Jonathan—

The tape has rewound and stopped with a click. I balance the remote in my hand, my thumb over the play button. I've lost count of how many times I've watched it already.

I push play.

As the camera reveals a room in a slow pan down from paint peeling from the ceiling, and the delicate opening notes I've played so many times rise in volume, white letters float in the lower left-hand corner.

"Joie de Vivre"
Mercurial Visions
Joie de Vivre
Directed by C. Eshelman

The abandoned room is shot through with shafts of light from broken windows, casting deep shadows of a solitary bed across the floor and up the wall. The wrought-iron headboard lists to the left. A thin mattress lies across the sagging frame. As the drums and guitar join in, a woman is revealed, lying across the bed, her hand covering her eyes, as if she is afraid of seeing something. A sheer black negligee lies bunched, high upon her thighs, so white they almost don't look real. It clings to her hip bones and drapes her thin waist. Her full breasts fill the low-cut top, the fabric hardly hiding her nipples. A black velvet choker looks almost like a wound on her pale neck. Her closed lips are bloodred, glistening. Her dark brown hair splays across the dun mattress as if she'd been tossed there.

I dissolve in next to the bed and sing, "Where there's love / There are ghosts." I kneel to kiss her as the camera closes in until our wet lips fill the screen.

Her name was Sarah something-or-other. She told me that she enjoyed the kiss—that it lingered after the director said, "Cut."

She reminded me of Amy so much that when we kissed, I thought I would feel electric again, as if it mattered. There I was, singing of a time with Jennifer, kissing a scantily dressed woman spread across a bed, looking so much like Amy, and—I felt nothing.

It was the same nothing as I feel now, watching my lips press against Sarah's, remembering when I wrote the song, remembering all the times I've sung it, remembering when I could merely think of the lyrics and prickles would rush down my back and arms. *Now nada.*

Each time I watch the video, I see all three of them—that girl Sarah, Jennifer, and Amy. *And I really can't give a good goddamn.*

I loved two of them, was obsessed with both, wrote about them, and sang about them. Shouldn't I feel a thrill, a titillation, a rise?

A year and a half ago, it was no different.

After shooting her parts, Sarah said she wanted to hang out. But I was angry she didn't make me feel like anything mattered, and so I said, "I'll call your agent," or some asshole thing like that. She looked so pissed. I would've smacked me. She should've. Perhaps that would have woken me up. Most of the reason I agreed to shoot the video at all was to jolt myself back to feeling that something mattered; I'd been trying to write songs for *Second Vision* and had been getting nowhere.

In fact, the whole time we were shooting the video, I'd had to force myself to obey the director's instructions to lip sync more authentically. "You're singing to your lover. You want her so much it hurts. Remember: she's the reason you stay alive."

I can't remember what it feels like to kiss Amy, Jennifer, or anyone. Love them? Want them? Please mister director sir, there's nothing left in here.

Still isn't.

Standing up, I let out a disgusted sound.

How could I think watching myself fake my way through an old song would inspire me? I should know better than to troll the past. It's so full of broken pieces. Of people leaving, last kisses, and unkept promises. Not exactly motivating.

We're due in the studio in a couple of weeks, and all I've got is a pile of embarrassingly bad lyrics, dead melodies, and, to salvage these, years of regret for inspiration.

Worse: I'm not sure that I care.

"Come on, man," I say to myself, and then I let out a long breath. *You've hit slumps before—worse than this one. You've always pulled out.*

Even in Ohio, when our band Arcade Land floundered, Scott played house husband slash manager, and I lived for 5:00 p.m. When the idea of tying a belt around a chandelier and going out kicking at the smoke-filled air turned itself into lyrics.

Then we risked it all to go the road for the Micherigan tour—including Jennifer. That's where I finally lost her. We'd been fraying, but after that miserable night at Crazy Mama's, there was no way back. I lost her completely on the car ride back from Toledo. I was trapped. Scott was relentless, hammering on me about all the problems she caused, swatting away my answers that she helped us stay afloat, battering me with her demand for more control, beating down everything I had to say, ultimately stripping my life down to a simple choice: her or music, sex or performance, her or him, like a diabolic metronome. *"What's it gonna be, boy?"*

Over and again he asked, until I stopped responding and turned up the music to drown him out.

Needle in, damage done though.

I started believing he was right, at least in part, and started thinking I could see problems that she created for Mercurial Visions—problems with no other way out than to make the choice: the band or her. I hated him for it. I hated that she'd said what she'd said, done the things she'd done. I hated being trapped in that car. This had been so much harder than with Amy. With Amy I *had* to move. She *refused* to. It was an irresistible force meeting an immovable object. The force moved on; the object stayed.

But with Jennifer, I hadn't moved. The only reason I had to ask her to leave my life was that I'd chosen music over her; there wasn't room for both. I hadn't seen this until Scott forced me to.

This killed me inside. I dreaded each minute, every mile that passed, all the way to Chicago. I was able to work up a perfect fury to help me when I got home. But she wasn't there. I hoped she'd decided to move home on her own. She'd hinted she would. I could avoid having to tell her.

Then she came home. I wasn't sure I could say it. I hoped she sensed it, and would understand and go.

When I finally forced the words out, I was lost. *Do I help? Leave? Sit in a corner and sob?*

Watching her pack was emotional leprosy; all I could feel was hurt, as if lesions were breaking out all over me, and then as if bits of my body were falling away: nipples, eyelids, lips, and skin, until I was left a skeleton—inhuman.

When she finally walked out the door, relief swept through me.

That's the best I've felt since. For penance, the angel from "Love Will Tear Us Apart" has judged that I may feel only regret, in one form or other.

I reach for our book of newspaper clippings. It's grown so much since Columbus. I'm not sure what I'll find here. Perhaps if I feel remorse intensely enough, the angel will finally take pity and let me go.

I flip through all the pages until I get past the Micherigan tour and to what happened after. I've read these articles so many times that I need only glance at the headline to watch my complete decay.

Bucktown Rag, October 23, 1989
[An excerpt from the "Who's Doing Whom
(Behind Whose Back)" column]

The writer insinuates that since Kenny is here all the time, Lynda moved out west, and Jennifer's gone that we've gone queer.

You got it so wrong. Kenny's no boyfriend. And Jennifer—she had to ... *I had to ...*

I sigh.

You never should have met me, Jennifer. You had the chance to get away.

I did ask you to leave, remember? The night you massaged my hands. First kissed me.

I flip the page quickly.

Chicago Tribune, January 8, 1990
(excerpt from Style section)
Living in Mercurial Visions

Hate this one. A tour of our loft. It it's not half what it was supposed to be. We couldn't afford a contractor so built it out ourselves. And it looks like it: cheap aluminum balustrade, not the wrought iron we'd wanted. Pinewood stairs, not the diamond-plate sheet metal we'd wanted. The only thing that's actually right is the poster of "Love Will Tear Us Apart."

Yeah, you, angel. You're all that got done right here.

I snort in derision.

I didn't want anyone profiling this place—not the half-assed version we were able to build on our own. But this was a few months before the release of Second Vision, *and Scott wanted the press. "There's no such thing as bad publicity," he kept saying.*

Yeah ...

The disk didn't deserve the publicity. Two stars? Isbister was kind. He was right, too, about what was wrong: me. It says so right here.

Chicago Tribune, March 10, 1990
Mark Isbister
Chicago Tribune Electronic Music Critic

Mercurial Visions Second Vision Wax Trax! 10-song CD
Two Stars
Releases are rated on a scale of one to five stars

I move my finger down to the written proof:

It's easy to pin down what's wrong.
The danceable rhythms are there. So are

the guitar and drum hooks. But Jonathan Starks, the heart and voice of the band, seems to have absented himself. The lyrics are standard-issue material—not bad for a lesser talent; a disappointment here.

His singing, his sonorous voice—that's there. But its guts—the feeling he put into singing—he left behind on the EP.

That is but for one song: "Suffer in Silence." This track has heartfelt lyrics and is sung as if he's right there and means every word. It's a song that no one would really want to have stuck in his head—a song of being wrong, of making an irreversible mistake, and of wanting to hide from it, to never hear of it again. It's a song to dance penance to—and the only reason to give this release a try. But prepare yourself; this is the true sound of regret.

I thump the last word with a fingertip.

Yes, angel. Everyone can feel it. Then it only gets worse.

New York Times, May 18, 1990
Mercurial Visions at Irving Place
Review by Ken Johnson

Mercurial Visions, the driving energy on dance floors for over a year, sold out this show, their first in the Big Apple, in a day. This is the Chicago outfit that broke the image of Second City music as merely blues, Al Jourgensen, or '70s rock ballads. The audience was packed with a mix of club kids in nightclub drag, and hipsters from the LES and Williamsburg. With Brooklyn's *Avatar* opening for them, and the audience having been worked up into a fever, the scene was ripe for a legendary show—one that came with bragging rights: "I was there when ..."

But front man Jonathan Starks forgot to show up.

The danceable rhythms were there, along with the drums and bass lines—but these are machines, computer sequencers. The human part of the band almost missed the whole show. Mr. Stark's lackluster vocals and mechanical keyboard playing forced Mr. Marshall's guitar and Ms. Mauer's vocals to prop up the whole band for most of the show. Finally even the heroic guitar and sensuous singing succumbed to Stark's absence until it was like watching a karaoke performance. The audience turned restless; some left.

Only when they played their latest single, "Suffer In Silence," did Starks finally prove he wasn't actually a mannequin. This penitent song, a raw admission to a lover of his complete failure, felt so vividly regretful it chilled the audience. They stood in place and watched like sinners in pews; heads and shoulders fell, one after another. In the silence after Starks released the final note, it seemed that everyone knew he had been exposed—that this was their own confession. It was a powerful moment, but it hardly made up for the previous forty-five minutes.

If not for this, there would have been no encore, not even for their über-hit "Joie de Vivre." Yet as they played it, Starks faded away again, as if he were lip-syncing to a cover of his own song.

I let everyone down.

Chicago Sun-Times, June 2, 1990
[from the "Around the Town" column]

You wonder why I've not been in public, guessing that I was sick. No, not HIV. I was sick. Of everything that happened. Come on. How can anyone expect me to show up an a music awards ceremony as an soulless skeleton? I needed to hide and prevent anyone from seeing how far gone I was.

Some writers have speculated I had a monkey on my back; the rare time my name comes up anymore.

Chicago Reader, July 7, 1990
[from the "New Music Beat" column]
Scott Marshall Starts on a New Project

Yeah, Scott. I understood. I was pitiful material to work with. But I needed help, and instead you started a new project, producing Unknown Vices. You ignored Mercurial Visions—our band.

Worse than that—Unknown Vices was a mistake, and you knew it.

Sure, Kenny's got talent—but not enough to drive a whole band. Not by himself. The rest of Unknown Vices wasn't there yet. I don't think they ever will be. They just don't have the stones. You shouldn't have forced them onto Wax Trax! Especially not with that single "Should've Done It."

The review's headline said it all: "Not Sure about Doing It."

The Reader *panned it. The single you guaranteed Wax Trax! was going to be a dance floor hit, like our first EP, flopped. Why did you keep forcing it when you knew it wasn't all that? You heard it, same as me. Merely trying hard doesn't make it good. Isn't that what you've said?*

And now? Wax Trax! is piling on more pressure. We have to recover from Second Vision and "Should've Done It" both, and I'm no better now than I was two years—

"Stop! This isn't helping," I say, slamming the scrapbook closed.

Something's gotta change. Feeling like hell about what happened isn't cutting it. Not anymore.

I look up at the angel on the poster.

"Haven't I done my time yet?" I ask it. "What else do you need me to do? I've admitted I was wrong. I've admitted Jennifer isn't Amy. No one is. See; I did it again. Now both are gone. Mercurial Visions, all I have left, is on the edge. This single's my one last chance. But I can't keep living in this one-dimensional space. Not anymore. Don't you see that?"

I point to the stack of stillborn songs on my keyboard.

"Give me a hint, won't you!" I demand.

In disgust, I walk away from the poster, sit down at the keyboard, and grab a sheaf of songs to review. *For the fiftieth time.*

A matchbook falls from between the pages.

Forgot about that.

Two days back, a girl scribbled her phone number on that matchbook, and I tossed it onto the keyboard when I got home.

This your idea of a hint, angel? The number of a starstruck girl? Struck by a collapsing star.

I scoff.

Number's probably fake. Or wrong. Or she won't be home.

But if she does pick up, what? I'm supposed invite her over. Have her wear that same skimpy red dress. And maybe …

"Maybe what, angel? Been so long since I've even cared." I shake my head. "Fine."

Picking up the phone, I open the matchbook cover: "Marci 555-9651." The *i* is dotted with a tiny circle. She's probably too young to have been in Smart Bar: nineteen, twenty.

I dial her number.

"Hello," a girl's voice says.

"This Marci?"

"Yeah," she says suspiciously.

"It's Jonathan. Jonathan—"

"Starks?" She squeals and then effuses that she didn't think I would call, and how excited she is to have met me, and how she had, this morning, listened to *Second Vision*.

I hate that CD, but I'm supposed to ask her to come over, so I fake appreciation and then ask, "What are you up to right now?"

"Nothing," she says.

"Perfect. Why don't you stop by? Hang. I'm working on our next single. I need a break," I say. "And inspiration." *Did I really say that? Did I have to?*

"Okay! Sure!"

"2017 North Ave," I say. "Just west of Damen."

"Next to the 'L,' right?"

"Yep. Fourth floor."

"I love your music," Marci says. "I just broke up. 'Suffer In Silence,' says it all."

You too, Marci? Coming here to rub it in?

"Do you remember that red dress you wore at Smart Bar when we met?"

"Oh, yeah."

"Wear it," I say. She's giggling when I hang up.

Shouldn't I be feeling sleazy?

A half hour later, Marci shivers in the light of the open doorway, the fur collar of her black leather jacket pulled up around her soft, round face. *Are you like most club girls—a mindless pretty doll? Or are you the one to surprise me? Wake me from this somnambulism I'm pretending is living.*

"Hi," I say. *The angel seems to think you are.*

"Hi," she says, biting her lower lip.

Inviting her into the loft, I notice the smooth tautness of the red fabric of her dress from her back and down to her long, firm legs, and I feel a twinge of anticipation.

Been a long while since I felt that. You were right, angel.

But then she starts looking around, up to the huge poster of the angel on Joy Division's "Love Will Tear Us Apart", and the high ceilings. And then, seeing the keyboard, guitar, and sound gear sitting in the center of the room, she rushes over and walks through them, running her fingers along the tops of everything, glancing at me, grinning like a child who's a bit slow—wide-eyed and gape-mouthed.

An ordinary club doll. I can't stand her. But you did feel something.

I prod myself along.

"Let me show you around," I say, taking her jacket and laying it on a couch. "You get the best view from up there." I point to the railed balcony for our bedrooms running the width of the loft. I lead her up the wooden stairs, and we lean against the aluminum balustrade, looking down at the expanse of the loft. I tell her what each piece of equipment is and explain how we set up for rehearsals, where I composed the songs for *Second Vision*, and that "right now I'm composing new songs."

Wide-eyed, she's rapt to every detail. I let our fingers casually touch. Her fingers cross mine and then intertwine, and that's the cue, as if I'm taking direction for a video. I know the plot; I'm to press my hip to hers. She'll press her thigh to mine. It'll be warm and firm. Next, a breath on her neck. My lips will graze her ear. She'll turn. We'll kiss. The dress will come off. I'm to latch onto one and then the other of those plump breasts and then lead her to the bed. Her dress comes off. Then my pants.

I need some help here, 'cause I ain't feeling it anymore. Like in the video, I imagine the director instructing me to act like I mean it. I'll do my best. Like last time.

I press my hips to hers, and exactly like the director wants, she presses her thigh to mine. It's warm and firm.

But I don't want to do this.

What am I supposed to say now? Sorry, but I'm not into you enough?

But I'm not evil. Only empty.

The front door opens.

"Cut!" my make-believe director yells.

"Hey, Jonathan," Scott says, walking in. "I'm back."

Thank you for interrupting. I don't know what to do with her.

Marci shrinks from the edge, crouching behind me.

"Yo, Jonathan!" he calls. "You home?"

I crouch next to Marci. "Well. This sucks. Sorry."

"That's Scott right? Scott Marshall—the guitarist. He's so"—she peeks around me—"big."

I lean forward, looking through the aluminum spires of the balustrade.

He's putting down his travel bags. Once he stands back up, he brushes his hair across his forehead. "You still sleeping? What the hell did you do last night? It's three thirty."

"Not sleeping. I was home last night."

"I have to call Wax Trax! today. We need to go over what you've got ready." He takes a couple of steps. "Someone up there with you?"

"Yeah. A fan. Big fan of yours."

She smacks my arm, grinning.

"Reeeeally now?"

"So she said."

"Did not," she whispers, biting her lip.

I listen to the clopping his boots make on the stairs.

Perhaps she'll like him. I'll slip away.

Scott's head pops up at the head of the staircase, and he grows larger and larger. Finally whole, he nods to Marci.

She stares at him.

"Scott," I say, "Marci. A big fan of yours."

"Hate to break this up, but we've got some work to do."

Marci's face deflates.

"Seems I've … lost track of time," I say.

"I could, you know, just … stay out of everyone's way …" she says. "I love you guys. Your guitar playing is … Wow."

"Well," I say helplessly, looking to Scott.

He actually looks flattered—not something I'm used to seeing. Marci's biting her lip, her legs nervously bouncing.

"I don't know. Depends on how our meeting's going to go," he says.

"We *do* have rehearsal later."

"So the meeting's not going to go well?"

Saying nothing, I nod at Marci, raising my eyebrows. "Rehersal?"

He gives Marci a long, hard look and nods.

"So," I say. "For now, we need to hash some things out. Alone. You can, you know, hang out at the Myopic. Right around the corner. Then come back for rehearsal. Meet *everyone*."

I'm sorry. I made a mistake inviting you.

318

"Sure," she says.

"Give us an hour, hour and a half," I say to her, nodding. "Head back. And Scott. Why don't you do the honors? Show her where it is. I'll ..." I motion toward the pile of songs on the keyboard.

"Sure," he says.

He leads her down the stairs from the balcony; they find her coat, and Scott snags his off the rack on the way out.

Eventually I start trudging down the stairs to the keyboard.

Feeling the disapproval of the angel, I stop and face her.

"You were wrong. Look what you made me do." I shake my head. "She's an innocent here. Getting tossed away."

Turning from the angel, I continue to the keyboard. "When are you going to let me free? I *never* wanted to hurt anyone." I pick up and start reading the first song. *Sophomoric.* I discard it and pick up the next and the next until Scott pulls open the heavy steel-wrapped front door.

My head drops. *Oh, here it comes.*

"Guy," he says, intimidatingly, like a bouncer, "could you please tell me what's going on."

"I've tried. Believe me. To have at least a single ready. But nothing. It's like someone has stolen my—"

"No, no, no, no," he says, wagging a finger. "We need these songs you've been promising. Eight. At least. It's in the contract." He slams his foot on the floor. "We're due in the studio next month, for fuck's sake! If we don't have at least a single ready by then ..." His hand rises to hold his drooping head.

I feel a stab of fear in my gut.

"But this." His mouth stays open for a moment as he raises his head and drops his hand. "No one *stole* anything. If you want to know why you're where you are, go look in a mirror. The answer's staring at you." He waves his hand at papers sitting on the keyboard. "Let's see what you *have* gotten done." His boots thump with each step.

"There's nothing much to look at," I say.

"Because you're too busy trying to nail teenagers."

"That's not ..."

"Not what?" He pulls the black leather coat off his broad shoulders, drops it on the keyboard stool, and then picks up the stack of song lyrics and notes I've been foundering on. His eyes scan each page before putting it down into one of two piles. He shakes his head slowly before drumming two fingers on the smaller one. "You got some music to go along with these lyrics? Recorded, I hope? At least sketched out? These others … toss 'em."

"I can't write anymore." *There. I've done it—spoken the words that I've been too terrified to think. Is that what you've been waiting for me to say, angel?*

"Well," he says, shuffling the few pages of the smaller pile together. He then taps them into a neat rectangle, and carefully lays it down. "Not like you used to. Of course, nothing's recorded either, right?"

I avert my eyes.

"So what are we gonna do now?" He waves his hand at the pile of misbegotten songs. "There's little I, or the girls, can work off of. Nothing, really. No lyrics worth talking about. That I can see. Unless you've something in your head you're not sharing. No music. Nothing recorded. Simply nothing." He takes a deep breath.

I click my Zippo open and shut.

"Look, I don't know what the problem is, but …" He pinches the bridge of his nose. "We are due in the studio, like I said, in a couple of weeks to cut the single for the album we're recording a couple of weeks after that. Fuck this up … We're done. *Poof.* Contract cancelled." He flares his fingers in front of his face like a magician.

"I know."

"*Second Vision* didn't sell. It wasn't good. This is it. *The* second chance."

"I know. I know," I say.

"Then act like it." Scott thumps his finger on the pile of notes. "This stuff … is not good," he says matter-of-factly. He takes a deep breath. "We all play with *your* lyrics and the melodies and rhythms *you* start us off with. No one writes like you, Jonathan. Not like you did."

"I've tried—"

"*Don't* say another word."

I stare at my shoes.

"You drive this band creatively. Without you, there's nothing to record. You can't merely *try*. We can't rehearse *trying*. I'm going to be meeting Kenny in a couple of hours to talk about *his* next single, 'Fantasy in Black.' Right now I've got to clear my head. Grab some coffee. So while I'm gone, look through this stuff. Find *something* we can salvage. We need a single. Without one, the whole CD won't happen. I'll call Wax Trax! later. Tell them ... something."

Scott picks up his coat, stands still a moment, and then turns. "You know, 'Fantasy in Black' is solid—much more like our first disc than 'Should've Done It.'"

"Yeah, and?"

"Well," he says, "I can talk to Kenny. See if he'd let us record it first."

I shake my head. "No. No, no, no. Uh uh. I'm not singing other people's material. I'm not a failure."

"We need a single. In a couple of days. It'll be our song."

"Not ours—his. I'll get something for us. I will." I nod vigorously. "I will."

"Do it, then," Scott says. Pulling on his coat, he leaves me alone with the angel again.

With a sweep of one arm, I send the piles of music sheets off the keyboard and into the air. With a sweep of the other, I send the ashtray into a column, shattering it.

The ash falls like dirty snow.

Chapter 48

A Hesitant Breath
—Jonathan—

"It frustrates the hell out of me," I say, turning my coffee cup around in its saucer. "I've got nothing for us."

Across the tiny table, Nancy languidly pulls a spoon around in her coffee. The neon sign hanging behind her glows "The Myopic" in the front window.

"Not even two days alone helped. Scott got back a couple of hours ago, and all I had was a pile of vague notes and stiff, contrived lyrics to show for it. I tried to push out at least a single. And—nothing. Nada." I sigh. "I couldn't find anything to latch on to. As if I'm adrift. Have lost whatever it is I need to compose."

"I don't think alone can work for you. You need to get laid."

I raise my eyebrow at her. *The angel already tried that.*

"No," she says. "Not what you're thinking."

"Not what I'm thinking? Sounds pretty obvious."

"You're thinking of the sex. But what you *need* is what leads to the sex and what happens once it's ended. The life cycle of an infatuation."

"You're prescribing obsession?" I snap my fingers. "Now, why didn't I think of that."

"Only for a night."

"A one-night obsession. Clear as mud, that."

"What do you think Amy was?"

"Nancy, hate to break it to you, but we were lovers for years."

322

"A single one-night stand at a time," she says. "Night after night."

I scoff. "Why not start sleeping with my keyboard. Make lots of software babies."

"You?" She shakes her head. "No. You *need* the instability of flesh: falling in and falling out of love, the ecstasy *and* the sorrow. In a word—women."

"Jennifer said that."

"You should have listened to her. She was right," Nancy says, looking slyly up. "What if she came back? Knocked on your door?"

I shake my head. "I don't … no. That. No."

"Why wouldn't you want that?"

"I was wrong. Everything was wrong. No."

"Three words: 'Suffer in Silence.'"

I can only stare at her smile. "I couldn't do that to her again. To anyone. Not for anything. To write? No." I shake my head.

"Something to hold on to, right?"

"I need it to be something else. Anything." *Except "Fantasy in Black."*

* * * * *

When I get home from the Myopic about an hour later, with nothing resolved, the numeral 4 glows on the answering machine. I push the oval button and listen to the tape rewinding as I drop my keys on the table.

The machine beeps. "Hi guys," AnnMarie's voice says. "We'll be at Gingerman later. A birthday party for Michele. If you remember her."

"Sure," I reply to AnnMarie's voice. *From a different life. Back when I cared about why she was always around Tanya's parties. When there were her parties.*

The machine beeps again. "Jonathan," Scott's voice says, "where are you? It's five thirty-five."

"Figuring shit out," I tell Scott's voice.

The machine beeps a third time. "Hey guys." It's Ron's voice. "What's up for next week? I need to schedule a couple of shoots. You gonna be rehearsing? Yes? No? Call."

"Don't know, Ron. Call when Scott's here."

Slipping off my coat, I walk toward the keyboard.

The machine beeps for the fourth time.

"Oh. Shut the hell up," I tell the machine.

"I called Jeff." Scott again. "He's pissed we don't know when we need to book the studio for the session. If there's going to be a session. We've got till next week to let him know." He sighs. "I need to tell him *something*."

I collect the scattered leaves of paper from the floor and flip through them. After the last page flits off my thumb, I drop the pile back on the keyboard. I then get up, wander to the window, and stare down into the dusk. The streetlights cast orange-white circles on the sidewalks. I drum the sill with my fingers.

"Okay, Jonathan. Time to wake up."

The stream of cars flows by below. A wind gust rattles the panes of glass.

I'm all alone here. No one gets it. Not Scott. Not Nancy. Not even the angel. I counted on you guys.

"Not gonna sing someone else's words," I say defiantly to the night.

The phone rings.

"Oh, fuck off!" I shout at it. "I don't know!"

It rings again.

"No, Scott. I haven't gotten anything done. I don't know, Ron. I just ... don't."

It rings again. I grab the phone.

"What?" I snarl.

A faint, hesitant breath comes from the other end. Then: "Hi."

"Jennifer?"

"Never thought you'd hear from me again, did ya?" Jennifer asks.

Chapter 49
Playing for Drinks
—Scott—

Greeting me when I arrive home from the meeting at Bulldog Road with Kenny are a shattered ashtray, scattered cigarette butts and ashes, and the click and pop of a Zippo. Following that sound to the balcony, I find Jonathan standing against the aluminum balustrade, wearing that impish smile of his.

"Oh, what have you gone and done now?" I hiss through clenched jaws.

As if he heard me, he jumbles down the stairs, his bus-driver shoes clomping loudly, and starts to say something. Instead he shakes his head, mouthing, "No." Continuing to the keyboard, he flicks the machine on, and climbs over the back of the stool. He plugs in his headphones, hangs them around his neck, and taps a pen on his lips.

"Okay," he says to himself.

Closing his eyes, he sits very still for a moment. Then he suddenly leans down, flips over a sheet of paper, and starts scribbling.

"Don't bother with the show, man," I whisper. "We've got 'Fantasy in Black' now. Kenny's stoked to sing it for us."

I walk by him, up the stairs, across the balcony and into my room. I throw my bag on the bed.

Now I need to talk to Nancy and AnnMarie. Considering Jonathan's got nothing, they have no real option but to get onboard. *With* Kenny as guest vocalist. It is his song. They need to hear this as soon as possible and make the actual choice. *No freak-outs. No drama. Simply business.* Then we go to Wax Trax! and sell them on this. *Course we'll need to rehearse the song. Here. That'll be tricky. But this will buy us the time we need for the rest of the songs.*

With or without *Jonathan.*

Coming down the stairs, I still hear the mute clicking of the keyboard's keys. He hunches over, working them with his right hand, pressing the headphones to his ear with his left. He stops, looks at his lyric sheet, and then starts again.

Sitting there like that, you're a bad rock 'n' roll cliché: skinny, with long, unwashed hair. How could I have ever ... I shake my head. *You're nothing like Sammy. Kenny? Well. Sammy'd approve of you. I'm sure.*

I enter the bathroom, walk to the mirror, and look. *If you ever wonder why you are where you are in your life, look in a mirror: the reason is staring at you.*

"Exactly," I tell my reflection. "It's up to you to get this done. Don't worry. I will. 'Persistence and determination alone are omnipotent.'" *Exactly like you said, Sammy.*

As I splash my face with cool water, the clarity of resolve calms me. *No more indecision.*

Dropping my head back, I take a deep breath.

"'Fantasy in Black' will kick ass," I tell my reflection. *It has to. Everything depends on it.*

In the mirror, I can almost see Sammy standing behind me. "I'll never break my promise. Even if you can't keep yours."

I look away, holding my fist to my lips.

I won't let anything take that away. "I promise you ..."

It starts feeling too much, and I leave the bathroom.

Heat shushes from a duct hidden in ceiling. I stand, letting it pour over me, warm and soothing.

Jonathan's still sitting at the keyboard, drawing his finger and thumb together repeatedly on his forehead. He taps on a few keys and shakes his head. He picks up the lyric sheet. He studies it for a moment. Then he starts clicking on the keys again.

I can't watch his delusion play out, so I go to the phone and call

Nancy. She's not there, so I leave a bland message about wanting to grab a cocktail. The same happens on my call to AnnMarie.

Then I pick up my Stratocaster from its stand and slip on the strap. I stand ready, legs apart, knees bent. The weight feels good on my shoulder. Not needing to plug it in, I pull off one of the picks taped to the body and run a couple of quick scales up and down the neck.

I start picking out the notes from "Fantasy in Black." With his headphones on, Jonathan can't hear. Even if he could, he's too busy pretending he can write to pay any attention.

It's up to me to get our mojo back. Like when we played Metro on the first night of the Micherigan Tour.

I remember the roar of whistles, claps, shouts, stomps, and cries for "Joie" blasting into the wing where I and Nancy leaned against one another.

I feel my heart hammering. My sweat-soaked shirt clings to my arms and back. I can smell her Aqua-Net.

"Metro!" Nancy shouts over the cheers. "Love it."

The cries of "Joie, Joie, Joie," grow louder, joining the rhythm of feet stomping. Looking across the stage, the yards of pocked hardwood, I see hundreds of flickering flames in the audience. Jonathan stands next to me, his hair tossed carelessly across his face.

I catch AnnMarie's attention, and nod.

She walks out onto the darkened stage. Cheers erupt, louder now.

Nancy slides out onto stage. She presses her body against the mic stand and strokes it, slowly, up and down.

I follow, grabbing my guitar.

Then Jonathan flows onto the stage as if dreamwalking.

Pulling my guitar over my shoulder, I stand, legs apart, knees bent, ready. The people are waiting. I feel them. They're about to feel me back.

Jonathan draws up behind his keyboard. Spreading his fingers over the keys like wings, he draws in a deep breath.

The lone keyboard begins, strong and invigorating. The lights blaze on.

The audience's roar of recognition bellows across me.

You can't imagine what that feels like, Kenny. The sound. It touches all of you—reaches so far into your past it might even raise the dead.

That's waiting for me again. Onstage. Waiting for us, Kenny.

It shoulda been you, Sammy. You promised. Why'd you go and get yourself killed?

Then the phone rings. Expecting it to be Nancy or AnnMarie getting back to me, I grab it before Jonathan looks up from the keyboard.

Instead Ron's inviting us to a birthday party for Michele, that enigmatic chick we used to run into all the time at Tanya and Randal's, and then after that, until we didn't. She'd been Jonathan's first candidate to replace Amy here in Chicago. Before he met Jennifer.

Ron made sure I knew she wanted Jonathan to show up at the Gingerman tonight, around ten.

Jonathan's still at his keyboard, drawing his finger to his thumb across his forehead. He hasn't moved in almost two hours.

Sorry, Michele. He's not going anywhere tonight: too busy putting on a show. The fraud.

When it's pushing nine thirty, the night has settled solidly on Chicago, and I decide it's time to leave for Michele's party, which I've not told Jonathan about.

He's been pretend-singing while I've really been ignoring him, drinking a vodka on rocks. I rise from my chair.

"You going to the Gingerman?" Jonathan asks.

"Gingerman?"

"Yeah. AnnMarie left a message earlier. Birthday party. I wanna go, but I'm starved and need a shower. I'll hook up with you guys there." He spins on his stool, pulling his hair into a ponytail and then letting it go. It flares out.

"I've ... no," he says, holding up a hand like a cop stopping traffic. "Later. Later."

I hate it when you don't act the way you should.

• • • • •

The jukebox at the Gingerman plays "Guns of Brixton" while a pinball machine, stuffed next to the hallway leading to the back bar, rattles and beeps. The high stamped-tin ceiling exaggerates the odd angles in the main bar. A dark, burled art-deco bar with three billowing, clouded mirrors takes up most of one wall. Art nouveau mirrors and sconces hang from the exposed brick walls. A stand-up piano collects dust silently near a bay window. Zines and handbills litter the sill. All the wooden tables are covered with gouges and cigarette burns.

It's full for a cold work-night, and I can't find our party among the bikers in leather jackets and the Goths with their hair dyed black or dark rust. The goths are only starting their evenings here before heading on to Smart Bar, Metro, the Wrigleyville Tap, U-Bahn, or even Club Lower Links.

Looking around, I move through the rickety tables and the smoke trails rising from ashtrays. The smell of stale beer hangs above everything.

Then I hear Nancy laughing from near the back.

They've pulled a few tables together and have already drained a couple pitchers of beer. Nancy's toasting with someone. Ron, camera hanging from his neck, is talking to Randal at the far end. The table is finished off with AnnMarie, Michele, and a few people I don't recognize.

After pouring myself a beer, I sit next to Nancy, near the birthday girl. Michele wasn't the usual Tanya hanger-on. She wasn't in need of anything, not vulnerable, older than most, not especially good-looking, but very stylish—tonight in a white leather dinner jacket with a ruffled red men's shirt, her hair slicked back and pinned with rhinestone clips. It never made a lot of sense to me why she was around.

Two women I've never seen before show up, and the birthday girl gets up to hug them.

Nancy leans over. "Jonathan coming?"

"Said he was."

"Oh," she says. "Too bad for you."

"Too bad for me?"

"You were using that special fantasy x-ray vision men have to see what's under her clothes. No Jonathan—no competition. But now ..."

"Actually," I say, "I was trying to figure out if Ron's ever going to get her to model for him."

"You're lying. But nah," she says, "not for Ron. For Jonathan, she'll strip. Model naked for him all night and the next morning."

"Speaking of whom," I say, "we need to talk."

"She's exactly what he needs," she says. "A new habit."

"Hey, hey," I hear Kenny say right behind me.

I turn. "What are you doing here?"

"Glad to see you too," he says. "Lynda told me."

"Lynda?" I ask. "She's in LA."

"She came into Borders today," Kenny says, brushing the bangs out of his eyes. "She's in town for some shoot or other. Mentioned you'd be here. Came over after I got off work."

"She's going to be here tonight?" I ask.

"That's what she said a couple of hours ago," he says, sitting down next to me.

"The more the merrier," Nancy says as her smile grows mischievous.

"Uh-huh." *Today's going from strange to freakish.*

"So what did everyone say about 'Fantasy in Black'?" he asks.

Under the table, I give his shin a quick kick.

"Ow, fuck!" He yanks his leg away.

"What's the matter?" I ask, glaring. "Leg cramp?"

"Yeah. Cramp," he says.

"Need more liquids," I say. "Here, have a beer."

Then, looking like a Victorian vampire, with a short forest-green cape flying wide off the shoulders of his coat, his long hair flowing behind, Jonathan strides in.

As he pulls up a seat at the table, the birthday girl taps out a cigarette. Jonathan draws his Zippo, and by the time the cigarette touches her lips, his fire waits. She inhales and glances at him from the corner of her eye, winking.

"Always," he says.

He's wearing that damned impish smile again, which means something's up, and he's itching to spring it on us.

I don't like this at all.

Jonathan grabs Nancy's and AnnMarie's wrists. "Right before I came. I was working on an idea for our new single. Got the lyrics. Still working on the melody. It doesn't *quite* work yet. But ..."

"What?" I ask.

He leans back. "Might be better than 'Joie.'"

"Some of us hate your idea of drama," Nancy says, looking directly at me. "Makes them ... nervous."

Kenny turns his glass in circles and stares at the rings of moisture it leaves behind.

I want to tell Kenny that this doesn't change things; I stop myself from reaching under the table and stroking his thigh to reassure him.

"It was like ... *poof,* there it was," Jonathan says, slashing his hand out. "Right after I got off the phone with Jennifer."

"Jennifer?" I ask.

"*The* Jennifer?" Nancy asks, looking genuinely surprised for a moment.

His eyebrows jump up and down, his expression pure Cheshire cat.

"How's she been?" Nancy asks.

"Oh. Started a West Coast office for Les Femmes," he says. "She's in Chicago, visiting for however long."

"What does ..." I start asking. "Does this mean you're going out with her again?"

"Oh, no. I burned that ship, to cinders, years ago. You of all people should know that. I'd like to say hi, though. Grab a quick 'Hey, how are you?' cocktail before she goes back to Seattle."

"Do you think you can?" Nancy asks.

"Absolutely. If it ever happens."

Kenny slams his empty glass on the table. "I'm outta here." He leaps up and starts pushing through people toward the door.

Everybody at the table stares at me.

I raise my hands and shrug, shaking my head.

What, has everyone picked today to lose his mind?

Quickly getting up, I go after him. Pushing a Goth chick to the side with my arm, I clamp my hand on his shoulder. "Hey—"

He freezes. "Hey what?"

"Let's get a shot."

"I'm leaving."

"First," I say, "let's have a shot."

"I've already told everyone in Vices. That's done. They're expecting—"

I twist him around to face me. "So he *talks* about a song. One he says doesn't even work. So what?"

"You haven't told him."

"It's not so simple for me. There's the band—"

"Fuck you," he says and tries to push past me. I clamp onto his arm.

"Let's get a shot," I say. "We need the girls. I gotta get them behind this first. *Then* him."

He tries to yank his arm free from my grip, can't, and then goes limp.

I turn him toward the bar. We belly up to the curving dark wood top, and I order two Jägermeister shots. He's staring straight ahead at the freezer painted with the Jägermeister emblem—a green stag and cross on an orange-gold background. The bartender pours out the two shots from a frosty green bottle, fresh from the freezer.

"To us," I say, holding the glass up in toast. He taps my glass, and we down the Jäger. It's sweet and sharply herbal. I feel the cold changing to warmth as it hits my belly.

I spin my shot glass and then pin it to the bar with my palm.

"Nothing's changed," I say.

Holding his shot glass over his mouth, he lets the last couple of drops fall on his tongue. "What about this new song?"

"We're doing 'Fantasy in Black.'"

"*His* new song."

"His song? What song?" I ask. "He said he has an *idea* for a song. One *he* said didn't work. In other words, he has no song."

"What if he gets it to work?"

"What if?" I ask. "Oh, no. Too many broken promises. I'm not going to let him lead me on like that again. No. We're doing your song, no matter if he finishes whatever he's talking about or not."

"Great," he says, with less enthusiasm than I expect.

"No, mister, we're in this together. You've gotta stand by me to make this work. The way we planned," I say. "You'll sing for Mercurial Visions. Period. I only need time to tell the girls the right way. Bear with this. Don't walk away, Kenny. Not now. We're too close."

He hasn't looked up.

"Jonathan can't pull it off," I say. "He hasn't written anything good in years. I won't deal with his on-again, off-again, prima donna crap anymore. I can't partner with a man like that."

His noncommittal nod gives me very little confidence, and his slouch less.

I lay my hand on his shoulder. He finally looks at me, and I can see he wants to believe me.

"Trust me," I say. "He'll let Jennifer come between us again, as always. He's done."

Kenny pops his lips. He looks vulnerable and unsure of what to do.

I lean back. "This is a big move. For both of us. We need to do it right. Just hold tight for now."

I order two pints and watch the streams of amber filling the glasses. With Jonathan's ex back in town, breaking it off with him probably got much easier. *She might take care of it for me.*

In the bar's mirror, I watch some people slither between the tables to our group. No one I know. The birthday girl hugs them.

"Let's go back," I say. "Show 'em nothing's up."

"I'll"—he points to his beer—"finish this here."

I squeeze his forearm. "Stop thinking about it. Come on. Have some fun."

Lynda appears in the mirror near our table in back. After a moment, Ron points toward my reflection in the mirror, and her eyes find mine. She slides through the tables toward us, hips and shoulders rolling as if she were on a catwalk, her long, curly red hair bouncing with each step.

Bad time for catching up.

She comes up from behind and hugs me, placing a quick kiss on my cheek.

"Surprise," she whispers in my ear. "Didn't think you'd see me this soon, did you?" She mouths "hi" to Kenny.

He waves two fingers back.

"Actually," I say, "I wasn't sure I'd ever see you again."

"Really?" she says. "We're trapped. We move in the same flow. We can't help but keep meeting each other."

"So," I say, "is that a good or bad thing?"

"Does it matter?"

"Possibly."

"My, you're grumpy." She pulls out a cigarette. "Light, mister?"

Jonathan's Zippo isn't around to beat me this time, so I reach over to the napkin caddie, pick up a book of matches, and strike one for her.

"How've you been?" she asks.

I tell her everything's just dandy, and she believes me, and her cheeriness, when things are so obviously not well, irritates me. That's so like her—unaware of what's outside her bubble of self. *No wonder I didn't care if you came around again or not.*

"So," she says, "why haven't you called all this time? You said you would." Her green eyes flick playfully.

"You always called me," I say. "Whenever you felt like company."

Right then, Nancy steps between us.

"Scott," she says, "you've got to come convince Jonathan to play 'Joie.'"

"What?"

"On the piano." She points to the stand-up piano near the bay window.

"That thing doesn't work," Kenny says, dismay spreading across his face.

"Bouncer says it does," Nancy says. "Come on. Michele wants him to, and he's being such a little shit."

"I'm outta here," Kenny says.

"Look, Kenny," I say. "Tomorrow we'll start getting things set for your next project." I wink. *No need to look so lost and unsure. We're not breaking up, here.*

Nancy grabs one of my arms, Lynda the other. They drag me back toward the table. I barely resist. *They'll see how bad he is now. It'll make selling "Fantasy in Black" to them all the easier.*

"Singer Man," I say, "what's this about you not wanting to play?"

"No." He shakes his head. "Really."

That smirk he's wearing says he'll do it. He only wants us to make a big production of it.

"You're being a shit," Nancy says.

"Another cocktail, anyone?" he says, holding up his glass.

"You're going to disappoint the birthday girl," I say, offering her up with my open palm.

She lets slip the merest smile.

You do that, girl—stroke his ego.

"I'm out of practice," he says. "I haven't played that song for ages."

"Never stopped you before," I say.

"Oh, come on. You haven't simply played it for us in," Nancy says, "well, ever. You can start tonight."

He reaches out for the pitcher of beer. I pin it to the table. "No more drinking until you play."

"Playing for drinks now. How low I've come."

Everyone looks expectantly at him—except the birthday girl. Aloofly, she sips her martini.

Leaning over the table, he pushes his face into her gaze. "Do you want me to play?"

"If you'd like," she says with fake indifference.

"I'd like," he says.

He strides over to the piano, followed by the rest of the party, including Michele. Once there, he cracks his fingers.

Michele stands next to him. Her fingers graze his shoulder.

Crossing my arms, I stand back to let him show off just how bad he's gotten.

Chapter 50

Daydreaming
—Jonathan—

Sitting in front of the piano at The Gingerman, I feel the birthday girl's fingertips grazing my shoulder. With everyone watching me, it's as if I am onstage again. Caressing the keys, I let this sensation sink in. *I miss this so damned much.*

Then a fleeting half-hope, half-fantasy of Jennifer walking into the Gingerman right now, as I'm about to play "Joie," slips through my mind, making me catch my breath.

"Are you going to play?" Nancy asks, "or only tease us?"

"Trying to remember how it goes." I purse my lips. "A prelude." I splay my fingers, slowly, over the keys and then tinkle out a clumsy "Chopsticks."

"How wonderful," Nancy says. "Brilliant interpretation. Never have I heard better."

I shift to the "Moonlight Sonata."

"You're disappointing the birthday girl," Scott says.

"The keys were dusty. I needed to clean them off first." Stopping, I listen intently to the sound of Jennifer's voice on the phone announcing she's back in Chicago.

The first chord of "Joie" flows easily, which melts into the first phrase, and the rest comes so effortlessly. I play "Joie" the way I did on the morning she and I recorded it—the morning I brought it to the office of Wax Trax! Now I sing it to her once again.

336

As usual when I play, time flows differently, as if it doesn't exist; it's always as if I've just started playing when the song ends and I find myself sitting at a silent piano, my fingers over its keys, with nothing left to play.

There is a smattering of applause. I let my hands fall to my lap, as a droplet of sweat trickles down my lip. I lick it. It tastes like life.

"I could really use a drink," I say.

The birthday girl bends toward me. "Thank you," Michele says. "That was lovely."

"Oh, yes," I say, remembering that I was playing for her and not Jennifer. "You're very welcome."

Turning away, Michele runs her fingers along the keys of the piano.

"Hey," someone says. "That's that guy from that band."

"Mercurial Visions," someone else says.

"Jonathan Starks. Hey, the whole band's here."

"Play something else," a woman says.

"I don't know," I say.

"Play!"

"Pop-up concert!"

"He's back!"

· · · · ·

The sounds of a windblown city loft late at night: the rattling of windows, a hollow rush at the door, muffled buses lumbering by below, the faint hum of cars, the distant rumble of the 'L' making its way between buildings along raised tracks. This greets me when I arrive home alone. I throw myself onto the couch. Through a gap in the heavy drapes, I gaze at the dull aura over the choppy skyline, including a sliver of the Sears Tower's light-speckled silhouette. Scents have impregnated my clothes and hair: Michele's musky-floral perfume, the malty yeastiness of beer, the sweet herbaceousness of Jägermeister, the rich reek of tobacco, the salty musk of my sweat—pungent, living smells. I breathe them in deeply as if they are magic vapors.

Letting a satisfying fatigue settle over me, I carefully line up everything that's happened today: a call from Jennifer, the birth of a new song, a party at the Gingerman, performing as I once had, and an unexpected kiss—right before Michele walked from the piano, she turned and brushed her lips on mine.

I feel that delicate kiss even now.

You're still such a cipher.

I don't know if I'm thinking of Michele or Jennifer, and that doesn't seem to matter right now.

• • • • •

The next afternoon, Nancy and I are sitting at the table in the loft with a half-empty press pot of coffee between us. Scott's out running errands while Ron sets up for a shoot in a half hour. Rehearsal's right after he's done.

"You're acting all different today," Nancy says. "It's the sex, right?"

"The sex?" I scoff. "Boy here's regrown his hymen. Been years."

"But sex is what you're thinking about, right? Or what you're avoiding thinking about."

"Don't think so." I shake my head.

She arches her eyebrow at me and takes a sip of coffee.

"Okay. Avoid. Yes. *Possibly,*" I say. "But not quite, either." I roll my coffee cup around in its saucer. "It's more about being on a precipice and looking down into the yawning gulf of a possible new life, and then stepping off into it and falling. Being embraced by your lover on the way down, in a way no one else can. Until you hit the bottom. It's over. Smash." I flare my fingers flat over the table. "Then we bounce back up." I raise my hands. "Or we die down there." I lay my hands flat on the wood. "Sex is merely a way of falling—a way of slowing down the descent. Even floating back up." I frown. "To avoid having to turn her into literature. A song. For a time."

I pop my lips.

"And here I am," I say. "Staring over that precipice again."

I catch my breath as I feel myself teetering over the edge of Jennifer's being back. I close my eyes to keep from tipping all the way over, the same way I'd pulled myself back yesterday afternoon when she'd called.

Again I feel the pull of the new song. I know it will better than "Joie," in the same way I know things while I'm dreaming, but it keeps slipping away, the same way dreams elude capture. This one, though, keeps coming back, teasing me.

Leaving Nancy to her smirk, I wander toward the center of the loft. I tap my fingers lightly on the keyboard and then run a finger down the keys. Leaving the machine turned off, I tap out a mute "Chopsticks." Then I let my fingers meander up and down the keys in silent scales.

I need to catch that song now—before it does fade completely away. A soft push of my finger on a toggle switch, and the green and red LCD lights of the keyboard wake, glowing.

Then I strike a chord and the speakers cry out, rending the late-afternoon stillness with a ferocity that startles everyone, including me.

I splash another chord into the air—my first flirt with the memory of the song that stands at the edge of my mind.

"Okay," I say. "Too direct. More foreplay then."

I send it a single note, a whisper, to beckon. The memory doesn't melt away but lingers, coyly. I send another note out, and the two seem familiar together, and enticingly, the song feels as though it's gelling. Quickly I offer three more.

Too much too fast, and the memory starts dissolving.

Frantically I imagine what it would be like to have Jennifer watching as I try to catch the memory of a song before it vanishes completely. My fingers start to move along the keys with more ease.

The memory shimmies but has stopped fading.

I pursue the memory with a phrase of notes.

A silhouette of the melody forms for a moment.

I try to grasp it with another phrase.

It eludes me yet again.

I keep offering it phrase after phrase, yet the true melody escapes capture, flirting, just out of reach of my memory.

My next variation, and then the next, and the next can't quite describe the melody's shape. I throw my hands up.

Nancy turns her sequencers on and starts a rhythm, which fills the space with beats like heartache. Now the melody makes sense. I hear it and can play it, and it's breaking my heart again, as if I were lost, without any way of finding home.

Ron has come over and started photographing us.

Scott opens the door and watches us with his arms crossed.

After Nancy and I run through what we have figured out so far a few more times, Scott slips off his coat.

Nancy and I stop.

"So," I ask, "what do you think?"

"Bleak but catchy," he says.

"Now, lyrics," I say. "I've got a few lines. Here." I tap the side of my head. "Let's fool around with what we've got. Let the rest of the lyrics come out as we play. It's about an ex-lover. Long gone."

"That's the bleak," Nancy says.

"Being empty. Killing time. Until they," I say, interlacing my fingers.

"Told you it's all about the sex," she says.

"Play," I say as I start, and she follows along.

"I'd like to do a song now called 'Daydream and Try,'" I say to the audience I picture in front of us.

Then, I sing words as they tumble onto my tongue:

Empty
That's all I am now.
Even despair
Has turned its back on me.
Apathy is all I have left,
But she could bring it back—
The confidence I had
When the two of us
Had been here together,
When we'd been happy,
When everyone believed in me,
When we were broke
And all we did was
Daydream and try

Chapter 51
The Songs We Write
—Jonathan—

It took me four days to get Jennifer to agree.

Spinning my Zippo on a tall table for two in the front bar of the Red Lion, I'm wondering if she's actually going to show up. Until last evening, I didn't think it would even get this far. I'd called her so many times, acting more like a stalker than someone who simply wanted to talk. First I tried her parents'. That was good for several messages. I can only imagine what her mother thought when she heard them. Eventually her stepfather answered and told me she wasn't there and to stop calling. That left me calling her work. As expected, I got the "She's too busy to come to the phone right now. Can I take a message?" routine, repeatedly. I could hear the contempt in the voice of the receptionist growing with each call. I'd leave a message anyway: I *needed* to see her. Not to excuse what I did two years ago; there's nothing that can do that. Nor to explain myself; it's far too late for that, even if I could.

My need is not to offer an apologia for what I did in the past but to reveal what she has done for me now and what that could mean for the future.

I'd been the walking dead before she called, but now I've written half the songs we need for the album. The rest? That's up to her. It depends on what happens between us now.

This I *need* her to understand. I'd even gone so far as to call Wendy's.

Once, I got her machine but didn't dare leave a message. Once, Wendy picked up: I hung up without a word.

Then, yesterday, around six, Jennifer was on the phone when I answered it.

At first I couldn't offer more than "Hi." I wanted to tell her everything the sound of her voice had done but knew that would sound insane, or like an attempt to seduce her. But it's neither crazy nor a lure. It's a hand out for help, a plea for something to hold on to—a tether to keep me from getting lost again. Yet this isn't something I could have said over the phone. I have to see her face, and she needs to see mine, to make any of this intelligible. So I forced myself to start talking—of nonsense and trivia, of new bands and cities—until I asked her to meet with me over a dinner.

"Promise: I'm paying this time," I said, and she chuckled, and while she said yes, I got the impression she agreed mostly to get me to stop calling.

Now I'm here, spinning my Zippo, and I think back over the four days since she broke our silence with her "Hi": the explosion of lyrics and melodies, songs almost composing themselves as I sat at the keyboard, stories completing themselves on paper, while teetering on the edge between everything and nothing: the insanity of Jennifer. Of her being close again. I haven't felt this real since we were together. *Before I betrayed her. Before I did what Scott wanted me to do—choose music instead of her. But did I ever really have to choose?*

I hold my hand up to stop that thought.

Doesn't matter. I made the decision. I did choose. Yet couldn't I have refused? Scott, couldn't you have not asked—

"No," I say, "can't do that. This time it was me who couldn't figure a way out for us. Not her. She's not Amy."

"What was that?" the waiter asks, having appeared at the table.

"Oh. Hey. Didn't see you standing there," I say, shaking my head. "Talking to myself. Bad habit." I wave the words away.

"So. What can I get you to start, then?"

"Um. Yes," I say. "I'm meeting someone."

"Okay ..." The waiter stares at me blankly.

"For me," I say. "Yes. To start—scotch. On the rocks. No, wait. A coffee. Yes. That would be better."

"Cream?"

"No. I need a real drink. Scotch—rocks."

Waiter gone, I turn to watch the doorway. I want to see Jennifer first so I can play calm and have her come to me. I tap my fingers to occupy my hands.

My drink arrives.

Running my fingers around the top of the rocks glass, I look out the bank of multipaned windows at the gray forms people carve out under the streetlights as they pass by. The Biograph Theater's marquee glows from the far side of Lincoln Avenue. It feels old-world—like London; I half expect fog to roll past and blot away the street, cars and taxicabs included.

The door lets out a wispy groan. The sound yanks my attention around. A tall man with a woman on his arm enters, and I breathe out, relieved yet more anxious; my watch reads 7:10. *Ten minutes late.* I imagine her working parking karma—wiggling the first two fingers of each hand like quotation marks.

In a fit of alarm, I shove my hand into my coat pocket to make sure, again, that the box of chocolate-covered espresso beans still sits at the ready.

Hanging my head back, I let out a long sigh of self-disgust. *Gotta chill, boy. 'S not prom night.*

I close my eyes and turn my attention to the indistinct music, the occasional bolts of laughter, the click and clatter of plates, the bell announcing that food's up—the comforting sounds of a restaurant.

"Still smoking unfiltered," Jennifer says. "Mean stuff."

I jerk my head forward at the sound of her voice. "If you're going to kill yourself—"

"You may as well do it with style," she finishes.

I stand. She's in a black leather jacket with a faux-fur trim, a slender low-cut top clinging to her willowy body as it pours into slim hips clad in faded blue jeans and a thick black belt.

You seem taller than I remember.

She's standing close by, so I open my arms slightly, checking for a hug, but her arms remain at her side.

Instead I offer her the tall chair across the table from me. I hold on to the edge of the table to fight off the sensation that I'm leaning too far over a precipice that goes infinitely far down.

"How are you?" she asks once I've settled into my own chair.

I nod. "You, of course, are looking … incredible."

"Flattery will get you nowhere," she says.

"There is a difference between flattery. And the truth."

"You are, of course, only telling me the truth."

"Pointing out the obvious."

"You haven't changed," she says. "Not a bit."

"I beg to differ," I say. "I'm growing a goatee. See. That's different."

"Not what I meant …"

"Do you like it?" I scrunch my fingers through it. "Still not sure about it."

"Well, you're certainly as vain as I remember."

"Oh, now really," I say, exaggerating a look of surprise. "Who, exactly, am I sitting across from?"

"Me." She grins, full of self-satisfaction.

"You. Yes. Indeed. It is. You."

"And you too," she says, picking up her menu.

"It's the same as when we …" I say, stopping before "came here on our first actual date."

She doesn't acknowledge what I almost said, though I'm sure she thought it too, and suddenly I'm not sure coming here was such a good idea.

"Yep. Looks the same. Smudges are new."

I smile. "Think I might have made that one." I point to a water stain on the back of her menu. She glances at it and politely raises her eyebrows in acknowledgment—no smile.

"So, um," I say, sensing that the chance to say what I need to is slipping away into the trite and overly polite, "what brings you back to town?"

"Oh. I needed a break—to see a friendly face … or three."

"Running an office getting you that down?"

"Yeah. So many people are lazy, stupid, or want to rip you off." She purses her lips. "I got used to getting tough, working shows here. But Wendy was around to handle to deep problems. There. Nope. I'm the heavy. That, sure. And, um ..." She looks down into her hands for a moment before staring at the trail of smoke from her cigarette.

"Um ...?"

"Nothing," she says, waving a hand. "Really. Things I needed to talk to Wendy about." She shrugs.

"Don't take this wrong," I say. "But I don't ... quite believe you. I know—I *knew* you better than that."

The waiter arrives, and we order more drinks and our food, and when he leaves, we're back to sitting across the small, tall table from each other in silence.

"Oh, before I forget." I reach into my pocket and bring out the small box, covered in light gray paisleys with a black-and-red sticker reading "The Myopic" fixed across the opening. I push the box across the table.

A smirk breaks over her mouth before she looks up with a question in her eyes.

"You mentioned once that you wanted to try them. At least that's what I think you said."

"Possibly. Very possibly." She snatches the box and rips the sticker in half with her finger.

"The forgotten comment, remembered."

She blanches as if I've stumbled over a dark secret. I try to remember what it was about these that was so important. Her eyes wide in alarm, she stares at me.

"Here." I reach for the box. "You don't have to eat them. I can toss 'em out. I ..."

"No. Not that. I thought you said ... something else. Nothing."

"So it didn't have anything to do with those—"

"How's Scott?" She pulls open the box and pops a bean into her mouth.

Without a word, we've decided to keep things safe and talk about everything except why she's actually in Chicago and what really we're doing here. Glasses empty. Food vanishes. I've struggled to keep from revealing that she's rescued me—partway.

Eventually there's nothing left to talk about except what we've avoided, which has been hanging off the edges of so many remarks. So it falls quiet between us again and feels like this will be the last silence before we say good-bye, and I've not had the chance to tell her how she's woken me from the sleepwalk life I've led since we lived together, and that I still her need help. It won't happen if I don't ask her tonight.

"So," I say, "what was the 'um' you mentioned before about why you're back here?"

Tapping her glass on the table, she takes a breath. "Ah, well. I had to ..." She takes a sip of her beer. "Had to break off my engagement."

That stung. I'm sure it showed on my face. "Hmm," I say. "That's, um ... too bad."

"No," she says. "Well, it's for the better. Only bad that it got there in the first place."

"Can only imagine."

"Took me too long to realize he was dating his idea of me: Jennifer, modeling exec from Chicago; not Jennifer, the woman who likes the Cure and *Twin Peaks*. It got so much worse when he found my name was on *Joie de Vivre*. I got the impression he started thinking I was a Laura Palmer and had some secret life up at One-Eyed Jack's." She scoffed. "Part of why I'm here."

"Sorry. That's so ..."

"Exactly."

"That's only part?"

"Yeah. You're not going to believe it."

"Try me."

"Notes for songs you never wrote."

"What?"

"When, um ..." She takes a deep breath. "You were always writing a lot of notes. Lyrics. Bits and pieces. About us."

"How did you get those?"

"Took 'em. When I left."

I look down into my drink, and swish the ice around. I take a drink, and only then can I look back up. "I'm surprised you didn't burn them in effigy."

"I tried to explain it to Wendy. Who *cannot* find out I'm here." She waves a finger at me. "As pissed as I was at times, I realized you saw me in some way no one else had. Has. I could see myself in your songs. I might not have liked what I saw every time, but at least it was real. Even if it was a catfight song."

"I never wrote a catfight song." I shake my head. "You were sure I would. Never even occurred to me."

"Nothing," she says, stroking her forehead, her hand hiding her face. "Stupid."

"Okay," I say. "So you read some old song notes. Then ..."

"I'd been planning on coming back to see Wendy for a while. But after what happened with my ex-fiancé, I took off without telling anyone. I think the songs might have nudged me. That's the only reason I'm here with you. You were a cold bastard. I hated you."

"I. Yes, I was. I don't even—"

"Don't. Just don't. I can't hear any lies right now, okay? It's good to see you, but only if you're honest."

"Completely honest then. Promise."

"But not too honest, okay. Not *yet*. I'm still feeling a bit ... raw."

"So I'll tell the truth and only the truth. But not the whole truth. Fine. Only do the same for me, okay?"

She smiles wryly. "Yes, Jonathan," she says, tapping the back my hand with a finger. "Honesty. To lay some out: It almost killed me when I had to break my engagement off. I loved him. But I had to choose between being me and trying to live up to being someone I'm not. I have to imagine that what you—No." She shakes her head. "No. I don't need to hear that—only that you know what that feels like. You do know, don't you?"

"Yes."

Nodding gravely, she looks out the window. "Enough truth telling. Too much is toxic."

Thus you slam the door on me. But you should know you make me feel again. So strongly I can hear music. Now you demand silence. Oh, girl, if only ...

Picking up her empty beer glass, she stares at the bottom and swirls it. "Empty."

"That's your third one," I say.

"So? You've had three," she says, holding up my glass, jiggling the ice at the bottom.

"So nothing," I say, taking my glass from her hand and draining the last liquid from it. "Want to get out of here?"

"Sure."

"Where do you want to go?" I ask.

"I don't care."

"You don't care?"

She shakes her head.

"At all?" I ask.

Arching an eyebrow, she shakes her head a bit slower this time, as if she's sending out a code she's counting on me grasping.

"Where's your car?"

She points. "That way. Couple of blocks."

"Here," I say, holding out my hand. "Give me the keys."

"I'm not drunk," she says. "Now, where am I taking us?"

"It's a surprise."

"Oh, no," she says. "I don't trust you."

"Oh," I say, gripping an imaginary handle over my heart. "Let me take out the knife."

She picks up the empty box of covered espresso beans. "You devoured half of this. And I'm supposed to trust you?"

I cock my head. "The loft."

"The loft?"

"I've got music. Coffee. Noshes for later."

She bites her lip. "Jonathan, I don't ..."

"Don't what?"

She reaches out and squeezes my hand. "Nothing. But I can't stay long."

"I've got things going on too, so I can't hang too late either."

Towing me behind, she leads the way out the door.

You already know what you did for me, don't you? Now you need it too—
to feel what we had again. Oh, Jennifer.

She leads us to a car I don't recognize, and somehow it surprises me
that it's not her old beater.

"New car to go with the new job," I say.

"Rental. Haven't been home yet."

I "huh" in agreement and don't ask why not; I can't risk waking up
some unpleasant memory that would send this night skittering off into a
heap of lost last chances. While we're driving, we decide to chat about a
lot of not much, but as we draw closer to the loft, the chatter slows until
we're staring straight ahead in silence. *Please be gone, Scott.* Without a
word, we park, enter the building, and climb the stairs to the loft. I take
out the keys.

"Is it like we imagined?"

"Close," I say. "You'll see."

"Scott here?"

"No idea. Haven't seen him since this afternoon."

"Good."

I open the door and step in, turning on the lights.

She follows me in and stares. "My god. I don't recognize the place."

"We've done some minor improvements in the last year and a half
or so."

"Yes," she says, "all of them—everything you said you'd do. The
drapes. And that balcony. The bedrooms—no ... 'sleeping dais.' That
was a favorite."

"I know," I say, hoping she'll ignore the angel on the "Love Will Tear
Us Apart" poster.

She runs across the floor and up the stairs. I watch as she stops at the
top of the stairs, turns, and throws a kiss out to the loft.

"Like it, Evita?" I ask.

"Don't cry for me." She vanishes.

"Jennifer," I call, "what are you doing?"

"Seeing who you really are."

I stroll up the stairs and throw open the drapes. She's kneeling on my bed, holding up a blue button-up shirt with the sleeves cut out from the body in a wide oval.

"Yep," I say. "Yours."

"You kept this?"

"No. Just didn't throw it out."

"There a difference?"

"Vast." My heart's racing as I lean farther and farther over the lip of a precipice that falls all the way to that bed, with her. I have so many songs I'll write about this. About everything it means. I can hear them. My mouth twitches.

Scott, don't you dare *walk in right now.*

Jennifer drops it next to the bed, which she turns to sit on. "A real bed." She bounces on it. "It's a lot like I had imagined it. But that shirt. I mean, really?"

"It's not like it was under my pillow or anything like that." I sit down next to her.

I catch the merest smile flickering on her lips.

I hear the first song; it's about being vulnerable and needing to be safe with someone you trust. Loving her.

Lying back, I reach out to stroke her palm with a finger.

"Jonathan," she says, "I'm not …"

"Not what?" I ask, sitting up, looking at her.

The next song's about taking advantage of the vulnerability of someone who trusts you.

"This is very … confusing."

I pull a finger along her jaw. She holds her breath until my finger slips off her chin.

The song after that explores the hurt that betrayal causes.

"Don't," she whispers, looking away.

"What's confusing?"

The next song explores a couple's downfall. Even if he can't help himself. Even if she can't. Suffering for her.

"Life," she says. "I don't know. I'm sorry."

She starts to stand

I guide her back next to me.

She goes without resistance.

The next song's about doing something wicked when you're not a wicked person, when you don't mean to—when you can't stop yourself.

She touches my cheek, shaking her head.

It'll explain the wickedness. Plead for understanding; that she's the key. And he can't lose it. Not again. Turning her into lyrics, melody, and rhythm. Preserving her. Us.

I kiss her. Her tongue burrows into me.

But he can stop this time. No matter his loss.

"Jennifer," I say, pulling back. "It's late. We've had a lot to drink. Why don't I go sleep on the couch? You can sleep here." I pat the bed.

She looks as startled as she did the night she gave me that hand massage, when I said no.

"I don't like the songs we're writing," I say.

CHAPTER 52

SWEEP IT ALL AWAY
—JENNIFER—

I slip out of the loft as soon as I wake up, and I head to my parents' place. I don't know what to tell Wendy about what nearly happened last night—especially since I'm making the drive of shame I would have made the next morning anyway: clothes tossed on, hair mussed, makeup smeared, no fresh pair of panties.

We only kissed. Once. Nothing more.

So why do I feel ashamed? So scudgy.

"God. I so need a shower."

After making one last turn, I'm driving down my parents' street.

Please, Mother, be gone. I can't do discussion right now. I don't know why I'm here, don't know what happened last night, and don't know what to expect now. So please, please, please—no mother. No stepdad.

I see the house. No lights. Both cars gone.

"Yes!" I slap the dashboard. "Empty house. Lucky Jennifer."

I park up the street, let myself in with my old key, and make straight for the shower. Turning on the water, I kick off my shoes, strip last night's clothes off, and step into the warm stream.

"Oh, that feels sooooo good."

I wash—my hair, and face, my body; I wash away every particle of what nearly happened last night.

What the hell was that all about, girl? Fly two thousand miles to get him into your panties? And he says no. Again.

Stepping out of the shower, I dry off.

"What are you doing here, anyway?"

I stare at myself in the mirror.

"Well. I don't know either."

I've no clothes here so have to put yesterday's back on. Then I walk out into the living room. She said she'd fixed the place up when I was gone—remodeled—but everything looks the same. Maybe she meant she remodeled my old room. Fixed it up.

Nope. Can't do that right now.

I drop myself into my stepdad's ugly yellow chair and flip on the tube. Stupid daytime talk shows: *Maury. Jenny Jones. Click, click, click,* and the channels flit past. Weight-loss infomercial. Black-and-white cowboy movie. Soap opera. A bad music video. A shampoo advertisement. *Good Day Chicago.* I stop clicking.

Why not? See what's been going on.

While watching an empty-headed blonde blabber on about some community organization in Humboldt Park, I think about my old room. My mother told me that she cleaned it up, made it into a guest room. *Wonder what she threw out and where she put whatever's left—the things she thought mattered. Whatever that could be.*

The blonde looks earnestly at the TV audience. "And now some breaking news about Charlene Pollard, the model who was thought to have been murdered three years ago. Her death was ruled an accident; she apparently slipped off her balcony after an afternoon of drinking."

The scene cuts to a cop behind a microphone.

"Charlene Pollard: Mystery Solved" appears in white at the bottom of the screen.

"Charlene? What mystery? You slipped. Fell," I tell the TV, explaining it to them.

The cop says, "When the current tenants decided to remodel the apartment Ms. Charlene Pollard occupied with Mr. Barthes, her companion, this was found, hidden in a bookcase." He holds up a small camera. "At first they considered it unremarkable. Probably a forgotten surveillance camera. But when the contractor found cables still attached, he examined further and saw they went to a remote recorder, and there he found a videotape. He played it to see if there was anything recorded. What was there caused him to bring it to the police. It shows the model Charlene Pollard's last minutes and reveals that she was neither murdered nor had an accident. Rather, she committed suicide, and this videotape is her suicide note." He holds up a compact videotape.

Charlene?

"Why didn't her companion, Mr. Barthes, present the tape to the police?" a reporter asks.

"He has told us that he was unaware of it. It seems Ms. Pollard either had it installed secretly or found it there. That's something we'll probably never know."

"Did she say she was trying to frame Mr. Barthes? Was it a domestic situation?" a second reporter asks.

"Though the circumstances are suggestive of that, there is nothing on the tape that indicates she was trying to harm Mr. Barthes. Her reasons, rather, suggest depression. Or extreme disappointment."

"She wasn't depressed!" I yell at the cop. "She wasn't! No. She partied with us. She had fun. Charlene, what did you do?"

"What, exactly, were her reasons?" another reporter asks.

"This is all we can say right now. The tape contains a lead we are currently following up on. We'll be more at liberty to discuss those details once that has been completely investigated."

The earnest blonde returns. "We'll be right here on Fox 32 to keep you informed on all the details as soon as they happen."

Good Day Chicago returns.

My hands tremble.

There is a sharp knock on my door.

I jerk in the chair, and turn toward the door.

"Chicago Police," a man's voice announces.

I'm frozen in place. *Why would police be here?*

The knock comes again.

"Um, hang on," I say, tottering to my feet. I walk unsteadily to the door. Opening it, I find two cops standing on the small porch. They are both wearing black leather jackets and have large automatics slung from their hips. Their low-set checker-brimmed hats hide their eyes.

"Um. Yes?"

"Are you Jennifer Gaultier?"

I stare blankly.

"Do you know where we can find her?"

"Me."

"Me?" the larger officer asks.

"I'm Jennifer. What's this ... I just got into town. I don't—"

"Did you know Charlene Pollard?"

"Uh," I say, nodding.

"Can we come in?"

"Uh-huh."

Turning back inside, I feel as if I've floated from my life and into an undiscovered Hitchcock film.

The heavier one introduces himself as Sergeant Luckac, and the other one as Officer McInerney. Officer McInerney leaves while the sergeant explains they found a videotape in Charlene's old apartment and that I'm the only person Charlene named in the video, other than Mr. Barthes, and that they need me to watch it.

"To see if she said or did anything that warrants further investigation," Sergeant Luckac says.

Officer McInerney returns carrying a compact VHS player–television, and after setting it up for me, they play Charlene's suicide note for me.

The soft-focused video reveals the room; there is a dark leather couch, a cherrywood coffee table, and a large-screen TV near the doorway leading to the balcony; the curtain is pulled back. Through the balcony's glass door is a good view of Chicago on a sunny afternoon. Charlene walks into the scene with two glasses, one in each hand. She stands in front of the camera. Everything about her is long: her legs, her neck, her waist. She's the idea of a model with arching blonde eyebrows. She gives a model's smile: wide-mouthed, full of straight, white teeth. She takes a drink from one glass and then from the other.

"Cocktails for the both of us."

She nods.

"Yes, both. There are two of us here. Can't you see us? Well, here, let

355

me point us out. Here's the innocent one, who still tries to believe." She nods her head to the left. "And the experienced one, who knows there's no point," she says, nodding to the right. "One still smiles very sweetly, like she used to; the other fakes it—like Dale Carnegie gone wild. So"—she takes a pair of sips, one from each glass—"can you tell the difference? Can you tell which one is talking now, pouring these cocktails of very expensive booze in the penthouse high above Chicago with the splendid view? The leather sofa, big-screen TV, and cut crystal are the finest. Like you see in the magazines. Oh, I hear you thinking: Wouldn't it be fabulous to be like that? To live like that? To live like in magazines—perfect and glamorous, always beautiful. Like Dorian Gray, but it's the world aging for you? Wouldn't it be wonderful to be like me—ageless in my living photograph world?

"Yep, you guessed it. It's the worldly one speaking. The innocent one is almost gone, barely able to smile anymore, her dreams lying broken in the corner, with me pretending she likes to live that way.

"See, this is what they told her: 'With looks like yours, you'll go far.' Look it; she did go far. She got the prize: me. And I got it all—exactly what they said she would."

She winks. "You know what I'm saying, Jennifer. 'Just smile. You can get anything you want.'" She winks again. "Shoulda moved in with you. Shoulda kept looking at the magazines. You see, once you step inside the photographs, once you are what other people want to be, you find out, well ..."

She takes a pair of drinks.

"So who am I now?" She sticks her tongue out and crosses her eyes.

She takes another pair of sips. "Ah, liquid courage.

"I shouldn't say this. She might hear, and I don't want to break the innocent girl's heart—what's left of it. I can't let her know that once you get what you want, once you're inside and you find it's still only you, there's nothing to dream of anymore. That's the worst part about being here, inside of a magazine: you've gotten what you wished for, but you're still the same. Glossy color and captions don't change that. I'm only me, protecting the little one. Until I can't anymore."

She walks toward the door to the balcony. "Stay where you are—on the outside of magazines, looking in.

"Oh, Richard? Nice guy. Too wrapped up in his work, though. Us? I guess like everyone else, we had our ups and downs. It's no different in here than out there. The problems aren't something we enjoyed, and they're beside the point, so we're going to stop talking about that now, okay? That goes to show another problem. All you voyeurs know *of* me, but not one *knows* me. Not anymore. Not even you, Jennifer."

She takes two more drinks and opens the balcony door and looks outside.

"Lovely day out. You should come over and take a look."

She beckons the camera and then gives a look of mock shock.

"Oh, right. It will be days later, and the weather will be different. But it is lovely today. You know, it occurs to me right now how the weather changes the whole background of this. Take a storm, with thunder— all ominous. Or a cloudy day. Or foggy. Or drizzly. All so depressing. Weather like that would fit your expectations—the expectations you've fed on from books and magazines and movies and TV. Today, though, this sunny day. It really is appropriate, if unexpected.

"I'm not depressed. No. I'm pissed that I got what I wanted, but it's not at all what it looked like. It's the same as you thinking a rainy day is more appropriate for a twenty-three-story dive. It's a fake—an illusion. I blame imagination. But not mine. Not completely. Someone has to make up these magazine spreads, make up these dreams out of so much nothing. People fashioning what we should want, even if it never existed. Can never exist. 'Cause they are all fairy stories. Only Rumpelstiltskin spinning gold out of straw. It makes me angry that I believed. I believed in it so strongly I became it. It sucks worse 'cause this is real life and there's no one to overhear him saying his real name. I'm losing my child—the innocent one, who still tries smiling. She's so sweet.

"I'm sorry, dear," Charlene says, patting her own shoulder. "Have a drink." She takes two big slugs.

"I'm not letting that imp take her. She can still try to dream; I won't tell her the truth."

She takes a long drink from one glass and walks back to the coffee table and sets the drained glass down.

"Here's to you. No, you. To us." She drains the second glass and sets it down on the table. "Sorry for not cleaning up. I'm sure you can understand."

She struts to the balcony door and gives herself a hug. "You always wanted to fly. Maybe if you believe strongly enough, we will. Clap, clap. Everyone clap. Don't let Tink die."

Charlene then steps up onto a chair and sits on the balcony railing.

"Everyone clap. Don't let Tink die." She waves. Leans back. Her legs fly up and vanish. There is only clear blue sky.

Officer McInerney turns off the TV.

Every part of me is shaking. I answer their questions, explaining that I didn't know she felt like this, that we were supposed to be roommates but we'd grown apart since she moved in with that man, and that I didn't see anything out of the ordinary—except everything. After getting the answers to their questions, the two officers simply leave.

I feel drained of feeling, as if I'm the one who's dead and the officers came to tell me they'd found my body. I stare at the spot on the table where the portable TV showed Charlene talking.

Charlene, what did you do? Jonathan, what happened? What am I doing here at all?

"Stop." *Too much, too fast. Time to slow it down, girl.*

"My old room," I say, forcing myself to think of something else. *Right. Let's see what mom left of me here.*

I get to the door of my room and only touch it.

"Whatever you did, Mom, it's fine."

Wrapping my hand around the doorknob, I twist and push open the door.

Nothing looks the same. My bed is there, along with my dresser, my nightstand, and my lamp, but it's not the way I left it. New yellow paint covers the walls, which have been cleared of all my posters and photos. A strip of floral print runs around the tops of the walls at the ceiling. There are new white sheets and a summery cover. It's bright, happy. I'd never been happy like that here. Not bright, shiny happy.

My mother has painted over all my disappointments and hurts with bright colors. It's what Mother wants to make-believe, like a spread from a homemaking magazine. I was the one who lived here, but there's nothing left of me.

For the best—can't idolize disappointment. Get it gone and get on living. Unlike Charlene.

"How could you do that, Charlene? Who were you? Really?"

I open the drawer on my nightstand and start poking around in the crap my mother put there: two pens, a pad of clean white paper, a small bottle of aspirin, and a bag of toffee candies.

I scoff. *It's a hotel room.*

At least she left the flowers I scribbled on the bottom of the drawer when I was nine.

She's refinished my dresser; it looks almost new, except for the deep gouges on the side I dug with a penknife rather than cutting myself. I run my finger along those dark indentations and then jerk my hand away.

"Nope. Not something to remember."

I'm not like Charlene. Not anymore. Not at all.

I open the top drawer: empty. The next: empty. The next: empty.

Right: hotel-room clean. For houseguests.

"Whatever, Mother."

The bottom drawer, though, is full.

Sitting cross-legged in front of it, I run my hand along all my rolled-up posters. One by one, I pull each out, roll the rubber band off, unfurl it, and try to remember why I bought it. *She* sang what I couldn't say. *They* understood. *They* showed me a different life—showed me what I could be. *They* lived in a sorrow I understood. *They* were who I thought I wanted to be—happy, admired, beautiful.

"But they're not really like that are they? Right, Charlene?"

I let the last poster fall from my hand; it curls back up like the others.

"Don't like light, do you?"

Lying at the bottom of the drawer is the letter I wrote to Jonathan right after he ended it. It's still sealed. Undelivered. Unread. Running my fingers along the edges, I try to remember what, exactly, it says. It's long—six pages.

I toss it back in.

I slam the drawer closed.

I needed someone to trust; then he went right for his bed. Worse, I wanted him to. Now I can't trust him or myself.

I sprawl backward on the floor.

"Stupid," I say, kicking the dresser. "Stupid, stupid, stupid."

I kick the dresser again. I want to destroy something. I yank open the bottom drawer, pull out the letter to him, and start tearing it to shreds. I rip up all the posters. I'll kill everything that was me. I'll kill all my decisions, all my stupidities, all my empty thoughts, my dreams of magazines and bands and fashion, and everything I was and wanted to be. I stomp on the pile of shreds; I kick them into the air.

Gathering an armful of the scraps, I march through the house, push open the back door, throw them onto the concrete porch, light an edge on fire, and then watch the flame spread. Soon everything is burning. I run back and scrape together the pieces left on the floor, and I feed the flames with them. I watch the column of smoke as it fades into the cold breeze, wiping out all that I was and all those dreams of what I *could* be like—what my life *should* be like.

"See, Charlene," I say, "I'm killing myself. But only the parts of me I can't be anymore. Not all of me, Charlene. You never, ever had to do that. You're weak, girl.

"Who the hell were you?"

Sitting on the cold concrete, I pull my knees up to my chest and hold them, watching the shrinking fire. I push the pile of ash and half-burnt paper together to revive the flames, making sure everything burns up completely.

The posters, photos, and letters, frail and blackened ash now, rise and blow away.

Then a thought jars me—I wanted to sleep with Jonathan last night. Some part of me wanted to. We'd only been talking, being friends, just having fun. Yet all the while, something had been prowling around inside of me, urging me, pushing me. I imagine it had his chameleon eyes—hazel, changing from blue to gray to green. They were eyes that made me feel not pretty, which I'd have hated, but completely wanted, for my thoughts and my opinions—everything. That was so thrilling, like walking along a precipice, teetering on the edge of everything I'd wanted—the world I'd seen in my posters. With a nudge, I'd have fallen in.

He was the key. I wanted him—wanted that—so badly, years ago.

Still wanting that after all this time disturbs the hell out of me. That's the part I'm trying to kill right now.

Last night I felt exactly the same as the first time I came over to the loft alone—the night we first kissed, when he refused to sleep with me. That was so impossible to understand. But I didn't understand the loft either: two mattresses, a stereo, a card table, mismatched folding chairs, music gear, and all that emptiness, with his keyboard sitting in the center, as if it were the center of his life.

It was. Still is. Always will be.

That's what I didn't understand then. All I saw was the emptiness; the concrete, brick, and steel; and how it looked like a glossy two-page spread of everything I wanted in life at nineteen. I could touch it. I felt as if I'd lose myself in that place—in him. With him, back then, I was able to forgive myself for old lovers, mistakes, and bad decisions. So much disappointment and pain went away with him; he made real my desires shown in my cutout photos and posters.

Then he yanked that away.

What's wrong with you, Jennifer? Didn't he sing of moments when love tears lovers apart? When it's irresistible and destructive? Why didn't you see that wasn't merely his art? It's his truth.

The phone rings, jerking me back to now.

What bill did you forget to pay this time, Mom?

The phone rings again.

I pick it up out of old habit.

"Hello?" I challenge.

"Jennifer?" Jonathan asks.

I should hang up.

"I'm sorry," he says.

"So am I."

"I ..." he says. "What happened—not what either of us needed. But did. Now—"

"No," I say, shaking my head. "Not ... just no. I gotta have some time."

The front door opens, and I hear my mother's high heels clacking across the floor toward me.

"Mom's home," I say. "I'll call. As soon as I can figure it out." I hang up.

"Oh, I thought you said you were going to be at Wendy's," my mother says.

"Hi, Mom," I say.

"What is that?" my mother asks, pressing her finger on the sliding glass door looking out over the patio.

"I'll sweep it up."

"But what is it?"

"Old things. Things I don't want anymore."

"You smell like smoke."

"I'll shower," I say. "Do you have an extra towel?"

"Of course. You know where they are." She opens the refrigerator door and starts pushing things around, making rattling noises. "Are you staying for dinner?"

"Hadn't thought about it."

"Well, I do need to know. I had only planned on Jean and me. If you're staying, I need to make something else."

"I'll eat out."

"Okay," she says, and then she starts pulling out a few sealed plastic bowls.

"Can I stay here for a couple of nights?"

"I thought—"

"Things changed."

"Oh." My mother purses her lips. "Sure. You know where your room is. But your father and I have gotten used to the quiet, so—"

"Won't even know I'm here," I say, pulling out my cigarettes.

"Your father and I quit smoking, so you have to do it outside."

I nod and walk to the door. I turn back to my mother. "Where's Sarabeth?"

"Around somewhere," she says, pulling the top off a green bowl and sniffing inside.

In the living room, I kneel to look underneath the couch and then under each of the chairs. I find Sarabeth curled up beside a heat register and pick up the fat, lazy thing as she mews softly. Petting and cradling her, I walk past my mother, busily pulling a spoon around the green bowl. I step outside and hold Sarabeth as she purrs. I nuzzle her.

"You don't want anything but love, do you?" I say. Feeling Sarabeth's warmth, I watch the breeze sweep the remaining ashes away.

Chapter 53

The Smooth, Cold Floor
—Scott—

I pull back a corner of the kitchen curtains in the apartment where Lynda's staying. A dull-gray morning awaits outside.

That "Daydream and Try" rocks has complicated things. Doing "Fantasy in Black" because it's the only single we have won't fly anymore. That makes selling it to get Kenny on as a guest singer a hell of a lot harder. And without his singing on a new Mercurial Visions single, his replacing Jonathan on the album looks all but impossible now.

It's not how I worked things out for us, Kenny. But—persistence and determination.

Jonathan was finished. It was an easy out for him and an easy in for Kenny. Then Jonathan goes and kills it with "Daydream and Try." Now he claims he'll churn out stuff like he used to.

But Jonathan's pulled crap like this on me one too many times. And I won't get fooled again. His games exhaust me, leaving me wondering when he'll turn into the mopey prima donna who can't function because of yet another woman.

Plus we've only heard one good song, pulled out of his ass at the last second. That's not an album. Sure as hell's not what I've already seen for the future. That's you, Kenny: our future. I promise.

I've given up waiting for you, Jonathan. Sammy couldn't wait *for me. Kenny won't have to. He'll sing "Fantasy in Black" in front of Mercurial*

Visions, right beside me. It's simply a matter of working out the details. Starting this afternoon.

I'm meeting Nancy at Mad Bar. I'm sure she'll understand that a single song from Jonathan doesn't cut it. Neither does talk. We need real songs, actually written. She likes Kenny. She'll be on our side. Plus she needs the band to work so she can live legit, long term. However she gets her money can't be legal. The band's a cover. That much I've figured out.

The whistle on the teapot starts crying, and I turn off the flame and then pour two cups of hot water.

"Scott," Lynda calls to me from the bedroom.

I slide a tea bag into each cup.

"Scott?" she calls again.

"Yes," I say, dunking the bag until her tea is "the color of early dusk." *Ridiculous comparison. About as ridiculous as me being here. I'm gonna have to tell Jonathan sooner or later.*

I wrap the string of her bag around the handle.

"I'm out of cigarettes."

"And?" I ask, placing her cup on a saucer and walking it into the bedroom.

She's leaning off the bed, revealing her back and hips, rummaging through the pockets of her jacket.

"I'm out of ..."

"So you said." I hand her a cup as she sits up and brushes red curls of hair from her face.

"Could you go get me some?" She gives me her I-might-let-you-have-me-if ... look.

"Your nasty habit."

She scowls and pulls the sheet over herself.

No more skin for Scott. He's been a bad boy.

I leave for my tea.

"What time is it, honey-bunny?" she asks after me.

"Clock's right there. On the nightstand," I say.

"I'm hungry," she says. "We've got time for brunch before I go to Charlie's."

I lean against the door frame, the paint cool on my skin.

"Can't take long though," I say. "We have to be in the studio in a few days. I have a call this a.m. Meeting later."

"We can get my smoky treats on the way," she says, letting the sheet fall away, revealing her body again. She curls her finger at me, beckoning.

"Thought you were hungry," I say.

"I am," she says, patting the bed beside her. "But for more than eggs." I scoff.

"You're such a prick," she says, reaching for her bra. "You know that?"

"We've both got work today," I say. "Right?"

"Fine."

Staying here longer than I must ain't worth it.

She pulls on her bra. "You gonna put some clothes on?"

After we grab a bite to eat, I call the executive producer at Wax Trax! and tell him we'll be recording "a song called 'Fantasy in Black'" and that we'll need to meet with him about it. We set the meeting for tomorrow. *Deed done. Next: break it to Jonathan.*

I call Kenny. His answering machine kicks on.

"Hey. Called Wax Trax! We're meeting, tomorrow, about 'Fantasy in Black.' Let's talk after rehearsal tonight. Out someplace. I'll let you know where."

I hang up the phone, button my coat, and leave to meet Nancy at Mad Bar.

Got things on track again.

The damp, cold wind blowing along Damen Avenue hits me as soon as I step outside. I pull my collar tighter.

Nancy's smart enough to see that even if we release "Daydream and Try," Jonathan's got nothing left. And Jennifer being back in town? I shake my head. Nancy knows the future needs to be planned for. She'll see Kenny's it.

Then it's on to AnnMarie. She needs the band too, but differently. She wears it like a disguise.

For Kenny and me, it's even more.

Sorry, Sammy. I don't have a choice. You didn't give me one. I wipe my face to sweep Sammy's face from my mind. *God, I'm so sorry. So very—*

"Hey," Ron calls to me from across the street, a stocking cap pulled over his ponytail. He waves for me to stop and trots across the street.

"What's this about Jonathan?" he asks, his camera swinging from his neck.

"What about him?"

"He's leaving town with Jennifer?"

"What?"

"So Kenny's taking Jonathan's place?" He shoves his hands deep into the pockets of his leather jacket.

"Who told you that?"

"He did."

"He said he's taking Jonathan's place?" My hands ball into fists. "When?"

"Hour ago. Saw him at the Busy Bee with some pretty boy. He said you were going to use 'Fantasy' something for your single. He's singing it."

I clench my teeth.

"When did he decide to leave?" Ron asks, fondling his camera.

"Hold up here. What did he say about Jennifer?" I ask.

"Kenny? Nothing. Nancy told me she was back in town and that she and Jonathan got together last night. *Together* together," he says, interlacing his fingers. "I figured that's why he'd leave. Almost makes sense that way."

"So," I say, "this stuff about Jonathan leaving ..."

"Figured it that way," Ron says. "Nancy figured as much too."

"Nancy figured what what way?"

"About why Kenny's replacing him," Ron says. "She was shocked when I told her."

"Stop." I hold my hands aside my head. "When did you tell her?"

"Ten, fifteen minutes ago. She was right there"—he points down Damen—"at Mad Bar. She said she was meeting you. I—"

I bolt down the sidewalk. *No. No. Not the way.*

"Hey," he shouts after me. "When do I shoot new band photos?"

Mad Bar is empty when I burst through the door.

"Hi there," I say to the bartender, my breath heaving from my run in the cold. "Did you see a woman in here? Dark hair? Blunt cut?" I ask. "She was with a guy with long black hair, goatee, a camera."

"Oh, yeah," the bartender says. "She took off. Left a few minutes ago. Right after the guy."

"Shit," I say, scowling.

"Aren't you …"

"No. I'm nobody." I rap my knuckles on the bar. "You have a phone?"

The bartender points to the back. I jog to the back, slip two dimes into the black box, and rap it with my fingers until her machine clicks on: "I'd love to hear from you," her voice says, "but I'm not here. Or can't get the phone. You know what to do next." The machine beeps.

"Nancy. Call me as soon as you get home. There's been some bullshit flying around, and I want to straighten it out. Call me. A-SAP." I slam down the receiver. "Fuck me." I walk back to the bar, pinching the bridge of my nose.

"She'd go home, right?" I ask myself. "Yes. Go home to think. Make calls. Right." I take off, hauling ass down Damen to her place.

I jam the button next to *Nancy M.*

Nothing. I jam it again and wait. Nothing. Twice more. I wait more. Still nothing. I walk to the side of her three-flat and strain to see into her windows. They're all completely dark.

"Where the hell are you," I say to the window. "Goddamn it!"

It's gotten very windy, and the wet cold cuts deeply. I lean against the wall, closing my eyes. *Goddamned Lynda and her movie-script life. She had to have brunch the morning after. I was supposed to be at Mad Bar, with Nancy. Instead, stupid people got to say stupid things to the wrong people at the wrong time.*

"This was so simple!" I shout.

"No," I say, correcting myself. *It's still simple, only not as easy. Because of diarrhea of the mouth. Now, instead of easy transition, it's damage control.* "Fuck."

I take several deep breaths.

"Fine," I tell myself. *So let's say she called Jonathan. Him I need to deal with now. Then Nancy. Then AnnMarie. Then Wax Trax!*

As I walk around the park, I jam my hands into my pockets and pull my shoulders up against the frigid wind.

Kenny, you've made this so much harder than it needed to be. The whole world probably knows about us now. Why'd I think you could keep a secret like I did for Sammy?

Doesn't matter. Like Sammy always said, persistence and determination alone are omnipotent.

When I reach the loft, I trudge up the stairs, wondering how far this has gotten. No matter what, I know I'm right to put saving the band above everything else. *Including Jonathan.*

On the fourth floor, I stop and take a deep breath. Pulling my shoulders back and standing tall, I slide the key in and twist.

"Let's get it done." I open the door.

Under a thin layer of smoke, the three of them sit on the couch—Mercurial Visions without me. They all turn at the sound of the door opening. I pop my lips.

"What's up?" I ask, striding in.

"We have a problem," Jonathan says. "Involving all of us."

I shake my head as if I don't know what he's talking about.

"'Fantasy in Black.'"

"Yeah?" I ask, shrugging. "That's that song I've been working on with Kenny, for Unknown Vices. We've talked about this before."

"Yes, we did. Last time, you suggested that I sing *his* song because *we* didn't have a single."

"Not so."

"Yes so. But now I hear—"

"Hear what?"

"Kenny thinks *he's* singing it," Jonathan says.

"Oh? And you believe him? Our former roadie? Onetime singer of another band?"

"Cut the crap," Jonathan says. "What's going on?"

He's glaring at me. Nancy looks down, picking at her fingernails. AnnMarie's expressionless.

"I told him," I say, "that I wanted to use his song *if* we couldn't come up with anything else *for* the single we're recording in a couple of weeks. But—"

"But what?"

"'Daydream and Try' changes that."

"Not what he said. And not what you said to Wax Trax! this morning," Jonathan says.

I cock my head as if I didn't hear.

"Yes, we know you set up a meeting with Wax Trax! without me. Yes, we know it's about recording 'Fantasy in Black.' See, they called. They had to push it back fifteen minutes. I asked, of course. One plus one equals you're going to tell them our *ex*-roadie's singing *his* song in *my* band."

"Our band!" I shout. "It's *our* band. Not yours alone. And you haven't really been in it for two years, Jonathan!" I stomp my foot. "Two years that I worked my ass off to keep us touring and keep us earning money while you curled up into a little ball like some prima donna, letting everything go to hell. You couldn't write for shit on *Second Vision*. You couldn't even perform. Read the reviews. 'The front man, lead singer was all but absent, and the guitarist did his best but finally couldn't overcome the mannequin's lackluster performance.' Yeah, I remember those lines. You felt it. And you." I point to Nancy. "And you." I point to AnnMarie. "The audience did too. They especially. Tell me I'm wrong. Tell me!"

They stare.

"What the hell d'you want me to do?" I cleave the air with my arm. "Let us die?"

Silence.

"This isn't right. I'm not the bad guy here. I'm the one trying to save the band. To pull the rest of us out of your self-absorbed implosion."

"*Self-absorbed* implosion? You mean my reeling. To recover from that choice I never had to make—the one you forced me to make."

"*Forced* you to make?" I thrust my finger at him. "Jennifer? You *chose* to leave her. No gun to your head. You kicked her out because you knew it was the right thing—"

"Bullshit." He shakes his head violently. "You trapped me, alone, in that car for days, filling my head with shit: 'It's either me or her.' 'It's the band or a woman.' 'Make a choice!'"

"Yes. Make *your* choice," I bellow. "Not *mine*. *Your* choice: some *woman* or the *band*. Stay with me or go with her. I saved you. Like I've always been forced to save you. I've always been there for you, Jonathan. Always. And you? You take me for granted. Sammy *never* did—never broke a promise to me either. Until you got killed."

"What?"

"I've protected you repeatedly. I saved you from Amy, then Jennifer. I kept you focused. I kept this band going for you, like I would have for Sammy. But Sammy's dead. *You?* You take me for granted. I'm sick of it, Mister Jonathan Starks. You won't do that to me again. You've rejected me for the last time. Kenny? Yeah." I nod, jabbing my finger at Jonathan. "He's going to be the singer in Mercurial Visions. Like Sammy should have been. Like you were supposed to be."

His mouth hangs open, full of silence.

Motionless, Nancy and AnnMarie watch like harrowed window display mannequins.

My heart thuds. My whole body's tense. I summon the sounds of a helicopter flying low overhead, toward a tree line. Then the eruption of napalm comes, engulfing the jungle, taking Jonathan with it. Over this scene, Jim Morrison is singing, "This is the end / my one and only friend / the end."

I mouth *"boom." The apocalypse. Now.*

"I think you'd better leave now," he says, in spite of being engulfed in an explosion of napalm. "The rest of us have to decide what to do."

"Not from my house." I crouch, my body tightening like a bow. "No one decides anything for me. Not for my band."

I lunge.

He springs aside like a startled cat.

Missing him, my shoulder slams into the couch. I knock it sideways, taking the girls with it.

They scream. Someone grabs my arm.

"Get off me!" I shout, twisting around, pulling AnnMarie with me, flinging her off my arm. Jonathan's brows are drawn together. He's seething but scared. I leap, swinging my fist at his unfaithful face. He shifts, fending my punch far to the side. I lose my balance and fall—hard—to the concrete.

Before I can think, he's pinned my arm behind my back, kneeling on it with his full weight.

My hands sting from striking the floor. I can't move. The concrete chills my face.

This isn't right. This cannot be the way it ends. *I promised.*

So I tell myself to relax. *This is only one day. One setback. The only thing that matters is persistence and determination. Just like you said, Sammy.* So with each breath, I push the rage out and into the cold, concrete floor. My heartbeat calms, my breaths come slower, more evenly.

No one's moving. I can hear only breathing.

"I think you'd better leave," he says, his voice strained.

I lie slack on the concrete.

"Now," he says.

"I can't get up," I say, coolly, evenly.

"Are you going to leave? You're a big man. I have to trust you. Or call the police."

I nod my face along the smooth, cold floor.

He lifts his knees off my arm. Putting my palms next to my ribs, I lie on the floor a moment. Pushing myself up, I keep my eyes pegged to the door. The girls have armed themselves with mic stands. *Certainly tells me what side you're on.*

"I'll be back, ladies," I whisper.

Walking directly out, I refuse to look at anyone.

"As conqueror."

Chapter 54

Persistence and Determination Alone

—Scott—

As soon as I hit the street, I walk directly to the 'L', hiking up my shoulders against a wicked blast from an Alberta Clipper. The wind's blowing down North Avenue, hitting my cheeks in a hard, brittle gush that feels sharp like slivers of ice. It stings. I turn my back, letting the wind whip the edges of my long coat in front of me.

"It doesn't end like this," I tell myself.

Right now I need a place to work from. *Kenny's. I'll crash there for as long as it takes. We can work from there. Even rehearse if necessary. Not as convenient as the loft, but we'll take that back soon enough. Mister Starks, you won't be needing it anymore. It'll be for my and Kenny's band. The new Mercurial Visions.*

This time of day, Kenny'll be at work, so I catch the 'L' at Damen and head to the Loop, where I switch to the Howard line and get off at the Chicago–State Street stop.

Finally reaching Michigan Avenue, I pass under the faintly orange glow of the lights of Borders. I push through the revolving doors. Passing the racks of magazines and the thin crowd browsing the displays of best sellers and tabletop books, I ride the escalator down. Sliding my fingers through the opening of my coat, I ease each button off, one by one. The long coat spreads open as I stride to the information counter, where Kenny is standing. My palms still tingle from striking the concrete.

His eyes grow wide when he sees me approaching. He backs behind the counter and grabs the computer screen, holding it like a shield.

I snap to a stop directly in front of him and his frightened-doe eyes.

"I thought you'd told them," he says. "This is my job. Please. I didn't mean—"

"What do you mean?" I smile and then tap my fingers on the wooden countertop. "I'm here to talk business."

Kenny regards me with suspicion. A natural-looking woman with her hair in a bun and a makeup-free face emerges from the doorway behind him. She glances at me and then makes a double take: an expression of do-I-know-you? appears.

"You're ..." she says, pointing.

"Yep." I nod. "Scott Marshall."

She beams. "Yes, yes. From—"

"Mercurial Visions. Exactly why I came to see your friend Kenny," I say. His expression pleads. "What are you doing tomorrow?" I ask him.

"Why?" he asks, his voice small, almost whispering.

"We've got a meeting. With Wax Trax! *tomorrow*. To tell them about 'Fantasy in Black,'" I say. "We'll need to be in the studio quickly. Like, within a week *at most*. And we might need some help from Unknown Vices. Probably will. We'll discuss that with Wax Trax! at the meeting."

"Um," he says, looking lost.

"Now, I need someplace to crash for a couple of nights," I say.

"What?"

"Nothing serious. We'll talk about that later."

"I don't ..."

"When do you get home today?" I ask.

"I don't—"

"You owe me. *Big* time."

His lips close pensively.

My nod beckons.

"Sure," he says, finally. "I'll be home about seven."

"We'll talk more when you get home," I say. "Especially about the meeting. Oh, let your roomies know. I don't want to get shot as an intruder. Capish?"

The girl looks at him, then me, and them him again, biting her lower lip.

He nods uncertainly.

"Remember," I say, repeating Sammy's favorite quote, "persistence and determination alone are omnipotent."

• • • • •

At seven, I knock on Kenny's apartment door. He lets me in.

In the living room, his two roommates are channel surfing. *Young do-nothings, good-for-nothings. Fashion and clubs and nice hair: stereotypical queens. Don't like you much.*

"Let's go into your room," I say.

The roommates look at each other with I-told-you-so smirks and then get back to watching TV.

Soon enough you'll be looking for a new roommate. Kenny'll be living in the loft with me.

"Let's talk some business," I say as I close the door. The room's small, but there is a chair, which I take. He sits on his bed.

"Can I have the phone?" I ask.

He hands it over, and I call Dave, my lawyer.

"So the meeting is tomorrow?" he asks.

"Yeah. And then we move to evict," I say, glancing at Kenny, my new front man. He's watching me with an expression of admiration. His eyes scintillate.

"That'll take a while," he said. "It's not hard—only slow."

"At least I have a place to stay." I look to Kenny.

He nods.

"I'll get that started," Dave says. "Now, as for the band—"

"We're meeting with Wax Trax! in the late morning for the single. Kenny'll sing that. That sets him up to be the new front man, with Jonathan no longer a member of Mercurial Visions."

"Once you get the contract, send it over to me. I'll make sure of all the details."

"As soon as we get it," I say.

"Sounds fine."

I hang up.

"Now," I say, turning to my partner-to-be. "About the meeting. And this is very important. You know these people. They don't like delays or confusion. This is why we're eliminating Jonathan. He's on the way to getting our contract cancelled. We're already way behind on the recording schedule. Tomorrow we're telling them the plan to fix all that. Giving them a way we can keep on schedule and use the studio time already blocked out, and prevent further delays for the release of the single and then the CD. You got that? Keys: No delays. No confusion."

"Yeah," he says.

"So I'll start. I'll explain how things will work so they know exactly what to expect. We'll record 'Fantasy in Black' and get the single out quickly. That you're replacing Jonathan on lead vocals *only* for this single."

"But—"

"We need to make it look effortless," I say. "Don't worry. He's gone for good. But we have to make this transition look as smooth and effortless as possible to Wax Trax! As if there's no transition at all. We'll present you, simply, as a guest vocalist on a single. All we've got to do is hand over the demos and talk like it's done. They know you'll show up and will commit to this. They know your voice from Unknown Vices, so this is an easy crossover for a single. Once it's done and they see it's a hit, *then* we tell them that Jonathan's tapped out, done, can't write, and can't sing, and you're there to save the day. You'll already have sung on the single. Simple. He'll just be gone. Make sense?"

"Sure." His tone shows little confidence and far too little enthusiasm.

"Hey. We need this to work more than we need to worry about anyone's pride. *We* know you'll be replacing him for good." I move my hand back and forth between us. "Our knowing that has to be enough for now. It's what we need to make this work. You understand that, right?"

"Yes. It's that … No. I understand. I get it. Be patient. You're right."

"Great," I say. "I'll tell them we've already got this worked out with Nancy and AnnMarie, of course, and that everyone's onboard. No dissension. No hesitation. When we show up to the studio, we'll deal with who's actually playing then."

Kenny nods, looking into the palms of his hands.

"Once we've got that done, we'll move to integrate or replace the other two with the Vices guys for the CD. *Then* we'll get Unknown Vices back up and running. It'll be like Al Jorgensen with Ministry, Revolting Cocks, 1000 Homo DJs, all his projects ..."

"Right," he says.

"Remember: you and I have to be completely in sync. Wax Trax! must believe in this: that they'll not have to spend more money, that we will meet all the schedules, and that 'Fantasy in Black' will be a hit. That Jonathan's gone for good. They don't need to know that yet. Let's get the single out. Then one step at a time. Simple."

"Sure."

He's still not looking at me, so I bend down to find his eyes. "Look, I know Unknown Vices' first CD wasn't what we'd planned. But this time, you're stepping into a spot in an established national act. You get the chance to avoid—"

"Scott, I get it."

"Good, 'cause I'm trusting you with my future here—*our* future. Speaking of which, you haven't told Chris about this, right? I mean, with you two involved ... You don't think she'll try to sabotage us out of some sense of loyalty to Jonathan?"

I shake my head. He shakes his emphatically.

· · · · ·

That night, I can't sleep. Because his roommates are still watching TV, Kenny and I are trying to share his bed. It's too small for us both. We keep touching each other. With the meeting tomorrow morning running through my mind, I'm stuck lying awake in bed feeling his body heat and sometimes his flesh.

Sleep, sleep, sleep.

I try naming types of animals in alphabetical order. I start drifting off but then feel him shift in bed or remember how Jonathan's face will look when I reveal my coup de grâce at Wax Trax!—that he's done and that Kenny's in.

I'm so tired.
I drag a hand down my face.
I don't have a plan for Kenny doing Chris. But she's snatch, and he prefers boys. Like me.

"Don't you dare be another Jonathan," I whisper. "He turned his back on me, ignored everything I did for him. 'Cause I don't have a *pussy.*"

Chapter 55

Just Like Sammy
—Scott—

When the alarm rips through the room, I sit bolt upright, completely awake.

"It's a day to reap," I whisper at Kenny, who gropes for the snooze button, still mostly asleep. *Sammy and I never got to do this.*

As I shower, I picture everything unfolding today, starting with packing the tape of the acoustic version of "Fantasy in Black" we recorded last night. Then I imagine how I'll lay it all out at Wax Trax!: we have a single already ready to go now. Jonathan's AWOL, so Kenny's stepping in as the new singer. Easy as pie. No schedules have to be changed—only a name on the CD insert.

Like a snake sloughing off dead skin.

After the meeting, I'll call the girls and lay it on the line. Then it's time to call the lawyer and get the former roommate handled.

In time, the loft will be ours—Kenny's and mine. And finally I'll have the kind of partner Sammy would have been. My whole body tingles like destiny.

We'll record the new CD and have a supporting tour ready in two, at most two and a half, months. *Bigger than the old* Mercurial Visions *ever had.*

Oh yes, Kenny. Today it starts. It's not easy, but it is simple. It only takes "persistence and determination," I say, stepping out of the shower.

After drying off, I comb my hair and flash a smile in the mirror. *Like what you see?*

So do I. And just you wait, mister: this is only the beginning—of everything.

As we wait for the car service to pick us up, I call Jonathan and give him his only warning.

"I'm coming over to pick up some stuff," I tell him. "My clothes, guitar, amp. The rest—the band's equipment, furniture, whatever—my lawyer will be dealing with. Including the loft. In other words, don't get too comfortable there."

"Dream on."

"I'll be there this afternoon *with* Kenny. Be gone when I get there."

He slams down the handset.

I sneer at the phone as Kenny looks at me the way Jonathan should have all these years: as if he's looking at the man who's going to take care of him.

About a half hour later, we're in the car on the way to Wax Trax!

But the meeting with the executive producer and owner Doug starts all wrong.

"Scott," he says, "I thought Jonathan rescheduled this meeting for later today. About a new single, 'Daydream and Try,' and needing—"

"What?"

"And we're not interested in talking about Unknown Vices. Not now."

"I know," I say.

"So what're you doing here, Kenny?"

"Well," I say before Kenny can speak. "We've got some news on the single."

"This had better be damn good news. We're already behind schedule."

"That's why we're here," I say. "We've moved the roadblock out of our way for the single. If you would."

Kenny hands Doug a demo tape, exactly as Jonathan did with "Joie."

"What's this?" Doug asks.

"The single."

"Where's Jonathan?"

"That was the roadblock. He had writer's block and couldn't come up with anything. But Kenny—"

"But Kenny what?" Doug asks, looking like he's just eaten moldy bread. "Where's Jonathan?"

"He's not going to sing on the single. Kenny—"

"Whoa, hang on here," Doug says, waving his hands. "We're two months behind schedule. I've made commitments. This is costing—"

"Nothing more. We're ready to go *with* the current schedule. No extra time. The single will go out—"

"No, it won't. No," he says, shaking his head. "Look. Your first disc rocked. Your second, not so much. And now, you want me to think this singer of a B-list band is going to be better than Jonathan when he's on? No. Scott, I have an agreement with you and Jonathan as Mercurial Visions. He's the face of the band: the voice—what people buy. Generation X without Billy Idol is nobody."

"Jonathan couldn't write. Kenny could. A great song. A hit. This is the solution. It's like Richard 23, Ogre, Al Jorgensen, and Trent Reznor—"

"No, it's not. You don't have one-tenth of the sales of Front 242, Skinny Puppy, Ministry, Revolting Cocks, or Nine Inch Nails. This isn't a game of musical chairs."

"I know it's not," I say.

"These are the types of surprises that tell that me a band isn't worth it."

"This is the way out. Jonathan is spent. Kenny has it—a hit. We're ready to go. No changes. One name on the liner notes."

"This isn't Columbia or RCA, Scott. We don't have the money— bottom line. No. This isn't working," he says, folding his fingers together. "I'm afraid we're going to have to exercise our right to cancel your contract. As of now, we no longer have a working relationship."

All I can see is his face, saying words that are all wrong.

"Thank you very much, Mr. Marshall," Doug says. "And good luck."

"No, I don't think you understand," I say. "We're—"

"Mr. Marshall, please leave. And take Mr. Magnum with you."

I stand there.

"Now."

Heat rushes into my face. It feels so hot. *How can you be so fucking stupid not to see Kenny is best for all of us?*

"If I leave now," I say, "no one will use that name again—for anything. No reissues. No best ofs. No compilations. Nothing."

Doug turns his back and calls the front desk. "Could you get security? And tell Adam that we're no longer working with Mercurial Visions. I don't want any calls from them."

"I own that name. Remember that." Turning, I wave for Kenny to follow me as I leave. I look at no one—at nothing. "You'll be hearing from my lawyer later," I say to everyone who can hear.

Outside we stand on the corner in the cold wind, the sky starkly bright. Kenny is silent and seems afraid to even look at me.

"I don't understand," I say. "Everything was so simple. Perfect. What happened?"

"Um," he says, tentatively.

"I don't know what to tell you about Unknown Vices."

"Actually," he says, "I was going to suggest we head back home."

I raise my eyebrow. "Home?"

"We can blow off some steam."

"Blow off some steam," I say flatly.

"Then, like you always say, we can make plans. You know, 'perseverance and determination alone.'"

I don't answer at first, because I can't be sure he's not mocking me, but then, when I see he's sincere, I'm surprised and grateful. *It's "persistence and determination."* I stay silent. *At last—someone who actually gets it. Gets me. Gets that I am right. You really are just like Sammy. Truly.*

"Yes," I say. "Yes. Very good. Yes."

"Sure, we'll get something figured out. You'll come up with something. You ran that band."

"You're *damned* right. We'll prove I'm right. To Jonathan. To Wax Trax! To everyone."

Things will be very different—better.

Chapter 56

Dizzy
—Jonathan—

"I'm coming over to pick up some stuff," Scott says on the phone. Then he shakes his lawyer at me through the handset.

I slam it down as hard as I can.

This was always your plan, wasn't it? The whole scene yesterday's something you worked out with your lawyer so you can claim I kicked you out illegally. Or some shit like that. To take everything over and put your boy in.

I dial information for a locksmith and call the first one.

"Yes, it's an emergency," I say in answer to his question. "Yes, I understand there will be an extra charge for a new lock."

After hanging up, I walk around the loft collecting the bits and pieces of Scott's existence, to purge him and Kenny from my life.

I pick up and carry an armful of Scott's albums to the elevator. I dump the vinyl on the wooden floorboards. Dust flies up.

Once the locksmith arrives, I show him the door, and answer his questions about the type of lock I want: "Stronger." He starts working.

Then I start up the stairs to the sleeping dais. *For more of my ex-roommate's crap.*

"Damn." *I called him an ex-roommate. And he is, as well as an ex-partner and ex-band member.*

But you, Jennifer—you're not quite an ex anymore. We're not lovers, but we almost slept together, didn't we?

383

I roll those words over in my mind again: *"We almost slept together, didn't we?"*

Great title for a song. Or at least a killer line.

I run down the stairs to the keyboard and sit on the edge of the stool. "So how *does* uncertainty sound?"

I close my eyes, listening closely, and let out a hum of pleasure and then a whimper of doubt.

An hour later, my hands tremble from the buzz of drafting a song. It's as if the world appears to us as black-and-white, but in truth it's full of color, and I've seen reality's full palette, just below the black-and-white surface. The sense of this vision always evaporates too quickly, leaving me with only black, white, and gray.

The locksmith pushes the door closed, and I can hear the new lock sliding home—the sound of Scott being expelled.

"There are your four copies," the locksmith says, holding them out to me on a single ring.

"Excellent," I say, taking them. I reach into my pocket and pull out a wad of bills. I count out fifteen twenties. The locksmith writes "paid" on the invoice, collects his tool kit, and starts down the stairs.

As I close the door, I find myself completely alone in all this space.

If Jennifer and I had known Scott would be gone, would it have been a mistake to get together again? Would our falling off the precipice still have broken us apart in the end? Or would we have floated back up and never touched the ground again, ever?

Two nights ago, we sincerely wanted to try. I wanted you. You wanted me. How could that be wrong now?

The place would be empty but for us; the blade that divided us, removed— not only from here but also from my life. Our lives. It can be if you want.

Yes, I should have protected us better—made us safe before. Instead I gave in. He thought you were nothing but a distraction. He never understood that our conversations, our moments together, our story—all the stories with Amy too—were the songs Mercurial Visions performed. That got him on the stage at Cabaret Metro. That gave him Kenny and Unknown Vices. Gave him everything.

"It's *always* been like this," I say, a chill flowing down my body.

But even that's not true—not completely. I've been lying to you, to myself—to everyone.

It really has been about the tumult. *You told me that, and I couldn't see it.*

"My god," I say.

I've been running this whole time, trying to escape the emptiness—first with Amy and then with you. I've been falling in and out of love so I can constantly relive the moments when everything is as sharp, hard, and fierce as when I sing.

You thought life was movies and magazines. I thought it was nothing outside of falling in love or hurting from love's end. Joy and despair, and all that nothingness in between moments onstage where the world burns away and I'm there, naked and pure.

"I am so sorry Jennifer. So, very, very sorry," I say, crumbling to my knees. "Please, you must understand: I couldn't see this back then."

"Back," I sing softly, "when we were broke and all we did was daydream and try."

After kneeling on the cold concrete for I don't know how long, the phone rings.

With a flick of my thumb, I wipe the last of a tear from my cheek and then stand to face what must come.

"No, Scott. You're not getting in. Not without these," I say, jingling the new keys at the phone. "See. Nine-tenths of the law, right here. In my hand."

I grab the phone before the machine picks up.

This needs to end today.

"Yeah?" I say into the receiver, challenging Scott.

"This Jonathan Starks?" It's Doug, our executive producer at Wax Trax!

"Yes?" I ask, confused at hearing his voice.

"Look, Mr. Starks. This isn't working out. Your project is already too delayed. We're not going to change the band's lineup this late. I've already explained this to Mr. Marshall: There will be no new *Mercurial Visions* single. No new CD. We're exercising our right to sever support for any further projects. We've concluded it's not worth our time to sue for breach of contract, so you'll be free to find another label after the stipulated time period. Our lawyer will send over the official documents explaining what rights you retain and what rights we retain. But please make sure Mr. Marshall understands that he is not to call or bring anyone by again. We're done." He hangs up.

Dizzy, I stare at the phone.

I want to vomit.

Eventually the phone complains to be hung up.

Chapter 57

Blowing Off Steam
—Scott—

I've lost Mercurial Visions—for now.

But I have him.

I smile at Kenny across the table.

After what happened, we decided we needed burritos and a couple of margaritas.

He nods back and drains the last of his drink. "I wanna get out of here ... get home ... blow off some steam."

We start walking the four blocks to his place. *Our place now. He did say "home."*

As we go, he's quiet, and that's good. He's not pushing me. This is a major move for us, living together. Sure, I'll have to put up with his roommates. With them getting home late only to flop on the couch and watch their shows until even later, and their sniggering, teasing looks.

At least we have our bedroom to hide in.

We walk into the apartment together, and his roommates leer at me as we walk past them and into his bedroom. They nod as if they know what's *really* going on. That pisses me off the most, because they know nothing about what's going on, 'cause *nothing's* going on. *We're only trying to figure things out, he and I. Together.*

"Now," he says, closing the door behind me. "Next we're gonna blow off some steam."

I feel unreal, as if I'm only watching this other man standing next to Kenny, who feels like he's fifteen again, and it's Sammy, not Kenny, standing there. He wants to grab the waist of Sammy's jeans, and pull them down, and then—*I don't know.* Sammy got killed before showing me. *But I can still learn.*

"Need to get ready first," Kenny says, sitting on his bed. Then he reaches under it, pulls out a box, and puts it on the bed beside him.

What's inside? Is this what you didn't show me, Sammy? I need to see it this time. Please.

He flicks open the clasps and then slowly lifts the top.

Holding my breath, I lean forward.

Nestled inside gray foam is a large 9 mm automatic.

I jerk back.

"My pistol," he says, lifting it out of the box. "Firing off a few clips is the best therapy in the world."

"I hate guns. I told you that," I say. *Take it away.* "I've never even touched one before."

"First time for everyone," he says. "The range is close by. We step in, get some targets—who or what you hate—*blam, blam.* Confetti. You win. You're the boss."

"Guns." I shake my head. "Killing—no."

"First off, guns don't kill; people do," he says. "Second, it's only pretend. Fantasy. Like Mistress Mayhem. Who's boss now? As for not liking it ... well, we're gonna make you a man today." He points the gun at the closet door, which is covered in a poster of Mercurial Visions. *"Bang,"* he says.

"Kenny, I thought ..." I cut the idea off before it's recognizable.

"Whaddya think?" he asks, giving me a coquettish look. "How'd ya think were we going to blow off some steam here, huh?" He winks.

"I don't know," I say. The room feels so small, as if it's pushing us together. *Sammy, why aren't you here? You promised to be here for me.*

"Oh, come on. Hold it." He holds it out to me, daring me to touch the long, hard shaft.

"No."

"It doesn't have a clip in it. It can't shoot."

"No," I say, taking a step back. The room's so small my back's already to a wall.

"Pussy," he says, reaching back down to the box. He lifts something shiny out. "This clip has twelve rounds in it. Nine millimeter. Blows the hell out of things when it hits." He slaps it into the grip. "Scott. Relax. The first time's awkward for everyone."

I wave it away.

"It won't go off if you only touch it, you know." He holds it out to me again. "Doesn't have a shell chambered. Think of it as foreplay."

My heart stutters, pounds. I shake my head.

"There's nothing weird about doing it." He steps closer. "First, safety." He points to a latch next to his thumb. "It's on, so it can't go off, even with a shell chambered." He pulls back the slide. It makes a metallic click. He lets go, and the slide snaps back into place. The hammer is cocked. "Now a shell is chambered," he says. He points the pistol at a poster and pulls the trigger. Nothing.

"It's okay." He pulls the trigger again, and then twice more. "See?"

"I can't," I say, feeling disjointed in our bedroom, alone. *With him pretending to be Sammy—no.* I shake my head.

"Then why are you here?" he asks, teasing. "All you have to do is switch this thing off," he says, sliding the safety down to off. "Start blasting away. It's better than sex." He licks his lips slowly.

"Sex?"

"Think about Jonathan," he says. "Or that asshole at Wax Trax!"

"Why? No. That's ... no."

"Come on. Just take it," he says, holding the gun out to me, chest high. "Hold it. Touch it a few times. Then we'll take off. Target practice. *Blam, blam, blam.* It'll change your life."

He's standing so close. *You're going to make me touch it.* I'm trembling not from fear but in excitement. *Why do I feel like this? Unforgivable.*

"What are you trying to do?" I demand. "I can't. No. You're not Sammy."

"Sammy? Who's Sammy? Some queen you've been hiding from us?"

I grab his hand holding the pistol and turn the barrel. I feel the safety click off.

"Don't *ever* say that about Sammy," I say. "He wasn't some faggot. He's my *only real friend.*"

I squeeze Kenny's hand to make him understand, which squeezes his fingers, including the one on the trigger, and then there's a glaring flash, a thundering boom.

I can't breathe, blinking away the afterimage of the muzzle flash. When I can see, I see gore covering the wall. Kenny's body lies crumpled on the floor.

"No." Ice fills my body. "No. No. No."

I bolt for the door.

One of Kenny's roommates opens the door right then. The solid-wood edge hits my forehead. I feel pain like a flash of light.

Chapter 58
Ready for a Fight
—Jonathan—

Hours have passed as I've sat on this couch, staring out the window at nothing in particular.

I know I should call AnnMarie and Nancy. *To let them know. I should start doing ... something. Putting a new band together?*

All I can do though is purse my lips.

Then a knock on the metal door startles me in the empty silence.

"What now? Hasn't this been enough for one day!" I shout at the door.

The knocking comes again.

"Piss off, Scott!"

Again comes the knocking—more insistently this time.

I stomp to the door, grab the handle, and pull to make sure it's locked fast. "Fuck off, Scott." I take the new keys out and jingle them. "New lock. New life."

"Chicago Police," says a man's voice through the double-thick steel door. "We're looking for Jonathan Starks."

I was ready for a fight, but they aren't here to evict me. Rather, they deliver news of Kenny getting shot and Scott being in jail, then they start with questions for me. I answer them as best as I can.

As they leave, the younger one, Officer McInerney, says, "You guys kick ass. I have both of your CDs."

I nod, I think.

I then look up at the angel covering her eyes on the poster for "Love Will Tear Us Apart" and think none of this should have happened.

Not to Amy. Not to Jennifer—my lovers—and not even to Scott, once my closest friend. Certainly not to Kenny, who'd only stumbled into this—our thicket of ignorance. This is not the ending any of us deserved. I should have seen something sooner and been able to stop this. Shouldn't I have?

How can it take so long to see what's so obvious?

"You're right, Angel," I say to her. "There really is too much sorrow to uncover your eyes."

CHAPTER 59

SUSPENDED IN CONTRADICTIONS
—JENNIFER—

It's been two days since Jonathan and I almost fell into bed together, a day since I watched Charlene tip herself over the balcony railing, and a day since I burned away the part of me that wanted Jonathan—the part of me that could have been Charlene.

And tonight I'm not hiding in my old room; my mother has knocked on my door, saying that Chris has arrived to pick me up.

I let Sarabeth run out first.

"I'll be back," I say, walking past my mother. "Not too late. And I'll be quiet."

I grab Chris's hand and lead her quickly out through the doorway. Climbing into Chris's car, I say, "I have to get the hell out of here. The last two days here have been too much."

"Stay with me," Chris says, starting the engine.

"I mean out of Chicago," I say. "I don't even know what I'm doing here."

"Visiting friends," Chris says. "Chillin' out."

"Chillin' out?" I scoff.

Then I realize Chris has makeup on.

That's about weird.

I take a closer look.

"Hey," Chris says, "I heard something about Mercurial Visions. 'Bout Scott."

"What?" I say, pulling back.

"Caught the end of something on the radio," Chris says. "Wondered if you knew what it was."

"Oh, no," I say. "I don't sleep with the lead singer anymore, remember?" She shrugs.

Two blocks pass in silence, and then Chris gets this grin like she's got a secret she wants me to ask her about, and it's probably about why she has the makeup on.

Girlfriend, I need to catch my breath here.

But her smile gets wider, as if she'll burst if I don't ask.

"Okay," I say. "What's up?"

"Guess who's been sleeping over?"

"Sleeping over?"

"We get naked."

"Oh, I don't know. Fey?"

"God no! Please."

"Well, I *have* been away for a while."

"You know him. Very well."

"Scott!?"

"That closet queen? Hell no."

"Okay, who? Just tell me. As long as it's not Jonathan."

"Kenny."

"Kenny?! The boy-girl, any-port-in-a-storm Kenny?"

"Yup."

"Chris," I say, "an awful lot's being going on. Don't mess with me."

"Kenny Magnum. Singer. Unknown Vices. Sleeping with … yours truly."

"Okaaaay."

"He's good in bed, by the way. Very good."

"Too much information, girl."

"And Scott is soooooo jealous," Chris says.

"Jealous?"

"Yeah, as in acting like he's Kenny's boyfriend. He hates me now. I think I just got myself uninvited to do any more artwork for Unknown Vices *or* Mercurial Visions. But he's worth it. Whoooo, the sex."

"I ..."

"Wendy called it years ago," Chris says. "The problem with Scott is that he can't admit he's as queer as a three-dollar bill. I swear he'll end up shooting someone. Probably himself. Can't deal with who he is. *Pow!*"

"No more suicide talk."

"Oh, yes. Shit," Chris says. "Sorry."

"Let's not. Not tonight."

"Sure. I ... Sure."

"So first stop. Las Mananitas, right?" I ask.

"Right."

"Then Smart Bar."

"I'm sure we'll run into people who're wondering what's up with you."

"Yeah, I know," I say, sighing. "Only wish I knew what to tell them."

"Come on. It's not that bad."

"I dunno."

"You've always made it through bullshit."

"Tired of having to."

"What can you do?" Chris asks. "If not this, then it's something. Is it ever any different?"

"I thought it was. Once."

"With Jonathan?"

"Yeah."

"He told you, straight up, love's like this," Chris says. "Something always happens."

"What about with Kenny?"

"Oh. Eventually he'll do something. I will. We both will. It'll end, I imagine. It could. I don't think about it. I mean, really; we all die. If that's all I thought about, I'd do nothing."

"Charlene didn't get it right," I say. "That's the cheater's way out."

"Oh, she pisses me off. I mean, you can't just return your ticket like life's a show. Plus you miss all the good parts—the ones that make it worth it."

"That was so weak," I say. "So not her."

"Not the her we knew," Chris says.

"Jonathan's not who I thought either." I watch the dusk skyline. Tall pillars of darkness speckled with lights pass slowly behind one another. "How about you? Are you who you say you are? Who *I* think you are?"

"I think I am. As much as I can be."

"I don't know what to believe anymore. About anyone. Everyone's always telling stories about each other, including stories about themselves. And none of the stories are the same. Or even completely true. It's like we're all a bunch of contradictory stories, none of which is completely true or totally wrong. Who we really are hangs someplace between all the stories, suspended in the contradictions."

$$\bullet \bullet \bullet \bullet \bullet$$

After a dinner of chicken flautas, rice and beans, and two margaritas, we're on the hunt for parking closer to Smart Bar. There's a lot of traffic on Clark Street, so we start looking for a parking space blocks before Metro. Everything slows to a crawl in front of its big black doors and glowing marquee. I haven't been here in ages, and I miss it.

I remember the time Mercurial Visions played here, which starts me thinking about Jonathan.

I shake my head.

Chris looks quizzically at me.

I mouth "nothing," and scan the street for parking, holding my fingers up in curling quotation marks, invoking parking karma.

"There," I say, pointing to a space on Racine, behind the Gingerman.

After parking, we walk through the alley between Metro and the Gingerman, and emerge on Clark and then wave to the bouncer as we walk past the black doors of Metro and through the gate of Smart Bar. We enter the tunnel. The graffiti skankers and demon-faced boys and girls painted on the passage walls, dancing under the pallid flickering of fluorescent bulbs, look like old friends. I feel the throbbing rhythm more than hear it. Then it's like old times and I'm nineteen and the past couple of years never happened. Still manning the booth, charging cover, Jennie looks the same with her long, black, blunt-cut hair, black dress, lipstick, and eyeliner.

I wave.

"My god, we all thought you'd died," Jennie says.

"Kinda did," I say. "In Seattle."

"Welcome back to Chicago," Jennie says.

Chris hugs the bouncer, and he lets us onto the fenced-in stairs leading down into darkness. The music thunders. Light splashes intermittently as people walk through beams of light coming straight down from spotlights in the ceiling. It's so familiar, like home. I look down the front bar, and I recognize several of the faces in the light splattering up from the bar. The light casts deep shadows over them, making everyone look demonic. I hang names on those I can—Paul, Missy, Mark, David, Sherry, Darlene, Gray, Bobby V, Rob, Kelly, Lynn—and I wonder if I actually know everyone here. Jack, the bartender, hands us our beers, Chris puts a fin down as a tip, I suck on the cold brew, and everything feels good and right.

Chris tells me she'll make the rounds to see who else is here, and she leaves me standing in the darkest corner of the bar, where I can watch but not be seen. It's always been my favorite spot. I notice people I don't know. *New blood keeping this place alive. Good to see.*

At the far end, Nancy struts up to the bar in a tight, short black cocktail dress.

"Oh, shit," I say, pulling back farther into the shadows.

She gets several drinks.

If they're all here, he's here. I need to get gone. Now.

"Chris, where are you?" I whisper.

As Nancy carries off the drinks, I notice she's not smiling. *What the hell's up tonight?*

Lurking in this deep shadow, I search for Chris, watching out for anyone from the band. The DJ has played "Mambo Witch," "Isolation," and "Stainless Steel Providers," but still no Chris, and I dread that she's talking to them—to him. Or maybe she's dancing. *She never dances. Not even when she's drunk. But she never wore makeup either.*

Oh, girl, where the hell are you? Get back now, I think as hard as I can. *Please.*

Then someone at the bar recognizes me in spite of the shadows, raises his beer glass, and nudges the girls beside him, and they wave me over, and now I can't escape, so I trudge over, and the questions start like a flood: Have I gotten married? *No.* Pregnant? *No.* School? *No.* How are the bars there? *Some are okay.* Night life? *Not like here.*

I hate answering these questions.

More people I used to hang with pile on, asking the same things, and more songs play, and Chris hasn't come to rescue me, and I'm dreading Jonathan finding me here, so I'm thinking maybe I should simply leave, but I've no car, and this is getting very frustrating, so finally I tell everyone I have to find Chris.

Breaking free from their questions, I weave my way through the bodies, keeping my head down to avoid being seen by anyone else I might know. I hesitate at the edge of the glass-block wall separating the dance floor from the main bar. Some Cubs fan who's standing next to me starts looking me over. He cocks his head as if he's going to say "Don't I know you?," so I quickly step around the corner toward the dance floor. The music grows more intense, the bass thudding through my chest. I search the silhouettes of dancers thrashing, jackets winging, cigarette cherries carving arcs to the rhythm. *No Chris. Not a surprise.* I look down the drink rail fencing off the dance floor. Small spotlights shine straight down, splashing off the glossy black wood. Trails of smoke climb the light beams. I scan the people standing behind the drink rail as they nod to the rhythm and sip drinks. *Again—no Chris.*

There is only one place left to look in the whole bar.

Making it to the far end of the bar, I can see the back alcove in the far corner—a large, square darkness. Chris has to be there, but I don't want anyone sitting in those shadows to see me.

I just want Chris.

So I steal a look into the alcove. At one of the tables, I see Chris shaking her head, looking distressed. She doesn't see me, so I have to take a step forward. Everyone looks troubled. Nancy shakes her head, and AnnMarie sits cross-armed but then leans down to listen to Jonathan, who sweeps hair from his lips.

I freeze.

He hasn't seen me yet, so I drop my shoulders, thinning myself, trying to disappear into the darkness so I can, quietly, escape.

Then Chris sees me. She stands up, pointing. Following her finger, Jonathan's eyes land on me.

"Aw, hell," I say.

He stands, ushering me to sit, looking very grave.

"He's dead," Chris says. She looks stricken.

"What?" I urgently want to flee but feel paralyzed with everyone watching me.

"Good you're here now. Come on. Sit next to Chris," Jonathan says, urging me to the table with a hand on my shoulder. I submit.

Chris leans close. I can see she's been crying. "He's dead."

"Who's dead?"

"Kenny," she says. "Kenny's ... dead."

"What do you mean? Dead?"

"Shot," she continues. "By Scott."

"Shot? Who? What's going on?"

"For starters," Jonathan says, with a dramatic thrust of his hands, "Scott's in jail."

I disbelieve him. Yet now everyone's lost expressions make sense.

"He shot Kenny this afternoon."

"My god," I say. Then I realize what that means. "Oh Chris, I'm so sorry. I ... I ..."

"Cops stopped by this afternoon," Jonathan says. "Questioned me. Unreal. They suspect a lover's spat. I think that's nuts."

This is all too much.

"Oh," he says. "Mercurial Visions ... broke up."

"Hold on ... what?"

"Jennifer ... I ..." he says. He drags his hands down his face, leaving a frown behind. "I'm sorry. For not seeing things. Everything could've been so different." He squeezes my shoulder.

In this darkness, everyone at the table looks like a specter, and the music keeps thumping through my body. Like shades, shapes of people mill around the alcove's opening. I feel like I'm in a cave, looking out from the world of the damned.

Chris is hunched over facing the wall. I wrap my arm around her, and can feel her sobbing. I lead her away from the alcove and what was Mercurial Visions. In the deep shadows and columns of light, I steer Chris through the faceless silhouettes as dark-dressed bodies jostle us, waving lit cigarettes around, the orange glows like tools of torture. The rhythm pounds over cackles, chortles, guffaws, and bits of conversation. The faces look menacing, leering, and angry. Smoke rises up the columns of light as if from pits of fire.

We make it to the stairwell. I feel cold air on my face, and I climb up and pull Chris with me down the hall, through the gates, and into the cold air of the night. It bites into me. Walking down Clark Street, I shiver. I take the car keys from her.

We've escaped, but Kenny's dead, and I need to spend the night with her—for both of us.

$$\bullet \bullet \bullet \bullet \bullet$$

It's still dark—around three, four in the morning. I've lost track of time sitting here with Chris. She's finally fallen asleep. I should be so tired I can't keep my eyes open, but so many thoughts hound me: I'm back in Chicago. Chris's boyfriend, Kenny, is dead. I knew him and partied with him. I liked him, I think. He was good for Chris. And he was shot dead. By Scott. Who's in jail. Mercurial Visions is gone. AnnMarie's little boy Malcolm is dead—hit by a car shopping for his fake mother's birthday. Charlene's dead—killed by Charlene, the jaded killing the hopeful. "Clap, clap, don't let Tink die." Nancy's a well-off escort. She told me right before I moved to Seattle that she gets all cash and special favors. Now she backs shows with Les Femmes. Ron and Wendy traffic in illusion. My homophobe ex was queer.

I'm so sick of tripping over who people *really* are.

Chapter 60
Sammy's Face
—Scott—

I hate the way hospitals smell. That's the first thing I notice when I wake up—the chemical stench.

Then I start remembering. The flash. The boom. The gore. All that blood. It's as if I've woken up in someone else's life.

'Cause this couldn't be my life. I kept my promises.

The next several days smear together into a series of scenes from a gritty crime show, except nothing's like it is on TV. It's slower, dirtier, and more confusing. Once the doctors say I'm fine, there are people taking pictures of me in handcuffs when I'm helped into the waiting cop car. They take mug shots and fingerprints, give me a jumpsuit, and leave me sitting alone in a room. Then come questions I can't answer to anyone's satisfaction. And there is waiting, more waiting, and more waiting.

My size plus a few angry faces keep the other prisoners from messing with me much.

Eventually Dave—my short, red-faced lawyer—posts bail for me. He's vaguely reassuring, telling me how "we'll say the powder on your hands is residual, blowback, from protecting yourself. The spurned lover was shot with his own gun." He nods. "I doubt there will be charges for anything in the end."

After handing me a bag of clothes, he slips me a wad of twenties and tells me to find someplace cheap to stay for now. "Think SRO. Try the

Hotel Hong Kong over on Ohio. It's not far. You'll need to work on getting something more permanent."

It seems I'm basically broke after posting bail. *I still have three boxes of T-shirts from the Micherigan tour. Collector's items for … some consignment shop. They'll probably end up as expensive rags. If I can ever get them.*

I scoff, stepping out into the gray afternoon.

The hiss of tires accompanies me as I trudge along Ohio Street in a misty rain. The streetlights give off damp light, making faint streaks on the wet asphalt. The Hotel Hong Kong stands tall over the street, towering over the one-story buildings and vacant lots surrounding it, making it seem impressive.

Pushing open the door, I stride past the three wooden phone booths that crowd the doorway to the attached liquor store and move down the hallway, with its stained red-striped wallpaper and flattened, threadbare red carpet. I cross the lobby—which reeks like hell—step up to the office, and look through the plexiglass window. It's a filthy little room full of old food wrappers, disheveled stacks of papers, and an ashtray overstuffed with butts.

The man inside turns from a small black-and-white TV and looks me over from inside his chamber with deep-sunken, dull eyes. In his stained, yellowing shirt, he's as grubby as the rest of this place.

"No noise," the man says, shaking his finger at me. "This respectable place."

"Right."

"Pay first."

"How much?"

"One forty a week," he says. "Up-front." The man glares at me, challenging me to disagree.

You must enjoy that power: able to torture us from behind your Plexiglas window, untouchable. A small-time tyrant.

Reaching into my pocket, I quickly count out seven twenties and push them into the plexiglass cylinder. The man inspects the money and counts it carefully, twice, and then shoves a card into the cylinder with a pen. "Fill it out."

Name: *Scott Marshall*
Address: *Here*
Phone: *none*
In case of emergency: *David O'Brian, ESQ.*

I exchange the card for the keys to room 917, a roll of wrapped-up toilet paper, and a greyed, fraying towel. The man turns back to his flickering little black-and-white TV.

Picking up my bag, I turn to the two elevators and walk past the shabby couch and two mismatched chairs furnishing the lobby. I punch the call button.

A skinny black man in a shabby suit watches me from the corner, smoking.

Don't tell me. The house dick.

The elevator doors clatter open. A painfully skinny man looks surprised to see someone on the elevator. His shirt's hanging open, showing skin wrapped tightly to ribs. He gives me a crooked single-toothed grin. The elevator's small. I take up almost half of it when I step in. I press the button for the ninth—the last—floor. The door closes, and the elevator groans, shuddering as it lifts me into the belly of the building.

It stops on the seventh floor, and the doors slide open, revealing a long hallway. Then a door opens halfway down long the hallway and a scream pours out. The skinny man turns and watches as a young woman appears in the poorly lit hall. A naked man appears right behind her and grabs the woman's hair.

The skinny man starts laughing and hoots, "Save me some."

I press the close button repeatedly until the door starts closing.

"I'll take sloppy seconds, baby," the man calls out as the door shuts off the scene. He laughs so hard it sounds like he's coughing up some part of himself. His breath stinks of Thunderbird and rot.

I close my eyes. The elevator clanks, grinds, and pounds, as if in torment. The man reeks. I can feel his body heat. He disgusts me. I try moving away, but my back hits the wall.

I rub at the ink on my fingers until the door opens again on nine—a deathly quiet floor. The occasional working lamp casts deep shadows into the corners like lurking phantoms.

I step on the floor as the elevator door closes behind me. I can hear the man cackling like Charon as he sinks with the elevator.

Moving down the hall, I read the numbers until I find 917. I unlock the door to stale air and darkness. I switch on the light. It casts a sulfur-yellow tinge over everything: the pockmarked walls, bed, table, and chair.

Stepping in, I toss the bag onto the bed.

Silence engulfs me. Even the noise of the traffic below is too far away to hear.

The TV is mounted high on the wall. I find the remote and turn it on to kill the silence.

White noise spills out, hissing and shushing as lines of snow drive across the screen.

In the bathroom, I run water over my wrists, cooling the chafing from the handcuffs. Then I rub my fingers under the water, trying to get rid of the remaining ink stains from the fingerprinting. At first the water gets streaked with black as it flows down the drain, but my fingers remain stained with gray. I scrub harder, the lather slopping over the edges of the sink.

"Fucking stuff," I say. I hold up my hands. *Won't come off.*

Cupping water in both hands, I splash it on my face. It stings. I look up into the mirror. Stitches run down the center of my forehead. My whole forehead's swollen and red. My face is ashen.

I leave the bathroom and take the three steps across the room to the two narrow windows covered by a cracking, yellowed shade. I pull down on the frayed pull-string. It slips from my fingers, flying up, rat-a-tat-tatting as it spins around the roller at the top of the window.

Through the grimy windows, I have a decent view of the city. I follow the line of the traffic along Ohio Street to the Kennedy Expressway. Then my eyes fall on the Coyote Building. Next to that, hidden, is the old pencil factory—the loft—everything I've spent the last sixteen years working for.

I pull the shades back down.

This isn't what we planned, Sammy. I kept my promises. For sixteen years. Now I'm completely alone, living out an idiot's tale.

I was fifteen the summer when Sammy's family moved to our trailer park, two spots over. His real name was Samuel, but I always called him Sammy. He was seventeen. Of course I'd heard the rumors. Everyone had. He was queer, and that that's why his family had to move here. He did act weird: kept to himself, spent all his time in his trailer, alone. The rumor was he had a *Playgirl* and was looking at naked men.

A couple of days after the school year started, this punk kid, biggest liar in the park, said he'd seen him looking at the pictures—said so right as Sammy got home from school, in front of all the other kids and his mother. The kids all laughed. Sammy's dad beat the hell out of him. He missed three days of school.

Sammy was so small and skinny. I felt sorry for him.

Since he lived two trailers over, we ended up walking to the school bus together most of the time. At first he acted scared of me. I was always big, even at fifteen. Eventually we started talking—about nothing at first. He was nice and not stupid like everyone else.

At school, he kept to himself. Tried to, at least. Other kids picked fights with him all the time and started calling him Playgirl. He wasn't my friend, exactly, but he'd get beaten up by these snotty-assed little punks I hated. The principal didn't do shit. Hell, I thought that prick actually encouraged them. Sammy's dad did nothing. I hated seeing it.

In late September, two punks had pinned Sammy on the ground, and a third was kicking his balls, saying he shouldn't have children.

That was too much. I punched that little bastard so hard I broke his nose: blood poured down his face. The other two ran as soon as they saw me turning toward them. The little prick had two black eyes for weeks. *No one* fucked with Sammy after that.

Sammy never said anything about why he was getting picked on so much or got called Playgirl, and I never asked. I didn't care. He wanted out of this hellhole as badly as I did, and he'd found a way out—he was going to play rock 'n' roll. He would make a living performing and get so famous that no one from this shitty place could touch him again.

All that time alone in his trailer he spent practicing electric guitar.

He said he never plugged it in 'cause it was too loud. He never played for anyone there 'cause they'd just laugh and tease him. He already had enough trouble. So he locked himself in his room and put on headphones.

But *man* could he play.

The first time he let me put on the headphones—goddamned if he didn't sound like what I heard on the radio.

I knew right then he was going to make it, and I wanted to get out with him.

Told me he was looking for a keyboardist and a drummer for the band he was going to start, but keyboards and drum kits were expensive. Guitars, though, we could find at a flea market for cheap. They almost never worked right, but I could learn fingering, strumming, and how to read music. Sammy said he could use a rhythm guitarist too.

Sammy taught me to play that winter.

We tried to keep it secret, but that didn't last long. I had to beat the piss out of more than one kid for saying I was his wife and calling us ugly names.

No one got it. We were friends. We both wanted to escape. He knew how.

Escaping here with him became all that mattered in the world. He was all I thought about. Seeing him. Being with him. Practicing with him. Making plans with him. I was afraid for him when we were apart. Especially when he was at home with his ignorant old man.

But as the year wore on, I realized he was graduating in June. I was only a sophomore.

I hadn't thought about it until the announcements started at school about the senior prom, graduation photos, and commencement. He was turning eighteen soon and escaping—*without me.*

The day he picked up his gown and mortarboard, he showed them off to me as we walked home from the bus stop. I told him I was afraid of what would happen now.

He stopped and said, "Hang on, man."

I stopped, and we let the other kids walk past.

"There's nothing to be scared of," he said. "Like I told you, I'm going to Columbus to get set up. I'll start a band for us. You'll come as soon as

you can. Remember: patience and perseverance alone are omnipotent."
He nodded, looking up at me. "Right?"

I pursed my lips.

"Right?" he asked again, giving me that expression he used when I
got frustrated while playing.

"Right," I said, nodding too. "I know."

"Nothing to be afraid of, right?"

"Yeah. You're right, I just ..."

"Just nothing. Patience and perseverance."

"Yes, I know. And if you want to know why you are where you are,
look in the mirror. The answer's staring at you."

"Exactly. Right like I said." He smiled and gave me a wink, and we
started back to the trailer park.

That evening, I was taking out the trash, and I heard him and his
father fighting inside their trailer. His father was a stupid, fat redneck.
And he was a lot bigger than Sammy. It started getting really loud.

I walked to the back of their double-wide.

His father was yelling that I was "never to come here again," because
I was "a faggot" and if I "only left you alone, God would cure you." Then
I heard his old man giving Sammy a wallop. Sammy yelped. Things got
knocked over.

I ran up and pounded on the door. "You inbred fuck!" I shouted.
"Leave him alone." I ripped off the screen door. "I'll kill you, you son of
a bitch!"

"Mind your own business, faggot."

I grabbed the door. "Sammy!"

That's when they showed up: his old man's trailer trash friends—
rednecks and hillbillies—six or seven of them.

"You need to go home, boy," the first of them said, lifting a section
of pipe. "Now."

The others showed off a tire iron, a baseball bat, and more pipe. One
pulled out a gun.

I stared at them in a cold rage.

"Sorry, Sammy," I said quietly, hoping he'd understand. I turned and
walked home.

I couldn't sleep that night. I sat in my bed and raged all night at how it should have been different. I knew we had to leave. Both of us, and as soon as we could. I imagined our escape. We'd run away tomorrow, stealing a car to get down to the highway, ditch that, and then hitch our way into Columbus. In two or three hours, it would be done.

The next day, my old man told me Sammy's family had gone to see Reverend Knox. "Wanted to see if Sammy's soul could still be saved. Get him to think right. Heard they were fixing to move again."

"Sammy didn't choose it. He's who he is."

"God *doesn't* make faggots!"

"Your God *does* make queers!"

"He chose perversion."

"You don't choose to fall in love with another man."

"How d' you know?"

I nearly put my fist through his stupid face.

It wasn't until that next Saturday afternoon that I saw Sammy again. He knocked on my window and whispered for me to sneak out and meet him down by the creek. Took me about ten minutes to get there. I lied about hunting for crawdads.

Sammy—he still looked bad. His face was red and swollen, and he had a limp.

"Your old man. He can't get away with this," I said. "Look at you." I reached out to touch Sammy's face. He winced. "I'll kill that inbred son of a bitch."

"No, Scott," he said. "Please."

"Let's leave now. Run away. Right now. Today."

"We'll get out of here soon. It's only a couple of weeks to graduation. My old man—I know him. He'll calm down. By then I'll have everything I need to set up in Columbus. Until then, you'll keep playing, right? Then we keep playing until we make it. Promise me you'll keep playing."

"Yes, Sammy, I promise."

"I promise to keep playing too, Scott. Until we get so big no one will care we're friends. So big no one can touch us." He looked so intense. "Promise me again."

"I promise, Sammy. I'll never stop playing until we're so big no one cares we're together."

I don't know how it happened, but his lips were pressing against mine. In that moment, the universe was perfect. I knew everything would happen exactly as we'd planned, inevitably. He would set up for us in Columbus. I would join him. We would play in a band together and get so big we wouldn't even remember this shitty little place.

In that moment, I was perfect. He was perfect. So were our plans. My skin tingled as if a million ants were crawling over me. I felt we were destined for this. I understood then why people rapturously cried out *hallelujahs* after one of Reverend Knox's church revivals, for I too had been saved.

That was the last time I ever saw him.

After we parted, he went missing. Four days later, they found him dead—beaten to death. By seven or eight people, the sheriff thought.

"One less of 'em to worry about," the sheriff had said, looking straight at me. "See what happens to a boy when he doesn't follow God's Word."

I curled up on that bed in the Hotel Hong Kong and, for the first time since that night, I cried.

"Sammy," I pleaded. "You promised."

CHAPTER 61

SHE SMILES
—JENNIFER—

At home on a hot July afternoon, I walk into the kitchen, where my mother stands next to the toaster, staring at a newspaper folded into quarters. The sundress I'm wearing flows out behind me. I give my mother a kiss on the cheek.

She regards me from the corners of her eyes with suspicion. Toast pops up from the toaster. My mother watches as I pull back the drapes, revealing how green it is outside.

"I'm moving to New Orleans," I announce.

"Is that where Jonathan thinks it'll be better?"

"I don't know what he think of New Orleans."

"Toast?" my mom asks.

"Sure."

"Then why are you following him there?"

"I'm not."

She scoffs and butters the toast with quick scraping noises.

"I haven't talked to him in three months. Since the day Chris's boyfriend got shot."

"It scares me that you were living with the man who did it."

"It wasn't his gun. It wouldn't have happened at the loft."

"Still."

"Still nothing. What's scary is doing things and not understanding why. What Charlene did is scary. Not seeing who you really are can be deadly."

"So do you know?"

"I think so. More importantly, I absolutely know who I'm not."

My mom sets the plate with the toast down on the table next to me.

"Thanks," I say, picking up one of the slices and biting off a corner. "I'm not who I used to be. Now I'm going to find out what that means. I figure I can take the bus. Start from scratch. It won't take me long to get a job." I shrug. "French Quarter." I take another bite. "Maybe I'll learn some French."

"Don't even try that with your mother. I know you too well."

"You're right about the French. Probably."

My mom snaps up the paper and shoves it under her arm. "I'm meeting Sherri at the mall. When you decide what you're really going to do, let me know."

"I'm moving to New Orleans."

"Yes," she says. "Leave me your address then. I'm late." Then she marches through the living room and out to the carport.

I don't care if you believe me or not.

I hear her car start, idle a moment, and then pull away. The sound finally disappears in the bright afternoon light.

I know, and who matters outside of that? I hug myself. I need to call Chris and Wendy. I'll call Jonathan someday. I'm sure he'd understand. I'd like that.

· · · · ·

It takes a few weeks, but I get all the arrangements made. Wendy's even kept me on as a talent scout and local presence. It'll be a start.

On a warm, bright Friday in September, I hug Wendy and then kiss her cheek.

The Greyhound man standing at the gate looks at my ticket. I push my boxes through the opening in the fence, and the driver helps me put them into the baggage compartment and then motions me to board, looking me over like men usually do. Ignoring him, I climb the stairs into the bus. I walk down the aisle, past seats almost as tall as my shoulders. In the back, I slide into a seat and look out the window.

Wendy waves.

A feeling of loss shoots through me, as if something has just died; then I feel giddy, excited, and nervous.

Wendy holds up her watch and points at it.

I bite my lip.

She grabs her tit at me and then laughs, waves, and walks away.

I fall back into my seat and draw my hands down my face.

"It's done. All me."

Ten minutes later, the bus crawls out of the berth, through the lot, up the ramp, and out into the air, and after the light turns green, Chicago starts melting away behind me.

Then it hits me—the terrifying, glorious feeling of being alone, by choice. I'm finally alone to build my own real life.

My heart races.

The sun shines.

The bus rumbles.

It's finally happening. I smile and laugh.

Chapter 62

One Night in Subterranean
—Jonathan—

The hard chill of late October has settled in. The leaves have all quit their trees, leaving them empty.

During the six months since Kenny was killed, I've found myself thinking back to everything that happened and wondering what might become of us. I suppose there's something I'm trying to find in the past to help me survive all these losses—or at least hint that I can.

Jennifer left a month ago to start anew in the Big Easy. Around the same time, I caught a short piece in the paper about Kolby, Green, and Michelson, Amy's New York advertising firm; an up-and-coming designer, originally from Columbus, had been picked to head some major international campaign or other. Turns out it *was* Amy. I haven't kept up with what happened to Scott. That lets me give the curt but honest answer "I don't know" whenever a reporter calls.

The band—we haven't named it yet—has been sputtering to a start for some weeks now. We—Nancy, AnnMarie, and I—have been looking for a guitarist who gets that we don't want to resurrect Mercurial Visions. Auditions have been sporadic and unproductive.

The biggest problem is me. We all agree about needing a new sound, a new identity, yet, every song that beckons me features some form of Jennifer or Amy. Sometimes I try to trick myself by giving her a new name, or hiding her face behind a new one, but we always end up tumbling over the precipice together, caring nothing of dashing ourselves on the

413

hard stone bottom at the end, as if no price could be too high to live so vividly, even as I stand in the ruins of who we'd been, alone once again, accompanied only by regret, as I do now, when there is only one thing left to do with her.

I feel trapped by the sounds of all this heedless, impetuous passion. I'm intoxicated by it as well, when I'm being honest with myself. I've made a career of turning it into songs, after all.

Added to my creative failures are the pressures of simply living life: lawyers arguing about who owns Mercurial Visions' catalog and publishing rights; the finances of paying those lawyers and their filing fees, paying for rent and for food and electricity—all these things with diminishing royalties and merchandise sales, and no tour income—plus simply getting my head around Kenny being dead and Scott being the one who pulled the trigger. Accidently or not.

At times I've thought about saying to hell with it all and going back to waiting tables, or trying to write commercial ditties, or getting a regular nine-to-five job. But that I've done, and it almost killed me. It would have, but for Amy.

See, Amy. I am trapped. I've never been able to escape you—probably never will.

So here I am, sitting in this big, empty space by myself, hating all this alone.

The phone's right there, a few steps away. It would be easy enough to get Amy's work number. I'd probably have to leave a message with her assistant.

Amy would eventually call back, of course.

When she did, I'd say, "Hey you. It's me."

What a great name for a song.

Once again I find myself seeking the edge, wanting to take that one last step with her.

No.

I stand, shaking my head. We've been trying too hard to breathe life into a new band—one that is ours, as free of the past as we can make it. One where I'm not forced to hurl myself and my lover into a private chasm, to finally smash us apart and then run my fingers through our entrails to retrieve words and melodies. That exhausts me, and in the end whoever I loved and whatever we were are always gone. Used up. Sacrificed. Consumed. Use whatever word; it inevitably leads to a vast emptiness. I resent this and wish it could be different. *Just once.*

I drum my fingers on the keyboard where I've been trying to coax something different out of the clamor of sounds cluttering my mind. The loudest are those that Jennifer and I came so close to living out when she was last here. The lyrics tell of luring her here and then betraying her trust by letting us give in to temptation. The melodies invoke the sounds of the few glorious minutes of being together, and then of us shattering apart once again, and then the sounds of regret take over—of being irredeemably broken. These are songs of our last moments together haunting us, hunting down all other memories we have of one another until none are left but those of our self-deceit and weakness.

I hated those songs then. I fear them now: If I write them, they'll become true for everyone who listens, no matter what actually happened. I'll have to live it repeatedly. *But you didn't betray her. Look what happened. So why not get something from it. After all, what real choice do I have? Isn't this who I am? Shouldn't I accept this? And write songs of what I know be best? We were famous when I did.*

Turning the keyboard back on, I dabble out a few phrases I hear clearly among the many that crowd me from every side.

Without hesitation, my fingers gambol along the keys into snippets of those melodies. *So easy.* Lines of lyrics whisper themselves to me. *I know you all so well. You remind me of what living can be when every nerve's alive.*

Running the tip of my tongue along bottom of my teeth, I spin on my keyboard's stool.

Then I start playing "Joie," the most beautiful sounds I've ever created.

Memories fly back of Jennifer when she lived here and I was so in love with her. Those, yes, but also memories of *how* I wrote it, of *how* I captured that sense of free-falling, as if there were no gravity.

I start singing: "When there's love, there are ghosts ..." I'm flying. *How I miss this—miss her. Miss being in love.*

Another memory then stirs, this one of the last time singing "Joie" punched through my numbness: one night in the Gingerman. At a birthday party. After an impossible call from Jennifer. I played it for the birthday girl, Michele.

I played *so well* for her after being barren for so long.

The scene unfolds in my mind—Michele looking stylish in a man's white leather sport coat. Later that night, she brushed her lips on mine.

I can feel their delicate touch.

I kiss at the air for them.

All the scents of that night had been so vivid. I try to breathe them in again now—those pungent, living smells: her musky-floral perfume, the hoppy maltiness of beer, the sweet herbaceous scent of Jägermeister, the rich reek of tobacco, the salty musk of my sweat—I remember each one so very clearly. As if I'm still impregnated with them, with her, and with that night, when I had no one else to play for.

No one else. But her.

Pushing away from the keyboard, I hurry to the address book and flip through the pages but discover Michele's not in there.

"Oh, what the hell is this?"

I'd only ever seen her with Tanya or Randal. The last time was over a year ago, at her birthday party.

Hoping he is still in touch, I call Randal. He says he hasn't talked to her in a long time but does give me the last working number he has for her.

"No idea if it's still good," he warns.

I try anyway.

The phone rings once, then twice, and then the machine comes on, confirming it's still her number.

Should I leave a message? Saying what? I tap my teeth together a few times. *No. Stupid idea.*

As I pull the phone from my ear, I hear the phone getting picked up.

"Hi," I say.

"Hi yourself," Michele says.

"This is Jonathan."

"I recognize the voice," she says. "To what do I owe this?"

"I was, ah, thinking about heading out tonight."

"And where were you thinking of going?"

"Berlin. It's Original Wave Night."

"When?"

"Whenever. I'm easy like that."

We pick eleven thirty. After hanging up, I think back to the desultory now-and-then flirts we've offered each other over the years—especially that delicate kiss on her birthday—and I'm right there again, overlooking a precipitous fall: one more step and I escape this empty sleepwalk existence.

Getting ready quickly, I rush to leave before I can change my mind.

At Berlin, I can't find her. *Fits perfectly, doesn't it; Amy's in New York, Jennifer's in New Orleans, and Michele's avoiding the whole problem altogether.*

Leaning against the bar, I stare into my scotch.

"So you're the smartest of us four," I say. "Doing the smart thing. Staying away."

Not that your being so very smart helps me out of my hole.

Don't be an asshole, Jonathan. She's saving us both a lot of pain.

I shake my head.

A moment later, a hand rests on my shoulder.

It's Michele. She's wearing that same white leather dinner jacket, with a ruffled red men's shirt and bell-bottoms. Her hair is slicked back and pinned with rhinestone clips.

I smile in relief tinged by trepidation.

Looking into my eyes as if she understands what is happening here perfectly, she brushes her lips on mine just as she did at the Gingerman, and then she takes my hand and leads me onto the dance floor, where our legs become intertwined and our hips press together as all our flirting turns physical and we act out what we'd do without clothes.

The DJ starts spinning "Sin with Me," and I sing along for her, melting into the rhythm and the warm textures of her body. After it ends, she leads me off the floor and out into the street.

I don't ask where she's taking me; I don't care.

Suddenly she pulls me into the narrow alley behind this clothing store called The Alley.

The streetlight coats Michele in a luxuriant yellow color, sowing flecks of gold in her smoky-gray eyes. She tilts her head one way and then the other, and then she straightens it back up. After popping her lips several times, she reaches a finger under my chin, and slowly brings my face closer to hers—close enough to feel her breath. Her finger holds me there. Her lips purse. The finger urges me closer until only wisps of our breath separate us. The finger drops away. She waits.

My head sinks toward her. We kiss.

I hear so many new songs clamoring at the edges of my mind; their rhythms drive the beat of my heart as hard and quick as "Sin with Me."

She pulls us back onto the street. I keep listening to the soundtrack in my head as we start down Belmont. Under the streetlights there, different songs muscle their way into my attention, drowning out the sounds of passion with the sounds of endings, when gravity takes back control and we hurl against the ground, splitting us apart. These rhythms mimic "Just Walk Away" and "Suffer in Silence," and quicken fear in me as they slash from anger to regret.

I refuse to hear to these sounds—these stories of the end. Michele's here. Now. I push everything from my thoughts but her.

You remind me of Amy. But Tanya hated Amy. How did you ever get invited to her parties in the first place? Let alone be a regular?

"You know," Michele says, breaking our silence, "when I first saw you, I thought you were just another one of Tanya and Randal's flaky friends."

I give a quick chuckle. "You have a creepy way of saying what I was thinking about."

"Sign of destiny."

The way she says "destiny" is thrilling. It makes me want to believe in destiny, if only for a moment, this one time.

"I've often wondered," I say. "How did you ever get hooked up with her? You're not like her regular people."

"I was on dates with them."

"On dates? With them?"

"Randal gave me as a birthday present to Tanya—for them both, really. I was at those parties to warm things up."

"A birthday present. Hmm."

"Sure. Tanya enjoyed girls from time to time; Randal liked the idea of a three-way. Like all men. Even you."

My shoulders rise slightly, and my palms turn up in vague agreement; she's not exactly wrong. Still, I won't completely admit to it either—too treacherous.

"So," I say, "when she got pregnant—"

"That was the problem indeed. But not the way you're thinking. When she got pregnant, he still liked his fun. He kept after me. Tried to get into my skivvies without her around. Tanya didn't like it, of course. That's what got them in trouble. Not the miscarriage."

"Slow down here."

"Oh, it's really not that interesting. Randal couldn't keep his pants on when Tanya had to. Now it's done. I'm not friends with either of them anymore. Tanya was jealous. She left. He's not that interesting—never was, frankly."

"But at the parties, you were flirting with me—"

"That's what parties are for: titillation, brushes with jealousy, jockeying for position, creating a mystery. Who will finally hook up with whom? And how? And when?"

"With Scott and me both."

"Scott? He was a prop. And soooooo queer for you."

"So I found out."

"You didn't see that?"

"Back then? No. Not at all."

"How could you have missed it?" Michele asks. "The way he treated the woman around you. He was so jealous. And possessive."

"If I'd seen it sooner, everything would've been different. Kenny wouldn't be dead. And Mercurial Visions—we'd still be playing. And, well ..." I shake my head.

She stops walking and regards me carefully, her head tilting to the side.

"You don't like boys *at all*, do you?" she asks, her finger making a couple of tight circles before landing on her lips.

"No." I shrug. "So?"

"At all—as in nada," she says. Her finger flicks back and forth and then rests on her cheek. "Oh, now. *That's* something I never suspected—a *truly* straight boy. That's like an albino."

"An albino?"

"Everyone's at least part queer. A lot of people are freaked out by it, so they do straight with all their might. Ten percent let it shine. Except you. You simply don't like boys *at all*."

"Um. Yeah," I say. "That's strange?"

She guffaws. "An honest-to-god straight boy—who's funny too. Wow, that *is* hot," Michele says. "But now, sorry to say, I do have to get some sleep. It's a school night for me." She kisses my cheek good-bye. "*I'll* call *you*. Believe me."

For weeks, we circle each other. We talk, have dinner together, and watch movies. We allow ourselves only brief kisses, fingertip caresses, and holding hands, while I constantly fight off the urge to ask her to the loft. I refuse to because of an ugly thought that intrudes when I'm alone: if I only push us a little further, let us dissolve into each other, save us from our solitude, she'll be my band's salvation; I'll stand on stage for her, spilling out songs with her name and her face woven into them.

I feel vile when this thought trots into my awareness.

She too seems wary of our hurling together, smashing pell-mell into each other's lives and bodies, and never asks me to hers. At least I don't have to decide if her place is safe.

As I keep my ugly thought at bay, I struggle to find the new sound for our unnamed band, and all I have to show for this is "Daydream and Try." One song doesn't start a band—certainly not with the expectations everyone has for us.

As more time passes with me empty of ideas, I find it harder to resist the lure of songs with Michele's name and her face woven into them. Oh, they would be so *very* good, these new songs I can imagine hearing at the edges of my mind. These could-be songs with Michele would be joyful, not regretful—what I need to feel now.

Then, one night in Subterranean, as Michele and I sit on a couch, I talk to her about my band, about creating music and my frustrations. I weave in hints at what we might do together, to probe the depth of her reluctance. I nudge the talk to us and what could be. As I do, the reluctance in her eyes softens, and then her smile widens, and as they do, I can make out the sound of our furious first album: a soundtrack for seduction, temptation, and the disintegration of one into the other. I can feel myself on stage again, singing of her. Of us. Ultimately of what we once were.

Everything sounds so familiar. Like my darkest fantasy.

My right arm has already found a perch, stretched along the carved wood backrest of our couch, grazing her shoulders; the music surrounding us here is rich and sexy. From the rim of her glass, a smudge of her lipstick whispers that I need to have her lips smear its color on me as well.

Be my lover. Live it with me. We'll feel like we're flying.

Picking up my scotch, I lean closer to her than I need to, and linger there, watching her shift her legs so her skirt spreads open as if she is testing me—making me choose, right here, what's most important to me.

Choruses from unwritten songs urge me to touch her. They crescendo as I put my glass down and lift my hand over the space she's opened for me at the bottom of her skirt. I look at the smooth skin of the inside of her thighs. It would be so warm.

I need this tonight. Need you as much as I ever needed Amy. I'll transform us.

Then I hear Amy's voice, giving me my only choices I have for a woman.

A sudden anger freezes my hand there above Michele's legs.

Next I remember Scott giving me my only choices for music.

I pull my hand back from over Michele's legs and set it on my lap.

A wave of disgust courses though me. At everyone. Everything. Including myself. For letting myself believe these stories I was being told, letting myself get trapped by them, like I'd allowed the white cubicles to trap me years and lifetimes before.

All I want is to get up and walk away.

I can't explain why. *I only know it's safer this way.*

I put my hands on the seat cushion to push myself up. I can't meet her eyes, so I look at the floor as I stand.

As I turn to leave, I remember a time I was just as disgusted at myself—when Arcade Land foundered, when Scott pretended to be our manager, when I tumbled into a world I never understood yet let its sterile white walls and 5:00 p.m. release define the limits of who I was. I'd believed those walls were as far as I could be.

Until I met Amy.

She shocked me back to life. Told me to turn her into songs. Then was I able to freeze moments, thoughts, and feelings into lyrics and string them together like crystals on a necklace of melody and rhythm, song after song.

Only to lose her. Then Jennifer. Then everything.

The desperate feeling sinking into me as I try to leave Michele in Subterranean is the same as the moments I'd thought of jumping off a chair, my neck in a belt, because I had no way back to who I was. This time no sterile white walls trapped me: I have. And the only way I can see of escaping is through Michele.

I finally force myself to look at her, and I see questions hanging from her expression, which quickly shifts to suspicion.

If I do not love you as intensely as I can right now, then what? There's no one to lose. Nothing to drive lyrics and melody. Nothing left to fill me out. I'll be nothing. Desperate, without a voice. Silently crying out.

This is the moment I understood what I'd failed to grasp all those years ago: the unspoken desperation in the eyes of everyone around me were songs they tried to sing, but they needed me to give them voice.

Holding my finger to my lips, I shush her.

"No," I say, laying it on her cheek. "Not what you're thinking."

We all need something to live for—a mirror in which to look and see ourselves reflected in a way that matters, to somehow matter, to someone. But the desperate ones gaze into mirrors that are warped by contrived oughts and shoulds, by impossible exemplars of perfection and exotica, by supernatural offers of life's higher purpose obtained after life has ended. These fun house mirrors merely feed an addiction to *higher* meaning—whet the need for ever more—like those that killed Charlene, ruled Jennifer's imagination, and deaden the eyes of anyone who looks in them too long.

The need to sing this for all those without a voice blazes inside.

Then the songs come. Songs years in the fermentation: a thousand new melodies bursting forth, crying out their lyrics, all screaming for my attention. I hear a lifetime of music unfolding: meaning woven from moments of living the best one can, through the tumult of hopes and dreams and fears and losses that fill every life with desperate acts, perdition, compassion, and a hope for redemption.

That night, perched on the edge of leaving, I look at her, and she at me. I nod.

The way she bites her lip lets me know she understands that our story won't be the same as all those we kept reliving when we were apart.

My fingers tap out a new rhythm on her shoulder; she shimmies in perfect time to it.

• • • • •

Over the next month, I wrote enough songs to fill three full-length CDs. A month later, our band, now named Merciful Release, gelled. In two months, our demo was ready. In three, TVT records inked a multidisk deal with us.

No one had to leave.

I still think back to our time together every now and then.

When I sift through all the things that happened to my friends and lovers, I always get angry—with myself mostly. Then regret takes over: I wish I could tell Kenny how sorry I am that I didn't understand in time to save him. Scott—my best friend—well, I failed him the most. Perhaps one day we'll meet. When we do, I hope I can find the words to let him understand.

I imagine I should tell Amy and Jennifer I'm sorry. Or not; they're alive and doing well from what I've heard. I doubt they'd have much use of our past anymore.

Oh, yes, Michele did eventually see the loft, not long after the TVT deal. I invited her over. We had coffee and talked of us and what might be. As we did, I ignored the angel that still hung on the wall, refusing to look.

Our first night together, Michele remarked that "Love Will Tear Us Apart" was a great song but a lousy way to live.

Since then I've only been able to love her, this woman named Michele, who listens to my music—and who now carries our child.

In quiet times like now, I sing a little song I keep only to serenade her:
There once
Was a man named Jonathan,
And a woman named Michele.
They were
Simply
In love.

Want more?
Go to: www.wlancehunt.com/music
Get access to playlists of the music on
YouTube, Spotify, Apple Music,
8tracks.com, and more.

Portrait of W. Lance Hunt by Charles Eshelman

ABOUT THE AUTHOR

W. Lance Hunt earned two bachelor's degrees from Ohio State University, cofounded the Rudely Elegant Theatre in Chicago, and helped produce an Emmy Award–winning film. After living in Mexico City, he moved to New York City, where he earned a Master of Arts in English from CCNY. Hunt works as a freelance writer and editor and lives in Brooklyn with his wife and son.